WICKED THIRST

THE ROYALS: VAMPIRE COURT
BOOK THREE

MEGAN MONTERO

CHAPTER ONE

TITUS

1000 years ago

"How dare you summon me." I ground my teeth together and spoke through thinned lips. I fought to stifle the growl that rumbled deep in my chest, then motioned to the gathering of rulers who'd been forced to this field in the dead of winter. "How dare you summon us *all* here!"

Outrage flowed through my veins, and I curled my hands into fists at my sides, barely resisting the urge to draw the sword from my hip. My blood magic floated around my fingers like a fine red mist. Yet I held my power at bay. A single move in one direction or another could start a war of epic consequences—a war the vampire kingdom was not ready to undertake, especially not against her. Standing here was like standing with the tip of a sword to my chest and a knife to my back, one wrong move and one would end up with a blade through the heart.

This gathering was overflowing with the most powerful leaders in Evermore. Magic hung heavy around us. I felt it run over my skin like a thick film. The sun had long since set and the temperature had cooled to a wintery chill. The moon shined bright on us all, turning the surrounding forest and open field into shadows blanketed in hues of blue. The grass was flattened into brown patches and the winter frost had set in. It crunched under my boots, and though this was not England, I had no idea where I'd been transported to. The lingering scent of snow drifted through the air and yet the weather dared not disturb her desires on this night. With every breath I took, fog blew from my lips. If I hadn't been wrapped in furs, the cold would've seeped into my skin, chilling me to the bone.

"How dare I?" Dracinda pressed her hand to her chest and smirked. She batted her eyelashes, playing coy, yet her undertone was clear. She was not one to be trifled with. "Do not court my wrath, vampire."

I let loose the growl I'd been holding back. "Do not court mine, Dracinda."

Dracinda was the most powerful witch to walk the Earth *and* the most beautiful, with her long silvery hair and huge blue eyes. She was comely in ways that would tempt even the most honorable of men to fall to her wiles. Rumor had it that she had indeed done just that many times over.

She, along with her sister, Danna, performed the most powerful of spells. Powerful . . . but terrible. They'd been a scourge on the land, and now they'd done the most impossible of all: summoned us unwillingly.

I stood among all eight of The Fallen, the angels destined to rule all of Evermore. The entire supernatural world answered to them, and they ruled with a harsh swiftness, meting out justice with the strength of their fists and the edges of their blades. When dealing with The Fallen, I'd learned there were no second chances. Each of them was adorned in full battle gear. Leather straps held their breastplates in place, weapons covered their bodies, and anger rolled off them in waves. Even in the dark of night, their hulking black wings were shadows against the sky.

Matteaus, their leader, stood at my side. He was slightly bigger than me, with a muscular physique, wild blondish-brown hair, and an angular jawline. His sapphire eyes blazed with fury as he gazed at the woman before us. He rested his hand on the dagger at his hip. I had no doubt there were many more hidden among his leather armor. "Your sins against Evermore are many."

"It takes a sinner to know one, is that it? Or has your ego allowed you the role of creator as well?" Her face turned stone-cold as she turned to Tristan, the member of The Fallen with influence over all forms of love. "I'd forgotten it was your hubris that brought you to your knees and earned you your fallen black wings. Do not dare to scold me of sins, for there are many among us all."

Tristan lowered his gaze to meet her eyes. His wings twitched and black feathers fell to the ground around his feet. He ran his hand through the long strands of his blond hair. Where Matteaus was tall and muscular, Tristan was trim and fit with long, lean muscle. When his gaze met hers, his breath left him, and for a moment I saw a man tormented by his own cravings. His eyes softened when he met her gaze, and he lowered his voice to a near whisper, "Dracinda, please don't."

She gave him a withering smile and backed away. Her long hair flowed down her body and caught the light of the moon, giving her that ethereal look that would bring any man to his knees. She had the appearance of heaven but was made of sin. When he looked away from her, she turned from him to stroll within the circle of those she'd summoned. We all stood equidistant apart, separated by floating balls of fire between us. They flickered and danced like torches, yet there were no wooden stakes holding them up. Smoke and embers drifted up into the sky and disappeared.

Her hair fanned out around her as she spun to face him once more. Her dark-purple cloak hung from her shoulders down to the ground where it pooled at her feet. "Don't what, lover? Don't tell the truth? Don't see fault in the way things are done? I recall at one time you all saw fault in the way things were done."

"And have been cursed since. We've seen the error in our ways. 'Tis not too late for you." Pain flickered over

Tristan's face at the reminder of how their own fate came to be.

"I see no error, lover, only the weakness of men and their cowardice in the lack of tenacity to fight for one's beliefs." She cupped his cheek. "I find disappointment in how accepting you all are of the lot you've been meted out."

His face turned stone-cold. "I find disappointment in the lack of compassion you show others."

She chuckled and spread her arms wide, giving him a devilish smile. "It's a hard life . . . I make the most of it."

So, the rumors are true. The witch entangled herself with one of The Fallen. I arched my eyebrows toward Tristen. When he glared at me, I turned my eyes back toward the witch. No use making an enemy of one of The Fallen. A man could only do so much when faced with his own passions, even if those passions were poisonous to the soul.

Dracinda was indeed a poison. She spun in a circle and smirked. "You all have an opportunity before you."

Alataris, the newly crowned King of the Witch Court, snickered. "What opportunity could possibly interest us?"

Her unwavering gaze locked on his. Interest flickered deep in her eyes as she sauntered toward him. Her long purple cloak dragged over the ground with each step she took. It was a slow, enticing seduction of a lad who was not prepared to confront a woman of her particular talents. "Such a young, ambitious king would surely be in need of a favor from one such as myself."

He was a young king. It was apparent in his smoothed-back dark hair and the soft planes in his still boyish features. Alataris was tall and slim with sharp features that showed even in the dark of night. His black cloak hung from his shoulders to just past his knees. He wore no armor nor held any weapons. It made me question how ready he was for the role of King. Evermore was a wonderful yet dangerous place to roam unprotected. He'd only been placed on the throne through the mysterious downfall of his long-reigning parents.

His lips turned up in a smirk. "My only ambition is to see my people prosper."

She arched her eyebrows. "Indeed. That is your ambition, and you'll accomplish it . . . by *any* means necessary."

His smile faltered for a moment when he glanced around at the rest of us, then he shoved it back into place. "I am nothing like you."

"Time reveals all. You'll do well to remember that." She winked at Alataris as though she knew a secret we all didn't, yet he didn't respond to her words or react at all. She turned to all of us. "Still, my troubles remain the same and you all have the option to help me solve them. In exchange, I will grant your people peace from myself and Danna."

"Your word is worth nothing among the honorable." I didn't bother leaving the venom from my voice.

She spun on me, and her long cloak billowed out around her. "This would be binding."

"And what is of that much importance to you? What could possibly make me believe anything would be so dire?" I adjusted my stance and kept my hand resting on my sword. No doubt her deadly sister lurked in the darkness, ready to attack. If given the opportunity, I'd take either of their heads. But Dracinda was not only beautiful, she was also deadly with magic and her sword.

Dracinda lifted her chin and threw her shoulders back. Magic crackled in the air, and she waved her hand. It was like pulling a veil off a hidden box. Where there was nothing in the center of the circle, there was now a lone bed covered in silvery satin sheets and thick furs. The smell of sickness hung in the air. My gaze drifted over the woman lying atop the bed. The sheets around her were stained a shade darker by the sweat slicking her body. Her white nightdress clung to her body along with the mess of blankets. Her midnight hair was sweat-matted to her head. Her body shuttered with a chill all while she continued to sweat.

My breath left me. "Danna."

"Danna." Dracinda walked around her like she would command us all to save her, to stop whatever sickness overtook her . . . but I would not. She motioned to her sister. "Save her."

Silence.

Danna's skin was sickly pale and death lingered around her. I felt it. We all did. Even Dracinda had to know her sister would not last this night. She dropped to her knees and took up her sister's hands in her own. "Hold on a bit longer, dearest."

When she rose to her feet and faced us all once more, there was a desperation to the way she commanded us.

"You are the most powerful beings to walk in Evermore. Save. Her."

Matteaus ground his teeth together. "I will not."

Dracinda hissed at his words. "Do you not know the wrath you court?"

He shrugged. "I do."

"I will plague this world for centuries to come . . . Any one of you can stop this now. Stop death from taking her." Her voice grew more urgent as Danna's breaths became shallower.

If Dracinda lost her sister on this night, I had no doubt she would spiral into the darkest magic. But the world would be better if there were only one sister to deal with. When death called, it would be answered, and it was calling out to Danna. This death was a kindness for the likes of Danna. Their atrocious ways should be punished by a much crueler way befitting their actions.

I lifted my chin and said the one thing no one here had: "Death cannot be stopped."

She glared at me. "You are a vampire . . . Death is nothing to you."

"We will not do this," Tristan raised his voice. "Her time has come."

"You would have me hate you?" Her eyes widened. "I swear I will hate you for all of eternity. Save her."

His eyes glowed with power as his body vibrated with emotion. When he looked down at her, there were unshed emotions in his eyes. The muscle in his jaw ticked as he spoke through thinned lips. "I. Will. Not."

When she looked to each one of The Fallen, they all stood firm, repeating the one line Matteaus had, "I will not."

She'd been denied eight times and each time she grew angrier. Tears pooled in her eyes when she turned to Alataris. "Come now, King. Are we not to be allies?"

"Your offer intrigues me, to be sure, but your allies have a way of coming to an early death, and I do not wish such an outcome for myself." He shrugged and waved her words away with a carelessness that only came with naïve youth. If he knew he courted her wrath, he would not take his denial so lightly. "I plan to enjoy the years to come."

"I vow you will not have an end with Danna and I by your side. You'll be the most powerful Witch King of all." Her words grew desperate as her sister's breath rattled in her chest. "I would give you the world if you would give me her."

Alataris smirked down at her with those deep black eyes of his, and for the first time I saw a hint of something . . . sinister. His words were slow and deliberate. "I will not."

Before she could say another word, black smoke billowed around him and he was gone, disappearing in a dark cloud. A scream ripped from Dracinda's throat. She dropped to her knees beside her sister and fisted the sheets on her bed. Strands of her hair fell over her face as she hung her head. "I have done all the magic I know."

Danna's eyes peeked open and she slowly lifted her hand to rest on Dracinda's head. "I will die this night."

"No." Dracinda shook her head as her tears slipped over onto her cheeks. "I won't let you."

A heavy sigh left Danna's lips, and for a moment I thought it might be her last breath. Long moments passed before she sucked in another breath. "There is naught to be done. Just be with me in these last moments."

"They will not be your last, dearest." She took her sister's hands and gave them a squeeze, then rose to her feet and turned on me. "What say you, vampire?"

I said nothing.

"Turn her."

I held my breath. *Dare I court the wrath of this witch?*

Power rose around her. Her magic flowed in bright lights from her hands up her arms. Wind kicked up, sending her hair flying about her face. She was deadly beautiful in a way that would ruin us all. She screamed over the sound of her storm of rage. "TURN. HER!"

I threw my shoulders back and tightened my grip on my sword. "I. WILL. NOT."

Tears poured down Dracinda's cheeks, yet she didn't sob, didn't draw in one hitched breath. She lifted her arms, and I felt her power about to slam into me.

"Dra . . ." A wheezing cough took Danna's breath away. "Come."

Her magic stopped and she turned back to her dying sister. Once again, she dropped to her knees and leaned on the bed beside her. "I am here."

"I'm . . ." Danna drew a slow breath, ". . . scared."

"No, no, dearest." She gathered her sister's hand into

hers and pressed it to her own cheek. "Hold on just a little longer."

"I fear," she let go of a slow wheezing breath, "I cannot."

"No. Fight this! We will find a way." She leaned over her sister and used her cloak to wipe the sweat from her brow. Her voice lowered to a whisper. "Sister . . . please."

When Danna's eyes slid shut and those deep, labored breaths started, I knew it was time. There was a specific sound to those last gasping inhalations. It was like the body was preparing to let go of the spirit for good. The weak vessel that her body was could not contain her any longer. Death had come for her. Dracinda jumped to her feet and ran toward me. She wrapped her hands in the lapels of my furs and fell at my feet. "I beg of you . . . turn her! She will live eternally in your kingdom. You will rule her, and me, as subjects. I vow it. I vow a loyalty only we can offer."

They'd committed crimes, murdered the innocent, stolen, and cast the darkest of magic. Evermore would be a better place without them, and if I courted her wrath . . . then so be it. I pried her fingers from my coat and took a step back, leaving her on the ground at my feet. "I will not, and none of my people will either."

Her eyes flared and anger ravaged her face. She sprang to her feet to stand and face us all. "Fools!"

When a single breath left Danna's chest and she did not draw another, we all stood there for long moments waiting to see if her chest would rise once more. When it didn't, Dracinda threw her head back, screaming the agony she felt at the loss of her beloved sister. The air grew colder, and the moon seemed to glow brighter. Magic crackled around her, and her eyes flared with wild madness. Tears poured down her face, yet she said nothing to any of us. A crazed smile spread across her face as if her last bit of sanity fled with her sister's soul.

Tristan stepped forward, trying to stop her from building her power. He held his hand up, and for a moment pink smoke seeped around his fingers. Would he use his influence to bring her to heel?

She glared at him as if in warning. No one, not even The Fallen, could control Dracinda. "Don't." When she turned to face me, her tears were gone. Her face was smooth with a coldness that sent a shiver down my spine. "Do you know what it is to love another more than you love yourself?"

I didn't answer.

"You will . . . Oh, you will." Her words were low, almost like a threat. "Love is a curse you will know well."

"There is nothing left for you here." I drew my sword as her magic lit up her palms.

She lifted her hands, and her power wrapped around me, holding me in place like chains I could not break. "Mark these words, avenge thy crime. Bound by blood in space and time."

"Let me go." I struggled against her to no avail. I couldn't move, could barely breathe.

Wind whipped through the clearing and wound around me, mixing with her magic. It grew impossibly bright and hot.

"From kin to kin, one wretched vine. A wicked curse seals a shaded line." Her lips drew up in an evil smile. "What was denied shall now be taken, for when thee love thee turn forsaken.

Deep in thy veins thy soul will burn. Forever more thy thirst shall yearn."

"NO! DON'T!" Tristan leapt in front of me, but she lifted her other hand and fired a ball of fire at him. His large body soared across the sky and crashed into the forest in the distance. Trees cracked around him and fell to the ground. Fire exploded over the dry, dead trees, nearly engulfing him in flames.

The other Fallen all leapt into action, drawing their weapons and running toward her. A tornado of power surrounded her, forcing them back just enough for her to keep her hold on me. "Breath by breath, thy mind unwound, to madness now thy life is drowned. And if fate shall deem thy love requited, don't speak the words or curse the blighted. For if on the wrist thy souls entwined, death shall call and forever find."

Power seeped into my body, and I felt my blood boil in my veins as it wrapped around my every cell and sank into my bones. Pain like I'd never known riddled my body, and my back arched so hard I thought my spine would snap. Light shined from my skin so bright it burned my eyes. Burning, so much burning, from the inside out. My mind whirled with the need to just survive. But I felt that all would be left of me was a ball of ash and dust. Drops of my own blood beaded my skin like sweat. It streaked down my face and into my eyes. It felt like acid with every blink and every move I made. My skin felt like it was peeling from my bones. Everything ached, and I felt my bones would snap beneath my muscles.

A bellow ripped from my throat, and I struggled against her hold, calling upon my own blood magic to make it end. Red mist flew from my skin, and with the little strength I had left, I shot it toward her. It smacked into her chest, and for a second, I felt the hold I could have on her. With my last bit of strength, I bellowed one word: "STOP!"

She released her magic, finally freeing me. I dropped to the ground and my legs gave out as I fell. The frosted ground felt like a balm against my burning skin. The breath felt tight in my chest, and a sharp ache spread through my body.

"What . . . what did you do to me?" I managed.

"The House of Shade will know love . . . and the pain it will bring for all eternity."

Blinding light filled the area and The Fallen charged forward, but it was too late. She was gone, leaving me there to live or die with the curse of love . . .

CHAPTER TWO

ZINNIA

"I just don't understand what the hell is going on." The school was eerily still this early in the morning. Most of the students went home for holiday break while the skeleton crew remained. Even most of the teachers were gone. Yet here I was standing in our meeting room in the basement of the school, wondering what the hell was wrong.

For some reason it felt colder, damper, and desolate now. The silence in the halls sat heavy in the air. Normally, I would've been sleeping and enjoying the comfort of my soulmate. Yet I couldn't sleep. There was something in the air that made the hairs on the back of my neck stand on edge. Magic was my existence, and I loved every bit of it, but why did it feel as though the balance was off in the world? It was as though darkness lingered around every corner. I shivered and ran my hands up and down my arms.

"Hey, couldn't sleep again?" Tucker, my soulmate, walked into the room holding a mug in each of his hands.

I couldn't help but give him a smile every time I saw him. If ever there was anyone on my side and by my side, he was it. He was perfection in every way, with his bed-tossed auburn hair and molten honey eyes. Though it was winter, he still wore a thin hoodie, T-shirt, and jeans. I took the cup and sipped at its contents. "Oh, it's cold."

"That's what I get for walking across the courtyard in the middle of winter." He reached out and placed his hand on the side of my cup. Warm light shined in his palms and warmth spread through the contents of my mug. Steam rose from the top and drifted up toward my face.

I sucked in a deep breath and sighed. "Thanks, babe."

He winked. "So, what are we doing?"

I groaned and slid onto one of the stools next to the table. "Something is wrong."

"Something?" His brow furrowed in confusion. "Care to be more specific?"

"I know it sounds crazy, but I feel it in the air. Magic is off." I rested my elbows on the table and gave a little huff. The world had a certain push and pull, a certain feel to it on any given day. But the last few days there was a build that I could not explain. It kept me up at night and made me feel restless during the day, like walking into a room and forgetting why you went in there in the first place. Everything was just . . . off.

"Like all magic, period?" He raised his eyebrows at me while sipping at his own drink.

"Yes . . . all of it. I can't explain it. I just feel it all around me. It's kind of like when you're alone in a huge dark house and you feel like something, or someone is watching you . . . like the creeps all over your skin." I sighed. "I'm not explaining this right."

"No, I understand you. We just have to figure out what it is."

"Makes my skin crawl." A shiver went down my spine. "It's icky."

"Icky?"

"Dark." I met his eye. "It's very dark."

A bright blue, swirling portal opened in the middle of the room, and I sat up straighter. Tucker turned toward the blue light and sipped at his drink. "This should be interesting."

"I'm hoping they found something to explain all this." I motioned to the map spread across the table. Every mark was a place where I thought I felt a magical flare-up, yet every time we checked it out, there was no sign of anything at all. "Otherwise, they're going to think I'm starting to go crazy."

Tuck shook his head. "No one thinks that."

No one would be able to open a portal right into this room unless they were one of our crew. Evermore Academy was protected by The Fallen and many layers of magic. If someone was coming in, they were granted permission, not just using their magic to infiltrate the school whenever they felt like it. Our enemies were many, so our protections had to be tight. Beckett sauntered out of the portal with Astrid at his side. He shook his blond hair out and sand fell to the floor around them. It sounded like grains of sugar hitting the floor. Astrid brushed her hands down her shirt and stomped her feet, sending even more sand to the floor.

Their magic filled the space, and I felt it run over my skin. I could tap into either of them and take whatever power they had to offer, but I wouldn't unless it was freely offered. Taking magic that wasn't my own was a slippery slope. As the Siphon Queen, it was my responsibility to keep the balance within myself and around the world. No one felt power the way I did, and I would be damned if I let it consume me the way it did my father.

Astrid could manifest anything her heart desired, which made her a hugely powerful ally. She was all fiery looks and attitude with her dark-red hair and bright emerald eyes. Beckett was powerful in his own right as one of the warlock heirs and a guardian of the Witch Queens. He could move anything with his magic. Yet he had a calm about him that made his magic feel like a cool balm against hot skin. It was almost icy like his ocean-blue eyes.

He ran his hand through his blond hair and strands of it fell back into his face. "What's up?"

"Did you guys find anything?" I wanted them to find something, but I also did not. If they found something dark, that would mean my suspicions were correct and something was very wrong. But when they found nothing, it just meant I was going to drive myself crazy looking for whatever I felt was wrong. It was a *damned if they did and damned if they didn't* situation for me.

Astrid shook her head. "Nothing. It's like whatever was there is gone now."

"I don't get it." I looked at the map spread out before me. I ran my hand over the points I'd marked. "I know they're there."

Astrid dropped down into a chair across from me and looked down at the points. "It was weird."

"Weird how?" I sat forward. We'd been checking out random flare-ups of magic for weeks now, but nothing ever came of it.

"It's like I could feel the power all around me, but there was nothing and literally no one in sight." She tossed her hair over her shoulder. "I mean, we were in the middle of the freaking desert, and there was absolutely nothing for miles."

Beckett nodded. "Nothing but sunshine, sand, and ass sweat."

"I'm telling you all something isn't right." The nagging feeling wouldn't leave me alone. Day and night I felt a shift in the world, a shift that could not be explained.

"I agree." Astrid nodded.

"I might not be able to feel what you do, but I believe you." Tuck reached out and ran his hand over my back in small circles.

Astrid glanced up at me. "We might have to bring some extreme things in on this."

"Extreme? Like what?"

"Like Ophelia and Maze." She met my eye. "Send them on the hunt."

I nodded. "You might be right. Nothing a little psycho and some psychic couldn't help."

"Does anyone else think they've been super weird lately?" Tuck glanced around at our blank stares. "I mean, more than usual?"

"They're both definitely up to something." Beckett nodded in agreement. "But we'll never know what until they think it's time to tell us."

"It's true. We just have to—"

The door flew open and slammed into the wall. Adrianne slid into the room with a sheen of sweat covering her ebony skin. Her chest heaved with deep breaths. Her long, dark braids whipped around her head as she skidded to a halt and nearly slammed into the wall. "You have to come quick."

I hopped to my feet. "What happened?"

"It's Niche, she's . . . she is not okay." She waved her hand, motioning for us to hurry. "You have to come."

Chairs scraped over the floor as we all sprinted from the room and down the stone hallway. Though the air was cold from winter, I felt my skin heat and my heart hammer in my chest as I pumped my arms trying to keep up with Adrianne. We ran up the stairs and across the courtyard toward the training room. It'd been ages since I'd been in the training room, but when we ran through those double doors, I found myself dragged back to those first days when I knew nothing of magic and the others weren't even my friends yet. Now we'd made a family and Niche was part of it. I didn't want anything to be wrong with her or anyone else in our crew.

Adrienne stopped just outside the door to Niche's office and placed her hand on the knob, then turned to face us all. "Just prepare yourself and remember . . . move slowly."

"You're scaring me." I didn't know what was behind that door, but whatever happened it'd spooked Adrienne, and she was all logic and patience. The only things that rattled her were her own clumsiness and her mother, Athena.

"Just . . . go easy." She turned away from me and opened the door. It creaked as it swung wide open and hit the wall.

The room was dim, with no windows and only a single candle in the middle of the room that bathed only some of it in warm light and left the rest of the room in shadows. Adrienne took a step back and let me go in first. All but one wall was covered in shelves, and each one held a dozen different pendulums—each made from a different stone. They all had their own stands where they hung and swung throughout the day. The last time I was in this room, they all moved in the same direction each time Niche asked me a question. Now they swung in wild circles as though the scattered energy was too much. I felt the power in the air, and it put me on edge.

Niche stood with her back to us and faced the one wall without shelves. On it was a huge map of the world. It was bigger than the one I had spread across the table in our meeting room. As the handler for the Witch Queens and their guardians, Niche had always been a guide of sorts. She trained our Guardians and kept on top of us all to become masters of our own magic. She'd always been so straight-laced with every strand of her fire-engine-red hair in place and her pressed lab coat. I couldn't remember a time when she didn't have her clipboard in hand to scribble notes across. Yet now her hair was piled in a messy ball on top of her head and her lab coat hung off one of her shoulders. It was so wrinkled it looked like she pulled it from a ball in the corner. Her body quivered from head to toe as she mumbled quietly to herself. I wasn't even sure she heard us enter.

"Niche." I barely touched her shoulder, and she startled and then spun around to face us.

"Oh good! You're here!" Her lips pulled up in a manic smile and she shoved her glasses up her nose like she always did. Except this time, they fell crooked across her nose and she didn't seem to notice.

I let my hand drop as I took in the map. It was covered in pins with red string running from one pin to another. It looked like a tangled spiderweb. Tiny Post-it notes littered the wall. Some made sense, others just had illegible scribbles on them. Tuck moved in beside me and lit a ball of fire in his hand. The whole room illuminated.

Niche flinched away from the offending light. "That is not necessary, Phoenix."

In the light I could see the dark bags under her eyes and the open food wrappers littering the floor. Astrid took a tentative step toward her. "Niche, honey, when was the last time you slept?"

Niche paused and pulled a pen from the nest on top of her head. "I can't remember . . . but . . . but you all have to listen to me."

"We're listening." I'd never seen her like this—so manic, so panicked.

"Magic all over." She began pointing at all the pins. "And . . . and we have no idea what it all is."

I lowered my voice and slowed my words so they were calmer than her hurried ramblings. I wanted to help her, but I didn't know how. It was difficult seeing her like this. "Niche, we know this. We've all been working on it."

"Yes, but you don't see." She ran her fingers over the bright-red strings and whispered, "None of you see."

Adrienne motioned to her. "She just . . . snapped. She's been saying that for the past two hours. *We don't see*, but she's not explaining what I don't see."

I lowered my gaze to meet her eye, trying to catch her focus or attention somehow. "See what, Niche? What are we missing?"

Wild laughter escaped her lips, and she began pacing back and forth. She dropped the pen and fisted her matted hair as her eyes bounced around the room. "It's all there. All the power! Like a sunken minefield in the ocean. All of it. Do you see it now? Do you!?"

I glanced up at the map, but all I saw was the mad ramblings of someone who'd exhausted herself to the point of madness. "I don't see it."

"She's not going to make sense until she gets some rest." Beckett eyed the pendulums all swinging in wild directions. He shook his head. "We need to get her to bed."

"NO!" Niche pressed her back to the wall and spread her arms wide over the map. Her eyes darted back and forth. "I'm not leaving."

"Easy fix." Astrid waved her hand and golden sparkles poured from her fingers. A small twin-sized bed formed in the corner of the room. "Look, you don't have to leave."

Niche's eyes widened and she slouched more into the wall. "No, it must be like this!"

I wrapped my arm around her shoulders and started to guide her toward the bed. "Come on. Just a few hours of rest and you'll be able to explain it all."

She fought my hold and Tuck moved to her other side, taking her hand. "You're going to have to drain her a bit."

I hated using my magic on my friends, but she needed my help. My silvery magic wrapped around her, and I felt the first pull of her manic energy shift from her body into mine. It felt like drinking ten espressos. I couldn't stop myself from shaking. But Niche visibly relaxed. Her eyes gave a long, slow blink. "Maybe I should rest for a minute?"

"Yes, you should." Beckett's blue smoke filled the room, and Niche was lifted from our hold. He floated her across the room and placed her on the bed. The blankets lifted up and laid over her.

She sighed as her head fell back into the pillows, then yawned. "But I have to help him."

"Help who?" I moved to her bedside.

Her eyes fluttered shut. "The magic . . . It's all converging in one place . . ."

"What?" My heart sped even faster. "Where?"

I spun around toward the map, trying to make sense of the lines. Astrid, Beckett, and Tuck all stood beside me staring at it as well. Niche gave another heavy yawn. "England . . . The House of Shade is in trouble . . . Grayson is in trouble. Death calls."

My body turned to ice. Only a day ago he came to us for help and now . . . and now I didn't know. I spun back toward her. "Niche, did he survive? Niche!"

It was too late. My power had done its job of knocking her the hell out. I nearly dropped to my knees to shake her awake, but Adrienne stepped in front of me. "She needs to rest. It's the only way we can have her back to help us."

I knew she was right. I knew I had to let her rest.

Niche gave one last sigh. "No one could survive this. . ."

CHAPTER THREE

DICE

"*L*ook, don't get me wrong, I love Christmas with you guys, but it's time for me to get to Piper. I mean, all the knives were awesome presents . . . if I want to . . . you know . . . slice and dice things." I followed Ophelia as she danced down the halls of her castle and sprinkled glitter over the dark stone floors.

"Or people," she pointed out as she danced around with all the joy an elf in the North Pole would muster in Santa's workshop. Kylian dropped me here days ago, and at first I found this strange castle creepy. Ophelia was terrifying and I thought Cross might kill me in my sleep. Since then, I'd grown to love the cold gothic decor. I even liked Ophelia, and maybe she was slowly becoming one of my most favorite psychopaths. I'd gotten to the point where I was pretty sure Cross would not kill me in my sleep . . . almost sure.

Ophelia's long hair was loose around her shoulders and

flowed and bounced with each of her moves. I'd grown used to seeing her in her black dress or sweaters strapped with weapons. But today she wore red and white-striped leggings and a bright-red shirt with Christmas lights on it that were set to light at random. Even her shoes had little bells on them. Every time she moved there was a little tinkering sound like a cat with a bell on its neck. For a moment I wondered if we could make this a permanent solution to a long-term problem. I never knew where she was, and she snuck up on me like a cat most days. Little bells would fix that real quick.

I cleared my throat and agreed. "Right, orrrrr slicing and dicing people. They're lovely and I—"

"—I know, right? I gave you only the good ones . . . pre-sharpened." She paused and winked at me like pre-sharpened knives were the best things ever. A wide smirk spread across her face, and she turned to start strolling away from me once more. "They never make them sharp enough. You have to do it yourself if you want a clean slice."

Okay. Why was I getting so used to these kinds of conversations after only a few days? The thing with Ophelia was she'd give the world to any of her friends at any point in time. She'd offer up their enemies on a silver platter . . . or just their heads. But Ophelia did everything on Ophelia's timetable. Somehow, I had to convince her to move on my timetable and get me off this island and to Piper. "And I am so grateful for that, and I'm sorry I could only put together a handmade thing, but there are no stores on this island—"

She spun around to face me, and a fistful of glitter flew

from her hand and landed on my shirt. Or the black T-shirt I'd been *given*. When Kylian dropped me here I had only the clothing on my back. *What an asshole move that was.* She tilted her head to the side and looked at the glitter mess. "Don't knock my present. You *made* it for *me* with your bare hands. That's the nicest thing anyone has ever done for me."

"Thanks." Cross grumbled below his breath. He was perched at the edge of the little platform where the empty throne sat. Dark strands of his hair fell over his eyes and into his face, but I still felt his eyes lingering on the two of us, like he couldn't stop watching her. Even I had to admit it was intense being in the same room with the two of them. Their quiet connection was nearly palpable. She moved, he moved. His eyes never left her, even when he was pretending to be preoccupied with other things.

"I mean, I thought a strangle wire seemed like something you'd like, but don't you think it's time for me to leave?" I'd made the damn thing out of spare wire I'd found lying around and two small, thick pieces of wood for handles on each end. Sure, I'd taken the time to carve the wood with funny faces because why wouldn't someone laugh at a funny tree face when strangling the life from someone?

"Leave?" Her brow furrowed as she turned and walked away from me. "Nope. Don't think so."

I followed her as she sauntered around the throne room, or as I liked to think of it now: the hall of Christmas trees, where she's lined the walls with dozens of them all decorated a different way. It was like the Christmas store blew up in here and threw up on all the trees. It would be fun, and I couldn't wait to tell Piper about my time here, but I had to go. It was time for me to get to her. Deep in the pit of my stomach, I knew she wasn't okay and that she needed me.

"Look, I know you don't get it, but I feel like she needs me."

"Oh, I get it." Ophelia nodded. "And she definitely does."

Cross chuckled from his perch on the stairs leading up to the throne. A crossbow sat beside him while he sharpened the points of his arrows on a stone. It would've looked like a peaceful thing to do if I didn't know that those arrows were meant to actually kill someone and not target practice. "Yeah, Maze with his creepy shit wasn't the most comforting. Blood on the streets! Blood on the streets! He's my friend, but he is one disturbing fucker."

I shook my head and ran my hands through my hair. Visions of that freaky fucker ran through my head all day long with his milky-white eyes and swirling neon power. It made the hairs on the back of my neck stand on edge. When I'd met Maze the first time, I thought they were common Salem psychics, but he was so much more. They'd led me to Piper once before, but this time it seemed they were totally against me finding her. Or at least Maze's visions were.

"No, it wasn't comforting at all, which is why I need to go there."

"Which is why you're not going." She walked over to a tree and sprinkled some glittering dust on it, and it grew three feet taller and fuller. Some of the decorations popped and fell to the floor, but she shrugged and seemed to like the broken glass ornaments littering the floor.

"What? Why?" I didn't want to sound like I was whining or frustrated. But the truth was that being trapped here was frustrating as hell. I hated being stuck here. The only benefit was the heat.

"Piper put me in charge of your little mortal ass, which means your mortal ass is going to stay put in the cushy castle . . . Jeeze. You should've lived here with my dad, then you'd appreciate how cushy it is now and want to stay." She glanced over her shoulder at me. "Bit ungrateful if you ask me."

"If one of your twenty-eight besties was in trouble, you'd be there in a heartbeat." I hoped if I appealed to the loyalty she showed to others, I might be able to convince her to do one of those crazy portal things and get me to Piper.

"Twenty-nine." She plucked a small dagger ornament from a tree and held it up toward the light.

I hesitated, feeling like I'd gotten lost in the conversation. "I'm sorry, twenty-nine what?"

"Besties." She turned and met my gaze with her own huge dark eyes. "You're number twenty-nine."

For some reason, that warmed me from the inside out. I pressed my hands to my chest and smiled at her. The only other friend I'd ever had was Piper. If I was being honest, I liked Ophelia. "Aww, I'm flattered."

She wrinkled her nose and moved to another tree. "Don't get emotional on me or you're off the list. I don't do tears."

"I wasn't crying." I glanced back at Cross, wondering if he was watching this wild exchange.

"In any case, the universe provides with all these friends, and it is quite exhausting," she said. "I never deny what the universe sends me, but honestly, you're kind of worse than a goldfish."

All Cross did was chuckle and shake his head.

I was so confused. "How am I worse than a goldfish?"

"At least if you put goldfish in a nice place, feed them, keep them in the water, they just keep on swimming and living. *You* insist on going to get yourself killed, and it makes the job of best friend so much more taxing."

Like I was planning on getting myself killed? "I feel like you could understand wanting to help a best friend."

"Anyways, about Piper." Ophelia sighed and turned to face me once more. "The answer is *no*. You're like a defenseless baby deer to the rest of the things in our world . . . in Piper's world. It'd be like shooting fish in the lake to kill you off."

"You mean barrel," Cross called from where he sat.

"Right. Barrel. Anyways, easily dead, easily killed,

totally murderable, like an easy practice kill." When she looked at me with those round dark eyes, it was hard not to think of her as innocent. Yet here she was telling me how killable I really was. It wasn't that I didn't believe her, it was that I didn't want to. If I was so easily killed in this new world of Piper's, then how was she also not in the same amount of danger?

"There's such thing as a practice kill?" I shook my head and held my hand up stopping her before she could answer. "Don't answer that."

"Look, twenty-nine, I don't want to see you trip over your feet and die." She turned to Cross. "They die that easily, right?"

He paused in his arrow-sharpening and brushed his hair from his face. He arched his eyebrow at her. "Mortals?"

"Yeah." She nodded.

He snapped his fingers. "Like that."

"I really don't know how parents let you out of the house like that, all not prepared to die to defend yourself." She paused as if thinking. "Feels like bad parenting to me."

"You think either of us knows anything about parenting?" Cross gave a dark chuckle. "With *our* parents?"

Ophelia nodded at him. "Good point. I mean, I had to help kill my dad . . . and your dad . . . and threaten your mom."

I watched this exchange between the two of them like it was a tennis match. My brain was not catching up to what she was saying. She killed her dad? And his dad? But the two of them acted like it was no big deal. I couldn't help but wonder if I'd actually dodged a bullet not having any parents at all, especially if these two got rid of the ones they already had.

Cross pulled a knife from behind his back and started sharpening it on his stone. "But you didn't kill Zinnia's mom, so bonus points."

Ophelia nodded. "Yeah, I like her. She's kind of like a second mom."

He scoffed. "To all of us. You think when she had Zin she thought to herself, *imma end up with like a dozen other kids and hope none of them die or kill the wrong person?*"

"She has to think that, right?" Ophelia bit her bottom lip as though deep in thought. She turned back toward me. "At least she was good at toughening up Zin. Your parents sucked. They kept you so . . . delicate."

"I don't have parents." I held my hands up and shrugged. When I was younger, it bothered me that no one chose me. I wondered what was wrong with me that not a single couple wanted me as part of their family, and I so desperately wanted a family. But the moment Piper and I decided to hang out, I knew we'd be the family both of us needed.

"Oh, lucky you." She shrugged and turned back toward the tree, searching for an empty spot. There were none. "Your survival skills *are* seriously lacking though."

She wasn't going to change her mind, and neither was I. There was only one thing I could do to get out of here and to Piper. "Fine, then, train me."

Her face lit up like I gave her the best Christmas present in the world. Cross jumped to his feet and shook his head. "Oh no, you don't know what you're asking."

"Yes, I do." I crossed my arms over my chest. If I was ever going to get off this island, I had to prove I could walk in their world.

"See, she knows." Ophelia beamed at him.

"You really don't, but at least she'll have potions to heal you." He backed away and turned toward the hallway. He took off sprinting down the hall, his magic seeping out behind him.

"Heal me?" My brow furrowed in confusion. "Where's he going?"

"To get the potions for healing, duh." Ophelia rolled her eyes at me.

Nervousness ran through my body. "Seriously? Like, he was serious about that?"

Ophelia's arm shot out and a knife sailed end over end right toward me. It grazed the side of my cheek and *thunked* into a tree behind me. I felt the sharp sting of the cut on my face, and when I pressed my fingers to it, warm liquid covered my hand and ran down the side of my face. I slapped my hand to my cheek, feeling the warmth of my own blood on my skin. "You cut me."

"Pain will teach you. And that's how you'll learn." Her face turned serious.

Cross ran back into the room holding two handfuls of potion vials. "Damn it, O. You could've waited until I got them."

She motioned to my face. "It's barely a scratch."

She pulled another knife that'd been hidden somewhere on her body that I couldn't see. *Shit.* I might've gone too far but there was no going back now. I wiped my sleeve over my cheek, trying to brush the blood away. *Piper, here I come.* "Well, bring it on."

CHAPTER FOUR

PIPER

"*I* loved you the moment I met you." Grayson fired the words out so fast my mind could hardly keep up. "I knew you would be it for me, and you always have been."

Bright red light flooded from under the sleeves of his coat and shirt at the same time as my own forearm started to glow. When I looked down, there was a mark there that I'd never seen before. Black lines that looked like vines ran from the back of my hand, around my wrist, and up my forearm. Sharp barbs poked out from each of the lines like barbed wire. I turned my arm, and there on my forearm were two roses. Their petals were a deep crimson. Each was tucked into intertwined vines covered in spikes. Blood dripped from the single spike touching the center of each rose. My jaw dropped at its gothic beauty. My heart soared at its simple yet beautiful perfection.

"Grayson?"

He ripped his sleeves open. Our marks matched perfectly. "You're my soulmate, Piper. I've always known you would be."

His body shuddered from head to toe and red veins forked out over the whites of his eyes. Dark circles surrounded them, and his skin paled until it was nearly blue. His fangs descended down past his lips, and when he looked at me, I felt like an animal about to be hunted. I didn't know what was happening to him, but he grew bigger, his muscles more well-defined. His suit coat tore to shreds and fell in pieces around him.

"Piper, listen to me." He caught my eye.

My heart hammered in my chest. "What's wrong with you?"

"Piper, I love you." His entire body shuddered as though the words themselves hurt to say.

"I love you too." I took a step toward him, but he held his hand up, waving me back.

"Good. Now do something for me." He froze. His eyes met mine, and a cold chill ran down my spine.

"An-anything." I wanted to go to him but every instinct in my body told me not to move, that this wasn't the Grayson I knew and loved. This . . . this was something else.

A growl ripped from his throat as he tensed his whole body to spring at me. "RUN!"

My eyes widened for a split second before he launched himself at me. I dropped to the floor and rolled to the side. His body soared over mine and slammed into the wall. It cracked under the force of his crash and a dent the size of his body was embedded into it. He dropped to the ground and shook his head. Before I could get up, he began to rise to his feet. A snarl ripped from his throat, and it sent adrenaline running through my body.

I scrambled to my feet. "Grayson, what the hell is wrong with you!?"

He moved to the side, circling me. His eyes weren't the warm mahogany I'd grown so used to. They were a bottomless black with red veins forking out in all directions. Strands of his dark hair fell over his face as he lowered his chin and locked his eyes on me. A hiss seeped from his lips, and he swiped his hand at the distance between us. He held his hands like they were claws ready to strike at any moment. I stepped to the side trying to keep my distance as we circled each other, and I held my hand out toward him, hoping to ward him off.

"This isn't you." My heart hammered in my chest and his eyes locked on the point in my neck.

I'd never seen his fangs so long and sharp. His tongue darted over the tip of one, and he made a little sucking sound. A single drop of blood trickled from the corner of his mouth. He didn't say a word. Yet when I looked at him, I couldn't help but feel the Grayson I knew wasn't here with me. He crouched down low, and I froze, getting ready for the attack. He launched himself across the room so fast he was nearly a blur to my vampire senses. I ducked under his attack and turned to the side a moment before he grabbed me. His nails raked across my skin, leaving deep cuts across my arm. Blood welled and trickled down my skin. Those red streams wound down my forearm to my wrist and dripped off my fingertips.

"Grayson, what the fuck!?" I pressed my hand over the cuts, trying to get them to stop bleeding.

He slammed into the wall and turned back toward me. A growl ripped from his throat, and he pushed off the wall, diving back for me. He wrapped his hands around my neck, tackling me to the ground. I slid across the floor with him on top of me and we smashed into the foot of Theon's bed. The mattress flew across the room and the bed frame splintered to pieces around us. We slid right through it and smacked into the other wall. It dented from the force that we hit it with, and dust filled the air. Grayson's hands were tight around my neck, and he wrestled me under him. He straddled my legs and pinned me down. His eyes were crazed with thirst. The air was stuck in my throat as he squeezed harder. He leaned over me, gnashing his sharp teeth inches from my face.

I clawed at his hands, but they were unbreakable vises around my neck. I wanted to scream to call for help, but no one would come and face this. My own fangs extended, and I hissed at him. I swung both my legs up, nearly folding my body in half, and wrapped them around his shoulders and shoved my heels into his sternum. With all the strength I had, I yanked him back. His body crashed to the ground and his head cracked against the floor. As his hands slipped from around my neck, his nails raked across my skin. The smell of my own blood filled the air as I pinned him down with my legs.

A wild growl ripped from his throat and his claws dug into the floor. He kicked his legs out and rolled to the side, flipping us both over onto our stomachs. I kicked out, connecting with his chest, and he flew back. My vampire strength was nearly as powerful as his and he crashed into the wall. I sprang to my feet just as he hopped to his. Blood trickled from his lip, and his eyes locked on mine.

I snarled at him. "You wanna dance? Then let's fucking do it."

He jumped toward me, and we grabbed onto each other at the same time, grappling for the upper hand. I spun around and yanked him with me. I wrapped my hands around his arms and slammed him into the wall. His eyes went wide with surprise at my strength. Even I was shocked I was able to put up such a fight against an older, experienced vampire like him. He was mine, I loved him, but this wasn't him. Something happened the moment he gave into our love, and now I had to figure out what before he killed me. Adrenaline pumped through my veins, and I tightened my grip on him. I spun to the side with all my might and threw him across the room. Before he hit anything, I grabbed a lamp off Theon's dresser and threw it at him.

Grayson smacked into the wall and the lamp exploded across his chest. Shards of dark ceramic fell to the floor around him. He bellowed at the cuts across his skin. The scent of his blood tingled my nose. It was a mix of the most enticing wine and chocolate. My mouth watered for a taste of him, and I ran my tongue over my lips. His eyes tracked the movement, and he hissed in my direction as though my desire infuriated him. He tensed as though he was going to leap forward, and I held my hand out. A fine red mist seeped from my palm and drifted on the air between us.

"Stop!" He froze for a split second, his muscles twitching with the need to move. It was like I was holding him there. I felt his body under my control and how it pained him to not have control of himself and be able to attack me like he desired. It was a heady feeling of realizing in this moment that there wasn't a damn thing he could do to me. Yet the power felt fleeting, like at any moment it would diminish and I'd lose control over him. I just had no idea how this was possible or how long it would hold.

What the hell did I do?

Not even a second later he leapt toward me, and I tried to catch him but the force of his attack knocked me off my feet. We crashed through the wall behind me and out into the hall. Rocks scattered across the ground and dust covered my body. He spun me around so his chest was pressed to my back. He wrapped his arm around my neck in a vise-like grip, locking my head there. The air cut off from my lungs and the lack of oxygen made my head feel like it was about to explode. I kicked my legs out, but they only scratched across the gravel left from the wall. My dress offered no coverage for my legs and scratches ran over my skin. I dug my nails into his skin, but he didn't let go. My vision wavered as black dots started to float around. I fought to turn my head to the side. Sweat covered my body. I hadn't been dead long enough to forget what it felt like for my life to slip away. But in this moment I was reminded, and the panic that came with my impending death was nearly paralyzing. I felt my life starting to slip—the lack of air, my blood slowing in my veins, and my vision nearly black.

I did the only thing I could think of, I opened my mouth and bit down on his forearm as hard as I could. His skin broke under my fangs and his heady taste filled my mouth. Grayson sucked in a sharp breath and a groan of pleasure escaped his lips. His grip loosened and I sucked in a deep breath through my nose. I locked my hold on his arm and held his arm there, sucking in the most delicious flavor of all: Grayson.

"Piper?" His voice wavered from behind me, and I immediately let go of him.

The moment my lips left his skin, he leapt away from me. I scrambled to my feet to face him. "Gray, what the hell is going on?"

"I—" he looked down at his hands, peering at how long his claws were. When he turned to me, his eyes roamed over the cuts marring my arms and legs. "Bloody hell."

He gazed round the hallway. Confusion riddled his features. I could only imagine what he thought seeing the wall in shambles and the two of us looking like we'd battled it out. He scrubbed his hand down his face as if he didn't know how or why he'd gotten himself to the Night Spawn headquarters. The hallway was oddly empty but for the two of us. It seemed like a lifetime since the ball happened, but it'd only been a few hours.

"Gray, look at me."

His eyes snapped to me, and there was a flash of recognition in them. I tried to take a step toward him, but he backed away from me. He ran his hand over his face and gave me one last glance before sprinting toward the mirrors they'd set up at the end of the hall for vampires who lived with the Night Spawn. He paused when he reached the mirror. When he eyed my injuries one last time, his brow furrowed and the muscle in his jaw clenched. Pain crossed his face, and he dove through the mirror, leaving me alone and bleeding.

"No! Grayson!" I sprinted after him, but a vise-like arm caught me around the waist.

I was pulled back and held away from the mirror he'd just gone through. I threw my elbow back, connecting with ribs. "Let me go!"

I had to go after him. Something was wrong with Gray. He clearly needed help. An *ooofff* sound came from behind me but the arms didn't drop. "Piper!"

I froze. "Theon?"

When I glanced back, his face was bright-red and his cheeks were puffed out like he was holding a breath he couldn't let go of. I tried to scramble away from his grip. "Let me go! He needs me."

"He's not himself, Piper. He's dangerous." He turned and tossed me back. He moved to stand between me and the mirror. He sucked in heaving breaths while motioning to me. "Look at you. You're lucky to be alive."

The scratches down my arms and legs were already healing from what little blood I took from Grayson. My dress was torn in all different places, exposing even more of my skin. Dried blood covered the shimmering cream-colored material and stuck to my arms and legs. I knew I looked like hell. I even felt like hell. Judging by the tenderness on my neck and face, I knew there were bruises there. I glanced over his shoulder toward the mirror I wanted to jump headlong into, hoping it'd take me to Grayson. But even I knew that would be a long shot. Mirror travel didn't work like that. We had to travel to other mirrors stationed in places we knew. I couldn't just travel to Grayson . . . or could I?

Theon offered me his hand. "You need help, Piper. You can't take a crazed vampire down by yourself. No one can . . . Even if you love him."

I'd gotten lucky this time. Whatever happened to Grayson was new and we were both still fighting it. I didn't know if it would get worse or if he would get stronger. But what I did know was that he needed help, the kind of help that required real firepower. I gave him a single nod. "Where to?"

"The only place with the power to help a vampire like Grayson . . . The House of Shade."

CHAPTER FIVE

SANCHITA

amn this dress, damn these shoes, and damn it all.
All hell had broken loose, and when I mean hell . . . I mean literal hell. *How could Marius have done this?* Attacking the crown and the Blood Borns was signing a death sentence for any of the Night Spawn involved. My heart hammered in my chest, and I knew I was in deep shit. I wasn't where I belonged, but I didn't know the way out.

"Come on this way!" Marius yelled ahead of me. A sea of Night Spawn vampires followed in his wake as he darted down dark tunnels leading from the castle. I didn't want to be here, didn't want to be a part of this, but I'd been swept away with the tide of traitors. One of his lackeys had a hold of my arm and dragged me along. I'd gotten separated from Prisha in the attack, and now I was in the bowels of the castle in a tunnel that looked like it hadn't been used in centuries. There was no light, dust was thick on the floor, and giant spiderwebs hung overhead. The tunnel smelled of damp earth, coppery blood, and sweat.

I jerked against the pinching grip. "Let me go!"

My voice echoed off the rough cave-like walls surrounding me. The beefy vampire beside me jerked me closer to him and lowered his voice to a hiss. His face was large and square-like with beady eyes and fat lips. "Walk."

He shoved me forward and I stumbled into someone's back. I spun around and shoved my hands into his shoulders . . . he didn't budge. Even with my vampire strength, he didn't move. He glared down at me and grabbed my arms, lifting me off my feet. My heels slipped off and clattered to the floor. My legs swung there, and I wanted to kick him in the groin, but I froze.

"Drop her." There it was. That smooth, confident voice I'd grown familiar with over the years.

Instantly my feet hit the ground and the pinching grip left my skin. I tugged my dress back into place and tried to dust myself off. When I looked up, Marius stood before me. He was much taller than me, with wavy brown hair that fell to his chin and a scraggly goatee. He wore that same damn leather jacket with the thick fur lapel. His eyes bore into mine as he spoke. "You're either with us or against us."

Against . . . definitely against. But I needed to buy myself time to find a way out of this and away from him. "I don't even know what this or *us* is."

"This is the future," he whispered from low in his throat and moved only inches from me. His hot breath fanned over my face. His dark eyes were wild with excitement. "I am the future."

Voices sounded from behind us, and I knew in moments the guards would be at our throats. Marius stepped back and glared over my shoulder. "We must away. Come."

I hesitated, trying to find a tactic to get away from him without losing my head. When I didn't answer right that second, he leaned away from me. His eyes blazed with fury. His lip curled into a cruel sneer. "You aren't ready for the future. And if you aren't ready for the future, you'll die in the past."

"I— I . . ." The voices grew closer and panic ran through my body.

Marius didn't say another word, he just turned away from me with his long leather coat billowing out around him. His wave of Night Spawn closed in behind him, following him. With their vampire speed they darted deeper into the tunnel leaving a slight breeze and the smell of blood in their wake. I sagged against the wall and sucked in a deep breath. Darkness swallowed me, but with my vampire senses, I could see in the dank cave.

Three soldiers appeared around me. One stood in front of me. He was large and imposing with big muscles and the look of a soldier who'd been living that lifestyle for an eternity. His jaw was square and bulky. He had a flat nose and dark, almond-shaped eyes. Before I could say a word, he grabbed my arm and spun me around, shoving me into the wall. Rough rocks scratched against my skin. If I were human, I'd be bruised all over.

"You're hurting."

Thick cuffs were wrapped around my wrists and leather binding curled my fingers into a tight fist. My fingers went numb, and my instincts screamed for me to fight against the pinching hold. I held as still as I could. The King's Guard was not to be trifled with. I knew it, everyone knew it. Everyone but Marius it seemed. The guard yanked me back and shoved me toward two others. Each took one of my arms and lifted me up off the ground and carried me down the hall.

"I didn't do anything." Panic made my voice sound higher than it really was, and I hated it.

"You were found in the wake of Marius' exit after he attacked the crown. You'll forgive me if I don't believe you." His voice was deep and gruff as he moved to walk in front of us.

I wanted to scream that he was letting them get away, but the shock of everything unfolding made me fall silent. The night had been too much, and suddenly I found my body sagging into their hold. My bare feet dragged over the ground. They picked up speed. My toes warmed from the friction against the floor as they moved faster through the castle. We ran through a dark maze of tunnels and pushed through a door, and suddenly I was blinded by bright lights. I blinked against how bright it was and white dots swarmed my vision. The doors banged shut behind us, and the two guards dragged me in behind the bigger leader.

"Jester, is this one injured, sick, or something else?" An older-looking vampire moved closer to us. He peeked around the big military guy and stared at me.

He straightened his glasses and sucked in a deep breath as though exhausted. I couldn't believe they had a made-vampire working in the castle like this. He was an older-looking vampire. His sire changed him when he'd hit what looked like his late fifties, and though the change made him strong and fit, he still held some maturity in his face and grey streaks in his dark hair. The wrinkles around his eyes were nearly smoothed out from the change.

I couldn't help but stare at him. Jester, I was assuming that was the name of the leader, glanced back at me with a hard look on his face. "Something else."

"There's too much." The doctor shook his head. "How could they . . . What I mean to say is the cruelty . . . the . . . the suffering they've caused."

It was then that I took the time to look around. Chaos filled the lab, injured vampires lay strewn across tables. Science equipment was shoved off to the side. Lab technicians hurried about. Their pristine white coats were spattered with blood. Each of their faces held the same panic that deep down inside I felt. Groans of the injured filled the air, their cries of pain and shock would forever be burned into my memories. They were vampires and they would heal, but their injuries were so substantial. They needed more blood, more help, more medical attention. All because of Marius.

Blood coated the floor, and the smell permeated the air. Instead of it seeming appetizing, my stomach rolled. It was the opposite of what tonight was supposed to be. They were all dressed in their Christmas ball gowns. The glitter and glitz mixed with the gore and injuries made it that much more horrifying. They'd all come here to celebrate, be unified, and show their love to the crown. Now everything was destroyed between the Night Spawn and made-vampires. I'd always thought Marius was shady, but now I knew he was a downright insane bastard.

"Then away with her." The doctor motioned to a door at the back of the lab. *No!* I didn't want to go back there. To whatever death trap they had hidden back there. It was bad enough out here among the injured, but back there gave me the feeling like I'd never return. A small whimper escaped my lips as the soldiers dragged me toward it. I tried not to look, I tried to search out anyone or anything that could help me, but all I was faced with was more troubling sights.

We passed by cells. Looking through the glass, I saw they held vampires that'd been overcome by the sickness. One stood there exploding into water only to re-form moments later. Another stood in the corner of her cell sucking blood from her own arm. I could feel the sickness within them all. The terror of not knowing where it came from or how it came to be sat heavy in my stomach. Would I get it here? Would my fate be to remain trapped behind these walls forever? Before, I thought it couldn't be explained. But now with the vampires infected with the sickness following Marius, I knew deep down that he was involved somehow.

They dragged me through the doors, and we were in a dark tunnel once again. "No, please, I'm telling you I've done nothing wrong."

Jester glanced over his shoulder at me. "That's what a liar would say."

"I'm no liar." I somehow managed to add a little venom to my words. I was a lot of different things, but a liar was not one of them. I prided myself on being honest.

They dragged me toward a dark cell, and the moment we reached the bars, they tossed me in like I weighed little more than a feather. I fell to the ground in a heap at Jester's feet. He squatted down in front of me and placed his finger under my chin. He lifted my chin until our gazes met. "I've put down a lot of vampires in my day. You might be the loveliest. Shame."

I yanked my chin back from his grasp. "I am innocent."

He stepped out of the cell and the metal bars slid into place between us with a thunderous clang. "We shall see. Atlas Savage will be with you in a moment."

A chill seeped into my skin, and I leaned back against the damp jagged wall. A shiver went down my spine. I didn't know if it was the state of the cell or the thought of Atlas Savage, the right hand of the King, the deadliest hand of all. The rumors were that he'd kill his own family, if he had one, for The House of Shade. Rumors swirled about how deep his connections ran and how far he would go for them. But I did not want to find out. I curled myself into a small ball at the corner of the cell.

"Hey, *pssst*." A low hissing voice traveled from across the way toward me.

I huddled in on myself. I didn't want anything to do with this. This place, this cell, was a side of the castle I never expected to find myself. Nor did I want to. I pulled my knees up to my chest and wrapped my arms around them. "Piss off. I've got nothing to say to you."

"You are no one," the voice hissed from the darkness.

"I am Sanchita, and I'll have nothing to do with you. Thank you very much."

A vampire slid into view in the cell across from me. He too was crouched on the floor but there was a madness in his eyes. His dark hair was all disheveled and greasy. Dark circles surrounded his eyes, and his skin was sickly pale, nearly gray. His clothing was ripped to tatters. He leaned on the bars and let his boney hand hang over the bars. "He will rule us all someday."

I glanced into the darkness down the corridor between the cells. "Who?"

The vampire slithered to his feet as if he were in a drunken stupor. He wobbled from side to side with a dark smirk on his face. "Join us, Night Spawn."

"Who is us?" I didn't know why I was engaging in this conversation. I had no intention of joining whatever the hell he was talking about. I wouldn't join Marius or anyone else who stood against The House of Shade. They wanted better for all of us.

He chuckled and wagged his eyebrows. He wiggled his fingers and black smoke seeped from his hand onto the floor like a creeping fog. I hopped to my feet and pressed myself to the wall. Panic flooded my body, and a chill went down my spine. Made-vampires weren't supposed to have powers like that. I didn't want it to touch me. I had no idea what it would do to me. But in the world of vampires, witches, warlocks, and more, anything was possible. A wild laugh escaped his lips as he watched that black smoke slither toward me.

"Stop it! No!" I scrambled back, trying to get as far away as I could.

A blur of movement shot between the two of us and my eyes widened. The breath caught in my throat. The very air around us changed. A dark figure reached through the smoke and in between the bars. He grabbed onto the other vampire's shirt and jerked him toward the bars, slamming his head into them with a loud banging sound. He jerked him back and forth three more times in rapid succession, slamming him into the bars with a loud bang each time. He did it until blood trailed down the vampire's face and his eyes rolled into the back of his head. When he went limp, the black smoke stopped, and the vampire fell in a heap at the dark shadow's feet.

He flicked his hand and blood splashed across the floor. When he turned to the side to look at his hand, I glimpsed his profile. His face was all sharp planes and pale, smooth skin. His eyes nearly glowed in the darkness. They were an odd coloring with dark brown around his pupils that faded to the most vivid blue. He lifted his hand and let his tongue dart over his fingertips, tasting the blood. He spat on the floor and wiped the back of his hand over his lips. I didn't dare move or breathe, and yet his eyes locked onto me.

"I didn't do anything." The words tumbled from my mouth before he even moved to fully face me. When he did, I sucked in a sharp breath. Atlas Savage. There was no mistaking who this was. I'd heard stories of him, with his white hair with black streaks and raven tattoo across his chest. His black shirt hung open just enough for me to spy the dark ink over his skin.

His face was covered in sweat and spatters of blood. Steaks of dirt covered his cheeks, giving them an even sharper effect. His voice was deep and gravely as he spoke, "Didn't you?"

"No." I wanted out of here and away from him now. This vampire was absolutely terrifying. That was when I heard the distinct sound of a drip, and another. In his other hand he held a sword with blood dripping from the tip onto the floor, creating a small pool. I hadn't noticed it before with him slamming that guy's face into the bars. But now that I had noticed, goosebumps broke out on my skin. "I swear I didn't do anything."

He ran his eyes over me from head to toe. "And the sickness?"

"Wh-what about it?"

He stepped in closer to the bars. "I don't have time for daftness . . . Do you have it?"

"N-no?"

He arched his eyebrow, and it made him look more sinister. "You don't sound so sure."

"I was just here with my sister and my friends. The Prince invited us personally. I had no idea any of this would happen, or that I would be dragged down here." I glanced around the cell, suddenly feeling like the walls were closing in on me. "All I wanted was to hang out with Piper and my sister."

"Piper?" His eyes snapped to mine. His whole demeanor changed. I didn't think it was possible, but now he was even more terrifying, with fine red mist seeping from his skin. The tattoo on his chest rippled as though it was going to leap right off his body. "Where is she?"

"I-I don't know. Don't you know?"

"I find your panicked reasoning tedious. Why would I ask if I already knew?" He sighed and then bellowed down the hall. "Jester!"

A moment later, the vampire who brought me here was at his side. "Sav."

He waved his hand toward me like I was nothing at all. "Release her. She's of no use to us."

The tight knots in my chest started to loosen. Jester glanced in my direction. "We found her in the tunnel in the wake of Marius' retreat."

"What were you doing there?" Atlas snapped in my direction.

"I got grabbed in the chaos, and they dragged me with them. I tried to get away, but it wasn't until your soldiers started to chase after them that Marius let me go."

He waved his hand and the cell bars slid open. There was nothing between the two of us. This close he could take my head before I even realized his blade had moved. The scent of blood and death lingered on him, and a chill ran down my spine. His gaze never wavered from mine. "Let you go?"

"I didn't believe in his cause." It sounded stupid even coming from my own lips.

He narrowed his eyes. "He just killed countless vampires on this night, and you expect me to believe he just *let you go?*"

"I'm telling you the truth. Please, if I could just speak to Piper, she'll tell you. I would never do anything to hurt The House of Shade."

"She has disappeared," he said through gritted teeth. "Last seen with Theon, a devout follower of Marius."

"He wouldn't hurt her." I didn't know why I sounded so sure of this. Theon annoyed me for all his devotion to Marius and his views, but I couldn't see him doing anything to actually hurt Piper. That said, I never thought Marius would take his ramblings this far.

"Take me to him," Atlas demanded.

"I-I'm not sure where he is." My eyes darted around like I'd find the answers here in this cell.

He reached out and snagged my arm and jerked me

toward him. "Then you will sit in here until your memory returns."

Bloody hell, this was going to be the death of me. Atlas Savage was going to cut off my head, or burn me alive, or turn me to ash just from looking at me. How was I going to say goodbye to Prisha? I turned to look at Jester. "If I die here, tell my sister I said goodbye and I love her."

Atlas gave a humorless chuckle. "So sure you're not going to remember."

"I have nothing to remember because I don't know, so I'm bound to fail," I admitted honestly.

"And if you succeed, then you won't die and you'll see your sister soon." Atlas leaned in closer, and I felt his breath fan across my hair as he spoke through gritted teeth. "If you fail, then you'll die, and I promise you'll see your sister that way too."

My stomach sank to my toes. If Prisha died because of me, I'd never forgive myself, even in death. I tried to show him no fear. "Seems like a win-win."

"Think hard," he growled.

We're all gonna die.

CHAPTER SIX

PIPER

"Come along, Piper. Come. Along." Theon wrapped his hand around my wrist and tugged me down the hall away from his room and the mirror Grayson leapt through.

I pulled back on his grip, yanking free. "I have to get to him."

He whirled around to face me. His eyes were wide with panic, and he motioned wildly to the portal as he spoke. "In case you haven't noticed, your boyfriend has lost his bloody mind. He's gone mad. There isn't a thing you can do about it on your own. You need help. The kind of help the King can provide. Grayson will be too strong for you."

When he looked at me with those deep, serious sage eyes, I wanted to give in and listen to what he said. He'd been a vampire far longer than me. He would know better. But my instincts screamed at me to go after Gray to help him. Standing here arguing with Theon was going to do nothing but waste my time and any chance I had of catching up with him. The urgency was so deep in the pit of my stomach that I was so tempted to knock Theon out and take off running.

Deep down I knew Grayson needed me, and I'd held my own against him before. He had the element of surprise the first time. Now he wouldn't surprise me. I would keep holding my own until we fixed whatever the hell this was.

"And I am just as strong," I said.

His face fell and he hung his head. "Piper, not for this. I saw him. The Grayson you know no longer exists."

The thought of the Grayson I knew not existing in the same world as me sent a searing pain through my chest. When I pressed my hand over my heart, Theon's eyes lingered on the soulmate mark winding around my wrist. He shifted from one foot to the other and ran his hand through his hair, tugging at the strands. His mouth opened and closed a few times like he didn't know what to say to me.

"Oh, Piper." His voice trailed off with a hint of sadness.

"Don't look at me like that." I squared my shoulders and glared at him. I'd gotten that look all my life with each new foster home I moved into—the pitying looks like they all thought I was something or someone to feel bad for. I didn't see myself that way, and I wouldn't have Theon seeing me that way either.

"I'm not looking at you like anything." He shook his head and strands of that dirty-blond hair fell over his forehead into his eyes.

"Yes, you are." I took a step back from him. "We are going to figure this out. Whatever happened to Grayson, I can help, and I can figure it out."

"Piper . . ." He groaned and his words trailed off. His eyes widened as he looked past me.

I spun around to see Night Spawn vampires flooding out of the mirrors. They didn't look like they'd been at a ball, but rather through a battle. Their clothing was ripped. Blood spatters covered the material and their exposed skin. But there was a look of shock on their faces, like they were shell-shocked, and it looked as if they were a panicked stampede running from something. Prisha limped toward us with Martin by her side. She leaned into him as he held most of her weight against him.

My jaw dropped. "What happened to you?"

"You look bloody awful." Theon took a step back from them as he looked them up and down.

Prisha's eyes flooded with unshed tears. Her emerald ball gown was shredded into strips around her legs. Her skin was scraped up as though she'd fallen or been dragged across the ground.

She narrowed her eyes at Theon. "As if you don't know!"

Confusion riddled his features and his brow furrowed. He wrinkled his nose and shook his head. "How the devil would I know?"

"Marius and his supporters attacked the ball this evening." Martin's lip pulled up into a sneer, and he too glared at Theon. "A lot of vampires were hurt and killed tonight."

I froze and my stomach dropped. "He did WHAT?"

"I lost Sanchita in the fray. I don't know what happened to her." Tears spilled over Prisha's cheeks and fell onto her dress, making the emerald color even darker in spots. "And now we have no idea what will happen to any of us."

I knew the relationship between the Night Spawn and Blood Born vampires was strained at best. Would this be the tipping point for war? It would be exactly what Marius wanted. This was nothing more than a power grab, plain and simple. No one wanted war between the factions. No one but him. He was using the majority to cater to his own whims.

"That greedy bastard."

"There must be some mistake," Theon muttered and scrubbed a hand over his face. He shook his head and met Martin's eye. "He can't have."

"Don't play daft with me. You're his progeny. You've been a devout right-hand man for decades. Can you think us so blind as to not see how you'd fit in with this plan? Perhaps a double agent?" I'd never seen Martin so angry. His normally perfectly styled blond hair was completely disheveled. His pressed suit was torn and wrinkled . . . and one of his shoes was missing.

Theon put his hands on his hips and sucked in a deep breath, then let it out in a long huff. His eyes widened as he shifted from one foot to the other. "This can't be true."

"Oh, you think me a liar, like you?" Martin looked like he was about to pounce on Theon.

"We have to get to the castle," Theon insisted as he wrapped his hand around my wrist and started to try to pull me along with him. He turned toward Prisha. "We'll find Sanchita, I promise."

"Don't fall for it, Piper." Martin got in Theon's face. "She's not going anywhere with you. And we will find her ourselves. We don't want your help, traitor."

I knew the vampires needed Grayson for this. He was the bridge between the vampire factions. If anyone could stop a war from coming, it would be him. More vampires came through the mirrors crowding the hall, all shoving into each other all to get away from whatever had happened at the castle. They shoved into us and his grip broke from my wrist. I stumbled back, but in that moment, I took my chance. I darted toward the mirror Gray had disappeared into. I didn't have time to pray that my power would work to get me through it.

I glanced over my shoulder just in time to see Martin tackle Theon to the ground as he tried to stop me. They wrestled on the floor as I pressed my hand to the mirror and leapt through. My thoughts were only of where Grayson could possibly be. The liquid was cool and slimy against my skin as I moved through it and fell into what looked like a tunnel. There was a pinpoint of light at the end of it, and I ran toward it with my vampire speed, thinking only of one thing... Grayson.

The mirror turned liquid and peeled across my skin on

the other side and fell away. I landed on my feet on top of loose gravel. I glanced around trying to acclimate to my surroundings. I was in some kind of tunnel. It was smooth and round and so very dark. My toe hit something metal, and before I could glance down, a bright light hurtled toward me at a racing speed. The ground vibrated and I realized the metal things at my feet were rails. The screeching sound of a train filled the air, and I leapt back against the wall. It sped past me only inches from my body. Wind whipped down the tunnel and my hair flew around my face. The sound was deafening and everything vibrated around me. I sucked in a deep breath and held it. I pressed myself to the wall and closed my eyes, waiting for it to pass.

I was a vampire, with all the benefits that came with that, but I had no idea if I would survive being made roadkill or not. Something about the force that it sped down the tunnel made me think being exploded by a train wasn't something a vampire would survive. Once the subway passed, I turned and sprinted toward the platform. I didn't know if Grayson would be here, but I had to try to find him. Adrenaline pumped through my veins. If I could have but a moment with him, I could fix this. Whatever *this* was. I had to believe I could. There was no other option.

I leapt up onto the platform and spun around searching for him. I didn't know if searching for him this way would work or if I was just standing in the tubes looking like a crazy person. I had to have looked mad with my hair in tangles and dried blood across my skin. My silky white dress was in tatters around me, and I had more skin exposed than not. My scratches had all but healed. The bruises were nearly faded. Grayson's blood was more than just my drug of choice, it was magical the way it healed me.

The platform wasn't crowded this early in the morning. It had to be nearly four. The air was cool against my skin. The smell of snow drifted from the street above. Cool air whipped down the stairs toward me as I tiptoed my way down the platform. Signs for where I was hung above my head: *Still in London*. Two men ran past me looking over their shoulders with fear fresh on their faces. My instincts screamed that it was Grayson who terrified these men.

I moved in the direction they ran from and found a shadow lingering in a darkened corner behind the stairs. A man's arms flailed helplessly, and a low growl drifted on the air. Grayson had his arm wrapped around the guy, holding him like a boa constrictor. His fangs were deep in his neck, and the sound of his sucking filled the air. I wrinkled my nose at the violence of it, how dark and dirty this was. The rules for feeding had changed long ago. Vampires didn't hunt their prey in the shadows of the night anymore, yet here Grayson was with a victim of his own.

The sound of the man's heartbeat slowed, and I knew death was nearly at his door. I stepped into the light, letting Grayson see me. "Grayson, stop!"

His eyes snapped up to mine, and I could tell he wasn't in there. Those lines forked out over the whites of his eyes. He growled at me and sank his fangs deeper into the man's skin. Any moment now he would kill him from the sheer amount of blood loss. Blood rushed through my veins as my panic took over.

I held my hand up and that fine red mist drifted from my skin. I tried to control it to tap into something deep within myself that made me want to stop this. I wanted it with all of my being. If he killed someone now, there was no turning back. He would forever be marked as a murderer, and it was not something even a cherished prince could survive. There would be consequences. I just wanted to keep him safe. With everything I was, I wanted to keep him safe. But if he did this now, all would be lost.

"Grayson, you have to stop now!"

He growled and jerked, trying to resist my power, but I forced more mist to seep from deep within. That red mist shot from me and wrapped around him like a cape. He opened his mouth and shoved the man away, letting him fall to the ground in a heap at his feet. He hissed in my direction but made no move to attack. Energy sizzled between us, and I didn't know what to do to stop whatever this was. But I knew if I got him home, they might be able to do something. "Come with me, Gray. We can help you."

He leapt at me and slammed into my body so hard the breath left my lungs. But I was ready this time and kept my feet. We skidded across the cement floor, leaving deep scratches in our wake. Our bodies twisted around and slammed into the walls, creating dents and crumbling the walls to the ground. He spun so quickly I lost my footing. My body went airborne as he threw me across the tracks onto the other side. I landed on the platform and then slid across the ground, my skin scraping at the rough surface. But I wasn't going to stop now. I sprang to my feet, leapt back to his side, and hit him like a lineman playing football. I wrapped my arms around him and threw him up toward the ceiling. He crashed there and the tunnel shook. The lights flickered above our heads. They popped and shattered, raining down on us like sparklers.

He crashed to the ground at my feet, and I stood over him. "Come on, Gray, I don't want to hurt you, but I will if I have to."

His arm shot out and he grabbed my ankle and jerked me down. He sprang forward and pounced on top of me. I held my arm up to block him, and he opened his mouth, baring his fangs. His teeth sank into my forearm, piercing my skin. My instincts took over and I shoved my body forward into his and struck hard and fast, biting him back. I pierced his skin, and his delicious flavor flooded my mouth. His grip on me loosened and I felt his fangs leave my arm, but I wasn't about to let go of him.

He groaned deep in his throat, and my name escaped his lips like a whispered prayer. "Piper?"

I withdrew my fangs and scooted off him. I knelt before him and caught his eye. "Gray, you have to tell me what's going on! What's wrong with you?"

He cupped my face in his hands, and when those warm mahogany eyes met mine, all I saw was devastation. We were only inches apart and I wanted to press even closer. I lowered my voice to a whisper, hoping he could hear how much I just needed him. "Let me help you."

"No one can help me now." He ground his teeth together and sucked in a sharp breath through his teeth. "But do one thing for me?"

"Anything. Just come with me, please." I wrapped my arms around his wrists and pulled him closer. This whole thing scared me. Grayson was in deep shit, and I felt helpless to do anything.

"Tell Atlas to keep his word to me." He pressed his lips to mine and fire shot through my veins. It was dark and desperate, like a *dead man walking* kind of kiss, like he believed it would be the last kiss we'd ever share. The world could have burnt to the ground around me and all I'd want was him.

The train came to a halt behind him, and I held onto him for dear life. He pulled away from me all too soon and stepped back into the train. The doors slid closed between us and his face fell. He threw his head back and bellowed to the ceiling. He dropped to his knees and fisted his hair. I'd never seen him so tortured, like there was no hope left in the world. The train shot into motion, and he was gone in seconds, leaving me there kneeling on the ground as he left me again.

CHAPTER SEVEN

THEON

"Have you lost your mind?" I rolled on top of Martin and shoved his shoulders into the ground. Chaos went wild around us. Night Spawn vampires gathered around us, watching as he growled and snapped his teeth at me.

He swung his fist at me, but it slammed into the side of my throat. "I'll rip out your bloody throat."

Pain shot through the side of my neck and up into my jaw. I choked on the air trying to leave my lungs. I coughed while holding him there. "Fucking hell, Martin."

I didn't want to hurt him. But I bloody well would defend myself if I had to. I wrapped my hand around his wrist and slammed his fist to the hard concrete. The ground cracked and dented beneath his hand. I held it there for good measure. "I did not betray anybody."

"Lies!" He jerked his hips up, tossing me to the side and leaping on top of me.

We rolled for control, grappling for the upper hand. Martin landed on top of me, and he wrapped his hands around my neck and squeezed. The air was caught in my throat. My lungs burned for breath. The pressure behind my eyes increased, and my head felt like it was going to explode. I pulled my fist back and shot it forward, connecting with his jaw. Martin's head snapped back. His grip loosened on my throat. I swung my other hand. My fist connected with the other side of his jaw and sent him flying off me. Blood shot from his mouth and splattered across the ground. Sweat slicked his body and trickled down his forehead. I scrambled to my feet as Martin popped to his. His chest heaved with heavy breaths, and he curled his hands into fists. His brows were drawn low over his eyes as he glared at me. I'd never thought prim and proper Martin would have the bollocks to attack anyone, let alone me.

Prisha leapt between the two of us, holding her hands up. Anger colored her features, and she raised her voice. "Stop! Do you not see we're quite possibly at war? The vampire factions are pitted against each other. We cannot do this to each other. Not now."

Martin straightened his sleeves and ran his hand over his hair. Even with the effort he made to tidy himself, he was still a mess. He sucked in a deep breath but didn't look at me. "Quite right."

"I've done nothing." I paused. thinking about what they'd just said. Marius was crazy but was he mad enough to take on The House of Shade? When did his ramblings become actual action? And when did I not notice how bad he'd actually gotten? "I find what you're saying hard to believe."

Martin crossed his arms over his chest. "If you're innocent, then go to the castle and see for yourself. I'm sure they will all take mercy on you."

Doubt weighed heavily on my mind. Marius was my sire. We were close, or so I thought. But I knew nothing of this plan. I knew nothing of his next move. I was under the impression that I was his right hand, helping to make the Night Spawn better for all of us, despite what the highbrow Blood Born vampires might think. But war? No, I didn't think it possible. Not even Marius would stoop that low. *Would he?*

"I have nothing to hide." I turned away from them only to find more vampires staring at me. The looks on their faces were full of the same emotions Martin and Prisha showed me: fear, anger, and disgust. Usually, I felt like I had nothing to prove in this world, nothing to prove to anyone. I was who I was. But if what they were saying about Marius was true, then I would have something to prove because my loyalty had always been with him. But this was beyond my loyalty. The House of Shade was not something to be taken on.

I hurried toward one of the mirrors The House of Shade had set up for us. They'd invited us into their home to celebrate the holiday, not to get attacked at the height of a time when we were supposed to be uniting and at peace. I sucked in a deep breath as I walked through the mirror and into the plain hallway that led to the castle. A chill went down my spine, and the hairs on the back of my neck stood on edge. An eerie feeling settled into the pit of my stomach, and suddenly what I thought would be unbelievable seemed entirely possible. Marius' venom for the Blood Borns had actually come to a head, and now I was on the wrong side of it.

Dried blood was streaked down the walls and over the floor. My pulse quickened in my veins. I rushed forward and stepped through the mirror into the remains of a war zone. The plush carpet was torn and stained with blood. Pieces of clothing littered the floor. Stray shoes lay there without an owner in sight. Voices carried toward me, and I didn't know why, but I ducked behind some of the fallen Christmas decorations. *Me*, hiding behind a downed tree and fake wrapped boxes. Glitter fell over my hand and onto the floor beside me. A string of lights tangled around my ankle, and I held still, trying not to draw attention to myself. The happy twinkling lights were a stark contrast to the smell of death lingering in the air.

Once the guards passed, I fought to untangle the lights without a sound. At this point I felt they'd kill first and ask questions later. I tossed them behind the downed tree and tried to move closer to the throne room. I tiptoed my way down the hall and toward where I knew the ballroom doors were. I wanted to push through those doors and see for myself how bad it truly was. But I didn't want to make my presence known. I peeked through the crack in the door, only to see the ballroom in complete disarray. There were huge cracks in the walls and floor. Bodies were strewn about the room, and the guards and lab assistants hurried in all different directions, cleaning up the mess.

Nausea churned in my stomach, and I pressed my hand to my mouth. Marius had done this . . . He attacked them. Anger rolled within me. If I'd only known, I could've stopped him. I could've stopped this. The damage was more than anything I could imagine. How could he? I never took his words to heart, and now looking back on it all, I should have. But years of listening to his ramblings had made me grow used to it. I tuned him out when I shouldn't have.

"Your majesty, they're going to want heads for this," a female voice came from within the room. "This type of savagery can't go unanswered. You know this."

Titus murmured in agreement. "Our justice will be swift, Eloura. I take comfort you were not injured this night."

"Ahhhh, it will take a lot more than a fledgling assassination attempt, my King. Let us not forget I have lived for many years and will continue to do so despite the attempts of Marius and his followers."

"We will squash this where it stands." A low growl rumbled from him, and it sent a shiver down my spine. King Titus was not one to be trifled with. He'd ruled the vampires for years without incident and always pushed forward into the future.

"Of that I have no doubt." She gave a dark chuckle. "Mark my words, there will be blood on the streets."

I couldn't see who was speaking but I knew enough to know if I stayed here much longer, it would be *my* head they'd come after and *my* blood on the streets. I was screwed and Marius left me behind to take the fall. *Bastard.* I turned from the door before I lost my life and took off running. There was no place for me now. Not here. Not the Night Spawn headquarters. Not anywhere. The only choice I was left with was to run.

CHAPTER EIGHT

PIPER

I'd never felt so defeated as I did the moment those subway doors closed between us. The look in his eyes would haunt me for eternity. I'd seen that look each time a kid got passed over for adoption at the group home. It was like they'd lost the dream of a family that could be. Losing a dream of what could be was almost as painful as losing what is. In that one moment, Grayson had that look, the look of a life that was completely over. I just didn't know why. But I was damn well going to find out. There was only one place where I could find answers: The House of Shade.

I staggered my way out of the subway and found a public restroom. I pushed through the door and checked under the stalls to see if anyone was there. As soon as I was sure I was alone, I stepped in front of a mirror over the sink and looked at myself. My hair was a rats' nest, my makeup ran down my face, and my dress was torn and covered in blood. I'd lost my heels somewhere along the way, but I didn't care. I'd walk through the streets barefoot if it meant bringing Grayson back. We had so much to talk about, so much to settle between us. It was an eternal life, but I'd be damned if I lived it without him now. I was going to give him so much shit when we fixed whatever the hell was wrong with him. We were soulmates and I loved him. Love was never perfect, hell this was far from it, but I wouldn't give up on him. Ever.

I pressed my hand to the mirror, and that red mist flowed from my hand and spread over the surface. It rippled at my touch, and I climbed on top of the sink, then stepped through the mirror and into the hallway. I marched down the hallway toward the other side of the mirror and leapt through, landing in the castle. My breath left me in a rush. I didn't think it'd be possible for the castle to be a chaotic disaster but here it was. I knew Martin and Prisha wouldn't exaggerate the situation, but to see it with my own eyes was startling. I wrinkled my nose at the overwhelming odor of blood. The hallways were desolate. After living in the castle, I knew it would never be this way unless something was really wrong. My heart sank at the thought. I'd left because Grayson broke my heart. But in the flash of a moment that changed for me. The second he told me he loved me and sank his fangs into me making me his it only meant one thing, he was now mine too. And I protected what was mine. Titus and Moira were always kind to me and now I would call on them to help us all.

I took two steps down the hall and nearly collided with

Atlas. His face was a dark mask of anger and determination that sent a chill down my spine. It was the kind of face he made when he was about to hunt and kill someone. "What's going on?"

"What's going on is you went missing, the castle got attacked, and now the Crown Prince is nowhere to be seen. I've spent what valuable time I have in the dungeon talking to simpering, inept vampires." Atlas looked like he'd been through a battle. Crimson blood was spattered across his skin and through the white strands of hair that ran back from his temples. Rips covered his black shirt and pants. His face was all sharp planes and anger.

A chill went down my spine. Sanchita had been missing for hours. "Is my friend down there? Her name is Sanchita. Have you seen her anywhere?"

He gave me a single nod. "She was found with Marius' group as they ran like cowards from the castle. They struck and ran. I plan on hunting them one by one until the very last draws his final traitorous breath. Your friend is being held for questioning."

What? How? Anger warred within me. I understood being cautious, but this was Sanchita we were talking about. She was a vampire who couldn't hurt a fly if she was ordered to. With wild, dark hair and a slight frame, she even looked harmless. Her abilities were minimal as far as vampires went. The Blood Borns could easily overpower her.

I tried to keep my voice even. "She's harmless, Atlas."

"That is of no concern to me. I have my own ends to

accomplish. It's of little consequence to me who gets imprisoned in the short term to get what I want." He waved a dismissive hand toward me like my concerns were nothing to him. He was about to step around me when I stepped to the side, blocking his way.

"And you thought she would be able to help you? She's not a warrior, Atlas. She's a civilian." Annoyance flooded my body, and yet I held still. There was too much happening with Grayson and the war. This was an easy fix, and I would see to it.

"By giving me information about you." He took a step toward me, towering over me. "I've been wasting my time looking for you, the female who tortured my only friend to the brink of madness."

No longer the brink.

"Well, here I am. You've found me. Now you can let her go." The soldier next to Atlas growled in my direction. But I was not going to put up with this shit, not when Grayson needed us all. This was wasting time and hurting others who didn't deserve it. I lifted my chin. "Now."

"I'm afraid that isn't your call or mine any longer." His words were so dismissive, like I would have no sway in this situation. But I was Grayson's progeny and that meant something in this world. It meant I had power, real power.

A growl rumbled in my chest. "You've made a mistake here."

The soldier took a step closer to his side and Atlas waved him off. "We're fine here, Jester."

I didn't like Sanchita being held against her will. Deep

down I knew they'd scared her for no reason. I didn't like how it made the crown look, or Grayson, or me. When Jester didn't move, I felt something rise in me, perhaps it was anger, panic, or the need to protect Sanchita. Power sizzled under my skin and the fine red mist flowed from my skin. It glowed like glitter between us. I called upon it, holding it there between us, daring either of them to step into it.

Jester took a slow, cautious step back. His eyes were locked on the mist as though it were acid that'd burn him. "Sav."

Atlas held his arm in front of Jester and pushed him back even farther. He took a small step back. "I see it." Atlas glared at the glittering mist between us. "It would be in your interest to put your blood magic away."

"Blood magic?" I turned my hand around, examining the mist seeping from it. "Is that what we're calling it? In that case, I think it'd be in your best interest to set my friend free."

"The nasty little time bomb of magic floating around you. Have you got any idea what it does yet?" He moved very slowly as though not to provoke me, even though I already felt pissed off and provoked.

I arched my eyebrows at him. "Made-vampires don't have blood magic. Or so I'm told."

"I've seen a lot of weird things tonight. You having blood magic is the least of them." Atlas reached out and let my mist hit his hand. He sucked in a sharp breath, then narrowed his eyes at me. He yanked his hand back and curled it into a fist as he lowered it to his side.

My mind lingered on Grayson's current state. As much as I wanted to stay here and test my newfound abilities on Atlas and his lackey, I didn't have time. I dropped my hand and took a step to move past them. Atlas took a step to the side, blocking my way. He gazed down at me with those intense eyes. They lingered on my appearance, but I would say nothing to him about the events of tonight. At least not until I spoke with Titus and Moira first.

"Where is Grayson?"

"I don't know." Not a lie, but I wasn't going to just tell him everything that was going on. I knew Atlas was close with Titus and Moira, but I was here to talk to them and *only* them. I didn't want any rogue vampires going after Grayson, not without a plan. Titus was levelheaded, but Atlas was dramatic as fuck.

"You're lying." He ground his teeth together and let his fangs extend.

"I'm not scared of you, Sav. So, move. I have business with the King. That's why I'm here." I didn't have time to stand here and bullshit with Atlas. Grayson needed me and all the backup Titus could offer, and now I would have to talk to him about Sanchita's release as well.

"Haven't you noticed the King is occupied, what with being on the brink of war? Now tell me where Gray is, and we both can be on our way."

Anger flowed through me, and I felt it moving to the surface. Mist exploded from me in a cloud of red smoke.

We were surrounded by it. I felt each particle like they were little strings I could twist and pull at any moment. I could only think one thing: *freeze*. Atlas froze, every muscle in his body tensed, yet he didn't move. He stood there, like my own personal vampire statue, yet his eyes tracked my movement as I walked around them. My powers were starting to make sense to me. I didn't know what they could do, but I was starting to find out.

"Remember this for next time."

I brushed past them and headed straight for the throne room. I threw the doors open wide and sucked in a sharp breath. The normally beautiful throne room was in shambles. Titus stood among the rubble with Moira only a few feet away. She hovered over a female vampire, holding her hands out while her blood magic seeped into the injured woman. It flowed in a pink mist from her hands. Mine was darker, more of a red wine color, while hers seems brighter and glowing. The lacerations marring the vampire's face began to slowly knit back together. The bleeding stopped and the skin wove back together seamlessly.

When Moira stood up straight, some of the vampires from the lab rushed forward and carried the injured vampire away. Moira swayed on her feet and pressed her hand to her head. Sweat trickled down her face, and her skin was sickly pale, nearly green. Titus was by her side in a moment. He didn't touch her but held his hand out for her to take. She placed her hand on his forearm, holding onto him for balance.

"It's only been a few hours, perhaps you should still be

resting." Titus' brow furrowed with concern as he gazed down at her. He was so large and imposing with his floor-length coat, muscular physique, and long hair. Wisdom and power rolled off Titus.

Moira gazed up at him and pursed her lips. She put her hands on her hips and narrowed her eyes at him. "You endured the same poisoning. Perhaps *you* should take your leave, my King."

Oh, sassy from Moira. This is new.

"I only worry for your health and safety." His voice was low and calm.

"And yet your health and safety outweigh the importance of mine." Her grip tightened on his arm as she swayed slightly, but she continued to hold a stubborn set to her shoulders as though saying she was going nowhere without saying anything at all.

I took a step toward them, and both their eyes snapped up to mine. Titus' red mist surrounded them in an instant in a protective barrier. When he recognized me, he drew in a sigh of relief and let his blood magic fall. His shoulders sagged slightly as though he were relieved to see me. It made what I had to tell them that much harder to do.

"Piper, are you well?"

"Yes . . ." I hesitated, thinking about Gray. "Well, no."

I didn't know how to tell them their most beloved son and nephew had turned into a monster. I couldn't explain how or why it happened. The words were stuck in my throat. It'd be like telling a parent that their child was involved in a horrific accident. It wasn't news that was easily broken. I felt my mouth open and close a few times as I struggled to find the words I knew would hurt them.

Moira glanced around the room and toward the door, searching for him. "Where's Grayson?"

A ball formed in my throat, and I fought the tears that wanted to spill over onto my cheeks. How could I tell them what happened? How could I say to their faces something was horribly wrong with their beloved son and nephew? I didn't know how to save him or fix this. "He's . . . he's gone."

"Gone?" Titus' grasp tightened on Moira's hand.

I held my hands together, wringing them in front of me. My nerves began to get the better of me. I'd held it together this long, but I couldn't reconcile the monster he became with the Grayson I knew. But they wouldn't be able to either. I'd been so strong, only thinking of getting him here, but now that I was here, the emotions I'd been holding on to were starting to come through. The cracks in my armor were showing, and I didn't know how much longer I'd be able to hold it together without crying. I sucked in a sharp breath. "Something happened to him and I don't know what it is. I need your help to find him and fix him. He's , , , he's not himself."

The doors flew open and into the walls with a loud bang. Atlas stormed into the room looking like he was going to light the whole place on fire. Red mist flowed from his body like a crimson cap, and the raven on his chest sprang from his skin and soared around his head in low circles. His eyes flared with anger as he looked at me. "How dare you use your blood magic on me."

Rage seethed in his words as he marched across the room toward me. My own anger and frustration rose to the forefront. It'd been the most terrifying few hours of my life, and I didn't need to be scolded by him. "How dare you get in my way!"

"Titus." Moira gave a light whimper. "Her arm."

All words halted and everyone in the room stared at the soulmate mark on my arm. Titus was at my side in a flash, holding my arm out to the side. His fingers were gentle on my skin, but his eyes were wide as he looked at the roses surrounded by black lines that looked like barbed wire. "He can't have. He wouldn't. I-I ordered him . . ."

His words trailed off as they all looked at each other and my arm. One moment they shared a look of shock, and in the next moment they fell into utter defeat. Atlas' shoulders sagged and he hung his head. His raven landed on his shoulder and ran its face over his cheek as though trying to soothe Atlas. Moira sucked in a breath, and she swayed on her feet. Her eyes rolled into the back of her head. Her body collapsed almost in slow-motion as she fainted, her hair tumbled around her head in wild chocolate waves, and the length of her dress bunched around her legs. Titus moved before she hit the ground. He was there, catching her from falling into the rubble left behind.

"Moira." He gave her a light shake. "Moira, wake up."

Her eyes fluttered open and tears spilled over her cheeks.

She squeezed her eyes shut and wrapped her hands in the lapels of his coat. She buried her face in the velvety fabric as she tried, and failed, to hold in her sobs. They racked her body, and she shook in his arms. "No, not again. I can't do this again."

"What? What's happened to him?" I turned toward Titus, but he couldn't look me in the eye. They all knew, yet no one said a damn thing to *me*, his soulmate. Titus just held Moira there, seeming unsure of what to do. His face was all hard lines and gritted teeth.

I faced Atlas. His face was a stone-cold mask. "What is going on?"

"Piper, this is very important. Tell me exactly what you saw," Titus insisted as he placed Moira on her feet but didn't let her go.

"Grayson . . . he changed in moments. It happened so fast. He suddenly got a little bigger, his muscles were more well-defined, red lines forked in his eyes, and he . . . um . . . he attacked me. Has he gone feral or something? Maybe he's sick like I was? Maybe he had some bad blood at the party?"

Silence.

I shifted from one foot to the other as the feeling of dread settled deep in my stomach. This was more than a case of bad blood or sickness. It was deeper. I felt it in my bones. Their reaction only solidified the panic I now knew was completely warranted. "Someone say something."

"Your majesty, I can see no reason to keep this from her any longer . . . He has fallen." Atlas pressed his lips into a hard line, like just saying the words pained him.

"Fallen?" I glanced around at them as panic ran through my body. I tried to hide how my hands quaked with fear. Deep down I knew this was bad, so bad it scared the people closest to my soulmate.

I felt like I knew him so well, but now this made me feel like I didn't know him at all. "What does that even mean?"

Titus helped Moira gain her bearings. He kept his arm wrapped around her side, allowing her to lean on him for balance. Quiet sobs racked her body as she struggled to breath. Tears fell freely down her face, onto her dress, and to the dirty floor. Titus forced himself to stand straight and meet my eye.

"The House of Shade has been cursed for a thousand years. And tonight, what you saw happen to my nephew, was the curse taking another member of our house." He cleared his throat and shook his head as Moira let out a light cry.

Anger and sadness warred within me. How could he never tell me about this? How was I just finding out right now that he was cursed? And why did I know that this was somehow my fault? "How do we fix it? How do we break it?"

Atlas scoffed. "You think we haven't tried to break the curse? Perhaps you think us sitting idle, watching the members of this house perish each time the curse befalls one of us?"

Perish? No, I refused to believe this was how Grayson and I ended. "I didn't mean—"

"—There is no fixing it." Titus' words were low and seething.

I wanted to scream that there had to be a way. Grayson was the life of us all. We couldn't give up on him this quickly.

Titus didn't look at me. He just turned to Atlas. "Find him and bring him home. Now."

Atlas said nothing. His silence sent a shiver down my spine. It made me uncomfortable, but I couldn't put my finger on why.

"I'm going too," I said. "He spoke to me. I can get through to him. I know I can."

"My dear, that belief will only break your heart in the end." Moira pressed the back of her hand to her mouth, and it looked like it pained her to just speak, as though she was already grieving him. "There is no happily ever after. Only sadness lies ahead."

I shook my head. *Fuck that.* "I won't give up on him."

He was my soulmate, my love, the love I'd been waiting for all my life. I was sure as hell going to kick his ass for keeping this secret from me once we broke whatever the hell curse this was. Moira could only look at me like her whole world ended.

"Then bring him home where we can keep him contained," she said sadly.

"I'll see to it." Atlas gave a single nod, and I felt something seethe under the surface of his words. He didn't look at either of them, didn't give Titus his unwavering bow as he always did. Something was off.

"As will I." Grayson was my soulmate. I would make sure he came home and we would fix this.

"I do not need your help. You've done enough," Atlas snapped.

"Take her," Titus commanded.

"Your majesty . . ." he tried to argue, but Titus silenced him with a single look.

"Do not question me. I have not the time nor energy to settle petty squabbles. Bring me my nephew. See it done or I will appoint someone else."

"Your majesty, I have one more concern." Now didn't feel like the right time but would there ever be a right time to bring this up?

He waved me on. "Yes."

"My friend, Sanchita—"

"—Now is not the time for this," Atlas snapped, interrupting me.

"Let her speak." Titus silenced him with a single look.

I sighed. "I don't want to bring this up now, of course, but she's being held in the dungeon and she shouldn't be there."

"She was found in the tunnels in the wake of Marius. Of course she should be there," Atlas growled.

"Your Highness, if you knew her like I did, you'd know she would never go against you. She must've gotten caught up in the wave of people running. It was chaos. I swear, you have my word that she is innocent."

"As if he doesn't have enough to contend with right in

this moment?" The venom in Atlas' voice was unmistakable. I'd never seen him so on edge before.

"Perhaps you will let me decide," Titus rumbled. "I will look into your friend, Piper."

"Thank you so much." It was one less thing I had to worry about.

Atlas' jaw dropped. "My lord, I can assure you—"

Titus waved his hand, silencing Atlas. "I will decide what is to be done. You have your own matters to attend to, do you not? More pressing matters."

"I will see to it," he muttered under his breath, then gave a slight bow. Before anyone could say another word, he turned and headed toward the door.

I hurried to catch up and fell into step beside him. "Can you do this?"

"I caught *you*, didn't I?" He didn't look at me.

"I'm not your best friend or your Prince." I grabbed his arm and dragged him to a stop. "What aren't you telling me?"

"Information is boundless, like the lost scrolls of Alexandria." He ground his teeth together.

"So, you're not telling me a fuck ton?"

"Precisely." He turned away from me and marched through the doors.

"Atlas." He didn't stop. "Sav!"

He paused with his back toward me.

I sucked in a deep breath. "What are you going to do?"

"The same thing I always do . . . serve the crown."

CHAPTER NINE

TITUS

The memory of bodies lying strewn about the castle were burned into my mind. Their lives were forfeit in a move I never saw coming. The lingering smell of blood tinged my nose along with the horrid stench of death. Not in a thousand years had the halls of The House of Shade been sullied in such a manner. The vileness of an attack on innocents sat like a twisted knife in my gut. Then, to lose my nephew to a curse just as awful . . . It nearly stole the breath from my body. My people trusted they were safe within the walls of my home, and I in turn should have protected them as such. Yet my people had been like lambs to the slaughter, dressed up for a night of horror. We gathered to celebrate the holidays, and now we would spend this night collecting our dead and mourning the loss of many, which I could only pray would not be the case for the nephew I felt was more like a son. I tried to push the thought away. I had to keep my hope that he would return to us and we would figure out a way to make him whole once more. Atlas was my most trusted warrior, and Piper, despite her lack of experience, was as stubborn as the day was long. She would bring him home. My only regret was that at a time like this I had to cast aside my personal desires to find Grayson myself and stay here to assure the safety of my people, to show them strength when I should have long before this.

Hubris and the belief we could all learn to get on was the downfall of this affair. Had I been guarded, had I taken heed of Grayson's words, this might have been avoided. Had I curbed Marius' ambitions, he would not have even dared to dream of such a thing. And now the regret was mine to live with.

"Don't." Moira drifted to my side and pressed her hand to my arm for the briefest of moments.

"Don't what?"

"Blame yourself. I dare say I see it in your face, and I cannot bear it." The effects of the poison still lingered within her veins. The pungent smell of it mixed with her subtle floral fragrance. Her already delicately pale skin held a bluish tint that was evidence of the crimes against her. A light sheen of sweat covered her body, yet she stood here by my side as she always had.

"No one could have known this, not the attack and certainly not . . ." Her words trailed off as pain covered her features. She sucked in a deep breath, trying to find her calm. ". . . Grayson."

WRONG. Her sadness and her sickness all made my

blood boil. My instincts bellowed at me that this was all wrong, yet I held back the relentless need for vengeance against any who'd hurt her or Grayson. Ours was a relationship of mutual respect. She was my most trusted advisor and the widowed mate to a most beloved brother. To say she was cherished among her people would be an understatement. To say I cherished her would also be an understatement.

"I'll endeavor not to, but blood has been spilt tonight within my home. You have been harmed. These things cannot go unpunished."

She folded her hands in front of her the way she always did when holding herself back. "The poison leaves my system even now. I will be well by tomorrow. And we need to save my son, Titus. I cannot bear to live in a world where he is not. I will wish for my own death daily. When I lost my own soulmate, he was the only thing to get me through."

Just the thought of my brother's death sent a deep sadness through me. I didn't want to feel the same about Grayson. I refused to believe all was lost. Times had changed and he had gathered so many powerful allies. Hope was not lost yet. "I will do everything in my power to break this curse. We all will. No matter how long it takes."

She nodded up at me but the sadness behind her deep, rich eyes nearly broke me. She held her chin up and gave me a forced smile. "I trust in you."

I didn't want to lose a fraction of that trust. "I will see to it all."

"I have no doubts." She closed her eyes, looking like she was trying to maintain her balance.

"You should be resting." My concern for her ran just as deep as the love I felt for my brother. She'd honored him by staying by my side as an unwavering loyal presence.

She looked up at me with that knowing glint in her eyes. "As should you."

I felt the lingering effects of the poison in my blood. Sickness turned my insides, and I too had a sheen of sweat over my body. My blood magic felt weak within my own veins. It was a feeling I'd never had in my long years of life. I'd come to rely on my own power as a way of being, and yet with the consumption of a bit of poison I was rendered powerless. The knowledge of that burned at the soul. A powerless king was a useless king. "I will rest when this is resolved."

"No rest for the King then." She sighed. "I will not rest until my son is returned to me."

"Then I too will not rest until we reach such a day."

My throne room was in ruin, blood spattered across the dark stone floors and walls. The flags representing The House of Shade were torn from the walls and gathered in balls on the floor. Early morning rays of light peeked in through the stained glass, casting the crest over the mess in the throne room. I bent down and ran my fingers over cracked stones. "I've never seen such power from Night Spawn vampires."

"Nor I. Something is unnatural about it." Moira watched as our soldiers began to straighten the room. "We have prisoners held in the cells in the lab?" Moira glanced back toward me. When I nodded, she sighed. "Atlas will suit that best when he returns."

"Agreed. But I will hold my promise to Piper and check to see if her friend is there."

"Indeed." She fretted with her hands, something she did only when she was nervous. Otherwise, she was the picture of what a royal should be. I wanted to offer Moira some comfort, but there was none to be given.

She sighed and pressed her hand to her head. "Then it will be handled."

"This cannot stand!" Clive marched through the doors and across the throne room with his usual entourage behind him. They all looked as though the poison had hit them harder than it had Moira and me, as though sickness might take them at any moment. Their skin was sickly pale, their clothing was more disheveled than I'd ever seen, and the bravado with which they normally conducted themselves was gone. Poison would do that to a person. Illness would knock even the most boisterous of people to their knees. Well, everyone besides Clive. He seemed to be full of piss and vinegar at the moment.

I groaned. "Did you think I would let it stand?"

This drew him up short. "You've got a soft spot for the Night Spawn, but tonight is unforgivable! Something must be done."

"I don't disagree." My mind was on Grayson, but I needed to try to focus for my people.

"They've been a drain for far too long." Clive shoved his hands on his hips.

I sighed and reached for the patience I didn't have. "Clive, make your point."

"Extermination." His face turned a bright red as he tried to shove his slick hair back into place. He normally dressed in old Victorian clothing, his way of maintaining the old ways, yet he'd lost his jacket, the linen shirt was torn and covered in dirt, and his pants were spattered with blood. Oh yes, he'd felt fear this night. Fear his arrogance couldn't overcome.

The sound of the cane tapping on the stone floor came first, then the distinct click of heels.

"Clive!" Eloura held her head high and shoulders back as she strolled into the room. Everyone seemed to turn and look at her at the same time. She wore a long navy-blue dress that pinched in at the waist and complemented her dark skin. Her normal smooth hair stood on edge and smudges of dirt covered her face. She glared at him with dark eyes and pursed lips. "Have we not suffered enough extremes this evening? You have ruined my sleep and demanded my return to this place unnecessarily."

"I'll not hear talks of peace. Now is the time for action. We meet fire with fire." He curled his hands into a fist.

"Foolhardy games are only suffered by fools," she snapped and jabbed her walking stick into the floor in front of her to punctuate her point.

"I want to know what's to be done!" He swung his gaze toward me.

My temper rose, and for once I let it. I'd spent years bartering diplomacy and in some ways it had failed. Now I had to deal with this while Grayson struggled for survival. "What's to be done, Clive? Shall I swoop in with a vengeance into the Night Spawn headquarters and commit mass genocide? I'm sure there are many rulers who've scarred the pages of history with such actions. But I warn you . . . I will not be one of them."

His color grew impossibly redder, and his cheeks puffed with anger. "This is not a slight we'll take. The Blood Borns will not allow it."

"I'm not saying it will be allowed," I growled low in my throat. "I'm saying I'm not an imbecile."

"Are you saying I am?"

"I wouldn't dream of it, though daft prick comes to mind." I towered over him. "It shall be dealt with. But a few rotten eggs do not make a rotten dozen. I will find the center of these problems and rip them out by the root. Nothing of this mess will be left."

"You had better see to it." Clive puffed his chest out.

"You dare to command your King?" Eloura shook her head. "Such disrespect is a punishable offense."

"It is indeed." I glared at him, wanting to see his head on a pike for the first time ever. I'd suffered Marius' ego, but Clive would be knocked down a peg or two. "My duties as King are clear, as are yours, Clive. Now stand aside and let me see to my kingdom. You are of no help in these matters."

Clive's jaw opened and closed a few times, and his eyes bulged from his head.

Eloura chuckled. "Your King has spoken. Do you intend to disobey him and commit treason?"

His head snapped around as though he'd been slapped. "I will not."

"Shame. It'd give us the excuse we needed to cage you up with the rest of the heretics," she muttered under her breath.

I turned to Eloura. "Are you well enough to take a meeting tomorrow?"

She gave me a low bow. "As you wish, Your Majesty."

I glared at Clive. "You are dismissed until you are summoned."

He opened his mouth to speak, and I silenced him with the wave of my hand. "Your opinion isn't necessary."

He closed his mouth, then spun on his heels and left the room. I felt Moira at my side, always there like a comforting presence who always had my best interests in mind. Even now, with our family under so much pressure, she was there. And I was grateful. Because as Eloura said earlier, we were on the brink of war and this time the streets of London would run red with the blood of our own...

CHAPTER TEN

PIPER

"Where are you going?"
Nothing.
"How are you going to find him?"
Silence.
"Atlas."

He continued to walk toward his room, collecting weapons and strapping them to his body. He'd already put a knife around his thigh and another in his boot. Then he slid some brass knuckles in his pocket. He kept his head down, never making eye contact with me. Yet with every step he took, his blood magic seeped from him, giving the room a red, misty fog effect. The tattoos on his body seemed to rise up from his skin and fall back flat. They moved over him like he was struggling to keep them in check.

Is this Atlas' way of showing emotion? No words, just inner turmoil spilling out uncontrollably over his skin?

He patted his hands down his chest, then over his pants. When he seemed to be happy with whatever it was that he was checking, he finally looked up at me.

"No one hears of this. Do you understand me?"

"Right, like I was going to announce my soulmate going absolutely crazy, making him a target in a volatile environment that none of us have any control over at the moment." I threw my arms up and let them fall back with a slap on my sides. "None of this makes sense. I don't even really understand what happened and now you're hunting down Grayson like he's some kind of war criminal."

One moment he was across the room, the other he was in my face, hovering over me all menacing. I sucked in a sharp breath but didn't back down from him. "This . . . is all your fault. I warned you to stay away from him."

Is he for real? "I left the castle."

"And yet somehow you've got the soulmate mark. A mark of love." The muscle in his jaw ticked. "*That* could only happen in person."

"I'm not going to apologize for that." I didn't back down. "It isn't perfect, but it is love. Were we messed up? Yeah, we were. But once we figure this curse the hell out, then we will get it all together, and I'll have a few choice words for him."

How could you not tell me?

Why the secrets?

And you pushed me away for this?

"Funny you believe that." His breath fanned across my face. "Wake up. This is not a fairytale."

"I have no choice but to believe it, because I refuse to believe he's gone for good. As his best friend, you shouldn't think he's gone either." This whole thing was so messed up. I didn't have a choice but to believe that everything would work out between us... eventually... because the thought of any other outcome was too painful to even try to process.

A growl rumbled deep in his chest and he bared his fangs at me with a light hiss, then stormed passed me to his closet. A moment later he threw a bunch of clothes in my direction. "Put that on."

I glanced down at my silky dress that'd been torn to shreds. I was borderline indecent with the amount of skin showing. "Where'd you get all these?"

He gave me a withering look. "Do you really want the answer to that?"

I glanced at the pile of clothing in my hands and could only guess the amount of vampire conquests Atlas had. Beggars couldn't be choosers in my situation. I'd left the castle and taken all my clothing with me. There was no way Atlas was going to let me make a pit stop. He wanted to hunt, and he wanted to hunt *now*. Besides, I'd gotten worse hand-me-downs than this before.

"Get dressed. I'll wait outside." He turned for the door.

"You expect me to believe you'll wait? No, stay right there." I stared at him until he held still.

He groaned. "You're going to undress in front of me?"

"If that's what it takes." I reached for the pieces of my dress and began tearing it off.

He spun around, giving me his back. "This is ridiculous."

The sound of ripping fabric filled the silence between us. There was a tiny crop top that was so small it'd serve as a bra for me. I shoved my arms through and wiggled the tight fabric past my bust, then I slid on a pair of jeans that were slightly loose but my ass was big enough to hold up. These two pieces did not go together, but I had only a few options.

"And how many different women's clothing am I wearing?"

"I fail to see how that's any of your business."

"Seems my love life is now your business." I pulled a loose-fitting sweater over my head that had rips carefully placed over the stomach and arms. I rolled my eyes. *Greaattttt.* "In my mind, turnabout is fair play."

"You mistake me, Piper. My involvement is not a choice. Anything to do with the crown is my business. Anything doing with a lifelong friend is also my business. Grayson and I have been friends for over a hundred years, and in one swoop you've ruined it for the lot of us."

I shoved my feet into boots that were too big. I'd never be able to keep these on. I turned and went to Atlas' dresser and pulled out a pair of his socks. I shoved my feet into them and tied them as tight as I could. His thick socks poked out of the top of the boots, and I shoved the jeans into them to get a bit more hold. I grabbed a pen off the top of the dresser and wound it through my hair to hold it off my face. I pressed my hand to the necklace Grayson had given me. It was to remind me to control my thirst, but now its weight around my neck would remind me of only him.

"Ready."

He glanced at me over his shoulder and sighed. "Help yourself, why don't you?"

"You didn't give me much of a choice." I wrinkled my nose and sniffed the borrowed shirt I was wearing. "Helpful tip, if she smells like a floral potpourri, she's going to be a stage-five clinger."

He arched an eyebrow. "Noted."

"Oh my god. She was, wasn't she?" My eyes widened and for the first time since everything went down, I smirked, trying to picture Atlas with a tiny female vampire clinging to his side.

He said nothing. He just groaned and turned toward the floor-length mirror and pressed his hand to it. The mirror rippled and moved like the surface of water. Before, the sight of it used to awe me, now I found myself growing used to this new vampire world I'd been thrown into. "How do you know where to go?"

He sighed. "There are places feral vampires are attracted to. We'll start there."

"So the curse turned him feral?" There was still so much I didn't know about the curse and how it worked.

"It's more than feral," he snapped. "Feral vampires can sometimes come back. The *curse* makes him feral but stronger and more violent too. In some cases, smarter . . . diabolical even. And he will not come back from this."

Annoyance ran through my body. Why did he keep insisting I give up hope? "How do you know?"

"Because I've seen it before. The House of Shade's numbers have dwindled over the years: cousins, uncles, aunts. One after another they fall to the curse of love, and I have put down one after another. I am the one who holds the silence and keeps the crown."

A cold chill went down my spine. "And now? What are you going to do now that it's your best friend?"

"What I must." He stepped into the mirror, and I leapt in after him. The surface peeled across my skin as I tried to barrel through faster.

When we entered the hall, Atlas didn't wait for me. He sped up so quickly that his body was nearly a blur. But I was stronger than I've ever been and keeping up with him was no problem. I pumped my arms, feeling the adrenaline course through my body. When we reached the mirror on the other end of the tunnel, Atlas dove through, and the mirror started to harden behind him. I skidded to a halt as he glanced back at me with a smirk on his face, as if that would stop me from following him.

I arched my eyebrows at him and placed my hand on the mirror, willing it to open for me. My blood magic spread over the mirror in a glittering red mist, and instead of the mirror turning liquid once more, large cracks forked out over the surface. The smile dropped from Atlas' face and he took a small step back. How dare he try to ditch me or dodge my questions. The mirror exploded outwards and shards of it shot toward him.

He ducked away and held his arm over his face to protect it. I stepped out of the mirror, the pieces crunching under my boots. "And what does *what I must* mean exactly?"

He sighed and turned his back toward me and began walking once more. I didn't know where we were exactly, but we'd come out in some kind of crappy bathroom. The walls were cream with dark-brown stains covering them. The white subway tile had a layer of muck on it that made me want to bathe in sanitizer. Wadded-up toilet paper and paper towels littered the damp floor. The smell of something foul hung in the air and I wrinkled my nose.

"Where are we?"

"A store in the shit part of town."

I followed as he yanked the door open and walked into a small corner store with half-stocked shelves, broken fluorescent lighting, and broken refrigerators. A lone man sat behind a counter with a register next to him. He didn't look up when the door flew open. He just kept flipping through the magazine that seemed to hold his attention. I waved my hand in front of him, but he just flipped to another page. I sniffed the air thinking he'd be a vampire, but all I smelled was human blood.

"He's very observant."

"In this part of town, no one asks questions and no one looks twice." Atlas pushed through the entrance and out into the cool morning air. He paused, glancing over his shoulder at me as I stepped out into the sun next to him. It was the day after Christmas and the air was freezing, yet when I felt the sun on my skin, I could feel the slight warmth in the rays.

As we walked down the street, I fell into step with him. I didn't know where we were going or how he knew where to find Grayson, and I didn't feel like Atlas was going to be forthcoming considering he'd just tried to ditch me by getting through the mirror before I could. He turned every corner like he knew exactly where he was going, like it was a maze and he had the only map.

The smell of blood filled the chilly air and I hesitated. Atlas gave me a sideways glance. "There's always prey to be had here. Feral vampires and newborn baby vamps are drawn to this place. The weak tend to be easy prey."

"The weak?"

We turned between two buildings, and there huddled in the shadows were groups of homeless people pressed to the walls. They had a messy encampment made of old tents, tarps, and boxes. The smell was overwhelming. But when we entered the alley, they all seemed to close in on themselves. They pulled tarps over themselves, zipped their tents, and huddled deeper into their boxes. Atlas looked at them, then pointedly looked at me.

"I see what you mean."

Farther down, street workers huddled and lounged against the wall, waiting for night to fall. They seemed to just stand there waiting for a man to pull up and ask them to hop in. It was a dangerous life, but I didn't dare judge them for their choices. Everyone had a story—a trauma or a responsibility. The smell of drugs, sickness, and other unsavory things filled the air. Atlas navigated the alley like he'd been here a million times before. He stepped over bodies and didn't even look at the faces of the people who were barely speed bumps to him.

He turned once more, and we were in what looked like a maze of alleyways. Atlas paused for a moment, sniffing the air. A growl rumbled in his chest, and he threw his arm out, shoving me back behind him. I nearly fell over with how quickly he did it. I tried to peek over his shoulder to see what had alerted him. A low hiss escaped his lips as he narrowed his eyes at the dark corner. It took a moment for my eyes to adjust, but the second they did, Grayson leapt from the corner and hit Atlas like a truck. He wore only a pair of dress pants. His chest and feet were bare. Dirt covered his whole body, and his hair was disheveled like I'd never seen it before.

Atlas stiffened a moment before their bodies slammed together like two trains colliding on the tracks. Grayson snapped his teeth at Atlas as he wrapped his hands around his neck and they both flew back into the wall. The brick cracked around them when they smacked into it. Atlas wrapped his hand around the back of Grayson's neck and spun around, slamming Grayson's head into the wall. It didn't even make him pause. Gray was as fast at Atlas, and the two of them spun around like a whirlwind.

"God damn it, Gray!" Atlas grunted as he threw a punch that connected with Grayson's cheek.

His head snapped back, and his cheek split open. Blood ran down his face and he gave Atlas a fangy smirk. Then he hauled his fist back and jabbed Atlas in the face. His brow split open, and blood trickled down the side of his face. Atlas shook his head and hissed as he threw another punch. They traded blows back and forth, each one hitting harder than the last. I wanted to jump between them, but I wasn't about to volunteer my face for that kind of beating.

Gray took a step toward Atlas. He planted one foot and then kicked him in the stomach with the other. The air whooshed from Atlas' lungs, and he flew back and skidded across the ground before crashing into a group of garbage cans. They exploded into the air and made a huge crashing sound. Garbage flew in all different directions, and the sound of broken glass filled the air. When he rose to his feet, he shook the rubbish off his coat.

"Gray, I know you're not yourself."

Grayson chuckled and held his hands out to his sides like he was enjoying this. I stepped between them. "Grayson, stop. I know you know us."

His eyes were wild, and his skin was that deathly pale that I hated. He tilted his head to the side, studying me. The muscles in his body twitched as he sucked in heaving breaths. He smacked his hands into the sides of his head and began pacing back and forth. He stared at the two of us as he paced, growled, and hissed in our direction. His eyes bounced from Atlas to me and back again. Agitation rolled off him.

Atlas' eyes widened, then narrowed. "Do you know us?"

His words sent Grayson into a fury. He leapt at Atlas and

threw him into the wall. Atlas hauled his fist back and cracked Grayson right across the face. He flew back into a dumpster, crushing it to a tiny, crumpled metal lump. Grayson grabbed the edge of the mangled dumpster and peeled two long pieces of jagged metal from it. He held them at his sides. They cut into the skin of his hands, but Grayson didn't seem to mind. Blood dripped down the sharp edges and fell to the ground.

Atlas pulled his sleeves up and ran his hands over the long sword tattoos on his forearms. Red mist glowed around the tattoos, and they seemed to peel from his skin and fall into his hands. The blades were long and terrible looking as they glinted in the sunlight. Fear shot through my body, and I felt my hands begin to shake. If I didn't stop this, they'd kill each other. They charged forward. Each one swung their weapons. Metal clanged against metal. Grayson slashed his piece across Atlas' mid-section and a line of crimson flowed down his side, coating his shirt in blood. Atlas spun and slashed his sword over Grayson's arm. Blood trickled down his arm and he lifted it to his face, taking a lick of the warm, flowing stream.

He grinned at Atlas and dove toward him. A moment before they collided, I saw the glare in Atlas' eye, the way they focused on Grayson's neck and the exact point he'd strike. His swing was strong and level as though he would take his head. Before I knew what I was doing, I dove forward and shoved Atlas back. Grayson slammed into my back and jabbed the metal forward. It breezed by me and went straight into Atlas' rib cage. A loud *oof* rushed from

Atlas, and he backed away with the metal jutting from his side.

Grayson's hand snaked around my body and up to my neck. He wrapped his fingers around my throat and began to squeeze. He sucked in a deep breath, smelling my hair. He hummed low in his throat. "Hmm. Divine."

I spun around and let my arm fly. My elbow connected with his jaw, and he soared across the alley. He smacked headfirst into the wall and dropped to the ground. Atlas was there with his sword poised at his throat. I leapt forward, shoving my shoulder into his side, sending him a few feet away. "No!"

When I turned back, Grayson was gone and I was alone with Atlas. When I faced Atlas, he stood there with two jagged metal pieces sticking out from his midsection. He glared at me and sucked in deep, sharp breaths.

"Trifle with your family, trifle with your deity, but do not trifle with me and the job I was meant to do." He staggered and leaned up against the wall as he wrapped his arm around his midsection.

"We need to get you to the lab. Back to the doctors there."

He shoved away from me. "I'll see to it myself."

"You almost killed Gray back there. You know that, right? So what the hell is your problem?"

"You! You are my problem."

I motioned to his wounds and my anger began to match his. I wanted to find Gray and bring him home, but I did not want to hurt him in the process. While we were standing here arguing about it, Atlas was bleeding out and Grayson was getting away. "You need to cope better or die mad about it."

He ground his teeth together. "This is your fault. His death will be on your hands, and I will forever curse you for it."

CHAPTER ELEVEN

PIPER

"What the hell do you mean it'll be on my head?" I had one of Atlas' arms draped over my shoulders, and he leaned only a bit of his weight on me as we walked through the tunnels under the castle toward the lab.

"You need to stop being so bloody naïve. The curse will take him. Face it," he gritted out between labored breaths. Blood misted from his lips and ran down from the corner of his mouth.

"You don't know that, and the fact you're willing to give up on your best friend says a lot about who you are as a person."

"I'm not a bloody person, I'm a sodding vampire, and I know what's in store for him." He hissed under his breath. "Death would be a kindness."

Blood seeped slowly from the jagged metal pieces jutting from his torso. It was dark and oozing as it soaked into his shirt and the top of his pants. When I kicked the doors open to the lab, everyone froze and stared at the two of us. Their jaws dropped.

Atlas groaned. "Generally, I'm not a patient here. I'm usually the reason they have patients."

"Right, you're the one bringing the others in on stretchers." I sighed and rolled my eyes. "He needs help, people!"

Three lab assistants rushed forward, and I handed Atlas over to them. The three of them nearly toppled under his weight. They stumbled and staggered as they directed him to one of the exam rooms. I followed behind him not really sure what to do, but I wasn't going to leave him alone until he explained and gave me his word he wouldn't try to kill Grayson. The doctor rushed in behind us, and I moved to the side watching as they hoisted Atlas onto the metal table. I was glad for once it wasn't me.

Atlas shoved the techs off him and growled at the doctor. He motioned to the metal jutting from his side. "Pull them out."

Doctor Stanbourn looked like he'd seen better days. He was a made-vampire, so there were only a few slight hints to his age when he was turned. But even now those looked more severe from the night. His salt and pepper hair stood on edge and the wrinkles around his eyes were accompanied by dark circles. Red stains marred what used to be his pristine white lab coat. His glasses were tucked into the pocket of his coat, and when he leaned over Atlas, he just appeared exhausted.

"What happened here?"

We shared a look and Atlas ground his teeth together. "Rogue vampire."

"I've never seen you injured before. Must've been a strong vampire." He hurried around the room, pulling supplies from the drawers and laying them on the portable tray that would wheel around the room.

He pushed it across the room and stood before Atlas. "Lie back."

Atlas relaxed his muscles and slapped away one of the techs who tried to ease his head down. "I'm not bloody dying."

The doctor cleared this throat. "I think I'll take it from here, lest one of you lose a limb."

Atlas hissed at them. "Right. Piss off, the lot of you."

The three techs scurried out of the room, leaving only me and the doctor alone with Atlas. The doctor picked up the medical scissors and cut away Atlas' shirt. He dropped the pieces onto the tray. With each strip, he revealed more of Atlas' skin. Dark tattoos covered his body along with a deep bruise that indicated he was bleeding internally. Those two metal pieces jutted from his torso, and rivets of blood ran down his sides. His muscles clenched and flexed in pain with every breath he took.

When the doctor picked up a needle and started to bring it toward Atlas' skin, he grabbed the doctor's wrist, stopping him. "Just pull them out."

"No need to put on a brave face here. The pain will be great." He hesitated with the needled poised.

The muscles in Atlas' neck tightened as he gritted his teeth together. "Be done with it so I can be on my way."

Sweat soaked his hair and had it sticking to his head. The doctor nodded to me. "Hold him down."

"I have command over myself." Atlas' face pulled into a hard sneer.

"And yet you need my assistance." The doctor didn't budge to help him. "You forget yourself. I've seen what you can do."

"And you think *she* can hold me down?" He glared in my direction.

The doctor scoffed. "And much more if she'd like."

"Do what you will." Atlas laid his head back and closed his eyes. "This is her fault. She best contribute in *some* way."

"My fault, huh?" I marched up to the table and grinned down at him. I pressed my forearm across his chest, pinning him down. When he tried to sit up, I easily pinned him there. I smirked down at him and gripped one of the metal pieces. "Ready, doc? On three . . . one . . ."

I yanked it from Atlas' side, and he let go of a deep grunt. He sucked in a sharp breath through his teeth and his nostrils flared. The tattoos on his body rippled as fine red mist seeped from him. He spoke through gritted teeth. "You said *three*."

"I lied." I dropped the piece on the tray on top of the pieces of his shirt.

"I always knew you were a cruel woman." His breath came in panting heaves as his muscles tensed.

The doctor pressed a gauze pad over the deep wound

and held it there. "Even immortals take a moment to heal from wounds such as these."

"I haven't got a moment," he snapped.

I reached for the other shard and yanked it. It didn't budge an inch. It stuck to a bone, and a growl erupted from Atlas as he tried to shove me from holding him down. "Bloody hell, woman. Have you no manners? A warning is required for such things."

"Then I require a warning next time you . . ." I glanced at the doctor and chose my next words carefully, ". . . *hunt* in such a way."

I couldn't tell him I deserved to know how he planned on hunting down Grayson and whether or not he was going to try to kill him. Because from where I was standing, that was exactly what happened. And I couldn't let him kill Grayson, not now, not when we'd found our love and lost it only moments later. I held the metal shard even tighter, and it started to cut into my hand.

"I only answer to the crown, and you are not it." The breath hissed through his teeth. "No dea—"

I yanked even harder this time. The metal came loose from his rib and slid from his skin. A bellow ripped from Atlas' throat, and his back arched in pain. Doctor Stanbourn leapt on top of him, trying to put pressure on the wound, but blood spilled from the opening. I dropped the piece onto the tray and noticed a tiny chunk of bone stuck to the end of it. I tried not to gag and nearly failed.

Atlas growled in my direction. "Don't you dare get sick over this. I'm the one on a sodding table."

I shoved my arm down and he slammed back into the table with a loud *thunk*. "Sit still so the man can work."

"In case it's escaped your attention, this bloody well hurts." Yet he let his body slump there, forcing his muscles to go limp while the doctor worked.

"I seem to recall pain meds were an option and you refused," I snapped back at him.

"Now that it's out, we no longer have need of you. Do we, doc?"

The doctor glanced from him to me and back again. He grabbed a thick bandage off the tray and pressed it to the wound. Blood seeped through, nearly soaking it instantly. "She's been of assistance."

Atlas glared at me. "Leave!"

"No!" I raised my voice to match his.

"NOW!"

"What the devil is going on in here?" King Titus boomed as he walked into the room. The doctor's eyes went round for a movement as he stared at the King who seemed to take up the whole room.

"I no longer need her assistance, Your Majesty." Atlas lowered his voice to a respectable volume.

The doctor handed me another gauze pack, and I pressed it to the wound. "And I respectfully decline his dismissal."

He hung his head, then gave it a shake. "You're fighting like petulant children on this night. Of all nights? The castle has been attacked, half the Blood Borns have been poisoned, half the Night Spawn have betrayed us, most of them are in our dungeons as we speak, and to top it all off, Grayson..."

He let his words trail off when Doctor Stanbourn began to stare at him. Titus waved his hand at him. "Leave us."

Without a word, the doctor handed me another pad to hold to the other wound in Atlas' side. I pressed and held it as tight as I could. Atlas flinched. "Not so hard. You're like a snake squeezing the life out of me. I don't fancy cracked ribs on top of this."

"You should be so lucky." I loosened my hold.

Titus gave a heavy sigh and lowered his voice to a deep whisper. "What of Grayson?"

"He is lost," Atlas said before I could even take a breath.

"He's not lost. He's still in there, I know it. We need to get him home."

Atlas looked down at himself. "One limb at a time then? He is too strong."

I scoffed and muttered, "Maybe for you."

"Audacity is not a good look for you."

I narrowed my eyes at him. "Neither is being a big old pus—"

"—enough," Titus broke in. "You will find him, and you will bring him home by any means necessary. Understood?"

I nodded, feeling satisfaction run through my body. It was good to have Titus on my side, even if no one else would be. Atlas gave a hesitant nod. "Understood."

Titus gave a simple nod. "You see to my nephew. And Atlas?"

"Yes, Your Majesty?" Atlas tried to perk up.

"No hunting until you're properly healed." He turned and was gone in a moment, leaving the two of us there to stare at each other with all the annoyance both of us could muster.

"Why did it look like you tried to kill him?" I barely whispered.

"Because I gave him my word I would if he fell to the curse." He closed his eyes and let his head fall back. "And I have never let him down, not once. I will not start now."

I tried to swallow around the ball in my throat. Everyone knew if Atlas wanted someone dead, they were as good as dead. But this was Gray, and we both loved him. "But he's your only friend."

"I know."

"How long?"

"How long for what?" He sighed and flexed his fingers as if sitting here waiting was the most painful thing that'd happened to him tonight.

"For you to keep your word?" If I knew how much longer I had, then I might be able to do . . . something.

No answer.

The doctor walked back into the room and checked under the gauze pads. "This is going to take some time. The wounds are deep. I fear there's organ damage."

"Get me up and going," Atlas demanded.

"I require more help and some supplies. I'll return shortly." He glanced from Atlas to me and back again. "Do try not to kill each other."

"If he behaves, he has nothing to worry about."

Atlas scoffed as the doctor left the room. I faced him once more, ready to question everything that transpired between him and Grayson. A glimmer of hope sparked in my chest. "So, he made you promise to kill him should he ever fall to the curse?"

He and I were gonna have words about that later. The list of things we were going to have words about kept growing and growing.

Atlas gave a single nod.

"Good."

"What do you mean, good?" His eyebrows rose up in shock.

I met his eye and held my chin up even though all I wanted to do was give myself a moment to freak out. But Grayson didn't have a moment, which meant neither did I. "It means now you can stop fucking around and help me. He may have made you promise to kill him . . . but he never made you promise to do it quickly."

CHAPTER TWELVE

SANCHITA

The cold dampness seeped through my dress and into my skin. It didn't help that I remained sitting on the floor of my cell with my knees pulled into my chest. Tears streamed down my face, and I did not know how to stop them. This night was supposed to be a perfect night with fun and celebration. I might have even met my soulmate among the many vampires attending the ball. Instead, I was trapped here, and I'd endangered both mine and my sister's lives. How could one night have gone so wrong?

A shiver racked my body and I huddled in closer on myself. I hung my head and pressed my forehead to my arms. This was a disaster of epic proportions. Not since I was turned into a vampire did I feel this low. Atlas was going to kill both my sister and me in one shot. It wasn't that I enjoyed drinking blood, but I wanted to have more time to live and see the world. Just to be young and see all that this immortal life could offer. Prisha and I had plans. I wasn't ready to give them up. I sniffed and wiped my nose on the back of my hand.

"Surely there's no cause for all these tears," a deep rumbling voice came from just outside the bars.

My head snapped up and I nearly tripped over myself trying to get to my feet. I held my hands behind my back, then I thought that looked suspicious, so I moved them to fold in front of myself. "Your Highness."

I bobbed a messy curtsy and tried to straighten my dress, but it all seemed so foolish at this point. I stood there in my bare feet covered in whatever grim was on the floor of this cell. My dress was torn and even now my body shook from the shock of it all. I was terrified. I didn't want to die, and I didn't want my sister to die, yet here stood King Titus . . . and my body shook even harder. I'd never heard of him sentencing vampires so quickly, but I'd also never heard of such an attack upon the castle. So, tonight could be a first of many things.

He waved his hand and the door slid open. This close he was even taller and more imposing, with broad shoulders, a barrel of a chest, and a very direct gaze that made me feel like I was being studied. I never realized the sheer mass of King Titus, but now that he was so close, I had to lean my head back to look up at him. He looked around the cell and across the way to the body lying on the ground in the other cell. The blood had congealed into a gloppy pool.

"Well, that's quite a sight."

"It-it certainly is, Your Highness." I tried to steady my

voice while not looking at that body. I knew I was a vampire, but killing people wasn't on the menu for me. I drank blood from bags that were donated. I didn't hide in alleys, hunting people down and taking random bites of them. I didn't even enjoy killing spiders that invaded my room, even though their invasion was an act of war.

"Atlas?"

I swallowed and nodded. Words were failing me at this moment. Not once had I ever pictured in my mind having a conversation with the King in a cell whilst standing across from a dead vampire. The King sighed. "I fear the tactics he uses are a bit extreme but sadly effective."

"Indeed, Your Highness."

"Piper tells me I should set you free, that you aren't a traitor to the vampires." He lowered his eyes to meet mine. "Is that true?"

Just hearing her name made me feel like I was able to breathe once more. If Piper had been seen by the King, then Prisha and I would be off the hook. *Maybe I won't die today.* I sucked in a deep breath and brushed the tears from my cheeks. "I would never betray you, Your Highness."

He stepped farther into the cell, seeming to take up all the space. "I would like to believe you."

"I-I would never cross The House of Shade or you, my lord." I lowered my eyes, not sure what to do or say. How could I reassure a King who'd been double-crossed only hours ago.

"And yet you were seen fleeing the castle in Marius'

wake. What say you on these charges?" His eyes were intense, like looking into deep pools of honey.

I swallowed and the words just tumbled out of my mouth in a panicked pause. "Everything happened so fast. The attack came in, and I just ducked and hid because it was totally terrifying, and then . . . and then vampires were dying ALL around me. I don't do blood, I mean, I do, because I am a vampire, but not like that. This huge vampire who I have never seen a day in my life grabs me from my hiding spot and drags me out the door. Or *a* door . . . I'm not really sure which one. Then I'm in this dark tunnel full of spiders and other things, being dragged along. By the way, you should think about cleaning those out. They're dreadfully dirty."

I paused and pressed my lips together, then opened my mouth and closed it once more. "I'm babbling."

"Please continue." He snickered. "This is one of the most entertaining conversations I've had all night."

"My apologies." I pressed my hands over my mouth and held my breath. I shook my head. I couldn't believe I was doing this in front of a member of the royal family. But I was in it now, so I let my words fly. "Then this meaty vampire picked me up, nearly tearing my arms off, and let me tell you, that was horribly unpleasant. I lost my shoes and then Marius threatened to kill me."

The King held his hand up, stopping my words. "You saw him?"

"I did."

"And he threatened you?"

I nodded and tried to imitate his voice. "If you're not with me, then you're against me."

He raised his eyebrows at my words. "And what did you do?"

I sighed and shook my head. "I'm not proud of it, but I pretended to be stupid and said I didn't know what he meant. But really, Your Highness, I knew exactly what he meant. I just didn't want to die tonight."

"Quite the little politician, aren't we?" He chuckled.

"I find when dealing with ignorance it is always best to play the role of the uneducated person so they feel they have something to teach you, then of course do what I think best anyways." I shrugged. I found myself getting more comfortable around him with each passing second, which I found to be odd considering he was the King and I was, for lack of a better word, a commoner.

"I can appreciate the genius behind that." He waved me on.

"Thank you. Well, once he was undecided where my allegiance lies, your soldiers showed up and scared them off, so they just left me there in the tunnel. That's when Jester took me and brought me here, where Atlas scared the hell out of me. I mean really, Your Majesty, he is an excellent choice to be your trusted enforcer."

"I like to think so."

"He's scarier than anything I've ever seen. I really thought myself and my sister were going to die for being in the wrong place at the wrong time." I sucked in a deep breath and my eyes widened. "Whoops, what I mean to say is—"

"— you were very clear." He strolled around the cell, looking at the bars and ceiling as though trying to see it through my perspective. He kicked at the damp ground and ran his finger over the slimy wall. "It's quite effective, putting traitors down here."

"I would think so." I sounded more enthusiastic than I meant to be.

"Places like this are necessary, unfortunately, to keep us all safe, even you." He nodded in my direction.

"Please don't mistake me, Your Highness, I completely agree. There should always be a punishment in place for those who would hurt us. Evermore is a violent place to live, and I've always liked the comforts provided by the crown. And that crown should be protected."

He nodded and the silence fell heavy between us for long moments. I didn't know if I said something wrong or if I said something right. But something in my gut told me I shouldn't speak at this moment. I needed to wait until he was ready.

"That settles that then." He turned and left the cell and started walking down the hallway. The door was wide open and I hesitated for a fraction of a second before rushing out to follow in his wake.

"I'm sorry, settles what?"

I nearly collided with his back at his abrupt stop. He turned on his heel and towered over me. "You will become the new Night Spawn Ambassador."

My jaw dropped, then I forced it shut only to let it drop again. "I'm sorry, what?"

"You will become the new Night Spawn Ambassador and we will work together to branch this new divide." He said it so simply, like this sort of job just fell into one's lap and I would know what to do overnight.

"How do you know I'm qualified for something like that?"

"Are you questioning my judgment?" he snapped back.

I shook my head back and forth so fast I nearly made myself dizzy. "No, of course not. But I hardly know—"

"—Then you will figure it out."

This night was more than I bargained for. I started the night by going to a fun party with my friends, and now I was standing in a dungeon being offered a major role in our society. I'd gone from standing at death's door to getting out of the hangman's noose, somehow, and now to getting a wild, life-changing offer from the King himself. "I'm flattered, Your Highness. But I—"

"—Are you turning me down?" His words seethed with power and a touch of shock.

"I wouldn't dream of it." I paused, choosing my next words wisely. "But I will need help with something this immense."

He put his hands on his hips and gazed down at me. "What kind of help do you require?"

There were only two people I could trust with a task this important. "Our numbers are divided, and we do not know who to trust."

He pressed his lips into a thin line and then crossed his arms over his chest. "I quite agree."

"So, it's only in good confidence that I think the job of Night Spawn Ambassador should be put on three of us, co-ambassadors if you will."

He nodded. "And who do you propose as the other two Night Spawn vampires I should trust in such a time of need?"

"My sister, Prisha, and of course Martin, whom you know to be extremely loyal to The House of Shade." I held my breath hoping he'd go for it. I didn't think I could do this without their help. It would be too much.

"Deal." He spun on his heels and began walking once more.

I froze. *What the hell did I just do*? I hurried to catch up to him once more. "But, Your Majesty, you hardly know anything about me."

He whipped around so fast it was a blur of movement. His blood magic wrapped round me like a thick blanket. It nearly smothered me. My body held there, unable to move even if I commanded it to. My blood slowed. I could hear my every heartbeat in my own ears, and everything was out of focus . . . everything but him. He held up his hand and his power drifted around his fingers. "It's an interesting sensation, is it not? To have lost control of your own will?"

When I said nothing, he waved his hand, giving me the ability to speak again. My insides flooded with nervousness. "It is."

"Can I trust you then, Sanchita?" He studied me like a bug under a microscope. "Do not lie to me."

His power rushed through my body, and I couldn't lie to him even if I wanted to. "You can trust me, Your Highness."

"Will you do your best to help your fellow vampires?"

"I will." My mouth snapped shut again because of his powers.

"Excellent. I believe you." He waved his hand and suddenly I was completely free. The blood magic surrounding me disappeared as quickly as it came. The only evidence of it would be the memory I had of losing all control to someone else. It was a good reminder of what the King was capable of.

We stood there staring at each other. "What now?"

"Now we send for your sister and Martin." He turned and started walking again.

"Just like that?"

"Though we've had a tough night, I do still have ways of getting what I want." He walked with his shoulders back and chin held high.

This time I fell into step beside him. I didn't know what to say so the first thing that came to mind was the first thing that came out. "Your power is very impressive, Your Highness."

He chuckled. "Thank you."

"Marius would do well to remember exactly that."

The King paused and all humor dropped from his face. "Indeed, he would."

CHAPTER THIRTEEN

PIPER

*A*tlas tried to rise up off the table. He bared his teeth at me and narrowed his eyes. "I don't do timelines. He asked me for my word. I gave it."

All I could do was glare at him. I knew what he was capable of. I knew he'd killed hundreds, probably a few thousand, but I didn't care. I refused to back down from him. When I didn't flinch back or even blink, he fell back onto the table sucking in panting breaths. He gritted his teeth and held the gauze tightly to his wounds.

Blood soaked through the gauze and seeped through his fingers. I crossed my arms, not making a move to help him. "He told you to hold still."

"How am I to hold still when you're standing there spouting idiocy in my general vicinity?" He nodded to the stack of gauze lying beside him. "You could take a moment from your single-minded mission to perish and hand me a bit more of that, unless you prefer to stand in the wake of the remains of my insides."

I rolled my eyes. "You're not dying."

"It bloody well hurts though," he snapped and hissed at me. "You could take a bit of responsibility for this current situation."

"Serves you right." I shrugged. "You're not a very good friend."

His body quaked in pain and sweat beaded his forehead. "Pardon?"

I walked over to the table and grabbed a wad of gauze and stood next to him waiting silently for him to move his hands. When he just glared, I stared back at him waiting . . . The more time he spent being trapped in here, the more time it gave me to think of a way to get to Grayson before he did. Atlas let his head fall back and dropped his hands. I pulled the sopping used-up gauze off his wounds and threw them on the tray beside us. They landed there with a wet, sticky slap. I pressed new pads over the holes and held them in place.

"Not so sodding hard." He winced. "Do they not teach new vampires how to control their strength in that night dweller cavern you reside in?"

"I'm pretty sure my strength is the only thing holding your insides in place. But I can let go and we can see what happens next. Would be interesting to find out how badly this could go for an immortal vampire who won't shut the fuck up for a second."

"Yet you're the one regaling me with tales of how love

will save all. Feels like a fortnight since you've closed your mouth."

"By the way, you're fucking welcome." The blood seemed to be slowing but not enough. If he were human, he'd be unconscious and half dead by now. I wondered if he'd ever get to that point or if the pure audacity he seemed to be oozing would keep him going.

His jaw dropped. "And what exactly am I to thank you for? Nearly getting me killed?"

Infuriating vampire. "Why are you so quick to just kill him? At least give him a chance. Give *me* a chance."

He rolled his eyes. "You *are* that bloody naïve. I am not."

I was sick of this. Grayson needed people behind him that would support him and get his ass home as soon as possible, not someone who was just going to try and hunt him down like he was some kind of deer in the wild. I stepped back from him. The gauze pads stayed in place, but the blood started to flow freely again without the pressure I'd been applying. Atlas snapped his hands over the wounds.

"Yes, let me rush to give my eternal thanks to you for getting me impaled by two rusty pieces of metal," Atlas growled. He looked down at himself, distracted long enough for me to find something in this room to use against him.

I pretended to pace the room while I looked for something to keep him at bay for just a little while until I could get some help. The second the doctor got him fixed up, he would return to the hunt and nothing would stop him this time. He'd be expecting my interference now, so there was no surprising him. I found a pair of stray vampire cuffs sitting on the counter. I grabbed them quickly and held them behind my back. I knew that there was a remote for them somewhere around here. Grayson had used it to free me only days ago.

"Let me also extend my gratitude for turning my only friend into a monster, the likes of which one does not return from," he continued. "You've yet to realize this, though I have. In my centuries of experience, I know this to be true. It is the daft who do not learn from the wise." He let his head fall back and his eyes closed.

Did he just call me stupid and himself wise? I wasn't even going to dignify that with an answer.

"Mhmm." There, only a few feet away, was the remote, lying on the counter among the containers of supplies. Usually everything was so organized, but after a night like tonight, I was surprised we even had clean bandages left. I grabbed the remote and walked closer to him.

He turned and narrowed his eyes at me. "What the devil are you doing?"

I lifted my hand and called on that inner well of power I knew lingered in the pit of my stomach just waiting to be used. Red mist flowed from my body and Atlas' body tensed like he was about to spring at me. My power surrounded him in a fine red mist that I felt settle over his body. I could feel his every move. It was like the magic was mapping him out for me and making it so easy to choose how best to use him. This power in the wrong hands would be detrimental to anyone.

I held my hand out. "Stop," I commanded.

He froze. His muscles strained against my hold but still he couldn't move. Anger flooded his eyes, and his face turned a dark shade of red. I could almost feel the hate rolling off him. I never wanted to take anyone's free will away, but in this case . . . Atlas had it coming.

"Lie back." I wasn't sure if I was using it the right way. There was no one here to teach me, but my power was almost like controlling an extension of my own body, like my mind and this mist were slowly becoming one in the same.

Atlas flopped back on the table. His eyes were wide with rage. His face had nearly turned purple. "I know it's hard for you to shut up and listen to me, being that I'm sooooo much younger than you and you're, well, old as dirt. But I know I'm right about this."

I proceeded to place the cuffs around his wrists. When I held the remote in my hand, it looked more like the key-fob for a car, with the lock and unlock features. I pressed the lock button and they tightened around his wrist and clicked into place as the magnet activated and smacked into the table with a slam. I slid the remote into the side of my boot. If I had it, it'd take that much longer for them to release Atlas.

I turned toward the door and called out. "Doctor! We need some help in here!"

Within seconds the doctor was back in the room. His

eyes darted between the two of us. "What's going on in here?"

Atlas flailed against the restraints as my power over him faded. "She's out of her senses!"

"I am not!" I was really going to have to work on how long my little magic trick would work. It'd be a lot more helpful through this whole thing if he would just shut the hell up.

The doctor took a step toward me, and I held my hand up, letting my blood magic seep around my fingers. "I wouldn't." He stopped mid-step. "You know what I'm capable of?" I twirled my fingers, and it danced above my hand like a flame.

He gave me a nod. "I have a fair sense."

"Then you know I won't hesitate if you get in my way." I liked the doctor, he was a good vampire and he'd helped me more than I could say, but he wouldn't get in my way, nor would anyone else.

"I do believe that. Yes." His voice was calm as he spoke to me.

"The lot of you are daft." Atlas struggled against the restraints but to no avail. They were made to hold *me*, and I was beginning to realize I was a hell of a lot stronger than they all knew. He glared at the doctor. "Let me out now."

"Not happening." I turned to the doctor. "I bet you could use some quiet while you work on him. Couldn't you?"

He hesitated. "I . . . suppose."

I smirked. "Good, then you can tell me where the drugs are that are strong enough to knock a vampire out."

"WHAT?" Atlas raised his voice. He jerked in his restraints. The table groaned yet still held. Blood covered his torso and dripped from the table onto the floor.

"Better hurry up, doc. He's bleeding an awful lot." I probably could've used my powers on the good doctor, but I didn't know if there would be side effects and wasn't sure if I could run out of them or if they would always be there. There was just so much I didn't understand but had to find out.

One thing at a time, Piper. One thing at a time.

The doctor gave a heavy sigh. "Second drawer on the left. There should be some syringes and medicine in there."

"I'll kill you. I'll bloody kill you both for this." Spit flew from Atlas' mouth as he thrashed and threatened us both.

"Actually, you won't." I hurried to the drawer and yanked it open. I grabbed a syringe and peeled it out of its sterile plastic container, then grabbed a bottle of medicine and held it up to the doctor. "This one?"

"Oh, I promise you I will. So long as the Earth moves around the sun, you will know my vengeance."

"Dramatic but okay." I waved the bottle at the doctor and raised my eyebrows at him.

The doctor nodded. "That's the one."

I pierced the rubber stopper with the needle and started to draw the liquid. "Atlas, think of it this way, when I save your bestie, you'll forgive me. Not right away of course, because you are a prideful son of a bitch, but when you get more centuries with him, eventually you'll come around."

"You do not know me!" He hissed. "Forgiveness is a virtue I do not have."

"That's enough." The doctor's eyes widened. "He'll be out for hours with that."

"Excellent." I pulled the plunger back a bit farther for good measure. I withdrew the needle from the rubber stopper and walked over to Atlas.

I leaned over him and his fangs extended as he snapped his teeth at me. I sighed and positioned the needle at the vein in his neck. "And you won't hurt the doctor because you know I forced him into this. If he hadn't told me, I would've used my power on him, and we'd be back in this exact position. Deep down, you know, and I know I'm the bigger threat."

His eyes widened as I jabbed the needle into his neck and pushed the plunger down. The effect was almost instant. Atlas' body went limp on the table, his eyes rolled back, and his head lulled to the side. I motioned to him. "Go ahead, doc."

The doctor rushed forward and placed more bandages over the wounds. He narrowed his eyes at me and gave a heavy sigh. "It'll be much easier now."

I winked. "I know."

"You truly do not fear him?" More techs hurried into the room and suddenly Atlas was covered in a sheet and being wiped down with some kind of liquid. I liked the way they took care to be sterile even though vampires were immortal. There was a level of respect for their care that the doctors and techs took that made me appreciate them more.

I shook my head. "Nah, like I said, I'm the bigger threat."

"Somehow I'm beginning to see that." He leaned over Atlas, examining the wounds.

"Oh, doc, they all will." And somehow I knew I wasn't wrong. My power made me stronger and faster, but my stubbornness would push me that much further and harder. "How long do I have until he wakes?"

"At least eight hours. At the most a day or two." He held his hand out and one of the techs placed a scalpel in it. "Are you going to stay and observe?"

"Not on your life." I turned toward the door. "I'm going to find someone who'll actually be helpful."

"Best of luck with that," he called after me.

I hurried from the lab and ran through the castle. When I first arrived here, I felt so out of place, but now I was beginning to get used to the dark, gothic interior and where the soldiers would be stationed. I knew the directions through the castle and navigated them easily. There was only one person who I knew would be on my side, so I hurried toward her.

Moira was walking out of the throne room as I was hurrying in. I tried to stop but nearly collided with her. She held her hands out and caught me by my arms. "Piper? Dearest, aren't you supposed to be with Atlas?"

I sucked in a deep breath and blew it out. "There was a small problem with that."

Her brow furrowed, and her fingers tightened on my forearms. "Is he dead?"

"Is who . . . oh god no." I shook my head. "Grayson is very much alive still, but I fear Atlas is not going to be the help we're looking for."

She pressed her lips into a hard line and dropped her hold on me. "Is that so?"

"Moira, I know you've lived years without your soulmate, but Grayson and I are just getting started. I need more time with him. I need to help him."

"I know the feeling." A haunted look passed over her face. "There is nothing worse than living without one's soulmate . . . To be alive and be so very far away."

"Will you help me?"

"Of course. I'll do anything within my power." She turned in the direction I'd come from. "But I'll be dealing with Atlas directly."

"No." I reached out and grabbed on to her, stopping her from leaving me. "I put him out of commission for now. But if I'm going to help Grayson, I need to know anything you can tell me. I know this will be painful for you, but will you tell me?"

Moira glanced around, looking to see if anyone was listening. "I'll tell you as much as I can."

I nodded. "Thank you."

She caught my eye. "All is not what it seems, Piper."

CHAPTER FOURTEEN

MOIRA

200 years ago

"I really don't see the point in me being here." I wasn't a great beauty, nor was I a great mind or had any particular talent that would make me stand out among the throng of eligible Blood Born vampire ladies. The life they offered was not a life I wished for nor wanted. A life of royal duty was not among the desires I had for myself. My powers only allowed for a small bit of healing, nothing as impressive as the others I was surrounded by, and that meant I was of no consequence in these matters. The King desired to find his Queen, and I was far from queenly.

"Moira," Eloura scolded me in a chastising tone, "you are as lovely as ever. The King would be lucky to consider you as one of his choices."

"Yes, but what if I don't want to be among his choices?"

I glanced around at the ladies all gathered in a smaller room of the castle. The walls were lined with books and a fire was lit in the oversized fireplace. Heat seeped from it, and I stepped closer, wanting to warm the rest of my body. There were two high-backed chairs and a smaller matching leather couch. The furnishings were dark and lush and fitting of the study.

Eloura chuckled and it was as robust as her personality. It rumbled in her chest, and she threw her head back, letting it free with not a care in the world. She was an old family friend. We'd grown up together and spent most of our days within the same circles of society. She was young, vivacious, and oftentimes outspoken on her opinions about anything and everything. She wore a light-pink dress that complimented her dark skin. It gave a look of innocence that was entirely misleading when it came to her personality. It was tight across her body and flowed freely from her hips to the floor with delicate cap sleeves. An accompanying pink bow wound into the dark curls on top of her head.

I was not so keen to be put together like the rest of the flock. My dress was plain, a darker brown that my mother insisted complimented my eyes. It was too tight around my body, pulling me in too much and pushing me up to make it look like I had more sizable breasts, which I most certainly did not have.

I pulled at my bodice and Eloura smacked my hand. "Don't fuss. It's unbecoming of a lady. No matches will want someone who isn't comfortable within themselves."

"I care not to be among the choices for the King." I folded my hands in front of me so I didn't continue to fuss. But everything was uncomfortable to me. My hair was flowing freely down my back and seemed to be everywhere, the dress was too constricting, and even the shoes on my feet were too tight. All to be paraded about like some prized piece of cattle for a man I wished nothing to do with.

"Everyone wants to be among his choices, Moira." She rolled her eyes as if the notion of me not wanting to be here was absurd. "Becoming Queen of the Vampires would be a great honor."

I shrugged. "But what if I desire a simpler sort of life?"

"You were raised in the highest level of the Blood Borns. This is how it is." She shrugged as though it were that simple.

I had to have been surrounded by at least two dozen women. They all fretted about with their outfits and hair. Their voices were practically abuzz with excitement. They all had their fanciest dresses in place, with perfect white gloves, fans, and all manner of accessories. It was a fashion show of all the most expensive dresses England had to offer. I took comfort in the knowledge that my dress was not the most beautiful to be had. It would draw less attention.

Eloura moved in close. "Besides, do you not think the King to be handsome?"

"I dare say he's very handsome indeed." King Titus was everything a vampire ought to be, yet he'd remained single for years. He'd taken plenty of lovers but had yet to commit to a single one. "Why does he choose to marry now? It's been years."

"I suppose even endless amounts of lovers would grow tiresome for the immortal." She snickered and lowered her voice. "But I've never heard a single complaint. He's been known to be very . . . *generous.*"

Heat flooded my cheeks. "Elouraaaa, we should not speak of such things."

"And why not? They will all talk of *our* talents. They'll say one of us plays the piano well, and the other paints, one can speak all the languages of the world, one will be the most beautiful . . ." She chuckled. "We might as well speak of their talents as well."

I pressed my hand over my mouth, trying to hide my laughter. "Very well. But even with the King's great bed sport, I find myself . . . uninterested."

Music started drifting through the doors from the other room and the excitement surrounding me was palpable. The women all twittered and moved closer to the doors. They pressed together and I found myself hanging back from the lot of them. Even Eloura was driven forward by her own curiosity. I spied a small crevasse between the giant mantel and bookshelf. I lingered back, and when the doors opened with a creek and they all started moving forward, I ducked into the little space and hid there. When their voices drifted away and the doors slid shut, I was just about ready to pry myself from the small space when my dress caught on something. I tried to reach back and yank it free, but it was stuck.

The door swung open again and I froze. My heart hammered in my chest, and I huddled back into the corner. If they found me now, this would just be embarrassing. I thought I was very smart for lingering back with the idea of hiding in the library for a few hours and then blending in among the decorations until the night was through. Now I was trapped and praying I didn't get caught lingering about the castle.

"I don't want to do this," a deep voice rumbled in protest. My brow furrowed in confusion. The voice was so familiar. Was it the King? I found myself trying to make my breaths shallower.

"No one is asking you to take a vow of celibacy or proclaim your undying love." This voice was smoother, more pleasant than the other. There was almost a playful tone to it. "But the family needs an heir, Brother."

"Then *you* bloody well do it." It was definitely the King's voice.

"No one wants an heir from the spare, Brother." He chuckled.

I'd always heard that Graymont, Titus' younger brother, had the lighthearted humor of the two of them. From my vantage point, I could see why. He seemed to be completely at ease while Titus seemed agitated and uncomfortable.

"What a load of bollocks." I heard the King's footsteps move about the room. "This is some kind of parade, and for what? So that I might pick the prettiest or smartest or most delicate. Is it not enough that I ensure the safety of our people? Why must this be the next step?"

"You know why? This is England after all. Monarchy runs deep in the blood here, whether it be vampire or human."

The King huffed. "And what of the . . ."

"You need not think on that now, Brother. We've both proven that the *physical* act of *love* does not trigger anything." Graymont spat the word *love* as though it were a poisonous word.

What were they talking about love being a trigger for? My curiosity made me hold still even longer. A wise vampire would have made herself known before either of them started talking. It was what propriety dictated on every occasion. Perhaps even overhearing this conversation would be considered a treasonous act. Yet I found myself enthralled by their words and wanting to know more.

"If we could but break it, life would be a lot simpler and surely hold more meaning for us all." Titus' voice was soft as he spoke, as though he yearned for something more, something better. It came as a surprise to me that this rake of a King wanted for anything at all.

"There is but one race we would be able to turn to for help, and their King is like the bone that poisoned the well. There's no telling who we'd be dealing with or what their ties would be. Our predicament should not be public knowledge. For the sake of the crown."

"I agree, but it is rather limiting."

I didn't understand a word of what they were saying, but I had to get out of here. Perhaps they'd leave soon and I'd be free of this confined space. I peeked around the corner of the bookcase to spot King Titus pacing about the room. He was tall with wide, strong shoulders and a muscular physique. He wore a perfectly tailored tuxedo accompanied by a cape that flowed down to the backs of his thighs. His eyes were a devastating honey color with flecks of mahogany in them.

"I met him once. Did I ever tell you?"

Graymont raised his eyebrows in surprise. "You met Alataris, the High King of Witches?"

Titus nodded. "I met him on that night."

"No." Graymont's jaw dropped. "Did he have something to do with our current problem?"

Titus shook his head. "No, it was all Dracinda, but I should've recognized the darkness in him back then. I regret that it escaped me."

"Indeed, what I wouldn't give to have a witch or even one of those dark warlocks to aid us." Graymont moved to the tray on the sideboard and poured himself a generous drink.

He was just as tall as Titus but sleeker and slimmer. He wore a fitted tuxedo of his own. His hair was a touch lighter, with wild waves fanning back from his face. His eyes were nearly the same color as Titus', a deep honey color with mahogany flecks in them. He moved with an ease I'd never seen before. The two were so similar that there was no denying they were brothers.

Titus scoffed. "Hardly a chance of that. I don't think the Witch King will be unseated anytime soon. And now this: my search for a bride." His voice was laced with annoyance and a touch of disgust.

I was so confused. Why would vampires need the help of a witch or those dark warlocks? Why would he even consider going to one such as that? Their powers and temperament were very unpredictable. This conversation made no sense, and now I felt silly and disloyal for even listening to it. But I felt trapped here. I reached back and tried to silently unhook whatever my dress had caught on so I could make a quick getaway as soon as possible.

"Look at it this way, having a child to love would be a . . . blessing of a sort. You can never love the mother, but a child would bring joy. Or so I'm told."

Titus made a sound of disgust in the back of his throat. "What does one even do with children?"

I gave my dress one final yank and there was a slight tearing sound. I pressed my eyes closed and held my breath, praying they didn't hear it. Their conversation halted and I heard them move in the room. *Bloody hell, you've gone and done it now, Moira.* I stood there frozen, knowing I'd been found and hoping they'd just ignore my presence. But only a fool would think so, and I was no fool. I blew out a breath and peeked my eyes open. Titus stood only a few feet away with his arms crossed and his face an unfortunate shade of red. Graymont stood next to him with a smile tugging at his lips and a light chuckle in his chest.

I stepped from my little hiding place and gave them a wobbly curtsey. "Your Highness. Prince Graymont. Good evening."

Good evening? That was all I could come up with!? They'd think I was simple and of poor manners. Titus glared at me. "What are you doing here?"

"I —"

He cut me off. "—Are you spying on me?"

"No, I—" I tried to explain, but he cut me off once more.

"—I don't fancy being spied on." His words were sharp and snapping. "This chamber was to be emptied. No one was to be in here. This castle is not a private residence where you can just linger."

"Linger?" My agitation began to rise. He wasn't even giving me a moment to speak.

"Yes, linger. It is not an open house for vampires to just roam free. You are to be in the other chamber with the other ladies of the court, not wedged here among my library eavesdropping on a private conversation." He put his hands on his hips, and for some reason I didn't feel intimidated by him when I should have. I should have been quaking with nerves, yet I didn't feel any.

"I was not spying on you." The words tumbled from my mouth. "You were meant to be in the room with the other ladies." At his raised eyebrows, I sucked in a deep breath and made my voice more even. "My lord."

Graymont chuckled and smacked his brother in the arm. "There you have it, Brother. *YOU* were meant to be with the ladies in the other room. But of course, she is correct and the folly lies with you and not this lovely creature."

Lovely creature? "Do not use your charms on me, my lord. They will not work."

He winked. "Of course not. Even so, it's clearly you who is at fault, good King."

"Indeed," Titus growled. "Then do tell me why are you here? In this room, at this exact moment?"

I held still, not saying a word. His brow furrowed and he motioned for me to speak.

"Oh, I was waiting for you to interrupt me once more, my lord." I folded my hands in front of me.

Graymont glanced from the King to me and back again. Laughter burst from his chest. He shook his head and held on to his brother's shoulder for support. "Well, she's got you there."

"I do not require sass in your answer . . ." He paused, waiting for me to fill in my name.

"Moira," I added.

"Moira," he repeated. "What I do require is answers. As your King, I command it."

There was something in the way he commanded me that made me want to be stubborn and resist him. Yet I was raised in this world and would comply. "I waited for the others to leave. I was going to read for a moment in front of the fire and then blend in after all the introductions were made."

Graymont walked over to one of the high-backed wooden chairs and dropped down into it. He held his glass to his lips and chuckled. "So, you had no intention of meeting the King tonight?"

I gave a heavy sigh. "No."

"But you have no problems with having an introduction between the two of us?" Graymont motioned between him and me. I smirked.

"Of course not. You're not the King." I tried to keep the teasing from my voice. "I just don't see myself as royal material."

Titus strolled over to the sideboard and poured himself a generous glass of whatever liquor had been mixed with blood. He seemed to watch me from the corner of his eye like he didn't trust my words. "And why not?"

"I have no interest in being your wife or Queen of the Vampires," I answered honestly. "It was intentional to wait out the night and return home with you none the wiser of my existence."

"This may be a first." Graymont took a deep drink. "A female who has no interest in a king."

I chuckled. "I'd see more merit in marrying the second son than the King."

At that they both froze and looked at me like I was something to be studied and not making perfect sense. Titus glanced at Graymont. "I think I'm offended."

"I do believe I'm quite flattered."

I took a small step forward. "I mean no offense, my lord. But the simple fact is I don't wish a royal life, and after hearing your rejection of love, I find my choice to be wise indeed."

"That was not meant for your ears." He took a sip of his drink, yet his gaze didn't waver from me.

"Nevertheless, I have now heard it. Trust, I will not repeat it to your potential brides, but with your permission, I will take my leave now."

I began to walk toward the door when he cleared his throat. "I did not give you permission to leave."

"Somehow, my lord, I do not think I'll be missed. There are a throng of ladies waiting to fulfill your breeding needs." I placed my best smile on my face.

Graymont practically fell out of his chair laughing. "I like this one. She's got a bit of fire in her belly."

My cheeks heated. "Thank you, my lord."

"You mock me." The King stood taller and seemed to fill up the whole room.

"No. I speak plainly. But do forgive me, my lord. I meant no offense. My bluntness does get the better of me often." I wanted nothing more than to leave this situation without getting myself in trouble with the King.

"Perhaps it is the reason you are not yet wed."

I shrugged. "Perhaps."

"Bravo, I do believe she's the first one we've met with some . . . spirit." Graymont gave his hands a small clap. "I applaud you."

"Do not encourage her, Brother," Titus snapped at Graymont. "Her demeanor leaves something to be desired."

"Or perhaps it's my resentment of being put on display like a prized pig for the King to choose from." *Complete idiocy, Moira. Complete and total idiocy.* "What I mean to say is, I'd very much like to leave."

"We have gathered that from your words." Titus motioned to the door. "Please do before you continue to wound your social standing and my pride further."

I hurried to the door and heard Graymont snicker. "She's rather perfect."

Titus scoffed. "Hardly, Brother."

"Mark my words, not everything is as it seems with that one."

I wanted to call back and tell him I couldn't agree more. But I'd already said my share, and I was sure I wouldn't be hearing from the King or his charming brother anytime soon, which suited me just fine.

CHAPTER FIFTEEN

PIPER

"Moira, are you all right?" I reached for her hand and took it into mine. I gave her fingers a light squeeze. I couldn't imagine what she must be going through. First losing her husband to this curse and then a most beloved son. I didn't know how she was even still standing.

She shook herself as if pulling herself into the present. "Yes, I-I'm fine. Just memories getting the better of me. Things I long since tried to forget."

"I can't imagine what this is like for you. And I know I'm asking a lot of you."

She shook her head and those long chocolate locks fell around her face in messy tatters. I'd never seen her so not put together. It was a bit unnerving for me. But I could see the strength she showed even now just by being here and helping. Even while Grayson was in such mortal danger.

She held my hands tighter, and when her gaze met mine, I saw nothing but determination.

"This curse . . . it is a plague on us all. It takes down one after another. Vampires are meant to be immortal. We are meant to be together for eternity." Her eyes welled with unshed tears. "And now it has taken my son, which I cannot bear."

"I'm going to do everything I can. I swear it."

She pulled me closer so we were only inches apart. "I know you will, dearest, but this curse is too big for just one to handle. You need help."

I nodded. "That's why I came to you."

"I wish I were enough." She lowered her voice. "You must go to Evermore Academy and seek out the Witch Queens. I know not who they are, but Grayson has made allies there. They're very powerful and might have exactly what you need to finally break this horrid cycle."

Excitement pumped through my veins. This could be a first lead. "Where is the Academy?"

"New York City. Do be cautious and keep your wits about you. While he may be friends with the Queens, they are very dangerous and might not take kindly to you just showing up. I don't know enough about them to tell you anymore, but it takes a powerful witch to cast a curse and it'll take an even more powerful one to help you break it."

"Thank you, Moira."

"I wish I could go myself. But I am the advisor to the King of the Vampires. If I go and there is a conflict, it means we'd engage in a political mess I couldn't clean up.

The witches have been in upheaval and there is a new ruler we don't know, but I want to go so badly."

"No, Moira, the King needs you here. I can go to the witches and plead our case. If they were half as fond of Gray as I am, then they will help us." I gave her hands one last squeeze and turned down the hallway.

"Piper!" she called out after me.

I whirled around. "Yes?"

"Do whatever you have to do to save him." She glanced down at her hands, breaking eye contact. "No matter what sacrifices must be made."

She looked so haunted standing there alone with the empty castle surrounding her. The silence of the hallway felt heavy between us. When she raised her eyes to look at me, all I could see was a lifetime of sadness. In another life and in another time, I could picture her with Grayson's quick wit and easy smile. But that was all gone now, and all that was left was a wife without a husband and a mother without her son.

"I will do whatever it takes. I promise." I knew I would. He was my soulmate. There wasn't anything I wouldn't do to give myself the time to kick his ass for not telling me any of this.

I hurried down the hall toward the mirrors that were set up for the party. Two guards were starting to take them down. I stepped in front of one and pressed my hand to it. I knew they wouldn't be here when I tried to come back. I wasn't familiar with the school, but I knew other places in New York City, and I would follow my instincts right to the witches. I stepped through the mirror and let its cool liquid smooth over my body. A few more steps and I stepped out of the mirror and into an oversized bathroom stall. I stood on the sink looking down at the dingy floor where toilet paper was strewn about. Some of it was left in damp wads around the bottom of the toilet.

I really need to think of better places to mirror travel to besides bathrooms. The odor was offensive and the sounds even more so. I hopped off the sink and pulled the door open.

"Hey! Did she cut the line?"

"Where'd she come from?"

"I need to go real bad! Move!" A woman rushed by me, and I snickered to myself as I passed the line of women waiting their turn. For such a busy place, I would've thought that Penn Station would've had a bigger bathroom. It was too narrow and just dark and dingy. Fluorescent lighting was a woman's worst nightmare, yet they seemed to put it everywhere.

I walked out past the police station at the half-moon desk right across from the big board showing where the trains were coming and going. The night had passed quickly and even at midday the day after Christmas the station still buzzed with activity. People were bundled in their winter hats, coats, and boots. As I walked toward the Seventh Avenue exit, I hurried past the delicious smells of the Krispy Kreme, pizza place, and Dunkin Donuts. I knew that once I'd been a vampire for a while, I'd be able to eat again. But I did not need another round of the lesson I learned before. I hurried up the stairs to the street. The wind whipped down, blowing my hair back from my face. People huddled into their coats when they hit the street.

It was nearly overwhelming with my vampire senses. Even in the middle of the day, the lights were bright, the sounds were louder, and the smell was thick in the air. If I looked to my left, Times Square blared as bright and hectic as ever. Across from the station were huge billboards that covered the fronts of the buildings. People moved in all different directions and the sounds of sirens echoed down the street. It wasn't Boston, but it was a busy city that I adored. I didn't know where I was going or what I was looking for, but I hoped my new sense would guide me to where the magic was strong enough.

I vaguely remembered what it was like to sit next to Ophelia. How the magic almost crawled over my skin. Deep down I hoped that it would also call to my own new blood magic. I closed my eyes for a moment just letting my senses be completely overwhelmed by the city and its surroundings. There was so much energy pulsing around me it was hard to tell what direction to move in. But there to my left was a glimmer of something different. Something more. I hurried in that direction, flying by people and things. As I passed the street vendors and little shops, I plucked a hat, gloves, and a scarf so I blended in better.

The closer I got to the area that called to me, the more I felt the power around it. It was like walking through a thick Boston fog. It tasted like powdered sugar on my tongue and smelled of morning dew. There was something fresh and clean that lingered in the air. I turned down another street and ran headlong toward it. My instincts carried me forward, and the world moved by so quickly I hardly knew where I was. When I stopped, I froze in front of two huge wooden doors. I gazed up at the dark building. It wasn't that it stood out, more that I could feel the power beyond the stone exterior. The top of the building looked like an old castle with turrets on the corners and stones at the top.

"Subtle. Real subtle." A building that looked like a castle which housed . . . Queens.

Not that I could say anything, I grew up without a home, and when I finally did get a fancy home, it was as a vampire in an amazing gothic castle. I knocked on the door, and it just echoed beyond the walls. For an academy, it was awfully quiet for midday. Did they leave for the holidays? I shook my head. They couldn't. I needed them now. I knocked again, this time harder. Some of the wood splintered under my knuckles but no one answered the door.

I glanced down the street, looking in one direction and then the other. No one would notice me if I moved quickly enough. I took two steps back and ran at the doors full speed. At the last moment, I planted my foot and launched myself toward the top of the wall. My arms pinwheeled and my stomach rose up into my throat. The top of the school came into view, and I dropped down and landed on top of the wall. My feet crushed into the thick stone as I dropped down into a crouch. A siren sounded and I jumped to stand.

"Shit." Breaking and entering was not my thing. "Not good, not good."

I hurried toward the edge of the wall that overlooked the interior of the school. Below was a courtyard with a light sheen of frost covering the ground. A large stone fountain with three tiers in it sat in the middle of everything. The water trickled lightly, making a pleasant sound I could barely hear over the alarm. I glanced around and still the academy seemed empty. There were only two floors and both were open and exposed the courtyard. Large columns were spread around the first and second floor. Stone archways connected the pillars, and a small half-wall made it look so picturesque. Multiple hallways ran off the courtyard leading farther into the school. I placed my hand on the wall and kicked my legs over, hopping down from the top of the wall.

A blast of magic struck me in my side as I dropped down. It felt like being hit by a sledgehammer and then blasted with fire at the same time. It sent me flying across the courtyard and I careened across the frozen grass like a tennis ball. I crashed into the fountain and the stone shattered around me. Water shot up into the air and rained down on me as I crawled from the rubble.

"What the fuck?" I shook my hands out, sending droplets of water flying in all different directions. I wiped at my eyes and blinked hard.

My blood magic rose to the forefront and a fine red mist surrounded me like a swirling vortex. Drops of water hung among the mist surrounding me. I pressed my hand to my side, and it felt so tender there I was sure some of my ribs were broken. I was lucky I'd bitten Grayson only last night, otherwise those would take me a long time to heal.

I glanced around and was faced with a woman with wild midnight hair and silvery magic whipping around her. Her eyes nearly glowed with the silver power surrounding her. Next to her was a guy with dark-red hair and a dark tattoo of a phoenix on his neck that peeked out from the top of his sweatshirt. He held a ball of fire in his hand that he tossed up and down like a baseball. A huge black dog-looking thing with a bunch of tails stood on her other side. Drops of drool fell from its mouth as it stared at me.

Another woman with long auburn hair and bright-green eyes stood on the other side of her. Golden magic hung in the air around her, except she stood there more casually and with a light smirk on her face. She let her eyes linger above my head, and I tilted my head back trying to see what she saw. A huge chunk of that fountain floated just above my head as if at any moment she could drop it and crush me from the top down. *Would a vampire survive death by crushing?* I didn't want to stand here and find out. A guy with bright-blond hair stood on her other side. With his ocean eyes and tasseled hair, he reminded me of a surfer I'd seen on TV.

I narrowed my eyes at the line of them. "Well, that's a fine fucking hello."

The woman at the center with the wild hair didn't flinch. "We don't take kindly to trespassers."

"Then perhaps answering your door would stop that." I didn't have time for this. There was too much power surrounding them for them to not be exactly who I was looking for.

"You're surrounded," the guy with the ball of fire called out to me. "So I suggest you state your purpose before you find out how bad this situation can be for you."

I was already in a bad situation. I wasn't trying to make it worse. I glanced over my shoulder to find a woman with dark curls that stood out from her face staring at me. Yellow bands of magic swirled around her and bounced on the ground in my direction. They glowed so bright it gave her dark skin a golden glow. Vines shot up around me like a cage and I fought the urge to just rip them all out with my bare hands. I opened my hand, and my blood magic flew across the courtyard and wrapped around her.

Her eyes widened and I arched my eyebrows. "Stop it. I don't like being caged."

The vines withered and died around me. They turned to ash and drifted to the ground. I dropped my hold on her and nodded my head. "Thank you."

"You have one second to state your purpose here or I drop this." The redhead narrowed her eyes at me. "We'll see if vampires can survive being crushed."

I gave a heavy sigh and pulled my sleeve up. "My name is Piper. I'm Grayson Shade's soulmate . . . and I need your help."

CHAPTER SIXTEEN

MOIRA

My body felt slow and heavy. Loss like I'd never known assailed me. The grief was so acute I found it hard to breathe, to even function. My heart was pained in the worst kind of way. It ached deep in my chest to the point where I thought it might stop all together. Yet all I could do was count each step I took along with each breath. If I just kept counting, then perhaps my breathing would feel normal too. No mother should have to watch their child deteriorate before their very eyes. No wife should lose a husband in such a way either. For all the blessings I'd been afforded—love, happiness, a son, a royal life—it felt like a blessedly cursed life filled with the greatest joys and the harshest sadness.

I didn't want to stand by and watch my son die the same way I stood by and watched my love die. I'd lived with loss for two hundred years, which had been made only bearable by the presence of my child. His easy smile saw me through the deepest hurt and the darkest nights. And now the ball in my throat made it so hard to breathe I felt as though I'd never draw a normal breath again. Grief did odd things to people. For me it was like a part of me had died the day I lost my love and had remained so. The hole in my heart was a dark reminder of what I'd had for the briefest of moments. Perfect as they may have been, falling in love was never my plan, nor was losing a love I never wanted. But Grayson had always been my light. My purpose. He made my life better simply by existing.

I took the steps slowly, climbing to a part of the castle where hardly anyone ever ventured. The hallways were empty here. The guards were only stationed at the entrance to this wing. A single crimson carpet ran down the long hall. A cold chill seeped into my veins from the stone walls. It'd been years since I walked through the doors at the end of the hall. The memories felt like drowning. But I *was* drowning. My boy, my beautiful boy, was dying . . . and I would have to stand by and watch. My mind was a whirl of prayers that by some miracle Piper would succeed where I failed so long ago. Unimaginable visions of seeing my son in his early grave assailed my mind, each one a torturous reminder of how I was reliving the past in the present. How would I live through this?

I didn't want to live through this. If he died, I prayed that the creator saw fit to take me as well. I pressed the door open and sucked in a deep breath. I expected there to be dust in this room, or the scent of stale air, but it was as pristine as ever, with fresh flowers lining the walls. I stepped up to the coffin standing in the middle of the room. My breath left me in a rush, and I placed my hand over the glass cover of the coffin.

At times I wanted to believe that Graymont was just lying there sleeping. The power of the coffin preserved him perfectly. Titus made sure to acquire it at a time when the vampires had little to no connection to the magic community. I only prayed that Piper could get through to them the way that Grayson had. I rested my hand on the coffin and gazed down at his face. He was so beautiful in death. It pained my heart to see him like this. His hair flowed back from his face, highlighting his perfect cheekbones and full lips. There was no doubt the men of The House of Shade were genetically blessed.

"We certainly have made a mess of things." I hung my head and silent tears streamed down my face. Tears I dared not shed in front of anyone else. Each one rolled down my cheeks and fell onto the lid with a tiny splash like raindrops forming a puddle. I sucked in a deep breath. "I- I don't know what we are to do now."

I leaned on the coffin, letting my arms fall across the lid. It was the closest I could get to him, to ever hugging him again. Everything was ruined now. My life was ruined. There was a time when I felt happiness, a tinge of excitement, and the thrill of new love. Memories I'd long since tried to forget assaulted me without my permission.

200 years ago

Wildflowers swayed all around me and brushed against the fabric of my skirts. My parent's estate loomed on the hills in the distance. Forest and rolling fields separated me from their prying eyes. I let my hair fall loose around my face and down my back. It was not the tradition of higher society to be so free with actions and looks. Yet I enjoyed roaming among the estate. The sun was warm on my skin and the lingering scent of the flowers I'd picked stuck to my clothing. I peeked up at him and met those deep eyes with their flecks of mahogany. I'd never noticed their depths before.

"You're beginning to make a habit of this, my lord." Warmth heated my cheeks. "People will soon start to talk."

His chest rumbled with a deep chuckle. "Would that be so awful? If others began to find out about us?"

I let the bouquet of wildflowers in my hand brush against the others we strolled by. "You tell me. I seem to be your best kept secret."

"Hardly, I find my regard is well noted by others. Even my brother, thick as he may be, has noted a difference." He plucked a daisy and handed it to me to add to the others he thought I might like.

"Ah, but what a reputation you must be giving me then. The secret mistress hidden in the countryside that you flit off to on a whim. What of your duties, my lord?" I found it difficult to keep the teasing tone from my voice.

"I think the word mistress is quite harsh for a close

friendship that I enjoy. If anything, I should be insulted you consider yourself so." He gave me a cheeky smirk.

I pressed my lips together to stifle the smile that threatened to spread across my face. "And yet here I've remained your secret companion for weeks, wandering among the forest and exploring the streams."

"Yes, like a tiny wood nymph prancing about through the greenery. I do so enjoy the sight of your little feet in the mud and the flowers in your hair. It's not something we see at court often. I find it quite refreshing." He moved toward the shade of the trees, and I followed his lead easily. "I can see why you didn't think you'd be suited to a royal life and chose to hide in the library that night."

I stepped over a tree root and he took my hand to help me as though I hadn't walked these forests all my life and knew every tree, stone, and flower. Yet when I was on the steady path, he didn't let go of my hand. "I find myself curious as to what it would be like to be required in court like you and your brother. Or what it would be like to give this up for the fast pace of London."

"Your curiosity pleases me." His fingers tightened around mine, and it sent a small thrill through my body. I didn't want a life in the public eye, but for him, I could almost picture it.

I beamed up at him. "Oh, we do aim to please, my lord."

"Would you like that?" He stopped walking and pulled me to a halt. His eyes bore into mine and for a moment I could see our future. Images of us spending hidden moments together among the chaos of court assailed my mind. We could hide in the library where we first met, or remain in the gardens, or spend the dawning hours lounging in bed together.

"I dare say I would." I bit my bottom lip and his eyes dropped down toward them.

He took a step and I backed up, then another, and another until my back was pressed to the tree behind me. He hovered over me so tall and imposing, yet I felt the safest I ever had in his presence. His eyes darkened and I felt as though he were trying to read my thoughts. "Do not toy with me."

"Would I dream of doing such a thing?" I tilted my chin up, hoping he'd take my lips for the first time.

"Many would." He inched closer. "What if I told you I could give you all you desire?"

"In truth, I would doubt those words coming from anyone else but you." I rested my hand on the lapel of his coat and felt the steady beating of his heart on my fingertips.

"What if I gave you all you desired but love." His face turned deadly serious.

I snickered. "I'd say we're well on our way toward an understanding, wouldn't you?"

"I do not jest, Moira." He shook his head. "My family, it's . . . complicated. I can offer you the world, my hand, my unwavering loyalty, and any other earthly desire you could possibly imagine, but I cannot offer you words of love, and I will not bite you or try to make you my soulmate . . . ever. So, what say you to a man who will give you all but this one thing?" He held his breath, waiting for my answer.

Then I will love enough for us both until you come to love me in return. Men often fought to hold on to themselves but even I knew we had something between us. I felt it in the words he spoke to me, the way he was so gentle with my hand, and the lingering looks when he thought I wasn't looking.

I wanted to keep the mood light between us as it always had been. Free and easy, so natural we moved around each other like two birds flitting through the trees at springtime. "I find it highly tempting. But there is one thing I am curious about?"

"Ask me anything." His voice was so grave, so serious. I wanted to see the smile tug at his lips and the twinkle in his eyes. I loved the way he played and joked, making everything that could be vexing seem so easily handled.

"Does this offer include you physically?" I whispered, knowing full well I was suggesting exactly what I was suggesting.

His eyebrows shot up and that smile tugged at his lips. "Ah, well, yes it would. The kingdom is in want of an heir after all."

He took a step closer, and this time my fingers curled into the lapels of his coat, holding him there so close to me. "Won't your brother be disappointed you've chosen me after that display in the library?"

"I dare say he'd find it to be quite a relief."

"Then perhaps I should be a secret mistress of the forest

no longer?" How could I pass up a life so sweet with a man so charismatic?

"Oh, enchanting forest creature," He tucked the strands of my hair behind my ear and let his fingers linger on my cheek. "I wouldn't dream of hiding you away from the world. Nor would I dream of holding anything back from you that I was free to give, physically or otherwise."

The world was at my feet, and he was giving it to me. I bit my bottom lip and pulled him closer. "I would be a fool not to accept such an offer, would I not?"

"Then perhaps you should put me out of misery and tell me, Moira, are you going to marry me or not, my enchanting forest creature?"

My breath left me in a rush and my heart soared. Nothing in the world could ever be so pleasing to hear.

I BRUSHED my tears off the top of the glass coffin, leaving streaks over the immaculate glass. "This life, this family, was well worth it. I would take this pain to live the joys that I have. But oh, dearest Graymont, we could really use you right now, your brother above all else. I know even in his silence he mourns your loss as I do. Wherever you are, please help Grayson through this."

I sucked in a breath and turned for the door, hoping that one mother's prayer for her child would somehow find his guardian angel and the past would not repeat itself.

CHAPTER SEVENTEEN

PIPER

The boulders hovering over my head disappeared into dust and rained down around me like falling snow. They all moved toward me like a wave. I held my hands up and my blood magic swirled around me, protecting me from whatever they decided to do next. I would make them all see reason, whether or not they wanted to. They hesitated, staring at my swirling magic. But the one that seemed to be at the center of it all, the girl with the wild black hair and bright eyes, seemed to be directing this madness.

She held her hand up and some of my power drifted toward her. It touched her skin and suddenly turned to silvery magic, and she absorbed it. Her eyes widened and a shiver went down her spine. "Whoa."

The guy next to her extinguished his flames and grabbed on to her elbow, seeming to steady her. His eyes roamed over her delicate features, looking for signs of trouble. So much concern for her behind one look. "Are you alright?"

"What a hit." She smirked at me while eyeing me with interest. "I think I'm going to like you."

"I think that's weird to say after the welcome I just got." I slowly dropped my hands and let my power drift back inside me where that well sat deep in my stomach.

"You're a powerful vampire that hopped over our walls and set off an alarm. How else were we supposed to approach you?" She arched her eyebrow at me as if saying *maybe think about what you just said.*

"Fair point." I sighed and shrugged. "But in my defense, this whole vampire thing is brand-new to me and I had no place else to go. Plus, I did knock, and I am desperate for your help at this point."

"I think you came to the right place." She moved in closer and extended her hand toward me. I took it. "I'm Zinnia."

"You're a witch? A Witch Queen? Because that's who I'm looking for." Power oozed off her like it was her natural aura, and I hoped she would be the one to help us. There was something so calm and capable about her that would make anyone think she was a queen.

"Yes, I think I'm who you're looking for." She turned to the guy next to her with all the flame powers he showed before. "This is Tucker. He's a phoenix, and the redhead over there is Astrid, Queen of Manifestation, and the blond guy beside her is Beckett, a general badass warlock."

My eyes widened and I gave them a little wave. "Piper. Just Piper the vampire."

It felt weird to introduce myself that way, but how else could I describe myself in this world? *Hi, I'm Grayson's progeny, but also soulmate, but also sometimes feral, but also on a mission to save the guy I love.* None of that seemed appropriate. But really, who the hell knew what was appropriate under these circumstances?

A woman dropped down from the opposite wall as though it was just like taking a step down from a small platform and not a great height. She held a bow and arrow casually at her side and pointed to the ground. She plucked at the string while staring at me. "You're lucky I didn't shoot you."

"Or are you lucky I didn't catch you trying to shoot me?" My instincts and senses were even stronger than I knew. I could see things flying at me from a mile away now. It was odd but so very welcome.

Her lips twitched like she was trying to hide a smile. She tucked a lock of her long, sandy blond hair behind her ear and my eyes widened at the tiny points. Her eyes met mine and I found her unwavering gaze to almost be unnerving. "She can stay."

"Um, thanks?" I wasn't planning on leaving without their help.

"Come on, let's get out of the cold and go somewhere we can talk." Zinnia motioned to a hallway behind me. "The Academy is pretty empty right now because of the holiday, but you never know who might be listening."

"That would be great." I turned to walk toward the hall but paused at the shattered fountain. "Am I going to get in trouble for destruction of property?"

Tucker sighed and kicked at a stray piece of stone on the ground at his feet. "No, but we are."

Water shot straight up into the air and sprayed in all different directions. It misted over us and the frozen grass. The redheaded woman, Astrid, stood just beside the shattered fountain, looking down at all the pieces. The water misted her hair, making those auburn waves seem even darker. "Not if I have something to do about it."

She held her hands up and gold glittering magic swirled around her before drifting over the grass like a creeping fog. The pieces of the fountain all lifted from the ground and floated in a million different directions. One by one, they all moved to fit together like puzzle pieces. Her magic flowed over the jagged edges, sealing them together like nothing had ever happened. Bright light shined from them and suddenly the whole fountain was back together perfectly. The sound of trickling water filled the quiet courtyard.

Tucker patted her on the shoulder as he passed by. "We really could've used you a few months ago. Matteaus would've loved for us to be able to clean up our own mess."

"Yes, but I'm here now." She winked and they started to follow him into the hallway. "He'll never know."

"Oh, he'll know." Tuck chuckled. "He just might not be as pissed."

I stood there for a moment, staring at the fountain and

looking for a crack or something. But there was nothing. My jaw dropped and Zinnia gave a light chuckle. "Magic. I know, right?"

"It's very impressive." She turned toward where the others had gone, and I fell into step with her. "So, you're the head queen? What's your power like?"

She gave a light chuckle. "You don't beat around the bush, do you? I can see why Gray would like you."

"I'm not sure the rest of his family sees it that way. But deep down I always thought we fit. You know?" From the moment I'd met Grayson, I knew there would be something between us. I tried to fight it and clearly so did he. But the universe had other plans. Finding out he was my soulmate only solidified the course of action I needed to take now.

She nodded and gazed at Tucker's back. "I know exactly what you mean."

"That's why I came here. I need the Witch Queens to help me, and I'm hoping that's you?"

"I guess you'd say I'm the Queen Witch, yes. My father was the High King of the Witches." She shrugged like it didn't matter.

"Oh, a princess first then." I chuckled. "He must be proud to have you as a daughter."

"I don't think so. He's dead." Her words were so emotionless, like his death was a matter of fact and not an emotional thing at all. But then again, I of all people knew how parents could suck.

Way to put your foot in your mouth, Piper. I didn't know

what else to say but to offer my condolences. "Oh, I'm so sorry."

"Don't be. I killed him. Well, me, Tuck, and my sister, Ophelia." She waved me forward as my steps slowed. It was the shock of all the information she just blurted out like it was nothing that made me stumble. How was killing your parent okay in this world?

I tried to go for the only thing I could think of. "Ophelia is your sister? I've met her. Did you know?"

Her eyebrows shot up in surprise. "Have you?"

"At the vampire castle." I nodded. "I kind of liked her."

"It's hard not to like the lovable psychopath. And I would say I'm surprised she was there, but somehow I'm really not. Our relationship with the vampires has always been limited until Grayson began to bridge the gap, so O being there is kind of very Ophelia."

"And you and she . . . killed your father?" What the hell was I walking into? And who the hell was I asking to get help from?

She smirked and gave me a sideways look. "You know your face kind of has subtitles, right?"

I tried to smooth my features and hide my shock. "I'm sorry. I just wasn't ready for murder."

She chuckled. "Well, don't tell my sister that. She'll be very disappointed in you. But my father was an evil man who used his powers to hurt the witches. He was a siphon witch, like me. I can take power from others and use it as my own. He took too much and used it for his own gains. A lot of good witches died under his rule. I was pretty much born to stop him, along with the other queens."

"Ohhh, hence your ability to take mine?" I followed her down the hall and we turned and went down a set of long, winding stairs. Cool, damp air seeped through the thick stone walls. It was only slightly warmer here than outside. But as we descended lower into the castle, it became warmer.

"Yours was like tasting blood and power at the same time." We walked down another long hallway. "What is your power exactly?"

"If I'm being honest, I'm new at this and my power is new to me, sooooo your guess is as good as mine. So far, I can control others' actions, but it's fleeting and whatever that magic was with the water before." I don't know why I felt so comfortable with her. But she had a calm, cool way about her that made me feel calmer in return, even if they had just attacked me and admitted to murder. In the world of witches and vampires, someone was bound to get killed.

She stopped before a thick wooden door and motioned to it. "This is where we stop."

I hesitated to open it. "What's in there?"

"This is our war room. We all meet here when there's a problem in the world of Evermore and we have to solve it." She stepped around me and opened it, letting the door swing wide. "And we're going to fix whatever happened because Gray is one of our own."

I followed her into the room and just stood there as all eyes swung toward me. There was one long table in the center of the room with a map of the world spread out over it. Red pins were stuck into different locations. It looked the way it would if someone was marking off all the places they'd traveled before. There were other tables pushed against the walls with random chairs spread throughout the room. A dusting of white sand was sprinkled on the floor, and the smell of sun and sweat lingered in the air.

I looked across from me, and there sat a guy with midnight hair down to his chin and glowing green eyes. Tarot cards swirled above his head, and I froze on the spot. Green smoke seeped from his fingers and churned with the cards. When he looked at me, his eyes went from milky-white to glowing green and back again. A tiny woman sat perched on the table beside him. She kicked her legs, letting them swing back and forth. She held a bag of chips in one hand and divvied them up between the two of them. One for her, a bunch for him.

When my eyes locked on her, I did a double take. There was something so familiar about her, something I couldn't put my finger on, but I'd seen her before, somewhere. The haunting feeling of déjà vu swam in my mind. "I know you."

"Yup." She nodded and her blond curls bounced with her movement. *Crunch, crunch, crunch.* The bag of chips crinkled as she yanked out more food.

I walked farther into the room. It was eerie how familiar she looked, like something from a dream or nightmare. Those dark eyes, that huge black trench coat, and those long blond curls, yet the memory escaped me from where exactly I knew her. "But I can't place where from?"

"I'm Tilly. This is Maze." She motioned between the two of them, then she brushed her fingers over her dark jeans and dusted the crumbs off her hands. She took a deep breath and met my eye. "Listen, I was only slightly demon-possessed when I kind of attacked you. But really, I was just hungry. I wasn't actually going to kill you or anything."

Then it hit me. The memories all rushed back. The night I was walking home from work to meet Dice. How scared and alone I felt. She hunted me. She chased me. She caught me. I nearly died that night from my injuries. It was catastrophic. "You're the one . . . you're the one who attacked me and put me in the hospital."

Astrid stepped in closer to her as though trying to protect her. She leaned in close to Tilly and I could tell there was a bond between the two of them, like Dice and me. If Dice nearly killed someone, I'd defend her with my last breath. Astrid lifted her chin and met my eye. "She wasn't herself."

"Yeah, I heard that, demon possession?" This world was far beyond anything I could think of. But Tilly wasn't attacking me now, and hell, I'd been feral for a time. I could only imagine the things I'd done against my will. So maybe demon possession was a bit like being feral? If that was the case, then I was in no position to judge, and a tiny bit of grace was in order. "So you attacked me because you were part demon?"

Tilly nodded. "Yep, demon-possessed. Plus, I was so hungry, and you had food. But I apologize."

"Food is always the answer." Maze reached into the bag and pulled out a handful of chips and shoved them into his mouth. Then he put his hand in his pocket and pulled out a brown paper bag with tiny stains on it. He turned it over on the table next to him, and the second he did, a one-eyed black cat charged into the room.

Maze put his arms on the table and surrounded the pile of tiny pizza rolls. "Back off. They're mine."

The cat leapt up on his knee and stared at him. They did this for long moments as if it were a test of wills to see who would win. Tilly sighed and rolled her eyes. She reached into the pile of pizza rolls and snagged one. Maze looked like he was about to whine at her, but she blew on it and tossed it to the cat. "Honestly, you two."

I was fascinated by the display. Maze stuck his tongue out at the cat and the thing turned around and stuck his tail up in the air and hopped off his knee with a little victory dance on the way out the door. He paused next to me and blinked his one eye as though winking at me.

Tilly cleared her throat. "I mean, I really am sorry now."

I shook myself and reminded myself we were in the middle of a conversation. "Yes, of course, apology accepted. Are you still demon-possessed or are we good? Should I worry you're gonna try to do that again?"

"Pshh, like I'd attack a super powerful vampire. I'm not stupid, Piper." She said my name as if I were already a close friend. Her voice was almost teasing, as though this was water under the bridge already.

I tried to go with her approach and just accept it. "I mean yeah, I guess it's cool now? I survived..."

Barely.

She looked me up and down. "Yeah, but not much longer after that."

I rolled my eyes. "Thanks."

"Vampire-Piper fits you." She winked. "And will continue to fit you."

"What?" My brow furrowed in confusion. What the hell was she talking about now? Will continue to fit me?

Maze sighed. "The rules, cupcake. The rules."

She sighed. "I knowwwww. Don't tell people what we see... blah, blah, blah."

Astrid sighed. "Ignore their creep asses. They speak in riddles a lot."

Zinnia motioned for me to sit at one of the chairs at the table with the big map on it. "I know it took you a lot to come here, and we all love Grayson and want to help. So just let us know everything you can, and we will figure out what to do next."

She was so calm on the outside, and I did not feel that way on the inside at all. Coming here was a last resort, and now that I was here, my nerves were starting to settle in and it was overwhelming to even be here in this room with all of them. There was so much power, so much magic. I could see why Grayson would hang around to ally with these people, but also for the sake of pure curiosity. Sure, vampires had blood magic but it was nothing like this. Nothing like the power all these people wheeled. It only made me realize just how brilliant he was to try and bring our worlds together.

The woman who tried to trap me with her yellow streaming power strolled into the room. She narrowed her eyes as she took a seat across from me. I wanted to say something like *hey nice power* or *thanks for not killing me*, but it didn't seem like the right time.

Zinnia motioned to her. "This is Tabi, our Queen of Elements."

"Nice to meet you." I gave her a wave. "I mean, nice to meet you again."

"Nice to meet you too." But the words almost seemed pulled from her.

Then another woman with model looks and long, streaked blond hair came in behind her. Zinnia nodded to her. "And Serrina, our Queen of Desires."

"Desires? Wow. I bet you know some shit." I slapped my hand over my mouth. I couldn't imagine knowing people's desires or making them feel desire for things. It was almost too hypnotic of a power to think about. "I'm sorry. Sometimes the words get from my brain to my mouth before my filter can stop them, and they've gotten a lot faster now that I'm a vampire."

"No worries." She gave me a secret smile. She was so beautiful it was difficult to look away. I'd never seen a person who actually looked like their power. "And yes, yes I do know a lot of shit. And right now, you're a bundle of nerves who just wants us to help you. It's almost desperate."

"Not to sound cliché, but I *am* desperate." The others all fell silent as I spoke. "Grayson fell to a curse that, from my understanding, was placed on his family ages ago. And no one in the vampire world knows how to break it."

They sucked in a collective breath and silence fell heavily. The blond guy, Beckett, was the first to speak. "Are you sure? It's not bloodlust or something else?"

"I'm sure." When they all just looked around at each other with sad faces, I got the feeling there was an unspoken conversation going on that I didn't know about. Their sadness was palpable but calm somehow. There was no outrage or shock in the room. It was as though they'd been prepared for this news. *Was that why they dropped their guard so quickly in the courtyard? They expected me?*

"Why don't any of you look surprised about this?" Their eyes darted but no one answered. "Are you all psychic or something? You saw this coming?"

Maze tossed a pizza roll into his mouth and spoke as he chewed. "Nah, only I can see what's coming."

"And he very annoyingly keeps it to himself," Beckett snapped in Maze's direction.

Maze shrugged. "*You* live with this madness and tell me how that goes for you."

Beckett opened his mouth to say something, but Tuck cleared his throat, stopping them all from talking. He turned toward me once they all fell silent. "Grayson came to us a few days ago, told us about the curse, and asked for our help."

My jaw dropped and I shook my head. "He did *what?*"

"He knew he was falling, Piper." Zinnia hung her head and her eyes shimmered with unshed tears. When she looked back up at me, I saw the pain she felt at losing a friend to something like this. She hated it almost as much as I did. "He wanted to see what we could do to help."

"And?" I held my breath. "Did you? I mean, were you able to find anything that could help?"

I held my breath, hoping against all odds that they'd found something that might ease this torture. Something that might bring him back to me.

"We're working on it." She nodded toward a stack of books in the corner of the room. "But we've found nothing so far."

I tried not to show my disappointment. They were his friends, and I knew they'd do anything they could to help. I just wished there was a solution at our fingertips rather than buried in an obscure book somewhere.

"What do the symptoms look like?" Tabi sat forward and rested her arms on the table.

Her words drew me from my thoughts. "He's stronger than ever, crazed, like it could be bloodlust but it's not. He's even slightly bigger. He moves so fast it's hard to keep up with him."

Tucker's hand balled into a fist on the table. "Is he lucid at all? Is he talking or is he a mindless animal?"

I thought back to the moments he looked at me with all

the anguish in the world. Or when he told me to run from him. "I know it sounds crazy, but he's in there. I know he is. There are moments where . . . I don't know. Moments where I swear he knows what's happening."

"Then first thing is first: we need to figure out how to break this curse once and for all." Zinnia was all command and attention. I could see the sadness in her face, but I could also see the determination to fix this shit. "Beckett, can you get Ophelia? I think we're going to need her for this."

"NO!" Maze, Tilly, and I said at the same time.

Zinnia looked to the three of us, and I pressed my lips together. I wasn't ready to tell them all that I'd sent my best friend, who was a human, to live with their murder happy friend.

Maze locked eyes on me, then turned to Zinnia. "She's handling business for me."

Zinnia glanced at the three of us. "Ominous."

"I always find it best not to ask questions," Beckett interjected. "We'll get the answers later."

Maze nodded and held the bag of chips over his mouth and dumped the crumbs in, then he threw two more pizza rolls in on top of the crumbs. "Precisely."

When she looked like she was going to question me next, I had to stop her before she got the words out. My mind scrambled to give them something else to focus on. "Besides, we have bigger problems. Atlas, Grayson's best friend, is going to hunt him down and kill him."

"WHAT?"

"Why?"

"How?"

"That's insane."

Their words all rushed out at once and I gave a heavy sigh. "It's some kind of messed up vow he made. Grayson made him promise that if he fell to the curse, then Atlas would put him out of his misery and kill him. It's a matter of honor to Atlas. And I can't lie, Atlas is pretty much a legendary assassin among the vampires."

"Not just the vampires." Beckett stepped in closer to the table and leaned over to rest his elbows on it. "If that guy wants you dead, you're as good as gone. He's like death himself."

"Who's like death?" Another guy walked into the room and the others all went quiet. "I didn't realize we were having a meeting."

"We were trying to let you rest." Beckett walked over to him and clapped him on the shoulder, then guided him toward the table with the others.

The guy had longer shaggy blond hair, a five o'clock shadow, and circles under his eyes. His eyes were so dark they were nearly black and they looked haunted. He gave me a half-smile that seemed to almost pain him. "Hey, I'm Logan."

"Hey, I'm Piper." I gave him a little nod, but I felt the power rolling off him. It was so enticing, like I wanted to listen to whatever he said, but at the same time so dark and twisted. I couldn't help but wonder what the hell happened to him that brought him such inner turmoil that it practically spilled out of him. The others clearly gave him a wide berth.

We all stood silent for a moment, then Logan gave a humorless chuckle. "So, you were saying someone is like death?"

"Atlas, Grayson's best friend. He's hunting him and I knocked him out for a bit, but he'll be awake soon, and when he is he's going to be pissed. We have to get to Grayson before he does."

Logan chuckled. "How exactly do you knock out death?"

"Umm." They all stared at me. "Pin him down and give him enough sedatives to knock out an elephant and pray it works?" They all laughed and shook their heads as though this were acceptable. "He was asking for it."

"I bet he was. If we could capture Grayson, it would help to get a feel for the curse and what it's doing." Zinnia glanced around at the rest of us. "Because so far Adrienne and Niche haven't found what this curse is, or who cast it, or how it works. There's like no record of it in any of our books."

"I'm sorry, who are Niche and Adrienne?" I glanced around the room feeling like I missed someone.

"They're not in the room at the moment. But Niche is our trainer, kind of like a guide to help us along the way. She's super brilliant. And Adrienne is one of our Guardians. She helps protect us. As a daughter of Athena, she's also crazy smart and knows more about Evermore and how it all works than any of us." Zinnia waved her hand over the map. "She's been working with us since the beginning."

"Hold up. Athena as in the Greek God Athena? That's like a real thing?"

Astrid shook her head and sighed. "Man, when Gray gets better, imma give him such a hard time about that lack of knowledge he gave you."

It wasn't my fault I didn't know. "I'm sorry?"

"Oh, I didn't mean it like that. But there is so much to learn about how everything works in Evermore, and it's overwhelming unless someone explains it all. Try to think about it like a hierarchy. At the top you've got The Fallen. They pretty much rule all of Evermore, which is every supernatural creature in the world, then right below them you've got the Greeks. They love to think of themselves as gods, but really they're just wicked powerful supernaturals who for a time made humans believe they were gods."

Beckett nodded. "And got into a shit ton of trouble for it too. That's why we have to keep our world a secret."

"Right, okay. Got it." I mentally took notes.

Astrid continued. "Then you've got all the other supernaturals of our world. The royals, like the Witch Queens and Vampire King, all answer to The Fallen and are responsible for their subjects."

"It's actually pretty clean if you think about it," Zinnia added. "But we all have a purpose. And to get us back on track right now, our purpose is to capture Grayson, and we all know what that means."

A collective sigh filled the room and Zinnia's was

among them. "Beckett, if you would please get Kylian here."

His lips twisted up into a shit-eating smile. "With pleasure."

He opened his hand and blue magic swirled all around him. He held it out and an oval shape began to take form, and my eyes widened. I thought mirror travel was weird. This was so much weirder. A swirling blue vortex appeared out of thin air. Beckett twisted his hand to the side and blue smoke poured from his hands and twisted the oval shape to hover high above the ground and face down toward the floor while being plastered on the ceiling. The magic swirled and twisted violently, and there was a collective cringe in the room.

"So violent," Astrid chided him. "He's going to puke."

"Wouldn't that be the point." Beckett wagged his eyebrows. "A bit of humbling for his cocky ass."

A huge guy fell through the portal. His arms pinwheeled and his body twisted mid-flight. He dropped to the ground, landing on his arms and the tips of his toes as if he were getting ready to do a push-up. His head snapped up and his dark hair flew back from his face. When he looked at me, his green crystal eyes flashed with annoyance. He sprang to his feet so fast he was a blur.

"You fucking rang?" Red smoke seeped from his fingers, and he seemed to take up the whole room.

A moment later a twin-sized mattress fell through the portal and landed on the floor with a loud *thunk*. Beckett lifted his hand and that blue smoke all filtered back to him. "Damn it."

There on top of the small bed was an even smaller woman with tiny green scales on her temple that ran down her neck and over her shoulder. Her head was a mess of short black hair and a single long braid that ran down the side. She was huddled on the bed wrapped in a blanket with pillows tucked all around her as though she made a nest for herself. She didn't open her eyes for even one second. She just continued to sleep. I didn't think I'd ever seen someone sleep so soundly in my life. I stared down at her, getting the hint that she was not from here.

When no one explained the sleeping women on the mattress, I tilted my head. "And this is?"

"Soto," Tuck, Beckett, and Kylian answered at the same time.

I tilted my head to the side to study her better. "That's it?"

"Yeah, that's it. She's my friend and that's all you need to know." Kylian turned to Zinnia, cutting off any other questions I might've had. He gave her a dark look. "What am I doing here, witch?"

"We need you to find Grayson." Zinnia got right to the point and matched his sharp tone.

He crossed his arms over his chest and took a few steps back to lean against one of the tables. "So, the leech needs me now. Why should I help?"

I was about to tell him if he wanted to keep his throat in his neck he would help. I wasn't against threatening, bullying, or even harming anyone to get Gray the help he needed. But Zinnia narrowed her eyes at him, and I knew she was going to get her way on this. "Because you live here, eat here, and generally are a nuisance all for free, and if you go home, you'll be thrown into a prison that you won't get out of. You have no place else to go, and you get to stay out of the kindness of our hearts. I'm not in the habit of my kindness not being returned, so you can either help or I will match energies with yours."

"Fair enough." He turned toward me with those uncanny eyes full of interest. "And who are you?"

"Piper."

His lips pulled up into a smirk. "Ahhh, Piper, we finally meet."

He licked his lips and looked me up and down with a satisfied smirk on his face that I wanted to slap off. I lifted my chin and hardened my gaze. "Yes, we do."

"You are a cute little leech. Well worth a curse if you ask me."

"You two know each other?" Tuck glanced from Kylian to me.

"We've had business," Kylian answered with a vague tone in his voice.

"What kind of business?" Tucker pressed.

Kylian shrugged. "The kind that's none of yours."

I didn't need him spilling our little deal about Dice. I was grateful for how he got her to safety, or at least with Ophelia, though I had no idea how safe that was. "Can you help us or not?"

He chuckled and winked at me. "Yeah, I can help you, little leech. But I don't need a whole contingent following me around to do it. I can catch one vampire myself. It's nothing I can't handle on my own."

"He's stronger than any vampire you've ever seen." I walked over to a metal chair in the corner of the room and picked it up. With my bare hands, I crumpled it into a tiny ball the size of a can of soda. "You're gonna want me with you."

Kylian's eyes widened, and he shoved away from the table and gave me a nod of approval. "Fine, then let the hunt begin."

CHAPTER EIGHTEEN

PIPER

"And I'm just supposed to step into that thing?" I stood just outside of Beckett's swirling blue vortex of death.

He nodded. "Yep."

"Feels like a trap." I crossed my arms over my chest and didn't make a move forward. The magic within looked so turbulent. It twisted and turned with blue smoke that felt heavy in the room. This was one rollercoaster ride I wasn't ready to step on. "You said Kylian was going to puke . . . I don't want to puke."

Astrid scoffed and stepped beside me. "Can vampires even puke?"

"I can assure you with perfect clarity that they really can." I nodded my head, trying to get the idea of my first meal as a vampire out of my mind and how Grayson stayed by my side through it. It was awful and not something I was looking to relive.

Astrid wrinkled her nose and made a sound of disgust in the back of her throat. "Noted."

"What are you waiting for?" Kylian silently came up behind me. I hadn't even heard his footsteps, which was shocking for me as I'd grown so used to hearing everything around me.

I whirled around to face him, and my fangs extended of their own accord. I hissed at him, then slammed my hand over my mouth. It was such a guttural reaction that I had no control over. "You startled me."

"Here now, what's a little hiss between friends?" He winked. "And we *are* friends, Piper."

I narrowed my eyes at him, trying to convey the message to keep his mouth shut. I wasn't ready to reveal how my fragile human friend got involved with an elven tracker, or how I'd hidden her in this world that she really didn't belong in. When this was all over, I was going to have to get her to a new, safe place to live.

"Yeah, we're friends." I tried to make my words sound free and easy, but they sounded as guarded as I felt.

Astrid looked back and forth between me and him. "You two are kind of weird with each other, you know that right?"

Kylian didn't bother to answer her. Instead, he turned to the rest of the group. "This isn't a school field trip, and I'm not a chaperone, so I won't be doing a guided tour on how to hunt a vampire."

I narrowed my eyes at him. "Meaning?"

"Meaning, I'm not taking all of you, so decide who's

coming and who's not." He pointed toward Beckett. "You're coming." Then he looked around the room at the rest of the group gathered there. "The rest of you . . . meh."

Beckett sighed. "You only want me for my power."

"So?" Kylian gave him a deadpan look as if saying *who cares why I want you here*. "Besides, you owe me for our little killing adventure before."

Killing adventure? This world was full of magic and violence I wasn't accustomed to but was steadily getting there. I couldn't decide if it was a bad thing that I kind of loved it. Maybe Ophelia and I had more in common than I thought, and maybe I was good with it.

Beckett held his hands up in surrender. "Just thought I'd make it known. I'm pretty too."

Kylian rolled his eyes. "You're not my type of blonde, pretty boy."

Astrid stepped between the two of them and pressed her hands to their chest, forcing them to move apart. "Better be careful or I'll start to get jealous."

Zinnia snapped her fingers to get everyone's attention. "Beckett and Astrid, you'll go with Piper and Kylian. We'll keep the hunting numbers small, and the rest of us will stay here and do as much research as possible."

Beckett waved toward the swirling portal, and I still hesitated. "How do you know where to go?"

"Kylian told me." He shrugged as if that were answer enough.

"Look, baby vamp, I'm not standing here all night

debating our quickest form of travel." Kylian looked me up and down. "Do you want your Prince or not?"

"Are you my fairy godmother now?"

"Yeah, better watch out where I stick my wand." He chuckled to himself.

Ashryn, his sister and the elf guardian of the witches, strode over to him and smacked him across the back of the head. "Don't be gross."

He rubbed the back of his head. "Only you could get away with that."

"You deserved it." She gave a casual shrug with one shoulder. "I don't think I've ever regretted hitting you."

"And here I was thinking you actually cared." He shook his head. "Sisters are useless sometimes."

"Except when breaking you out of jail." She narrowed her eyes at him.

I raised my eyebrows. "You know, every time I learn something new about you all, I start to question whether or not you're actually the good guys. Murder, jail, killing sprees . . . Might be a bit much."

Zinnia chuckled. "I could see how that might make you question things, and if we had more time, I'd give you all the details. But that's a story for another time."

Beckett took a step toward the portal. "Just trust me, Piper. I got you."

"I don't think I have much of a choice." Portaling would be the fastest way to get to Gray.

Kylian was the first to go through the portal. He threw

his shoulders back and stepped in without hesitation. I sighed and followed, stepping into the swirling magic. It wasn't anything like mirror travel. This wasn't walking from destination to destination. This was like floating in nothingness. I was surrounded by soothing warmth like floating in a pool, and then suddenly I was on the other side stepping out into a dark street. I knew the smell of this land well . . . and the feel of the dampness in the air and delicate falling snow.

We were back in England.

Astrid stepped out behind me. "You should've been around when he was annoyed at me. Rollercoasters don't have anything on a moody Beckett."

"I am not moody," Beckett protested as he stepped from the portal and right behind us.

"Right, and those portals from the early days were so calm and serene." She crossed her arms and pursed her lips.

Beckett kissed the top of her head. "You survived."

I snickered and turned to walk beside Kylian. "How do you know this is where he'll be?"

We were in the middle of a small town in the midlands. I could tell by the homes that reminded me of town houses. They were clustered in groups of three or four standing side by side down the narrow streets. At the town center, there was a simple main street that was dark but for a small pub. The smell of liquor and blood permeated the air and drifted on the wind. I froze and the rest of them didn't move.

Kylian knelt to the ground and pressed his hand to the cobblestones below our feet. Burgundy smoke seeped from his fingers and drifted over the ground. The stone cracked beneath his touch and crushed in on itself until it transformed into a long, thin dagger. I tried to hide the shock from my face as he stood straight with his newly made weapon. But I must've failed horribly because he chuckled at my face.

"I didn't think elves had witchy powers."

He wrinkled his nose. "Elves are creatures of the earth and as such are tied to it."

He said it so simply as if that was all the explanation I needed, but before I could ask follow-up questions, the door to the pub flew open and five people ran out screaming. Some of them fell in the street with bite marks on their necks. Blood coated the sidewalk and sirens blared in the distance. I ran headlong into the pub and felt the others hurry behind me. When I ran through the door, I froze. It was an utter disaster. People huddled in corners and under tables while others lay lifeless on the floor. The lights above flickered, and the TVs hanging in the corners of the room were shattered. Music skipped over the same three lines of song as though a record was being played on repeat. Broken glass, food, and furniture littered the narrow room.

When I looked deeper into the room trying to search out Grayson, I knew he was gone. His scent was dull and nearly undetectable. I hurried through the room listening for heartbeats to see how many he'd killed with his thirst. Not a single one had perished, though their injuries were grave, and if they didn't get help soon, several of them would perish this night. The others ran through the door and stood frozen, their eyes wide at the carnage. The sirens moved closer. Kylian bent down, pressing his fingers to a man's neck.

"Well, at least this one is alive."

I motioned to the whole room. "They all are. Barely."

Astrid sighed with relief. "What are we gonna do? If the humans find them like this, Grayson will be in a shit ton of trouble."

"But how do we fix this?" I looked around. It was clear a monster had ransacked the place, or a wild animal, and the midlands didn't have wild animals like this.

Astrid opened her hands and golden magic poured from her to cover the ground. "If we had Logan, we could convince them it was a gas leak or something."

Beckett opened a portal right away and stepped in. A moment later, he stood there with Logan by his side. Logan hardly showed an ounce of emotion when he stepped through the portal and looked around. He gave a low whistle. "And what's on the agenda for tonight?"

"We need them all to believe this is a gas leak or something like that," Astrid instructed quickly.

Logan opened his hands and dark orange power seeped from his hands and covered the people around us. He closed his eyes, and the people cowering under the tables and hiding in corners passed out, falling to the floor limply as though in sleep. He walked around slowly, letting his power run in all directions while Astrid did the same. Gold and orange power mingled together, and I couldn't see two feet in front of me. I waved my hand, trying to clear the magic from my face. A moment later the power faded, and the room was back to normal. Kylian walked into the room. He carried a man on each shoulder.

"You got them from the street?" My voice raised with disbelief.

He dropped them on the floor, and they fell with a loud *thunk*. "Payment for clean-up is extra."

I narrowed my eyes. "I'll add money to your meal plan at the school since you like to mooch off them."

He gave a dark chuckle. "Very funny, baby vamp."

When the blue lights flashed outside the door and the sirens were on top of us, Beckett opened a portal. "Everyone in."

Astrid waved her hand, and I watched as the skin at their necks knitted back together before my eyes.

"You can heal people?"

She shook her head. "It's a glamor. I can't heal, but I can hide the damage."

She turned toward the portal and ran toward it. The others all followed. I hesitated and looked back at the poor people all knocked out. Beckett cleared his throat to get my attention. "We'll find him, Piper."

"I know."

"Just prepare yourself. This isn't going to be the last time something like this happens."

My throat tightened, and I swallowed. "I know."

He placed his hand on my shoulder and gave it a little squeeze. "I'm sorry, Piper. But this will be the hardest hunt you'll have to engage in. And I wouldn't wish this on any soulmate."

CHAPTER NINETEEN

MOIRA

I'd spent a lifetime with my features placid, my words soft, and my clothing modest. Even now the material itched at my neck and pulled tight around my shoulders. The boning in my dress poked into my sides with every breath I took. The material, though light and flowing, just tangled around my legs. Everything about it agitated me. Or was it standing here beside Titus and feeling helpless that made me realize how uncomfortable everything else in my life was? I sat perfectly, I spoke perfectly, I held my emotions at bay. Ever the elegant royal, I made this life the best it could be. But now all I felt was annoyance at the very act of being here, and yet I held still, taking in the conversation around me.

We were in a part of the castle that Titus rarely used, yet I knew it was intentional that we hid here. The room was a smaller dining room with a large wooden circular table. The chairs were high-backed with thick wooden arms on each one. The cushions were plush underneath us, and I could tell that some of our guests were not accustomed to it. It was the way I'd been when I first arrived here.

Sanchita and Prisha moved their chairs closer together as though just being next to each other was soothing to them, and Martin took his seat across from me as if he owned the space around him. He gave me a warm smile as he pulled his iPad out and used the cover to make it stand on the table. He slid his fingers over it, and the blue light of the screen illuminated his face.

"Thank you for having us here." He met my eye and there was something so strong and pleasant about him that for the first time in a while I smiled.

"I think you all are just what we need."

Sanchita's eyebrows rose, and she pressed an earnest hand over her chest. "Thank you so much, your, um . . ."

I lifted my hand, stopping her from calling me *your majesty*. "Just Moira, please."

"I couldn't agree with Moira more." Eloura strode into the room with her head held high. The cane she used tapped the hard stone floor with each step she took. She moved farther into the room and placed her hand on my shoulder. "Good to see you, old friend."

"I'm pleased you're here with me." It was about time that Eloura took her place among society as well as taking the reins with the Blood Borns.

Titus walked in behind her and shoved the doors closed

in his wake. He spun around to face the table. "Good. My most trusted advisors have assembled."

At his words the others all showed signs of their surprise. Prisha and Sanchita wore the same jaw dropping expression while Martin nodded and smirked to himself. It was like he knew this was where he belonged, and he was just waiting for others to catch on to that fact. Eloura too held her chin up, giving the King an *about time you noticed* look.

I motioned for her to take the seat beside me. "Please join me."

"With pleasure." She pulled the chair out, and her dress rustled as she took her seat.

Titus paced back and forth behind his chair, looking down at us. "As you all know, last night the attack on The House of Shade changed the course of things. Now we must react appropriately."

Sanchita raised her hand, and Titus motioned to her. "Please speak freely, We do not need to raise our hands."

"Your Majesty, the Night Spawn are worried that The House of Shade will retaliate against them even if they weren't involved with Marius."

"The trouble is the Blood Borns are going to want to punish this offense," Eloura countered, "which I agree with to a point. The problem is the lines are muddy."

"Not to mention Clive will use this as an opportunity to try to overthrow you and oppress the Night Spawn," I added. They all looked at me. I shrugged. "What? It's true."

"That's very insightful of you," Eloura murmured.

"He's not to be trusted," I snapped, and Titus raised his eyebrows at me. I met his eye. "What?"

"I don't think I've ever heard you so . . . robust before." His voice was low and calm.

"Perhaps I've been quiet for too long," I countered, and the others at the table watched the two of us go back and forth.

"I welcome it." He seemed pleased I had more to say, and that was enough to make me want to say less.

Sanchita raised her hand again, and Titus motioned to her. "If we're going to do this, you must speak."

"The only way to make this work is to know who's with us and who's against us. If we are going to punish the traitors, then we can't just go around hurting innocent vampires. It has to be a precise strike."

Her words fell heavy in the room. Martin slid his fingers over the screen in front of him. "We can try to determine that through some of their habits and purchases."

Titus sat forward, and I could read the shock on his face as he shifted in his seat. "You can do that?"

Martin looked up from his iPad. "I can do anything you need, Your Majesty."

Prisha nodded at him, then turned to the rest of us. "Sanchita and I will go snooping in the Night Spawn headquarters. We need to see how deep this sickness goes. We've been thinking, and Marius is tied to it somehow. We just don't know how. Made-vampires aren't built for that kind of power, and I wonder where it's coming from."

"I agree with you all. But we can't have you putting yourselves in danger," Titus interjected.

Before any of them could argue, I cleared my throat. "They are old enough to do this and can be trusted. If we can send Grayson out to fight with the witches, then they can do some snooping around their own familiar surroundings. It won't look out of place and won't set off alarms the way it would if the Blood Borns did."

Titus pulled his chair out and dropped down into it. "I can't be doing with sending them into unnecessary danger."

"But it was okay for Grayson?" My voice was almost argumentative, a distant cry from the soft tone I normally took with him.

"No, of course not—"

"— Then they are more than capable."

Titus held his breath for a moment, looking taken aback by my words. But why shouldn't they be able to do what they say? He blew out a breath. "I do believe it is imperative we find out who can be trusted in our world."

"Seconded." Eloura tapped her cane on the ground. "I will look into the Blood Borns. The creator knows they expect me to get all the gossip. It will be easily discerned within days."

Sanchita started to raise her hand when I gave her a slight shake of my head. "Martin will dive into their records while Prisha, and I will be able to start to figure out who betrayed us with Marius. They've all but disappeared."

Titus stared at me with those mahogany-flecked eyes that reminded me so much of Grayson's and Graymont's. The three of them were so similar. Right now I found it difficult to meet his direct gaze, yet I sat there and held it. He didn't look away. "Then we must proceed from there and find out how deep this goes on both sides. We cannot fight an enemy we cannot identify. But you will take backup with you. Jester will go."

"I agree."

Sanchita swallowed. "The . . . the soldier guy who captured me?"

Titus nodded. "He is more than capable, and he will blend in."

"I think we can do—"

"—This is how it will be done," Titus said, cutting her off.

"Very well, Your Majesty." She nodded in agreement with him.

Titus rose to his feet. "Then so be it. We will meet back here in three days' time."

He stormed from the room, and though I felt he needed me, needed to talk to me, I just didn't have it in me to follow him. I barely had any of this in me anymore.

Eloura rose to her feet and headed toward me. "I take my leave and return with all the *gossip* one can stand."

"As always you are a comfort, old friend."

She paused next to me and placed her hand on my shoulder. She didn't look down at me to catch my eye. She squeezed her fingers and whispered, "You will always have my friendship."

I patted her fingers. "It is a good thing, because I will always have need of it."

She slipped her hand from mine and walked out the door. I leaned back and rested my arms on the chair. I felt the weight of the world on my shoulders, and all I could do was sit there and shoulder it.

Martin and Prisha quickly followed, giving me a little bow as they left. But Sanchita hung back for a moment. "Your Maje . . . I mean, Moira, may I ask you a question?"

I waved her on. "Please do."

"You weren't born into this world of royal courts and such."

I nodded. "No, I was of course a member of the Blood Born class, but it was never my intention to become royal. Things like this kind of just get thrust upon us. Don't they?"

I knew Titus put her in this position, much to her own shock, but I could see why. Sanchita, Prisha, and Martin were all forward thinkers. They wanted what was best for the vampires, and Titus needed vampires like that surrounding him, especially now.

Sanchita gave a slow nod. "Yes, I feel like this is very sudden, and I'm not quite sure how I'm supposed to be operating. Or how I'm supposed to behave?"

A smile played on my lips. I remembered a time when I too felt the same way and the panic almost changed the course of my own history. "There is only one thing you can do."

"What's that? Please, I need any advice you can offer." She rose from her chair and moved closer. Once she was beside me, she leaned against the table, waiting for me to say more.

"The only thing you can do in this situation is lift your chin and move forward in the best way you know how. Be honest, be forthright. Holding your tongue, especially now, will not serve the King or the vampires well. He seems to like you and with good reason. You are in touch with what is going on right now and that is important."

She shook her head. "But what if I overstep or my sister oversteps?"

I chuckled. "There is no doubt that you will. Because you are young and opinionated. The only thing I will say is to move forward with honest intentions and do it in the most respectful manner possible. The King favors honesty over protocol." She swallowed and her deep brown eyes looked like they'd shoot from her head at any moment. I reached up and gave her hand a pat. "You will find your way. Just be confident."

"Thank you, Moira. I will try." She lowered her voice. "I fear I worry more than Prisha does. And Martin is used to being in the castle and dealing with . . . well, everything."

"Yes, he's gifted in that way." I rose from the chair, feeling the stress ache all over my body. Between my son and the duties of the kingdom, I felt as though my insides were aging, though it would never show on the outside.

Sanchita stepped forward and wrapped her arms around me, squeezing me tight to her. I hesitated. It'd been ages since anyone hugged me like this. I found myself wrapping my arms around her and pulling her closer, just holding her for a moment. Something inside me shifted, and I wanted to let my tears fall endlessly. It was as if the tight control I held was slipping bit by bit. With one hug I nearly fell apart.

I pulled back and cupped her cheek. "Go and do wonderful things."

She nodded and glided out of the door, leaving me there in this room by myself. I fell back into the chair and rested my hand against my head. I knew how she felt. I knew what it was like to take a step into a world you didn't feel you belonged in. I knew the feeling all too well. I'd felt it in this very room in a time long since forgotten.

Two Hundred Years Ago

I COULDN'T BREATHE. The dress was too tight, the veil too thick, the walls too close. White, everything was so white. I sat in a high-backed chair trying to catch the breaths that wouldn't come. Sweat beaded my brow and ran down my back into the layers of my dress. I shoved the veil out of my face and tossed the flowers on the table. My mother, a slight woman with brownish-red hair, paced back and forth in front of me.

"This is the choice you've made, Moira." She pressed her hand to her stomach. "A royal life none-the-less."

"Yes, Mother, I know. If I could but have a moment to myself. All will be well." I gave her my best smile.

My mother wasn't so easily fooled. She pursed her ruby lips and crossed her arms over her chest. "There'll be no frolicking among the trees for you anymore after this. Nor will there be walking barefoot through the mud. Honestly, is this what you really want?"

I loved him. "Surely marriage doesn't have to be viewed as the end of all things. It's simply moving on to a new phase."

"Do tell yourself that," she snapped.

I rose to my feet and pushed her toward the door. "They will need you outside for the ceremony, Don't keep them waiting, Mother."

In truth I craved a moment to myself. Her words were echoes of my own worries. I could hear all the vampires gathering in the throne room where we were to be married. I had to stand in front of them all and take unbreakable vows. The mere thought of that sent me into having panicked breaths.

Perhaps I couldn't do this? Perhaps I was wrong. Perhaps this wasn't meant to be? Doubt like I'd never known flowed through my veins, and the need to run back to my home and safety of the fields and forests was nearly overwhelming. Alone in the room, the walls seemed to close in on me. I went to the door. I pressed my ear to it, hearing no one. I reached for the doorknob and yanked it open, ready to make a run for it back to my home and back to the safety of the life I knew. Who was I to think I could possibly manage in such a position in life?

I was two steps out the door when I nearly collided with a huge vampire. He reached his hands out steadying me and I sucked in a sharp breath. "Graymont . . . I—"

"—Looked like you were about to run out of this castle as fast as your feet could carry you." He gave me a warm smile, and suddenly I felt foolish.

"I must admit, I was feeling a bit panicked." I blinked up at him, feeling like the words and feelings were silly now.

"Have you got doubts?" The smile fell from his face.

I shook my head. "No, I just . . . what if I fail at this?"

He guided me back into the room and closed the door. "Fail at what?"

"My royal duties. What if I fail the people?" As the words were pulled from my mouth, I felt a knot tighten in my chest. The possibility of failing at so much responsibility was daunting to say the least.

"How could you possibly?" A light smile played on his lips as though this was a silly notion.

"I do not jest." I put my hands on my hips.

"I have discussed this thoroughly with my brother, and he has all the faith in the world in you, as do I. And, well, if you have the faith of a King, there is not much else needed but the backbone to take the place that is rightfully yours."

I sucked in a deep breath. "Yes, you're right. Of course."

He kissed me on the cheek. "Now, shall we attend a wedding, or have you decided to run off?"

I sucked in a deep breath. Knowing that Titus also had faith in me brought a calm to my nerves I hadn't felt before. I nodded. "You know it's bad luck to see the bride before the wedding."

"I hardly think that applies to me." He winked, ever the playful vampire.

A light knock came from the door and then it opened a crack. Familiar brown eyes peeked around the door as strands of wavy brown hair fell into his eyes. "What are you lot doing?"

"Marius, old friend, leave it to you to be pushing for punctuality." Graymont shook his head with a light chuckle.

Marius stepped through the door and let it fall shut behind him. "Well, there is a whole room *full* of vampires waiting."

"A whole room? You don't say. Intimidated to be around *all* those vampires?" Graymont teased.

Marius waved toward the door. "Of course not, but really, the wedding can't take place without you. It would ruin all appearances if you two didn't show up."

I smiled and a light giggle played on my lips. "Indeed, you are right. We have a wedding to attend."

I SHOOK my head and turned for the door. How naive I'd been. How full of hope I'd been. How . . . unprepared I'd been for the future and this new reality where hope scarcely existed.

CHAPTER TWENTY

GRAYSON

*T*hey say the descent into madness is a slow and steady decline ... they lied.

Thirst burned my throat like a smoking hot poker that scorched me from the inside out. I pressed my hand to my neck, hoping the pressure would somehow stop the fire within. All it did was cut off the air to my lungs. *If only I could die like this.* Death was not a luxury I'd be afforded at this time though. Atlas' face flashed through my mind, and I was reminded of his vow to me. It would only be a matter of time before he found me, so death may not come when I prayed for it, but it would come in time. There was comfort in that.

My stomach felt sloshy like I'd drunk my fill and then some. I knew I'd taken blood on this night, but the memories of how I'd done so were fleeting and hazy. I heard the echo of screams in my ears, felt the ache in my hands from the destruction I wrought, and scented the blood that wasn't my own. Flashes of throwing furniture and feeble humans ran through my mind. Guilt, madness, and pain all warred within my body, each one taking their turn to torment me. My heart was a pit that twisted in my chest, and at times felt so empty I was a mere shell. At other times, it felt so heavy I might suffocate under the weight of emotions I could no longer endure.

I tried to gain my bearings. I looked around at my surroundings and had no idea where I was or how I'd gotten here. The night sky began to lighten to purple, and I knew the sun would soon come. I crouched down in a heavily wooded area and leaned back against a tree trunk. The bark bit into my back, but I couldn't stop myself from rocking back and forth against it. I pressed my hands to my temples, hoping to squeeze the torturous voice from it. The cool air did nothing to calm the raging fire I felt burning in my throat, down my chest, and through my body. I was sure I killed innocents tonight, innocent people who didn't deserve to take the brunt of my madness. If I were a Night Spawn, I'd have met the sun by now. But my royal blood made it impossible to die that way. At least until my best friend finally found me.

I shook my head, unsure if he already started hunting me or not. The memories were foggy at best. I knew we'd fought. I felt the injuries to my body. They were slow to heal and ached all over. I'd been thrown but then again so had he. The smell of blood that was not my own filled my nose, and when I looked down at my hands, they were coated in crimson. I bellowed and pulled at my hair, throwing my head back against the tree. I looked to the sky, hoping my prayers for death would soon be answered. Piper had to suffer this, and I would not drag her down with me. She was perfect in every sense of the word. She didn't deserve what I'd done to her. I squeezed my eyes shut and was tortured by visions of striking out at her, hurting her. I'd covered her body in scratches and bruises.

Fuck. I bit her . . . like a bloody animal.

"Kill me. Please. Just kill me." I murmured the pleading words to myself as I rocked in the darkness. The forest around me had gone still, the animals all aware of the bloodthirsty predator that roamed through these obscure paths.

Now, now, there's no need to die. What a waste that'd be, the voice that plagued me all this time whispered through my mind. It was not my own and I had no idea where it came from or if it was even real. But it was smooth and deep, lulling me to do things I'd never think of on my own. Depraved things, things that would surely earn me a death sentence from The Fallen. It was so . . . enticing. I could hardly stop from listening to its tempting lulling tone.

"No!" I smacked the sides of my head. "Shut up! Shut up! Shut up!"

Sure, I'll quiet if . . .

The words trailed off and I held my breath, waiting for the voice to finish the sentence. If I could but get a bit of quiet, I could find a way to end this. But the bouts of lucidity were few and far between, and each time I'd fallen to the voice it'd been when Piper was there to see me, to witness the monster I'd become. I looked down at the soulmate mark that I would've been so proud to wear had this cursed life not taken me from her.

"If? If what?" I rose to my feet, yelling my words to no one in particular.

I stumbled forward, tripping over tree roots. Low-hanging branches scraped against my skin and pulled at my hair. That voice gave a deep chuckle, like my behavior was entertaining. This wretched state of being was funny to it. It relished my suffering. And I hated it more for the poison it spread through my mind.

If you do me this favor, vampire . . .

Visions of what it wanted me to do filled my mind. One after the other I saw exactly the steps it wanted me to take, the grotesque things I would be pushed to execute. I shook my head. "No! I won't do it!"

The visions came faster and stronger. One after another hit me until I lost my breath and fell to the ground. Pain exploded behind my eyes, and I rolled on the ground clutching my head. Mud coated my chest and what was left of my trousers. My mind slipped from me, and I once again belonged to the voice, belonged to *him*.

I chuckled and nodded, feeling the last tendrils of sanity slip away. I found peace in the voice and the things it wanted me to do. The pain was no more, and my thirst felt delightfully wicked. Laughter rumbled in my chest, and I spread my arms wide over the ground, loving the cool earth at my fingertips.

Those whispers and images came so fast it was all I could see, all I could hear. "Yes, yes of course. I'll do it."

CHAPTER TWENTY-ONE

PIPER

"I don't understand how you know where the hell to go." I stepped out of the portal with Kylian right beside me. "Can you explain it to me?"

"No."

"No? Just like that?" I looked around. "Like, what makes you think he's going to be in the middle of a field in the middle of the night in winter when we just found his leftovers in a pub?" I motioned to the wide-open field with all the dead brown grass. The trees were shadows against the purple sky. The sun was beginning to rise. Soon it would be a new day, and we were no closer to capturing Grayson.

Kylian rolled his eyes, sucked in a breath, and blew it out slowly. "Because I do."

I shook my head and muttered, "Makes no sense."

"Let me ask you this, little leech." Kylian turned to face me with those vivid, crystal green eyes. His voice was laced with exasperation. "Do I ask you how you do all your little blood magic stuff, or do you just do it?"

I searched my mind, trying to think of how to answer how my magic worked, but I couldn't put into words what it felt like to tap into that well that sat deep inside me. It was too difficult to even explain. My mouth gaped open, then I snapped it shut.

"I find it's best not to ask questions." Beckett moved from the portal and stood on the other side of me.

"*Thank* you." Kylian threw his arms up and let them flop down to his sides. "If we're through with the twenty questions, I have a job to do."

"Fine." I crossed my arms and pressed my lips together.

Kylian began to walk out into the field, lifting his knees higher to step over the tall brown grass. I followed behind him and Beckett.

Astrid caught up to me and fell into step beside me. She nodded her chin toward Kylian. "Don't pay attention to his moody ass."

"I'm trying not to." The truth was I wanted to know *everything* about Evermore. How the magic worked, and the world, and anything else that I still have encountered. Being around them made me realize how small the bubble I'd been in with Grayson actually was. Deep down I loved Evermore even though it was incredibly violent. The violence was balanced out by how magical and enchanting this world was.

"When we get this figured out, you should come and

hang out at the castle with us. You'll get to see a lot of cool things then." Astrid smiled up at me.

"I would love that." I nervously reached for the necklace Grayson had given me only days ago. I wrapped my hand around the pearl and fiddled with it on the chain. I glanced down, checking the color. It was still a creamy white, and yet I dreaded the moment it would change in color. This necklace would show me if I was moving close to my thirst taking over and needing to feed. The problem was I could only feed from Grayson. Only *his* blood would keep me from going feral.

Astrid let her eyes swing up toward me again. "You seem nervous. Don't worry, Piper, we'll find him. Kylian is the best."

I was nervous about losing control, nervous about what we would see once we found Grayson, nervous about how the hell she was going to save him.

"That's right. I *am* the best," he snapped over his shoulder toward us.

Logan, who brought up the rear and was silent until now, gave a humorless chuckle. "And oh so humble."

Astrid began to laugh and glanced back at him in surprise but said nothing. I slowed a bit to let Logan catch up to us. I didn't know what to say to him, he seemed to have a dark feeling about him, and I got the notion that whatever caused it was fairly recent.

When he caught me looking at him, he sighed. "Vampire, you're very transparent."

I shook myself. "I'm sorry, what?"

"I was a prisoner of the unseelie for some time." He didn't stop walking.

I tried to keep up with his pace while processing his words. *What's an unseelie? How long was he a prisoner? How did he survive? How did he get away?* "Umm, what?"

"You were wondering what the hell is wrong with me and why the others so obviously baby me, though I don't want or need it." His voice was level. There was no venom or annoyance to his words. Yet I could tell that the way the others treated him with kid gloves grated on him.

"Ah, well, I didn't want to ask . . ." I lied, even though I really did want to ask all the questions.

Kylian stopped in his tracks and turned to fully face me. His eyes bore into mine and the muscle in his jaw ticked. "Oh, *now* you don't want to ask questions."

I was getting sick of his attitude, but before I could snap back at him, something moved in the corner of my eye and I stilled. The others noticed my stillness and went motionless as well. I sucked in a breath through my nose, scenting the air, and there it was, the smell of wine and chocolate surrounding me with the hint of blood. *Grayson.* He was here and I knew it. I felt it in my very being. My eyes darted, but I saw nothing.

I spun in a circle and lowered my voice. "He's here."

"Of course he is." Kylian lifted his chin with a *I knew I was right* air.

I darted toward Kylian and shoved my hand over his mouth. "Shut up. I mean, he's right here."

He took his finger and hooked it around my wrist and pulled my hand away from his face. "Don't touch."

"Then don't be a douche." There was a noise in the distance. I turned toward it, then took off running. I pumped my arms, running faster and letting the world blow by in a blur.

"I really hate when she does that," Logan muttered under his breath, but with my vampire hearing, I could easily catch it as I left them behind.

I found a small patch of forest that separated the large fields and ducked down low behind a tree trunk and some dried bushes. In the dead of winter, it was difficult to hide when there were so few leaves. There before me was Grayson, not looking like himself at all. He walked round the open field with a bucket in his hand and a crappy broken wooden paintbrush. My brow furrowed in confusion. What the hell was he doing?

He slopped the brush around in the bucket and started to write something on the ground. His eyes were wild with madness, and he chuckled. A moment later he mumbled to himself as he moved over the dried field. The others came up behind me. Their footfalls were louder than I'd prefer, but with vampire hearing it was nearly impossible not to catch.

"What the hell is he doing?" Kylian's voice came from right beside me and I startled.

Well, they all *were* louder, all but him. I gave him the side-eye. "You're creepy as hell."

"Thank you." He nodded toward the field. "Now what's he doing?"

"I'm not sure . . . painting something on the ground?" Then it hit me, the distinct smell. "He's painting it in blood."

Kylian's eyebrows shot up and his face paled. "No, he wouldn't."

"Are you forgetting? The leech you know is not in there." Beckett crouched lower. "He's gone, and we have no idea what that damn curse is doing to him."

"We need to stop him, NOW." Kylian rose to his feet and pulled that stone dagger from his waistband. His face turned dark and determined.

Panic rose in my chest. "What are you gonna do?"

"Stop him from doing what he's doing, that's for damn sure." His grip tightened on the knife. "Whatever I do to him, he'll heal. If he finishes his happy little painting, then we're all fucked."

What?

Astrid crouched down and crawled closer to get a better look. She lifted her head and peeked over the bare branches, trying not to draw attention to us. She lowered her voice and whispered, "What is he doing?"

"From what I can tell, he's about to summon some hell demons." Kylian shook his head. "You all are always fucking about with things you really shouldn't."

"The curse wasn't a choice, you ass." I fought the urge to punch him. The Grayson I knew would never in a million years summon hell demons.

Logan rose to his feet and moved to Kylian's side and watched Grayson's every move. "We have no choice. We have to stop him now or The Fallen will show up and put Grayson to an end before we can even capture him."

"How long do we have?" I sprang to my feet as adrenaline flooded my body.

"Moments. The Fallen respond quickly. As soon as a demon emerges from that spot, they'll be here to kill them and possibly Gray for summoning them." Dark-orange smoke seeped from Logan's hands. "I can try to calm him with my power."

I shrugged. "Couldn't hurt."

Beckett held his hands up and his blue magic swirled up his arms. "We need to move now."

"Don't have to tell me twice." When I looked out over the field, all I could think was this wasn't him at all.

The Grayson I knew was suave, strong, and confident. He was always put together to the point of cockiness. This thing that huddled in the middle of the field in filthy torn clothing and muttered to himself was not him. The others all stared at him, and I felt the need to remind them why we were here.

"Hey," I snapped, "this is the curse at work. He's still our Gray in there."

Astrid placed her hand on my shoulder. "We all know that. It's just shocking to see it for the first time."

"Well, let's not let it continue on. The faster we capture him, the faster we can fix him." I couldn't shake the nagging feeling that the longer the curse held on to him, the further he slipped away.

"That's what we're here for." Astrid nodded, and I felt her power weaving around us.

I gave her a nod and stepped out from our hiding place, and I saw Kylian mutter a curse under his breath. The moment I was out in the open, Grayson's head snapped up and he wrinkled his nose as if he was smelling my scent on the air. I took a step toward him.

"Hey, Prince Grayson! What the hell do you think you're doing?"

His eyes locked on mine, and the moment I saw how black they were, I knew he wasn't in control. He shook his head and went back to his drawing. "Not real. She's not real,"

"I'm real!" I ran out toward him, pumping my arms faster. I stopped just a few feet from him and held my hands out. "Look at me."

He tilted his head to the side in an eerie movement. It reminded me of the way an animal moved when it was confused by something. He took a step back and looked me up and down like he'd never seen me before. "No, it lies."

"What? I'm not lying." I took another step toward him to try and close the distance between us. I so badly just wanted him to touch me, to recognize me. If we could share one real moment, he might snap back to me the way he had before.

A wild chuckle burst from his lips, and he threw his head back. He looked to the sky and smirked as though there were someone standing behind me. "You mustn't yell. Yes, yes I will finish it."

"Gray, who are you talking to?"

But he was too far gone in his own head, hearing voices that weren't there. He bent down and swiped the cruddy paintbrush over the ground, then stood up and admired his handy work. He threw his arms out, tossing the bucket of blood and brush off to the side. Blood splattered in the grass. I thought he was about to dance among the chaos when his hand shot out and his fingers closed around my throat. Pressure gathered in my chest, and I could hear the others running out behind me.

He lifted me up off the ground by the throat and held me there. "What are you doing here . . . Piper?" He hissed my name, and it sounded nothing like his real voice. This voice wasn't smooth or velvety. It was deeper and slightly rough with an enticing hint.

My legs dangled and swayed. I wrapped my hand around his wrist and squeezed hard. The bone in his wrist cracked. He flinched but kept his hold. I scratched my nails over his skin and blood trickled down. Blue smoke shot up between us, and Grayson's grip was ripped from my neck. His nails raked across my skin as I fell to the ground and landed atop his weird drawing. The damp blood stuck to my hands as I lay there on the ground. Grayson sailed away from me and landed outside the circle he'd drawn. Mud and dirt shot up from the ground in a thick dark cloud.

Kylian sprinted toward me, waving his arms and motioning for me to move. "Get out of there! Move!"

I scrambled to my feet feeling the drops of blood running down my neck. I pressed my fingers to them, then pulled my hand away only to watch crimson beads fall to the ground at my feet. The painting illuminated a bright red and the ground cracked beneath my feet. I scrambled back, trying to get out of the circle, but the light only grew brighter. Steam so hot that it burned my skin rose up from the cracks. A scream ripped from my throat, and Kylian dove across the opening and wrapped his arms around my waist. His shoulder slammed into my stomach, knocking the air from my lungs. My feet lifted off the ground and we soared out of the circle and landed on the dead blades of wheat, which were not as soft as they looked. They were straw-like and poking.

We rolled to the side, and dirt and grime coated my body along with Kylian's. When we came to a stop, I lay there for a moment staring up at the sky as it faded from purple to a pinkish color. My chest heaved in time with Kylian's panting breaths.

I turned my head toward him and let it fall back into the muck. "Thanks."

"Never . . ." he sucked in a breath, ". . . walk into a summoning circle again."

"Noted." I nodded.

"SOME HELP OVER HERE!" Beckett's voice carried over the sound of the grinding and cracking earth and we both shot to our feet.

Flames burst from the circle, and the sound of screams

echoed from beneath us. My eyes widened. "Like, actual hell!? Like real hell demons?"

"What did you think I meant?" Kylian bellowed back at me.

Beckett had Grayson trapped in a blue sphere that was hovering over the ground. He rolled round inside of it, snarling and ramming his body into the sides, but it bounced back to its shape, holding him there. Sweat beaded Beckett's brow, and his hands shook with the effort to hold him within the bubble. "Our boy is stronggggg."

Logan stood just to the side of the bubble and let his power wrap around Beckett's in an orange swirling mess. "Calm down, Gray."

But his power over emotions wasn't enough. Grayson was still fighting to get his way out. His body looked impossibly bigger, his eyes were black with rage, and those red veins forked out over his skin. His clothing was shredded, and every time he rammed his shoulder into the bubble, it split the skin on his arm just a little more. Red streaks dripped down the inside of it. Beckett and Logan fought to hold him while the world rocked around us.

"You guys! There are arms shooting up from the ground." And they weren't human. I wanted to back away and run in the other direction. But I couldn't, I was part of this now, and I'd dragged the rest of them into it with me. I would stay and do whatever needed to be done.

These things coming from the ground were skeletal with dark skin, like they'd been charred, and long claw-tipped fingers. They dug into the crumbling ground as though they were about to lift themselves from their hellish pit.

I held my hand toward Kylian. "Dagger."

He tossed me the stone dagger. "That's mine."

"You'll make another." I turned from him and raced with my vampire speed across the cracking ground, jumping from one unsteady opening to another. I swung down and severed their hands as quickly as I could, knocking them back into the pit. The ground was littered with limbs in my wake. They spasmed and twisted on the ground like fish out of water.

Astrid marched away from Grayson and let her power roll over the earth like a wave of golden glitter. She lifted the blood painting off the ground and forced it to disintegrate into thin air. But the hell demons kept on coming. They punched at the dirt, forcing their way up toward us. Heat and the smell of rotting flesh surrounded us. She used her magic to force the ground closed and to smooth it over. She gritted her teeth, and her body quaked with the effort it took for her magic to work over this horrific scene. Just as it was almost smoothing over, a large tentacle shot from the earth and wrapped around her ankle. I charged forward but it knocked her off her feet and flung her up into the air, holding her.

It swung her around like a rag doll and her screams drew Beckett's attention. He turned from holding Grayson to look at her. "ASTRID!"

His power faltered for a split second and Grayson shot from the bubble, exploding it into pieces. Energy rippled out from the bubble like a tidal wave. Logan and Beckett flew back, sailing across the field in opposite directions. Logan hit the ground and skidded across the dirt, sending debris flying all around him. He clawed at the ground, trying to stop, but he came to a screeching halt when his back smacked into a tree trunk. His head smacked into it, and he lay there in a heap not moving. Beckett surrounded himself in blue smoke and soared into one of his portals. It opened on the ground where he'd just been. Beckett charged out toward where Grayson had just been, but it was too late. Grayson was free and he was on top of Beckett in an instant. He grabbed Beckett by the throat and threw him up into the sky.

"CATCH!" he called out, and another tentacle slithered from the earth and caught Beckett around the waist as he soared high in the sky. Kylian and I stood there watching this thing swing our friends around. Grayson winked at me, then took off running in the opposite direction.

I took a step in his direction and Kylian snapped, "Don't even think about going after him."

"I wasn't," I lied and turned back toward the flailing tentacles. "How the hell do we kill it?"

"Like this." He bent down and pressed his hands to the ground, and burgundy smoke slithered from his fingers. The dirt packed in hard and transformed itself into two identical swords. When he stood, he tossed me one of his newly made swords. He swung his around in a circle and wagged his eyebrows. "You ready?"

I nodded. "No."

"Vampires have natural strength and ability. Use it." He took off running and the sword he made grew in length. He leapt so high and far I was surprised he wasn't a vampire himself. He bounced from one tentacle to the other using his momentum to climb higher. He swung his sword, hacking at the tentacles as he climbed. It sounded squishy and slime-like as he hacked and cut at whatever got in his path.

"Thanks for the lesson." *Well, here goes nothing.*

The ground rumbled as a monstrous roar came from below, and I didn't want to stick around to find out what the hell those things were attached to. We needed to stop this now before anything else emerged from below. I ran between the tentacles and used the double swords as best I could, hacking and swinging at the tentacles like my life depended on it. Really, like all our lives did. Slime coated my arms and dripped down my legs. Blood ran in streams down the tentacles and sprayed around us. The smaller demons continued to try and emerge from the ground as we fought to save Beckett and Astrid.

Suddenly, blue smoke poured from Beckett, forming one of his portals. It swallowed the tips of the tentacles, severing them from the body. They were gone, disappearing into his swirling portal. A moment later it opened on the ground beside me, and they stumbled out flicked pieces of slimy tentacles off their bodies. Astrid kicked a particularly large piece off her leg and huffed as she threw her auburn hair from her face. It was knotted and matted around her head and looked like she'd stood in a wind tunnel.

Anger was plain on her face as she marched up to the opening and threw her arms up. Golden magic exploded over the opening in one large wave. It covered the crevasse and forced the ground to smooth over. The cries died out, and the demons were all trapped deep beneath the ground. Pieces of limbs and tentacles littered the ground, and the smell of burnt flesh still clung to the air . . . or maybe it clung to us. We stood there for a moment, all staring at the field that Astrid had forced shut.

"Well, that was . . ." My words trailed off. "There really aren't words."

"How did he know how to summon demons from hell?" Kylian snapped while looking at me.

I pressed my hand to my chest. "Me? How would I know?"

He motioned to the direction Grayson ran in. "He's your soulmate. You'd think you'd know a thing or two."

My eyes widened and anger flared in my chest. ". . . About summoning demons. Really?"

"Alright." Logan groaned as he staggered to his feet and made his way toward us. He pressed his hand to his head and pulled it away. Blood coated his palm and he groaned and shook his head as he took slow, deliberate steps. "This is a whole other level that none of us could know about, especially Piper. How would a brand-new vampire know anything about this?"

"Logan is right." Astrid nodded. "We need to look into this whole thing."

"Yes, but right now we need to get out of here before The Fallen show up and catch us here. If they do, we're going to be in deep shit." Beckett pointed toward the sky, then opened a portal just as quickly. "Like now."

In the distance, four figures with black wings soared toward us. Their silhouettes were so dark against the rising sun, but I knew what that meant. The Fallen had arrived and we needed to be gone before they landed. I hurried toward the portal and dove in, not even daring to look back for fear of being caught and risking their wrath.

CHAPTER TWENTY-TWO

NO ONE

*E*very step I took echoed off the rough-hewed walls around me. I thought I was deep in the pits of the Night Spawn headquarters, but this felt like a different place entirely. We'd moved through a maze of tunnels and walked for long minutes. The cement floor was flat and the walls were rough as though they'd been dug out of the ground by hand. The smell of damp dirt lingered where the tunnels were dark and silent. A chill ran up my spine, and I wrapped my arms around myself and blew out a breath. Marius strode in front of me with his shoulders back and chin held high. I envied his confidence. His thick leather coat billowed out around him with every step he took. His wild hair swayed and moved with him, and for a moment I was distracted by how the strands moved.

He glanced back at me over his shoulder. "This is the point of no return."

"I know." I swallowed around the nerves in my stomach.

I'd been a vampire for less than a decade, but I couldn't feel more out of place among them. I didn't share their extreme strength or speed. The only thing we had in common were the fangs that seemed to descend of their own accord whenever I felt strong emotions. I was a human with pointy teeth who couldn't return home and felt as though I had no home anywhere. I'd been lost among the shuffle until he found me.

Marius dropped back to walk next to me. He threw his arm around my shoulder and pulled me into his side. He beamed down at me. "You're joining us, and now you will always have friends, a place to belong."

I gave him a half-smile and prayed his words were true. "Yes, Marius."

"And let us not forget the power you'll wield. Your true vampire nature will come out." He pressed his fingers into my shoulder and gave it a squeeze. "I'm so very proud of you."

The knot in my chest eased at the sound of his words. It was a rarity for anyone to say they were proud of me. When I was a human, I'd been small, feeble even, easy prey, and easily distracted by books. I preferred them over anything else. They were an escape from my existence, and I found that fact to be true even now as a vampire. The only benefit was that I could read even faster now.

"Thank you, Marius."

He turned down another tunnel and led me toward a metal door. There was a window next to it as though I was walking into an interrogation room rather than to receive my new powers and join his army. I didn't particularly feel one way or the other about The House of Shade, though Marius said otherwise, I just wanted someplace where I felt I belonged. Eternity was a long time to wander the Earth alone, and after nearly a decade, loneliness was a monster I no longer wanted to face.

"No need to thank me, child." He opened the door. "We are, of course, as one. And after your transition, you too will be one with us."

He walked me into the room, and I was greeted by the oddest stench: sulfur. It stung my nose, and I took a small step back, but Marius was there to move me forward into the dark room. I got the eerie feeling this was a mistake. It was too dark, too secluded. I'd been all over the Night Spawn headquarters and not once had I ever felt like there wasn't a vampire around. But here it was damp and silent. The air was stagnant yet cold. The walls were thick rock. Only the one wall with the window in it was made of cement. I couldn't hear past my own racing pulse.

"Perhaps I need to think on this a bit more." My voice sounded small, even feeble to myself.

"Now, now, my dear, you trust me, don't you?" Marius smiled down at me, and he turned me around to face the door as he took a step between me and it, blocking me from leaving.

"Of course I do." He was the first one to pay attention to me, the first one to take the time to talk to me about what my hopes and dreams were.

"Then you are ready to become one with us." He placed his hands on my shoulders and gave them a squeeze. "I am confident in this."

"Right, okay, yes." I closed my eyes for a second and took a breath, then blew it out. I smiled up at him. Finally I would belong. Finally I would have a place. "I'm ready."

"Lovely." He dropped his arms and took a step back toward the door. "I'll be just outside, and when it's over, you'll be a completely new vampire."

Completely new? Did I want to be completely new? Not really. I just wanted to find a place where I fit in as myself. But if this was some weird kind of initiation or blood magic, I was sure I could stand it to have a place to belong. Families were made every day, after all. They didn't have to be just blood-related.

I gave a nervous chuckle. "I mean not *all* new, right?"

"You'll be the best version of yourself." He took another step back. "Young, strong, and *powerful*."

He moved out of the door and smiled at me. "Welcome to the true Night Spawn."

"But what if I like who I am?" I just wanted others to see what I saw in myself. I wasn't sure I wanted a big change. Perhaps just a few things. I knew my strength was lacking. My speed was not what it should be. It stung to know I wasn't even close to what I should have been.

The door slammed shut between us and I heard the distinct click of a lock. I reached for the knob and gave it a twist. Nothing happened. I pulled at the door. It didn't budge. I knocked on the door. The room went dark, and I was left in total blackness. I spun around, listening to the blood rush in my ears.

"Umm, hello? You know, maybe I don't think this is a good idea."

A low growl rumbled from within the walls. I spun again. *I am not alone.* "Marius, I don't want to do this. Okay? I-I don't think this is meant to be."

But the door didn't open, and I knew he was standing outside the window watching. I felt hot breath on the back of my neck. Goosebumps rose over my skin. I whirled around and I was met with two glowing amber eyes. They looked like a wild animal's eyes reflecting in the night. I tried to move but I froze, my fear holding me hostage. I opened my mouth to scream. and a large hand wrapped around my face and covered my jaw. The fingers wrapped around the back of my head and pulled at my hair.

It lifted me off the ground. I swung my dangling feet through the air, desperate and confused. Suddenly, it slammed me down. My skull cracked back against the floor and black dots swarmed my vision. I tried to clear my mind, but it was slow coming. Warmth spread across the back of my head and flowed over my neck and shoulders. The smell of my own blood hit my nose, and I found the strength to struggle against the thing pinning me down. I swung my arms out and kicked my legs again, but again I connected with nothing. The hand over my mouth was like a solid vise, but its body was formless. It was like kicking at air.

Black and gray smoke filled the room in a spiraling funnel. It twisted and moved like a snake coiling in all different directions. The lights above flashed back on, blinking at me, then they turned to flicker like a strobe light. Panic and fear rushed through my body. I didn't want this. Whatever *this* was, my whole body screamed that it was wrong. The smoke hovered over my face, and for a moment a face appeared in it. It opened its mouth and long shark-like fangs descended. Drool stuck to both the upper and lower teeth, and a whimper, muffled by the thing's hand over my mouth, escaped my lips.

It snapped forward and the mouth of the smoke covered my face completely. The hand moved away, and I sucked in a sharp breath. Blackness swarmed my vision, and I felt it shove its way down my throat and into my body. I choked on the sulfuric taste and my lungs seized. My back bowed as pain exploded through my limbs. Every cell in my body exploded, and it felt like they were reforming anew. Fire and ice raged in a war inside me. Sweat and shivers racked me from the inside out. Moments turned to days that felt like years and went back to seconds again. I was lost, gone in this cloud of gray and black smoke. I wanted to scream for help, but I knew there would be no answer.

Slowly, ever so slowly, my will to fight, to survive,

slipped away. My body stilled and I lay there letting this happen to me. It was a violation of the deepest kind. My soul, my life, my memories all fell to the back of my mind where they were locked away until they were nothing but lost in the dark, smoky fog. I was nothing, my cells burned to nothing. My life was nothing.

It slowly withdrew with a growl, and I didn't move. The smoke left my body a shell of itself, and the pain of fire and ice remained in my veins. I dared not move, yet my breaths began once more, and I felt the cool, damp air run down my throat. Slime covered my face and limbs. Sulfur clung to my hair and arms. Still, I had to remain so still in the hopes that if I didn't move, I wouldn't feel anymore.

The door clicked open, and the hiss of fresh air filled the room. Still, I couldn't move. Marius knelt beside me and pinched my chin, forcing my eyes toward him. "Who are you?"

I thought. I scanned my memories for a hint of who or what I might be. There was nothing. My mind only showed me hazy images that were not clear. My brow furrowed, and I swallowed, searching for the words. It felt like razor blades in my throat, and I tried to swallow again.

He pinched my chin harder. "Who. Are. You?"

But there was nothing left of what I used to be. There was only this, only right now. I cleared my throat. "I am no one."

He shoved my head back, releasing my chin. "Welcome to the new Night Spawn."

He didn't meet my eye, he just rose to his feet and

started for the door while calling over his shoulder, "We'll see if you're worth anything to me. Now get up."

Get up? I didn't know if I could. The pain remained so acute it hurt to breathe. Who was I? What was I? Deep down, I knew that whatever I'd been before no longer existed, and I truly was no one.

CHAPTER TWENTY-THREE

PIPER

We ran through the portal and ended up in the courtyard of Evermore Academy. I hunched over and sucked in deep, heaving breaths as we stood next to the fountain. The silence of the courtyard was so different than the chaos of being in that field only moments ago. In England the sun was just rising, but back in New York it was already midday. Though it was winter, it was a perfectly clear day with the sun shining down on us. Still, it was chilly, and my breath fogged as my chest heaved with nerves.

"Did that just happen?" I spun around and looked at the others. "I mean, did we really just fight off . . . demons?"

"I don't think it's something we should mention or be proud of." Beckett glanced toward the sky, looking more paranoid by the second. The bottom half of his shirt was ripped, and I could see deep scratches over his torso.

Demon slime clung to his dark jeans, making them darker and shiny in some spots.

My eyes automatically darted upwards to follow his gaze. "I wasn't feeling either of those things. I'm just kind of shocked. Never in a million years did I think demons existed."

"I mean, I knew everything existed, but If I'm being honest, I am shocked too." Astrid hunched over and rubbed at her leg where the demon had wrapped its tentacles around her and flung her around. "And sore."

"None of you are built for that kind of battle, especially not with hell demons." Kylian let his gaze roam over us as he shook his head. He ran his hand over his hair, and when he pulled his hand away, slime coated his fingers. He flicked it down toward the ground, leaving a wet wad right next to the fountain. "We're not even supposed to know they exist, let alone fight them. The Fallen won't be pleased."

"Maybe they won't know it was us?" I said while trying to keep as calm as possible. But as the question left my mouth, even I found it hard to believe that they wouldn't know it was us. These were actual fallen angels. They'd been here for thousands of years. How could they not know . . . everything?

Logan scoffed as he rubbed at the back of his head. Dried blood had gathered where he'd hit it against the tree. "Not a chance."

"So, how much trouble are we in, do you think?" As if on cue, shadows of giant wings blocked out the sun and ran across the courtyard. I tipped my head back only to see them circling and swooping over us like crows circling a dead carcass. "It can't be. We just left there."

Kylian gave a humorless chuckle and pointed at me with the tip of his sword. "We got here that fast . . . You don't think they can? They're the Fallen. The world is their oyster."

Logan gave a low, slow whistle. "We are so screwed."

Astrid held her palm up and a paper with scrolling writing appeared there. She wrapped her fingers around it, and it burst into flames. She let the ashes fall to the ground without saying a word.

The others all seemed to know what she'd just done, but I didn't see how the paper being set on fire would help us. "What was that?"

"I was warning Zinnia that we're in trouble—"

One of The Fallen suddenly dropped to the ground in front of us. The ground dented with his landing and my eyes went up . . . and up. I was used to Grayson, Atlas, and now Kylian who stood over six feet tall, but this angel was massive. He was closer to seven feet tall with wild tousled hair that had hues of brown, blond, and red streaked through it. I sucked in a breath and held it as the fallen angel in front of me glared at us with the most vivid sapphire eyes I'd ever seen. Tiny flames danced over his dark black wings, making the oily feathers appear even darker.

. . .

I took a step back and nearly collided with Kylian. He placed his hand on my lower back, holding me there. He lowered his voice to a whisper. "Steady."

"I can't." My nerves were shot, I'd just fought demons and now I was facing the wrath of fallen angels. They were bigger than I expected and more dangerous looking. I'd thought angels would have some kind of bright inner light, with radiant peace. But this one only radiated power and danger. The energy around him was so strong I wanted to move away from him, but at the same time couldn't seem to stop myself from staying where I was. The swords in my hands suddenly felt heavy and out of place.

I handed them to Kylian. "Take these."

"What am I gonna do with them?"

"I don't know, get right of them?" He didn't take them back, but he grazed his finger over each blade and they turned to dust in my hands, falling to the ground around my feet.

"Matteaus—" Beckett stepped forward and began to speak, but when the angel held his hand up, Beckett slammed his mouth shut.

Steady? How could I be steady facing this . . . this Matteaus being? The power that simmered around him made my skin heat. Another fallen angel dropped down beside him, and though there was a smirk on his face, I didn't think he found any part of this funny. The smile was humorless and cold. His eyes were a dark hazel at the center that turned to the most vibrant sage-green I'd ever seen. Messy brown strands of hair fell all around his face, almost highlighting how beautiful he really was. His lips were full and shapely. He was so beautiful my jaw nearly dropped.

"I don't think he's taking commentary at this time." The beautiful angel pulled his wings in toward his back, and for a moment I found myself mesmerized by the deep-black feathers that were tipped with a green that matched his eyes.

"What Mika said." Matteaus didn't move as the others all landed around him.

Mika crossed his arms over his chest and glowered in our direction. "I, however, can only think one thing: what the actual fuck were you thinking?"

"We weren't." I hesitated. "We kind of just acted."

"You expect these young ones to think before they act?" Matteaus rolled his eyes.

"Fair point." Mika nodded in agreement with him.

How could I rebut that? We ran into the situation headlong without thinking. When I was about to apologize, four other angels all landed around him. One after another their giant wings caused gusts of wind to fill the courtyard and sent my hair flying back from my face. Their presence sent shivers up and down my spine. We were in deep shit, and all I could think was that Grayson was in even deeper.

Matteaus sighed and it came out more like a growl. "We're not all in attendance."

I thought he meant all The Fallen, and he was right, we were missing one, but I had no idea which one. But when he waved his hand and suddenly the rest of our crew was standing behind us, I got what he meant. He meant the other Witch Queens and Guardians. They were all here now: Tabi, Ashryn, Serrina, Maze, Tilly, Ophelia, a guy who looked nearly as dangerous as The Fallen, a girl with white-blonde hair and gloves up to her elbows, and also a freaking tiger. *Why a tiger?* The others didn't seem put off by the arrival of so many people or even a freaking tiger. I shook myself, trying not to stare, so I forced myself to face The Fallen.

Zinnia moved to the front to stand next to me with Astrid on her other side. She lowered her voice. "Thanks for the fire message."

"I tried to warn you," Astrid whispered back.

Do you think we can't hear you?

The words brushed through my mind like someone had spoken them out loud. I glanced around at the others to see if they'd also heard him. But when I looked back, they were all stoic and unmoving. Tilly hid behind Maze, pressing her body behind his until she was nearly invisible. All I could see of her tiny body was some of her wild, wavy blonde hair popping out from behind his back. Beckett inched closer to Astrid, and the backs of their hands barely touched, but it seemed like enough to soothe them for the moment. This situation was just adding to the shit storm we were already in with Grayson.

They all hear me. The voice spoke again this time with an ultimate authority that I couldn't deny even if I wanted to. *Turn around, Piper.*

When I snapped my head back around, one of the angels with wild black hair hanging past his shoulders stared at me with dark-purple eyes. He was slightly bigger than Matteaus and had larger muscles. A thick scar ran through his eyebrow, and when he arched it at me, it almost looked like the tip of a knife. Though it was winter, he wore a black tank top and black leather pants with heavy biker boots. I found it odd there was a pair of headphones wrapped around his neck at such a time. When he smirked at me and pointed to his temple, I knew it was he who spoke into my mind. *We're here for you, Piper. You're in over your head.*

Yeah, tell me about it, I thought back at him, and his eyes widened and his lip twitched as though he were fighting a smile.

He wasn't wrong. I was in way over my head—with this world, with them, with Grayson. It felt like at any second I was going to drown. I didn't think any of the other Fallen would know just how overwhelmed I felt, but this one did. It was difficult to look at him, and when I tried to turn my attention toward the others, I met eyes with the only female Fallen. I felt like her outside was such a contrast to the turmoil I felt rolling through my insides. She was calm, cool, and collected. Her hair flowed down her back in long dark waves that she braided from the crown of her head all the way down. Her eyes were sharp and observant but the stormiest gray I'd ever seen. Her tiny frame was strapped down with so many weapons that I couldn't tell which leather strap held which weapon. Knives, swords, a whip, and even throwing stars were all strapped to her. She didn't wear *jewelry* as accessories, she wore *weapons*.

"Kadeion," Matteaus held his hand out toward her, "the paper please."

She nodded her chin toward the angel next to her with a silver mohawk and a lizard perched on his neck that seemed to change colors every few seconds. "Taliam, you have the paper I gave you?"

"Right here." He pulled a folded envelope from his pocket and handed it over to Matteaus. Taliam wasn't as muscular as the others, but he was nearly just as tall. His body was all long, lean muscle. He wore ripped black jeans and a graphic T-shirt that read *'Feral'* across the front of it.

Matteaus didn't look away from us as he took it from Talium. He opened the paper and took his time reading it. After long, silent moments, he sucked in a deep breath and began to read out loud. "Dear Matteaus, I must say after weeks with this lot, I find them to be quite capable and impressive. Their magic grows daily, and as you and I have known each other for nearly all two hundred years of my life, I hope you don't mind my saying I think you will find allies within this lot as they grow. I know I have. I admire their tenacious abilities, their sense of justice, and their infallible moral codes. They are a testament to all that is good and right. Yours, Grayson." He crumpled the paper and threw it toward Taliam who caught it as though the move were planned. He sucked in a deep breath. "The Vampire wrote that to me only weeks after knowing you, Zinnia."

Her jaw dropped. "I-I had no idea."

"That's right. You all have no idea." His voice boomed in

the courtyard, and I could only imagine how the students would have scurried away had school been in session at this very moment. "You are all failing him."

His words fell hard on them, but I felt them deeper in my chest. I was failing my soulmate. I knew I was. I wanted to plead my case and ask for help, but I didn't even know where to begin. "But the curse—"

"—The curse has been in place for years and nothing has been done to end it." He crossed his arms over his chest and the muscles in his arms bulged.

Mika shook his head. "One of your own has fallen. What will you do about it?"

"Your minds are also weapons. Do not forget that," Kadeion added. Her voice was sultry and smooth with a seductive timber I did not expect.

"We are trying." The words slipped out of my mouth before I could stop them.

Matteaus swiped his hand down his face and the movement showed just how exasperating he found this whole thing. "Try harder."

Another angel landed a moment later with a large sack in his hands. He stood next to Matteaus, and I leaned toward him, unable to stop myself. He smelled of blood and chocolate with a touch of wine. He smelled like Grayson. But he looked nothing like him with his blond hair and turquoise eyes. He handed the bag to Matteaus and moved to stand at the back of the group. *Why did he smell like everything I desired?*

"Thank you, Tristan." Matteaus grabbed the bottom of

the sack, then turned it over, dumping the contents on the ground at his feet. Demon limbs spread across the frozen grass, and I took a step back as the twitching pieces flailed. Matteaus opened his arms, motioning to them. "And now we have DEMONS!" His voice boomed on the last word, and I flinched back. He marched toward us through the body parts, and they squished under his boots. "Summoning demons is not something we take lightly. So, tell me, why isn't Grayson here? Why isn't he contained?"

"He's stronger than we thought?" Beckett muttered as he shifted uncomfortably.

"Let me be clear, which of you knows how to summon a demon? And who taught *him*?" He seethed.

"None of us," Zinnia answered. "Honestly."

Matteaus glanced over his shoulder to the one who'd spoken in my mind earlier. "Aidenuli?"

"They're not lying. They don't know." His eyes roamed over the line of us standing there.

"You are the most powerful of your kind." Matteaus glared. "He should have been caught by now."

"The curse is driving him. It's like he's listening to the voices in his head and can't ignore them." I didn't want to argue with Matteaus, but they had to know none of this was our fault. We were trying to catch him. "He's unpredictable and doing things I couldn't even imagine. When we got to that field, none of us thought we'd be facing demons. None of us wanted to, but we did so no one else would get hurt. We stopped them."

"Very well," he grumbled. Matteaus opened his arms,

and the twitching limbs all caught fire. Flames burst up between us, and I moved even farther back. I felt Kylian at my back and the others closing in around my sides. Matteaus took a step forward and walked through the wall of flames. The scorching fire seemed to almost part around him. "Atlas rises in two days' time, and he will not be stopped. His vow is unbreakable."

"But he's his best friend. I don't understand why he won't just hold off on this." I could never kill Dice, not in a million years.

"Because some friends understand it's a kindness to be put out of your misery." The flames danced behind Matteaus, and I could see the others through them like flaming shadows with their dark wings. "We will not interfere. You have two days. Piper, if Grayson kills a human, I will have no choice but to kill him myself. I will not risk our redemption on the vampire, no matter how much favor he's garnered with us."

I opened my mouth to say something, anything, to beg for more time or beg them not to kill Grayson. But the clock had started. I could practically hear it ticking. In two days, Atlas would wake and he would hunt. In the meantime, Grayson was running rampant with voices in his head he couldn't resist. What if they told him to kill humans? What if he was out there right now about to do it and there was nothing I could do to stop it? Gray's neck was in the hangman's noose, and it felt as though it was being tightened around my own neck. If he died, there was no doubt in my mind I would want to die too.

"I suggest you hurry." He flapped his wings and took off toward the sky.

The flames grew higher and embers drifted up into the air, then a sharp wind whipped through the courtyard and they were extinguished in an instant, leaving no evidence of the demon limbs behind.

I hunched over and put my hands on my knees and nearly threw up right there. Zinnia ran her hand over my back in slow circles. "Breathe. I know they're a lot."

"Did no one else hear what they said?" I straightened my stance and put my hands on my hips. "Two days."

"We will find a way," she tried to reassure me, but the panic was setting in.

"And what did he mean by saying he wouldn't risk his own redemption? What does that even mean? Aren't angels supposed to help people?" It was so hard to even process what just happened.

Astrid sighed. "The Fallen fell from grace thousands of years ago. They've been trying to earn their redemption ever since."

"Redemption? They've been here ruling us for all that time . . . you'd think by now they would have."

"We don't really know how long it's been exactly or what they did to become fallen in the first place. But we do know they're fighting for something bigger ,and they're supposed to protect the humans, so if Grayson kills one, they won't have a choice in the matter . . ." Zinnia let her words trail off as the others gathered around us and formed a tight circle.

"So, I see we're all screwed again?" The girl with long white-blonde hair and black silky gloves up to her elbows crossed her arms.

"Nova!" Zinnia hurried across the little circle and pulled her in for a quick hug. "I didn't think you'd be allowed back up here so soon!"

"Apparently The Fallen's summoning trumps deals with Hades." She sighed, then opened her mouth about to say something else when the ground opened beside her and a man popped out. He was tall and slim with inky hair to his chin and bright-purple eyes. Nova pursed her lips, and when he moved to stand next to her, she kicked him in the shin.

He gritted his teeth, and the muscle in his jaw ticked. "Is that anyway to greet the person you like?"

"I'd like to punch you next time." She huffed.

He held his hand out toward her. "There's always a next time for us."

"Ew." Yet she placed her delicate, gloved fingers in his palm.

"Zinnia, always a pleasure." He inclined his head toward her, and the ground opened up beneath them. They both dropped into the hole, and it closed up over them just as quickly as it appeared.

My eyes widened but I didn't say anything. That was the least crazy thing I'd seen all day. But Tabi took pity on me and explained, "That was Nova, our Witch Queen of Death. She kind of made a deal with Hades, and now she's trapped down there until we can figure out a way to break the deal."

"*That* was Hades? I thought he'd be . . . bigger."

She shook her head. "No, that was his son, Liesin. They have some issues to work out."

"I'll say." She straight-up kicked him the moment he got here. *Definitely issues there*.

"We must be off too." Ophelia grabbed on to the guy standing next to her. He was all warm golden eyes with a *could kill you in your sleep* vibe. "Cross has things to do."

Before I could say anything to stop her or ask how Dice was, she reached into the pouch on her hip and threw a vial on the floor at their feet. Zinnia held her hand out. "But wait, We could really use your—" Ophelia and Cross jumped into the shimmering air the potion caused, and they were gone in seconds. The portal between us closed. Zinnia sighed. "—Help." She threw her hands up. "I just can't with that sometimes."

Ashryn turned and punched Kylian in the arm. He flinched back and rubbed at his shoulder. "What the hell was that for?"

"You're supposed to be the best." She narrowed her all-knowing sage eyes at him. "Do better."

"Thanks," he snapped back at her. "I am trying. The leech is fast and stronger than any of us anticipated."

"Perhaps I could persuade him to stop? Figure out exactly what he desires and we can use it against him?" Serrina offered, and I wanted to jump at any and all ideas they had.

Logan shook his head. "No dice. My charm didn't even make a dent on him. I might as well have tickled him, and if I'm being honest, I don't even think he knows what he himself desires. He's running on instinct and anger."

Tucker held a ball of fire in his hand, and he stood there thinking, mindlessly tossing it up and down like a baseball. "I don't think this curse has any reasoning to it. But what I can't wrap my head around is why he would summon demons and how would he know how to do that?"

"That's what I don't get. There's got to be something in his head that's driving him. But is that how a curse would work?"

Zinnia shook her head. "Not typically. Usually, the magic just does what it's meant to and that's it. It doesn't give directions on how to summon demons."

"But how do we know that knowledge isn't lingering in his mind? I mean, he's an older vampire. He might know?" I ran my hands through my hair and tugged at the strands in frustration. "Or I'm trying to apply logic where there is none. And now we're facing a crazed vamp with two lifetimes of knowledge in his head and a stupid amount of strength."

Beckett nodded. "I could barely trap him with my power. It was difficult. He's stronger than even I thought."

I wanted to say I told you so, but it didn't feel like the time or place for people who were trying to help me.

Tabi sighed and crossed her arms. "I wish there was something more I could do, but unless you want to drop him into a vat of water, or pit of vines, or fire, or bury him alive, there's not much that I think will hold him."

"As much as I love the sound of all of that, I think he's already close to madness. I don't think we want to push him any closer, and trapping him that way might do it." I couldn't even imagine doing any of those things to him. We might as well kill him if we were going to torture him like that. I turned toward Maze and Tilly. "What about you two? Look at your cards or dive into your visions. Tell us what to do."

Beckett and Logan both shifted awkwardly, running their hands over the backs of their necks as they shared a look. Maze chuckled and his eyes turned milky-white as he gazed at me with a wide smirk. "Careful what you wish for, little vampire."

"Psychics aren't really good at giving direct answers," Beckett interjected, "It's more like you have to just take what they say with a grain of salt and that's about it. Usually, however you think things will play out, it doesn't really end up that way."

"What he fails to mention is our powers can affect the outcomes if you all know too much, so we need to be precise in the information given." Tilly reached into the pocket of the oversized trench coat that she wore and pulled out a bar of chocolate and handed it to Maze without even looking at him. He dug into it as if he hadn't had a meal in three days.

"Well, we need something to go on. Because, and I don't

care if I offend you, Kylian, just hunting him down without a plan of how to trap him isn't going to work."

"Ugh." He placed his hand on his chest. "I'm crushed."

"You're an ass." He didn't appear crushed at all. I looked away from him and at the others. "If there was some way to get through to Gray, I know he's in there. I've seen it. Even when we were there, he spoke my name. Though it didn't really sound like his voice."

"What'd it sound like?" Beckett leaned forward. "I wasn't close enough to hear him."

"It's hard to describe." I hesitated trying to gather my thoughts on how to describe it. "But it's like there's something in his head talking *to* him and *for* him. I don't know much about curses or magic, but something or someone is pulling the strings behind it."

"It would stand to reason." Zinnia nodded. "We just need to find out who and how it was done before he kills anyone or summons more demons."

I shook my head, thinking about what just happened. The sight would haunt me for years to come. "We walked right into a summoning."

"I can't even imagine what that was like." Zinnia wrinkled her nose. "I kind of don't want to."

Astrid pointed to her ripped pant leg. "Yeah, getting thrown around by one wasn't exactly fun."

"Neither was hacking at all that slimy crap." I just stopped myself from gagging from the memories of the smell and sights of that charred skin. Their screams would echo in my ears for a good long while. "I'm going to have nightmares about it."

Tilly shrugged. "Oh, I don't know. A lot of answers can be found in dreams."

We all turned to look at her. She winked at me. Maze wrapped his hand around her and tugged her away from the group. "Let's go, little trickster. You know what they say, loose lips sink ships."

"Yeah, but who needs a ship when you can drift off all alone?" She let him tug her away. "Besides, ships are crowded."

That crazy one-eyed black cat scampered across the courtyard and leapt up on his shoulder as they walked away.

I turned back toward Zinnia. "What did any of that mean?"

Tucker chuckled and shook his head. "I don't know. But we need to find out, and I know just where to go."

CHAPTER TWENTY-FOUR

PIPER

"Okay, but just don't make any sudden movements or loud sounds." Zinnia, Tuck, Astrid, and Beckett all stood with me in front of a large door. The others had returned to their meeting room to wait for whatever information we got. They'd led me through a training gym and right to this door.

"Is there some kind of skittish animal behind the door or something?" I didn't want to take another step forward before I knew what we were dealing with. "Or like a monster?"

A light giggle escaped her lips, and she shook her head. "No, nothing like that. This is kind of the brains of our operation, and she wasn't feeling well before, so I'm hoping she's back in fighting shape. But in case she isn't, we're just going to take it easy."

I nodded. "Right, got it. No speedy vampire stuff."

I glanced down at the necklace Grayson had gotten me

to keep me aware of my thirst. I'd nearly forgotten about it, but even now it had a light pink hue to it, and I knew I'd need to drink soon. But when Zinnia reached up and knocked on the door, I shook my head, getting my mind back on the task at hand. My thirst could wait . . . for now. When the door slowly opened, I took a step inside and was immersed in dim lighting. The room was remarkable. Magical things were everywhere, and I had no idea where to look first.

There was an entire wall full of pendulums all swinging in the same direction. The other wall held a large map similar to the one in Zinnia's room. Books lined the walls and were strewn all over the floor. There were shelves with crystals, vials full of glowing liquids, and athames of all shapes and sizes. It was like a witch shop hidden at the back of their gym. It was also quiet here, so quiet I could feel the stillness around me. A woman with messy fire engine red hair walked out from behind a cabinet. She held a book in her hands as she read and walked at the same time. When she looked up, she startled at the sight of us standing there. She jumped and pressed the book to her chest. "What are you doing sneaking here? There is such a thing as knocking."

I wanted to tell her that we did knock, but I kept my mouth shut and let Zinnia handle this situation.

"Niche," Zinnia spoke softly as she motioned toward me, "this is Piper. She's here from The House of Shade. We've got a problem with Grayson, as you know, and we need your help."

Niche pushed her glasses up her nose and held her book to her chest. "Honestly, Zinnia, you don't have to be so gentle. I'm fine now. Just lacking some sleep. And we've been researching for hours and still haven't come across a single record of this curse I keep hearing about. We usually have records for that sort of thing, especially something as big as cursing an entire family line, which would take, pardon my language, a shit ton of power. It's very frustrating."

Her words sounded sincere, but her hands shook as she placed the book on the table in front of her. She sighed and straightened her white lab coat with quick, jerky movements. Zinnia and the others all moved to stand around the table with Niche.

I took my time moving to join them. "It's nice to meet you, Niche. And thank you for your help, even if nothing has come of it yet."

"You as well." She turned toward Zinnia. "Now what is this about? We have to keep digging. I know we'll find something. I just know it."

Just then another woman moved from behind the shelf and walked into the room. She held even more books, and when she dropped them on the table, they landed there with a loud thump. Her long dark braids streamed from the top of her head all the way down to her hips. She was exquisite with dark skin and eyes as equally dark. She wore a thick, light-gray turtleneck and dark-blue jeans.

She gave me a shy smile. "Hey." She waved. "I'm Adrienne."

"Piper." Then I remembered Zinnia had said they had the daughter of a Greek working with them. "Oh, you're the daughter of Athena?"

She gave a heavy sigh and looked away from me. "Yeaaa, Mom is . . . something else."

Touchy subject. Noted. "It's nice to meet you."

"What brings you all here?" She glanced around at the rest of us.

They all swung their gazes toward me, and I hated to admit I was slowly starting to get used to people looking at me like this. "So, we know that Grayson is cursed, but every encounter with him gets weirder. I think there's something or someone in his head, which might be part of the curse . . . I think. But I can't be sure."

"I've never heard of anything like that before." Niche set her hands back on the table in front of her. "But it's an interesting concept."

"Is there any way we can get into his head and see what's going on? Like, is there a spell for that? Something that would make me be able to see or hear his thoughts? Because if I can, we might be able to get an idea of who's doing this and how to stop it." I was a vampire, what did I know? I was just throwing out ideas. This was Evermore. Anything was possible. But if anyone knew how to do this, they would know.

Niche glanced toward Adrienne. They seemed to have a look pass between them, as if they were having a silent conversation no one else was a part of. After a moment, Niche stood up straight and pulled her glasses off. She pinched the bridge of her nose and gave a heavy sigh. "There are spells to get into someone's head, of course."

"Great, let's do that."

She shook her head. "It's not that easy, Piper. These spells are complicated because the mind is a complicated place. The person could fight the intrusion or it could break their mind. In this case, it sounds like his mind is slowly breaking already. You could make it much worse—to the point where even if you managed to trap him and get into his head, there'd be nothing left when you're done."

I sighed and placed my elbows on the table, using the support to put my head in my hands and rub at my eyes. "So, let's not do that."

Niche gave me a pat on the shoulder. "The conscious mind is a tricky place to be."

"But what if it wasn't the conscious mind we were toying with?" Adrienne chimed in with a little smirk.

Niche's eyes went wide. "You don't mean . . ."

"I do mean." Adrienne nodded.

"It's possible."

"I concur it could work. It'd be tricky but could work."

"And how about full sentences for the rest of us at the table who have no idea what you're talking about." Astrid swung her arm around, motioning to the rest of us.

Niche straightened her stance and hurried away from us, calling over her shoulder, "I've got the book for that. Adrienne, you explain."

"If we can't mess with the conscious mind, then why

not the unconscious mind?" She gave a broad smile like that one question would explain it all.

I glanced at the others, and they all had the same blank look I did. "You mean like knock him out and jump in his head then?"

She shook her head. "No, not knock him out. That won't be enough. Dreams. The mind is at rest then and the unconscious mind takes over. If you slip into one of his dreams, it will not be as jarring to his brain. It'll be more like walking through clouds rather than taking a wrecking ball to a mountain."

"Okayyy, so how do we slip into his dreams? And will that tell me what we need to know?" Dreams were an odd thing. For me, they were sometimes so vivid that they appeared to be real. At other times, they were so abstract I hardly remembered them.

Niche ran around the corner and hurried back to the table. We all jumped back as she slammed a huge book down. She opened the pages, and the binding practically creaked as she thumbed through the pages.

"I know it's in here somewhere." She made a sound of frustration in the back of her throat. "Adrienne, would you please?" She slid the book across the table to her.

"Of course." Adrienne held her hand over the book and the pages flew open and flipped themselves quickly.

Zinnia sucked in a surprised breath. "Adrienne, I had no idea you could do this."

"I've been working on my powers with Niche for a

while. Apparently, books are my thing." She gave a little chuckle and shrugged. "Who would've thought?"

"Do I detect a hint of sarcasm?" Beckett teased.

"My mother is Athena. What do you think?" She rolled her eyes as the pages kept flipping. When they abruptly stopped, she smiled at us. "Got it."

The book lay flat on the table, and a picture projected above it like a movie would on a screen. It glowed a dim white color, but I could see the image perfectly. It reminded me of pictures of space with the Milky Way. It was all flashing lights and shooting stars. "Dreams are the windows to the soul. We dream our fears, our deepest desires. We even see loved ones in dreams, or people we've lost. They can be flashes of nothing and long stories of lifetimes, which makes them incredibly difficult to navigate. And before you ask, no."

Am I the only one who doesn't know what she was saying no to? "No what?"

"No, you can't just jump into them with a spell. You're going to need an expert. Someone who can navigate through dreams more quickly and accurately than a spell could ever do. Someone who won't cause harm while doing so either."

Tuck gave a humorless chuckle. "And who do you think has all these skills that we need? Not who you think I think you need, right?"

When Niche and Adrienne just looked at each other, he swallowed. "Right? Guys, come on, right?"

"Why does this not sound good at all?" My eyes went from Niche to Adrienne and back again.

"Because the person you need is not a person at all." Adrienne flicked her hand, and the pages turned once more.

There on the projected image was a man with dark, navy-blue hair that had silver glitter running through it. His skin was a lighter blue that looked like he had twinkling stars as freckles. Two small, white-tipped horns stuck up from his hairline and matched the wings on his back, which were the shape of a bat's and started off darker but grew lighter at the tips. The image flickered. One second it looked like he was smiling, and in the next like he was frowning.

My brow furrowed. "Who is that?"

"You have got to be kidding me," Tuck snapped. "No, this is a bad idea."

"There is no other choice." Niche shrugged, "Well, if you don't want to break Grayson's mind, that is."

"I would very much like to *not* break my soulmate's mind please."

"Then you're going to need him." Adrienne motioned to the image. "You're going to need Morpheus, the most powerful dreamer there is."

CHAPTER TWENTY-FIVE

PIPER

"You have got to be shitting me." I stood outside a warehouse in the middle of nowhere. The outside was covered in simple tan, metal panels with grooves in them. There were no windows and the only doors were a set of glass double doors in the front that had black paper over the windows. But that wasn't the most alarming part of this whole thing. A huge sign sat on the top of the building with bright-red block letters that read, '*Sleep Matters!*'

"I shit you not." Tuck sighed. "He's a bit eccentric."

"Aren't all the Greeks?" Astrid rolled her eyes. "At least in my experience they all are."

"And temperamental, and touchy, and think they're just the greatest at everything," Zinnia grumbled.

"So, this is gonna just be greattttt." I took a step forward, and the others all filled in behind me as Beckett closed our portal.

The parking lot was empty. At this time of day I wondered if the warehouse would already be closed. I reached for the door, yanked it open, and stepped into a waiting room—a very, very small waiting room. The chairs were old and broken down with ripped vinyl and chipped wooden arms. The carpet was torn and worn in different spots. I walked up to the window where a receptionist sat flipping through a magazine. She didn't bother to look up at me as I approached her.

"Umm, excuse me?"

"Yeah?" She flipped the page and chewed her gum loudly.

"We're here to see," I lowered my voice, "Morpheus."

She pointed toward the waiting room. "You don't have an appointment, so you'll have to wait."

I didn't want to sit in those miserable chairs. "How long is the wait?"

"Until I say so." She popped her gum and flipped another page.

I didn't have time or patience for this. We were here to help Grayson, and with barely two days left, I felt seconds ticking by. When I glanced back at the others, they all seemed to read my mind. Zinnia gave me a single nod while Astrid smirked and gave me a wink. Tuck and Beckett took up positions at the back of our little group, acting as lookouts.

I lifted my hand and let my blood magic flow from it to land on her in a fine, misty cloud. "We want to go in now. Let us in."

"I'm going to let you in." She reached under her desk and pressed a button.

The lock on the door on the other side of the room buzzed, and I moved toward it, pulling it open. Beckett gave a dark chuckle from right behind me. "That little power of yours really comes in handy."

"For now." I marched through the door and into a huge, open warehouse. I paused, trying to get my bearings.

There were mattresses spread in perfectly even rows one after the other over a space the size of a football field. White machines with robotic arms all hovered next to each mattress, and they were testing everything. To one side, a bowling ball was being dropped on a mattress repeatedly. In another row, tiny robots jumped up and down on foam-topped mattresses with glasses of wine sitting on them. Some remained pristine while others spilled instantly. I kept walking, trying not to get too distracted by how weird this all was.

"So, he quality-tests mattresses?"

Tuck groaned. "Yeah, but that's not all."

"What else is there?" I turned down a row of waterbeds and froze. "Wow."

All those robotic arms held long, sharp blades, and they repeatedly stabbed the waterbeds. In the middle of the aisle stood Morpheus. He was taller than expected, with broad shoulders and long muscles. He had one of those travel pillows wrapped around his neck and wore silky baby blue pajamas with sleeping pandas all over them. Bright-pink water shoes finished out the outfit, and I found myself staring at him.

Just then the bed he was standing at the foot of popped from one stab and water sloshed over the floor and onto his shoes. "Damn it! The lack of quality is astounding. Honestly, how is anyone supposed to hit the REM cycle with utter crap?"

He turned away from that disappointing bed and moved to the next. I startled at his bat-like wings and couldn't look away. It appeared he had knitted covers for each wing that had black feathers sewn on to them. When he swung around, feathers fell to the floor around him and floated in the puddles on the floor. He marked something off on his clipboard and shook his head with a disappointed sigh.

I lowered my voice. "Should I just go up and talk to him?"

"Give it a minute." Tucker crossed his arms over his chest.

"Why do you know this guy so well?" This whole time Tucker did not seem thrilled to be here or to be dealing with Morpheus, and the curiosity was killing me.

"TUCKERRRR!" Morpheus boomed in our direction. He spread his arms wide, and his wings extended out, the motion littering the floor with more of those feathers. "What brings you here to visit me?"

Tucker motioned to me. "This is Piper, and she needs your help."

He looked me up and down, then turned away to walk

in the opposite direction from us. "I don't have time for vampires."

"Umm, why not?" I followed behind him as he moved toward a door at the back of the warehouse. I was trying not to be offended by the fact he was straight-up rude and said *no* based solely on the fact that I was a vampire.

"Talk to your girl, Phoenix. Nighttime waits for no one, and I have things to do." He opened the door and walked down a long hallway with windows lining it on each side. I tried not to look in them as we passed, but it was kind of like walking down the hallway in a hospital. I couldn't help but look through and see what was going on. In each room there was a person lying in bed with those electrodes strapped to their heads. The wires ran from their heads over the edge of the bed to a machine that seemed to be tracking something and scrawling on paper. It reminded me of a lie detector.

Tucker took big steps as we followed behind Morpheus. "He thinks vampires don't dream enough. Hence the saying, *sleep like the dead.*"

Morpheus whirled around on us. "That's right. You're boring. I find most vampires to be so. Their dreams lack . . . imagination or anything fun. They hardly rest. Tell me this, as a human, how many hours a night did you sleep?"

I glanced around at the others. "Umm, I don't know? Maybe six or seven hours I guess?"

He made a sound of disgust in the back of his throat. "You know women need like ten to twelve hours. If you want your mind to function, sleep matters. Stupid mortals really know how to ruin my fun."

"Really? I thought it was eight hours?"

"I'm not impressed with your friends, Tucker." He rolled his eyes. "That ridiculous study was conducted by men and only *on* men, when in reality, women do so much more throughout the day, so they require more rest . . . which means more time with me. Which means more fun. Which means better REM sleep."

"Oh, umm, good to know. I'll make more of an effort to sleep?" I shrugged, not really sure what to say or how to get back on topic. I wasn't here to discuss sleep or how much I needed or how it worked. The way I saw it, I wasn't going to be sleeping any time soon anyways, at least not until Grayson was back to himself, safe, and with me.

"We're not here for that," Tucker snapped at Morpheus. "We need your help, and we need it now."

"Of course you need my help. Look at the bags under your eyes." He pressed his hand to his chest. "Everyone needs my help."

"Greeks," Beckett muttered like it was a vicious curse.

Astrid elbowed him in his ribs. "Not helping."

Tuck cleared his throat, getting Morpheus' attention. "Look, I'm going to be straight-up with you. We have a vampire who's been cursed and he's gone mad. We need to get into his mind through his dreams to figure out who or what might be doing this to him so we can break it."

"Well, why didn't you say so in the first place?"

Morpheus gave Tuck a wide smile for a split second before he dropped it and glared at him. "No."

"You owe me." Tuck crossed his arms and arched his eyebrows at him.

Morpheus shrugged. "You put someone to sleep for one week, and suddenly they think you owe them."

"My family thought I was in a coma. You fill the Phoenix Queen with panic and tell me it's not a big deal." Tuck turned to Zinnia. "You know how moms are, imagine mine hovering over me for a week because I didn't wake up."

"Admit it." Morpheus wagged his eyebrows at Tuck. "It was a lot of fun. Dreams are pleasurable."

"I thought one night hanging out was like a single night of sleep, not a week!" Tuck threw his hands up.

Morpheus stepped into one of the rooms and walked over to the machine. He ripped the paper off and began to read it. He strolled back out into the hall and didn't look up from his paper. "Time can move differently in dreams sometimes. Sometimes not."

"Wait, so I could be in there for a week?" I didn't have a week to spend frolicking in the. dreamworld. I barely had two days. I wouldn't put it past Atlas to kill Gray in his sleep and think it was a kindness. "I don't have a week."

"No." Morpheus crumpled up the paper and tossed it over his shoulder. "Because I'm not going to help you."

"Enough of this," Astrid snapped. "If there's one thing I know, it's that everyone has a price. So, what's yours?"

"Feisty thing." He made a clawing motion between him and Astrid as he hissed. "I like it. The socialite has balls."

Astrid put her hands on her hips and tapped her foot impatiently. "And yet I'm still not hearing your price just for you to play tour guide."

"Tour guide? Ah, I'm offended. It takes a lot of power to navigate such difficult worlds like dreams." He snickered as he tapped his finger on his lips. "But there is one thing I'm *dying* to do . . ."

As if on cue, Beckett's cell phone began to ring. When he pulled it out, he raised his eyebrows in surprise but quickly answered it. "Maze? What's up?"

His brow furrowed in confusion, then he held his phone out in front of him and pressed the speaker button. "Go ahead. We can all hear you."

Maze cleared his throat and said one word, "Deal."

Morpheus clapped his hands together. "You'll let me walk your dreams then?"

"For one night and one night only in exchange for your help with Grayson." Maze's voice sounded more amused than serious.

"Deal." Morpheus leaned closer to the phone. "Oh to see the things you've seen and will see."

The sound of something crunching in Maze's mouth filled the silence and then he spoke with food in his mouth. "I'm not finished."

"Please, of course, proceed." Morpheus nodded toward the phone as if Maze could see him.

"This will be your one and only time in my head. And

you will stop trying to enter my dreams from here on out. I find it exhausting keeping you out."

"I don't know what you're talking about." Morpheus' eyes darted to the side while his words were met with only silence. I found myself holding my breath, waiting for Maze to say something, anything, to get this done. Still silence. Morpheus made a sound of impatience and fidgeted. "Finnneeee. You have yourself a deal."

Beckett held the phone closer to his mouth. "Maze, are you sure about this?"

Maze gave a dark chuckle. "Yeah, I'm sure."

"That is one ride I would not want to get on," Zinnia muttered to Tuck.

"Me either," he whispered back.

"Have fun, Morpheus." The line went dead, and Maze was gone.

Morpheus turned toward me and smiled. "Are you ready to find your little friend, vampire?"

"Absolutely." I didn't trust this guy as far as I could throw him.

CHAPTER TWENTY-SIX

PIPER

*M*orpheus hovered over me. "Lie still, vampire."

I was in a twin-sized bed with a thin sheet pulled up to my hips and a single pillow behind my head. The sheets were crisp and clean compared to how dirty I felt after the events of the day. I tried to make my body as still as I could, but I was nervous. It was one thing to swing a sword at some demons, it was entirely another to jump into someone's head and not know how it was going to go. I didn't want to hurt him any further, but if this was how I was going to help him, then so be it.

"You know I have a name. It's Piper. My name is Piper. You don't see me calling you by your description. Like, take me into Grayson's mind, powerful dream person."

Morpheus chuckled as he hopped into the bed right across from mine. He had it lined up so our heads were almost touching. He gave a heavy sigh, and I could hear the springs creaking as he got himself settled in. "This is going to be jarring. But then it'll be fine, and I'll get you where you need to be."

"Great." I nodded and glanced at the others standing on the other side of the glass wall. I forced a reassuring smile, but it felt shaky like my insides. Walking into the unknown wasn't something I liked doing. I loved knowing where I was and what I was doing. I loved having a perfect plan. But this was not perfect. This was exploratory surgery to find a problem no one knew the cause of. I gave them a small wave, then closed my eyes and sucked in a deep breath.

Morpheus tilted his head back, looking at me upside down. "Oh yeah, one more thing I forgot to mention. If you die in his dreams, you'll die in real life."

"Wa—" One minute I was in that room, and the next I was free falling. I felt my muscles twitch and bounce as my stomach flew up into my throat. I was in a swan dive off a cliff with clouds soaring by me.

A scream ripped up my throat, and suddenly Morpheus was next to me, gliding around me in slow circles. He held his arms out and smirked at his wings. "When I have my wing feather sweaters on, don't I look like a member of The Fallen? I'm going to apply to join them. I think my skills are valuable."

My arms pinwheeled and I thought I might throw up. The ground was speeding toward me, and I didn't know how to stop from smacking right into it. "Morpheus!"

"What? You don't think I would fit in?" He twirled

around me with his giant bat wings spinning like a ballerina. "I think they're pretty great. I mean, the feathers could stick better."

I was only feet away from hitting the ground and dying in Grayson's dream. "Morpheus!"

"Ugh. Fineeeee." He rolled his eyes and snapped his fingers. A glowing tube rose up from below me and opened. It was bright like neon lights or fiber optics. I dropped into the tube, and it caught me in a curve. I slid through it, riding my momentum like a waterslide without the water to ride on. My stomach twisted and turned with each curve. The lights flashed as I passed, and they made me even dizzier. I pressed my hand over my mouth as I slid in the tube, trying not to vomit. It curved upward and I shot out of the end like a cannon.

I thought I was going to soar through the air like a bullet, but instead I came to halt. I was floating but had no control over what direction I moved in or how. My legs slowly went over my head and my hair flopped over my face. Morpheus put his hands behind his head like he was floating in a pool. "It's a great time, right?"

"Can you please?" I tried to right myself but only ended up spinning farther away from him. "Just get me there."

"See why I don't like vampires? So boring. I'll come back for you when I'm done."

"Wait what?" He snapped his fingers, and I landed in a dark tunnel with a light at the end of it. It was smooth and looked to get smaller at the end. I spun in a circle. "Morpheus! Where am I?"

No answer.

"No, I won't be doing that." The voice was a whispered echo down the hall, and it was so familiar that I ran headlong toward it.

"Gray, I'm here!" There was no answer, only my own words echoing back at me.

There was another murmuring voice, but I couldn't make out the words. I ran faster and came out at the end of the tunnel into a wide-open space shrouded in fog. Grayson stood with his back to me, and I sucked in a sharp breath. This wasn't the crazed vampire I'd seen earlier. No, this was the Grayson I knew and loved. He wore a simple white T-shirt and dark pants. Yet he didn't turn to me. He didn't seem to even hear me.

I stood still, not knowing what I would find. "Gray?"

He turned to face me, but he looked right through me. "Piper?"

"I'm here." I was so close I could reach out and touch him, but he couldn't see me. When I tried to touch him, my hand came up against a barrier surrounding him. It was cold and jelly-like. I tried to call on my blood magic to see if I could break through, but this was his dream and I had no power here.

The voice murmured again, and Grayson shook his head. "I bloody well will not."

I closed my eyes, trying to hear what he heard or see who he was talking to. Slowly it came into tune like trying to find the right station on the radio. There it was, this voice that did not match Grayson's at all. This voice was deeper and even smoother than Grayson's. It was so enticing, like a whispered suggestion I couldn't say no to. I found my entire body relaxing as I listened. I imagined this would be like the moment before being hypnotized, like walking into a haze but wanting to be there.

"Do this one little thing for me." The words were so smooth I felt my limbs go heavy as they relaxed.

Grayson pressed his hands to the sides of his head and pulled at his hair. "LIES!"

"Return my Dracinda to me." He sounded like he smirked as he spoke. "And I will free you to return to your life."

I sucked in a sharp breath. Who was this Dracinda? And who was this voice with enough power to free Grayson from this hell? I wanted to yell that he would do it, that he would do anything to be free, but there was no yelling out to a voice I wasn't meant to hear. How could I answer for him? There was more murmuring and I lost the voice's words for a second. I knew he was talking to Gray in that enticing voice, yet I couldn't make it out.

Grayson shook his head. "Titus would never."

Why? Why wouldn't he take the deal? I wanted him back so badly it hurt. I reached out to him, trying to move closer, wanting to wrap my arms around him. But I couldn't move. I was trapped here just yearning for a moment of clarity with him. Here he was lucid, here he was himself, here he was perfect. If I could just get to him and make him see me, I could tell him not to lose hope and that we were all working on it. He just had to hold on a bit longer.

"Grayson, please." A ball formed in my throat, and I fought the urge to cry.

His head snapped up. "Piper, are you there?"

He took a step toward me, and for a moment I swore he looked me in the eye. I stared at those deep mahogany depths, feeling grief take a hold deep in my chest. We were so close yet so far from each other. "I'm here."

"Where, love?" He spun in a circle, searching me out once more, but we were divided by some kind of force. I couldn't help but think how ironic it was that we'd just gotten each other only to be torn apart again. So close yet so far would soon become our motto.

A hand wrapped around my upper arm and squeezed. "Come on. We have to go." Morpheus' skin looked paler than before, and he pressed a fist to his mouth.

I jerked my arm, but his grip was too tight. "No, it's not enough time."

"It's never enough, cupcake." Before I could argue, we were moving again, soaring through the world at a blinding speed.

"What the hell? Go back." I tried to fight, but I was not in control of this ride.

He shook his head. "Can't."

I opened my mouth to say something else, but he just narrowed his eyes at me and snapped his fingers. With that one snap, I sat straight up in bed, shooting up so fast I made myself dizzy. I kicked my legs over the side and turned to face Morpheus. "How dare you!?"

He hunched over the side of his bed and vomited all over the floor. "I couldn't."

The door to the room flew open as Zinnia, Tuck, Astrid, and Beckett raced into the room. Beckett chuckled as he leaned over Morpheus. "How was your trip through Maze land?"

Morpheus gagged and hunched over, trying to suck in a breath. "Never." He heaved. "Ever." He gagged. "Again."

Tucker raised his eyebrows. "That bad?"

"Chaos." He waved us away as he flopped back on the bed out of breath and sweating. "Utter chaos."

"Serves you right." Even Astrid couldn't hide her amusement.

"Be gone with you." His words sounded like a threat, but the fact he still hadn't moved and his body quaked with each breath he took made me think he couldn't do anything at this very moment.

"Poor Maze," I whispered as I rose to my feet and threw the sheet back on the tiny bed with all the annoyance I felt.

"Poor Maze?" Morpheus swung his gaze toward me. "No, poor me."

"Like she said, serves you right." Zinnia hooked her arm with mine. "Did you get what we need?"

I wasn't sure, but I got a strong dose of my soulmate for far too short of a time. "I don't know, but I got a name, and I think that's something we can start with. If I had more time, then I might've gotten further, but dreamwalker here showed up and pulled me out."

"You've been gone for some time." Astrid wrinkled her nose at Morpheus as he groaned and curled into the fetal position.

"How long?" Panic assailed my body. *Please don't let it be too long.*

Zinnia hesitated. "Two days.

"WHAT? Atlas will be—"

"Awake." Tucker finished for me. "My sources tell me he's awake. We have to go now."

"Good. Now leave me here to die with this madness." Morpheus threw his arm over his face with all the drama of a 1950's actress.

"Greeks can't die . . . can they?" I couldn't remember if anyone had told me that little fact or not.

"No." Tucker turned for the door. "But one can dream."

"I can hear you, asshole," Morpheus bellowed, yet still he didn't get out of the bed.

"I meant for you to hear me, prick," Tuck called back.

The rest of us followed him out, leaving Morpheus to groan and recover on his own. "You love me, really"

Tuck looked to the sky and groaned. "No, no I really don't."

Zinnia still hadn't dropped my arm. "Now, tell me, what do we need?"

"I really hate to say it, but I think I need Kylian."

CHAPTER TWENTY-SEVEN

THEON

"And this is where I find you?" Marius strolled up to me, motioning to me as I sat here. I didn't have the energy or patience to even look at him. What he'd done would affect us all from now on. Our lives would forever be changed because of him. The Night Spawn would live at the razor's edge, and if he kept on going with this treachery, it would be war—a war we did not want or need. He glanced around with a heavy sigh, looking as if finding me here was such a boring disappointment to him. "Not surprising. You always were rather . . . emotional."

I turned my face away from him and gazed out over the graveyard where I'd buried my family so long ago. My parents had loved me, my brother had loved me, and yet my maker, whom I spent over a century with, never had. I'd spent years devoted to him, thinking we were working together to help the Night Spawn. Now I could see his selfishness and it disgusted me. I shifted my weight away from him, debating if I wanted to leave now or give him a moment to explain himself. Not that any explanation could justify his actions. If I left, there was nowhere else for me to go to find a moment of clarity.

I'd always found this place to soothe me in times of trouble. It was the only place I could be close to my family, and now I really could use their wisdom and guidance. The wooden bench I perched on now was dilapidated and falling apart, yet I stayed there gazing out over the stillness of the cemetery, searching for solace. It'd been years since they'd buried anyone this far out in the country, and I liked the quiet of how undisturbed it now was. The moon shined down with bright light that lit the headstones with different hues of blue. Clouds passed over the moon, casting large shadows throughout the open space.

"Are we not speaking then?" Marius stood beside me with that stupid leather coat of his billowing out and dragging over the frozen grass.

"Of all the things to have happened, why did you not speak of the attack with me?" I rested my arms across the back of the bench and slouched down.

He took the space beside me and spread out in a similar position. The wooden bench creaked under his weight. "Because I am aware of how your mind works."

I didn't turn to look at him. "And what's that supposed to mean?"

"It means I'm aware you don't have the wherewithal to do what needs to be done." He turned to face me. "You are weak."

I scoffed and rolled my eyes. I'd never shown an ounce of weakness until I ran from the castle after the attack. "Because attacking at a ball shows strength? Half those vampires were Night Spawn. Many were injured or even killed in that attack."

He waved my words away. "They were not loyal to the cause."

"Loyalty." I shook my head. "And where is your so-called loyalty?"

"Do not question things you know nothing about," he hissed toward me, and I pressed my lips together. Silence hung between us, and I wasn't going to be the one to break it. He was the first to speak, and he continued in his condescending tone. "The House of Shade must fall, and this is the first step among many."

I rose to my feet and began walking away from him. This wasn't something I wanted to be a part of. There was no place I was safe after being so close to Marius, and there was no way that I wouldn't be labeled a traitor, or worse, sentenced to death. He put me here. He'd ruined the life I'd built. His actions would take me down with him, and I hadn't even gotten a choice in the matter. The bitterness I felt toward him tasted stale on my tongue. I didn't make it three steps before Marius was in front of me.

He pressed his hand to my chest, stopping me. "And where are you going?"

"Somewhere I won't be killed for your bloody actions." I shoved his hand away from my chest and tried to step around him, but he blocked my way.

"Join us." When I didn't answer, he ran his hand through his hair and turned away from me. "I will not beg of you."

"Beg of me?" My anger flared. "How about consult with me before you ruin us all?"

"Ruin?" He whirled around and shoved both his hands into my chest, pushing me back. "I have brought greatness to our door, and you insult it?"

"Greatness?" I shoved him back. "You have brought death."

He pushed his body into me, bumping his chest against mine. His breath fanned across my face as his fangs descended in his mouth. "You're either with me or against me."

"Is that how it is? Either with you or death? Such black and white lines you draw to justify your actions." My hands curled into fists, and I fought the urge to hit him.

Before he could act, a blue light appeared across the cemetery from us and began to expand to a circle. We both dove for cover behind two side-by-side headstones. Marius crouched lower and narrowed his eyes at me. "You've set me up. What is it!?"

"I didn't ask you here. You found me, you daft prick. How should I know what it is?" I hissed back as I peeked around the side of the headstone.

Piper marched out of this blue, swirling portal-looking-thing with a tall elf hot on her heels. She glanced around the cemetery and whirled on him. "He's not here."

"Don't doubt my skill, leech. You're trying my patience."

His eyes glowed a crystal-green in the darkness, and he walked over to one of the headstones and placed his hand on it. Burgundy smoke flowed from his fingers and covered the stone like a thick fog. It crumbled to the ground in an instant. He knelt and placed his hand on the rubble, and two short swords and one long one emerged. He took the two short ones and threw them to Piper. "You needed these last time. You might need them again."

She glanced down at the dark stone blades in her hands and to where the headstone once stood. "That feels so wrong."

"What? They're dead. It's not like they're using the headstones." He shrugged.

"You're a real ass sometimes, you know that?" She looked down at herself. "I have no place to hold these."

"I got it." Another girl with long, dark-red hair emerged from the portal and waved her hand over Piper. She covered her in golden magic, and an instant later Piper was in dark-black jeans and a black tank top. Leather straps were wrapped up and down her arms and around her hips.

She slid the swords into holsters at her hips and nodded at the redhead. "Thanks."

"Such power they wield so easily." Marius' voice was almost reverent as he spoke. His eyes were wide, and I was familiar with that look. He coveted them and their power. The gears were turning behind those dark eyes, and I could almost smell the envy rolling off him.

Piper turned to the tall, dark-haired guy just as a guy

with blond hair walked through the portal. Blue smoke swirled from the portal around his hand, and he seemed to draw it back into himself. The smokey magic twisted around his body before disappearing into his palm. He dusted off his hands and moved in closer to the redhead.

Marius leaned forward. "Such company our Piper keeps."

"Piper is not for you," I whispered so only he could hear.

He growled. "Everyone is for me."

"Where is he, Kylian?" Piper snapped at the guy next to her.

Kylian, the dark-haired one, pointed toward the trees in the distance. "My guess would be there."

"You guess or you know?" she asked as she walked by him.

A black raven flew overhead, and the shadow of its wings glided over the headstones. Piper's eyes widened as her hands shook. "He's here."

Who is she talking about?

Atlas melted from the shadows of the trees like a shroud of darkness, like death himself, like the shadows were where he belonged. The darkness was a friend he knew well and lived with all his life. If the rumors were true, then Atlas was so loyal to The House of Shade that his family paid the price for his loyalty. His black shirt and pants only helped him blend into the night. In one hand he held a sword. The other hung loose at his side. He stood there for a moment, then he tilted his head up to the moon.

It bathed his face in blue light, and he closed his eyes. He sucked in a deep breath and blew it out slowly.

The sound of a branch snapping echoed off to the right and his eyes flashed wide open. Piper's head snapped in the direction of the sound, and they both took off running at the same time. Atlas moved like a ghost. His movements were an effortless, silent glide as he leapt over headstones and gained more speed. Piper pumped her arms, trying to get there before he did. She moved so fast her arms and legs looked like a blur to me. It was fast even for a vampire.

Marius wrapped his hand around my wrist and yanked me with him as he followed and kept hidden behind the headstones. When we were close enough, he pulled me down next to him behind a thicket of trees and brush that would cover us. "What do you know of this?"

"I know nothing." How would I know why the right hand of the King and the soulmate of the Prince were clearly hunting for the same thing? Or why it seemed dire to each of them.

Marius dug his fingers into my skin. "Do not lie to me."

I yanked my hand free. "Out of the two of us, I am not the liar here."

When I heard a familiar voice muttering to himself, my head snapped up. *Grayson?* He was pacing back and forth among the brush. I'd never seen him like this before. His hair was a mess, his clothing was torn, and he looked like he was talking to someone but there was no one near him. He was the opposite of the smooth-talking Prince I'd grown used to. This vampire was . . . mad.

When I saw him before, it was a passing glimpse. He wasn't talking to himself or disheveled. I thought he might've slipped for a moment, not gone down the rabbit hole . . . I was wrong.

Atlas was so close. He sprinted toward Grayson with his sword in hand. He leapt up into the air and held his sword over his head like he was going to bring it down across Grayson's neck. My breath caught in my throat, and I couldn't turn away. It was like watching a train about to crash. *NO! What the devil was happening here?* A moment before Atlas swung his sword, Piper dove for him and wrapped her arms around his hips, knocking him off course.

She hit him like a rugby player would, driving her shoulder into his stomach. They tumbled a few meters away and fell to the ground. The other three who were with Piper hurried to surround Grayson. They moved in closer like they were going to attack. Glittering, golden magic wound around the redhead's hands. That blue smoke flowed from the blond guy and crept over the ground toward Gray. The elf, Kylian, swung his sword in a loose circle at his side. A manic laugh ripped from Grayson's throat as red mist exploded out of him and they all froze. The mist spread over them in a thick wave and wrapped tightly around them, holding them in place.

Piper and Atlas wrestled on the ground. That mad laugh escaped Grayson again. I watched his eyes go full black as red veins forked out over his face and down his neck. I glanced to Marius. This was not the ammunition or knowledge he needed right now. It would only add fuel to his fire.

A wide grin spread over his face. "The Prince is crazed."

Grayson forced the three surrounding him to kneel before him, their bodies quaking with the need to fight. Their muscles twitched and magic seeped from their hands and pooled on the ground around them. Grayson hunched over Kylian and raked a nail over his skin. A drop of blood welled at the base of his neck. Grayson drew back his lips and his fangs extended like he was about to strike.

"NO! Gray, don't!" Piper called out to him, and he hesitated.

His eyes widened, and he stumbled away from Kylian, shaking his head like he didn't know up from down. He pressed his hands to the sides of his head and hunched over, roaring with anguish. He rocked up and down for what felt like forever but was mere seconds. All at once he straightened his stance and spun to face Atlas and Piper, who were still struggling on the ground. When he glanced at Piper, he hissed, but he took off running in the opposite direction. The others remained frozen with the effects of Grayson's blood magic. Atlas rose to his feet above Piper, grabbed both of her shoulders, and shoved her to the ground. He turned to follow Grayson, but Piper was scrappy and hooked one arm around his leg and the other around his hip and threw him back to the dirt.

They both scrambled to their feet and drew their swords. They circled one another, and I was shocked how naturally Piper held those swords at her sides. "Atlas, don't do this."

"I keep my word," he growled at her. "I will not fail him!"

He swung his sword. Piper lunged forward and threw her own swords up, blocking his strike. He spun quickly and crouched down and swung his sword at her midsection. At the last second, she jumped back, and the blade missed her by inches.

"He's in there! You saw it! He hesitated."

"Take your lies somewhere else," he said on a snarl.

He swung for her chest, and I sucked in a sharp breath. Piper arched her back and the sword missed her by less than an inch. She turned and leapt forward, jabbing her swords toward him as he spun away. They were going to kill each other, and I had no idea why. They both loved Grayson, yet there they were circling each other, looking for how best to kill one another.

"Enough!" Golden magic wrapped around the two of them like a lasso around their waists. They flew up in the air and were held there.

Red mist seeped from Atlas, and the tattoos on his body rippled as he struggled. "Release me!"

The redhead marched between them and held her hands out. "This is stupid."

She flicked her wrist and Piper landed on the ground beside her while Atlas soared across the cemetery. He fell to the ground and crashed into a headstone, which crumbled to dust. He lay there motionless for a moment.

Piper rounded on the redhead. "What the hell, Astrid? He's trying to kill Gray."

"Yeah, and when you save Grayson is he going to thank you for killing his best friend?" She put her hands on her hips, and though she was smaller than Piper, she stood up to her without hesitation.

Piper's shoulders sagged, and she shoved the swords back into the holsters at her hips. "If he wants to kill Grayson, then he's in my way. Don't stop me again."

Astrid motioned to the blond guy, and he opened up a portal right in front of her.

Kylian pressed his hand to his neck. "I'm not thanking you for stopping him."

"I would expect nothing less." She waved toward the portal. "After you, princess."

Marius wrapped his hand round my wrist and yanked me to my feet as they walked through the portal and left us. The swirling blue light was gone, and the cemetery was back to being lit only by the moon.

I tried to yank my hand away, but he held on tighter. "What's this about?"

He jerked me around and pressed my back to his chest. His lips were so close to my ear I could feel his hot breath on my skin. "The castle is weak. The Prince has fallen."

Before I could react, he reached up and twisted my neck violently. The distinct crack of bone sounded through my head, and my muscles went limp. I fell back against him, begging for my body to move . . . Nothing. He'd snapped my neck in an instant. I couldn't move. *Bastard*. I blinked up at him from my place on the cold, frozen grass. He grabbed my foot and dragged me toward where Atlas lay beside the broken headstone. He flung me there next to him. As I lay there unable to move, unable to fight back, hatred for this traitor bloomed in my chest. Marius squatted down next to me, and his face filled my vision.

"You'll heal from this, but not before he wakes." He shoved his hair from his face and patted my cheek. My head lulled to the side. He chuckled and adjusted my head so I was looking at him once more. "Remember, Theon, if you're not with me . . . you're against me."

He rose to stand up straight and pressed his lips together as he looked down at me. "We will get past this. In time, I'll forgive you."

He turned and walked away from me, his coat billowing around him, and I wanted to rise and kill him then and there. I wanted to lash out and make him feel the panic I now did.

I will NEVER forgive you.

CHAPTER TWENTY-EIGHT

ELOURA

"How can we claim to be safe? How can the crown protect us when they couldn't protect us under their own roof? I pose this question to you." The show that Clive put on at his own home knew no bounds. He was comfortable here, and when he spoke, he acted as if he were center stage.

His words were smooth as always. He enjoyed posing questions in such an innocent manner to the Blood Borns. It was his manipulative way of planting the seeds in others' minds in the hopes that they themselves would start to question things. When others began to nod in agreement with him, I knew the tides needed to change or the King would have a rebellion on his hands.

I grabbed a glass of champagne from the waiter as he passed by. I swirled it around, keeping an eye on Clive as he spread *his* poisonous words too. These smaller parties were limited to the heads of the major Blood Born families.

Among them were the richest and most powerful to walk the Earth. Governments were made to rise and fall in rooms like this, rooms where blood and champagne flowed while deals were made over hors d'oeuvres. Empires rose and found ruin on the whims of these vampires, and not only in the vampire world but the human one too. It was all profits and power here.

I held my glass to my lips and gave Clive a light smile as I took a sip and moved in closer to the circle of partygoers he'd surrounded himself with. "Oh, I don't know, Clive. I've found the last three hundred years to be pleasurable enough."

He gave a light chuckle and smoothed his hand over his dark, slicked-back hair. "I have no doubts you have, Eloura. Your family has been among the top five most profitable within our circles, if I recall."

"Top three." I smiled as the others began to turn toward me, showing their interest. I gave a little shrug. "But who's counting really? Are we all not fortunate in our wealth?"

Clive returned with his own sly smile. He inclined his head toward me. "Indeed, but it's difficult to see the harsh realities amidst such splendor."

He wasn't wrong. Even now the string quartet played and vampires whirled around the small dance floor. Laughter and liquor were in abundance on this evening. "I do find we live a privileged life. Do you all not agree?"

The crowd around us nodded and murmurs of agreement fluttered all around. Privilege oozed off each of them, from the fancy jewelry encrusted with diamonds, emeralds, and rubies to the brand-new clothes for every function we attended. And in the Blood Born society, there were countless functions. Clive threw his head back and gave a hearty chuckle. "Precisely, and I know I would love to keep it that way."

"After thousands of years, I don't think there's a fear of losing any of it." I took another sip, and the bubbles tickled my nose.

"Not if things don't change." He glanced around at the others. "Only our known ways are a safe way of protecting our lives and lifestyle."

"Ah, but how boring for the immortals. If we are to live for eternity, then wouldn't it be in our best interest to keep things . . . surprising? Besides that, I'd like to see the vampires thrive as a whole. Spread the wealth, so to speak." I downed the rest of my drink, and a waiter appeared by my side in an instant. He took it with his perfectly shiny silver tray.

"I'm not sure I would enjoy a loss of wealth. Especially for it to go to those who are ungrateful for it." Clive chuckled and the others joined in with him. They were the kind of fake laughs that grated to hear. He wiped away a fake tear as though his joke was so funny it brought him to tears. He waved his hands, signaling for everyone to quiet down and of course they did. "I would say recent events would show how ungrateful the Night Spawn truly are. Titus has let them go unchecked for far too long. Like spoiled children, they should be given boundaries, of course."

I scoffed. "But they aren't chi—"

"Sir." One of Clive's attendants slid in beside him and whispered in his ear so none of us could hear over the music. The smile faltered on Clive's face, but he quickly put it back in place as he waved the man away. He turned back to his group of admirers with a half-smile. "If you'll excuse me . . . Please do enjoy the festivities."

He gave a slight incline to his head, then slithered away. The group closed the gap where he'd just been standing and turned their attention to the music, food, and dancing. It was all mindless drivel. When I turned away, I spotted Clive disappearing into the small hallway off the side of the main ballroom. There was something about the way he looked over his shoulder, the way he wanted to make sure no one was watching him, that gave me a suspicious feeling. I gave him a moment, then wound my way through the occupants of the ballroom. When I approached the opening, I marched into it without hesitation.

It was dimly lit by sconces spread every few feet with flickering lights. Gold-foiled wallpaper covered the walls. The rug was thick under my feet and muffled each of my footsteps. I followed Clive's clawing cologne all the way down the hall and turned to the right to walk down another. I tiptoed every step of the way until I came to a door that was cracked open just enough for me to make out Clive's annoying voice as he spoke with a man whose voice I didn't recognize.

"Mr. Cristiano, I believe our business is soon at its end."

I'd never heard another vampire use that tone with him. It was a mixture of exasperation, annoyance, and finality.

"I just need a bit more time," Clive pleaded as he paced back and forth.

"And yet you think it appropriate to use my money to throw this little gathering?" The sound of a lighter clicking filled the silence between them, then came the distinct smell of cigar smoke. I had no idea who this person was, but I had the sudden desire to find out.

"In a few days' time I will have the highest seat of power in the kingdom, and you will have the benefit of such a friend." Clive tried to sound so smooth, like a salesman making promises they never kept. It all sounded sweet but ultimately would not pan out.

More smoke drifted out the door toward me, and I wrinkled my nose.

The vampire sighed. "Thus far I've yet to see your advances, and I'm bloody tired of waiting for these favors and payments you promise."

"Just a bit more time, damn it!" Clive slammed his fist down on a table.

"Do not think to raise your voice to me. You may be one of the higher brow Blood Borns, but I own you, and I will be collecting one way or another. I have no preference or interest in politics. It'll either be blood or money."

"I swear I am this close to getting everything we want," Clive pleaded. "I have several of the most prominent families ready to back me in a move against Titus, and once he's unseated, I'll have more wealth than we can ever dream of."

"No, Mr. Cristiano, that's what *you* want." The sound of a chair scraping across the floor made me peek through the door even harder to get a better look at the mystery man. "What I want is my money."

"And . . . and I'll get it to you." His voice was threaded with panic.

I peeked through the crack in the door only to see Clive pressed up against the wall with a fair-haired vampire standing in front of him with a knife pressed to Clive's throat. He lowered his voice. "You seem to forget that while vampires are immortal, they die every day."

He pressed the knife up under Clive's chin and blood trickled down the shiny, silvery blade all the way to the hilt.

Clive's throat bobbed as he swallowed nervously. His eyes widened and he went up on his tiptoes. "With interest!"

The man stopped pressing his knife upward. "I require forty percent."

"Twenty-five," Clive countered, and I couldn't help but think how stupid the vampire was to negotiate from a position of weakness. But Clive was always the rabbit who tried to catch the snake.

The man gave a deep chuckle and took a small step back. He pulled the knife away from Clive and slid it into the holster at the small of his back under his suit coat. "And yet you'll still be giving me forty."

Clive gave a heavy sigh. "Very well. Partners."

"Not partners, you'll be paying a debt." He gave a dark chuckle. "I rather fancy having a king in my pocket."

Clive moved from my vision, but a moment later I heard ice hitting a glass and the sound of liquid being poured. "And I rather fancy being a king and returning things back to the way they belong."

"Whatever that means," the man said, dismissing Clive's words.

The ice clinked on the glass as Clive raised it to his lips and came back into view. "It means that my desires will benefit us both in the end."

The man walked up to Clive and clapped him on the shoulder. Yet he never turned to face the door so that I could ascertain his identity. "Your greed knows no bounds. It's to your detriment and my gain."

Clive chuckled as if this were a joke and not the truth. "We'll see."

"There's no *we'll see*. You had better keep up your end, or I'm afraid the future looks bleak for you."

"My future never looks bleak. I'm Clive Cristiano." Somehow, over the course of five minutes, he went from begging for his life to bartering for it and then to claiming he's the best thing since electricity. His ego knew no bounds, but I would relish the day when all the pieces fell into place. Because there was no doubt in my mind Clive would die . . . I would see to it.

CHAPTER TWENTY-NINE

ATLAS

"There are many things in this world I find intriguing: how the sunflower raises its face to the morning rays, how in a world of perfect symbiosis one cannot believe in a higher power, and how humans find the existence of the supernatural to be nothing but a mere myth. However, as of late, I find how you came to be lying beside me in a graveyard the most interesting of all."

Theon lay on the ground at my feet with his head lulled at a hard angle to one side. Whoever broke his neck had done so with enough force to render him helpless. Which, given the current state our world was in, rendered me intrigued. Theon was believed to be among the traitors to our kind. His reputation for being a staunch ally of Marius had been solidified over the years. I reached into my pocket and pulled out a small, square folding mirror that I carried with me in case of emergencies. I placed it on the ground next to him, then pulled my cell from my pocket. "I need medical and transport. I'm sending my location now." I hung up and quickly sent my coordinates, then closed the phone. Theon just blinked up at me with those wide green eyes. I squatted down over him. "You interfere with my hunt."

Though if I was going to roll with the honesty I prided myself on, I found the intrusion to have occurred at the perfect time. The hunt was taxing to my soul. I found little value in the world or beings around me. Only three vampires had my loyalty, only three vampires had my respect, and only one had my friendship, a friendship that'd seen me through things I cared not to dwell on. A friendship that indeed brought value to my world. Yet now I found myself in the position of failure. It was not a position I was used to occupying. I excelled at the hunt, I excelled at the kill, I excelled at the execution of orders. But this vow was the hardest one of all to keep. I was not a man who thought of futures nor believed that I had one. The only future I saw for myself was loyalty to The House of Shade, and now I was failing that too.

Like a wounded animal or terminally sick creature, it was a kindness to end their suffering. No one should have to live through the pain and anguish of such a life. I knew this was the kind of torture that Grayson felt. To not be himself physically or mentally or to hurt innocents would be the deepest kind of pain he could feel. Yet I could not find it in myself to do the right thing and end his suffering. With such a weakness, I didn't deserve to be called a friend. Each time I encountered him, I found myself pulling punches, hesitating to deal the death blow, or even worse, I would fear his loss so intensely his pain might as well have been my own.

How could I do this? But how could I not? I made a promise! A vow! A vow I wanted to break with every fiber of my being. I'd tussled with Piper, but it was a half-assed attempt if I was being honest with myself. Deep down, I wanted her to win. I wanted her to be right, even though Grayson was no longer in there. I didn't want to kill the belief that he still might be able to be saved. The desire to see him saved was overwhelming. In truth, I didn't want to give up on my friend.

Theon made a small grunting sound at my feet and blinked several times at me. "I find the blinking unhelpful. Do stop it. You look absurd."

More blinking.

I pointed my finger in his face. "Do not make me regret saving your life."

The mirror glowed and a vampire dressed all in black shoved his way out of it a little at a time. He placed his arms on the ground beside the mirror and pulled the rest of his body through, all the while grunting with the effort it took. He was slim, with a chiseled face and dark eyes. When he was fully through the mirror, he knelt down and reached back in to pull out a large duffle bag. "I hate coming through tiny spaces like that. It does no favors for my bollocks."

I rolled my eyes. "Just do as you're told."

The vampire swallowed and his eyes widened. "Atlas?"

When I arched my eyebrows at him, he swallowed and held his hands up. "Apologies. I'm new."

"Clearly." I looked toward the sky, where the dark-navy had begun to turn to purple. The first rays of light would surely burn Theon to death if we didn't move this along. "You want to hurry this up before the sun chars him to death?"

"The emergency?" He looked me up and down.

My patience held on by a thread as I pointed to where Theon lay on the ground at my feet. The vampire tripped over himself as he opened the bag and started pulling things out. Another vampire came through the mirror, and this one was a smaller woman with wide blue eyes and dark-blonde hair pulled back in a tight braid.

She shook her head when she looked at the other vampire working. "Oi, rookie, don't fuck this one up. Relax and do what we trained you to do."

She too had a large duffel bag with her that rattled with supplies. She reached in and pulled out a fold-up mirror and began to lay it out over the ground. It expanded into a six-by-six foot square that would make it easier for us to travel through with an injured Theo. My mirror was for emergencies only.

She glanced in my direction, and in a clipped, direct tone she asked, "Are you injured?"

"No."

She said nothing else, just went about preparing Theon to be moved. I stood there gazing off in the direction Grayson had taken off. I could hunt him down, I could find him, I could kill him, but the prospect of doing that only made me feel weary down to my bones. I was a solitary sort of soul but that had always included Grayson. Even in his current state, I found solace in knowing my single, only friend still walked the Earth along with me. Slowly, I felt myself begin to mourn him. It was a deep sadness that I would carry with me for the rest of my days. It made me question if the rest of my days would be worth it without my only friend. He made the days seem tolerable, his humor always surprised me, and no other on this Earth understood me the way he did. We had an unspoken understanding between the two of us. His death would dim the world, and it would never be the same . . . *I* would never be the same. It was selfish, and yet with each passing day, I found myself praying that Piper was right and would find a way. It was an odd sensation to root for one's only failure.

"We're ready." The smaller vampire caught my attention as the two of them lifted Theon on a big, flat yellow board they'd strapped him to and began to descend into the mirror, which rippled around them as though they were stepping into a lake.

Theon's eyes widened and he kept blinking them at me. "As much as I love your efforts to communicate, I find the attempts tedious." He rolled his eyes, and I tilted my head to the side, studying him. "Now that sentiment I understand."

I followed them through the mirror, letting the cool liquid run over my skin and peel back just as quickly.

Bright white light momentarily blinded me as it always did when we entered the lab. But this mirror opened right into the heart of it, which at this present moment I was grateful for. I turned toward the first lab assistant I saw and stepped in his path, stopping him from walking. His hands shook and he dropped a tray of test tubes onto the floor. They shattered at my feet and tiny shards of glass scattered over my boots. He tipped his head back, looking up at me. His mouth dropped open, and he snapped it shut only to let it drop open once more. I scrubbed a hand down my face.

I don't have time for this. "If I wanted you dead, you would be."

He nodded so emphatically that his teeth chattered. "Yes, of course."

"Go tell the King I'm here and requesting his presence." When he stood there frozen, just shaking and staring at me, my patience met its end. I wrapped my hand around his upper arm and walked him past the research tables, past the holding cells for the vampires overcome with sickness, and right to the doors. I planted my foot and kicked them open with the other foot. They both flew wide, slamming into the walls with a bang. I tossed the assistant out. "Go, now."

He scrambled away, and when I turned around, all the other techs were staring at what I'd just done. I growled and they went back to their microscopes and lab work. They all pretended to bustle about as I passed, but I could still feel their eyes on me. I marched down the hallway toward the exam rooms until I came upon Theon's. He lay there strapped to the board with that brace around his neck.

Doctor Stanbourn hovered over him and was flashing a light into his eyes. He held his finger up. "Follow my finger."

Theon followed the doctor's finger with his eyes. He gave another round of infernal blinking and tiny grunting noises. "For the last bloody time, no one understands you. Might as well shut it."

The doctor pointed at Theon's neck. "Your handiwork?"

"If I wanted him dead, I would've ripped his head clean off and left the body there to burn to ash."

His eyes widened, and he moved to the other side of Theon. He pressed his fingers to his neck, feeling the bones. "It's a clean break."

"How long until he recovers so I can kill him properly?" I never wanted to kill my best friend, but I'd happily kill Theon.

"Why bring him here to get well if you're only going to kill him in the end?" The doctor straightened his stance and ran his hand over his salt and pepper hair.

"I'm a big softy."

A smile spread over the doctor's face, and he licked his lips, trying to fight it. "Indeed, a word I would use to characterize you."

If I hadn't felt like I was drowning in melancholy, I might've given the doctor the smirk that remark deserved.

As it was, I could hardly find joy in anything, perhaps I never would again. I pressed my lips into a line. "What's the course of treatment?"

Titus marched into the room and everything halted. I turned and bowed out of respect and habit just as the doctor had as well. Titus gestured to Theon. "What's the meaning of this?"

"It's a gift, I believe."

"I'm not sure what would make you think I wanted a broken vampire as a gift, but this is dark even for you, Atlas." He moved closer to Theon and bent low over him, looking at the way his neck bent to the side.

"Not a gift for you, Your Majesty. I believe it was a gift for me. He was left like that at my feet when I was looking for the Prince."

Titus' eyes darted to me at the mention of Grayson, but he said nothing. Instead, he stood straight to face me. "Why would anyone break Theon's neck and leave him for dead at your feet?"

"You assume being laid at my feet means death?"

When he only stared at me with an *of course* look on his face, I gave a single nod. "Fair assumption."

"So, we have Marius' right-hand man with a broken neck in our lab." Titus rubbed at the stubble covering his chin and gave a little hum. "Interesting turn of events, wouldn't you say?"

"The most interesting one I've had all day," I agreed.

Titus turned toward the doctor. "What is the plan of action here?"

The doctor crossed his arms over his chest and glanced from me to Titus. "I will have to use one of the healing potions Ophelia left behind for us. I can straighten the bone, and the potion should help the healing process move rather quickly."

"Excellent, then I'll be happy to question him." I strolled over to Theon and bent over his head so he could see me clearly. "And you'll be very helpful, won't you?" More of that rapid blinking. "I'm going to assume that's a yes, because a broken neck will seem like child's play compared to what I will do to you." A small grunt. "Good." I patted his chest.

Titus turned to the doctor. "How long until he's fully healed?"

"I'd say a comfortable estimate would be three days. As he's a prisoner, I'll be sure to keep him restrained at all times."

Titus nodded in agreement. "Until we know how or why he came to be like this, I think that's best. See that he gets the best treatment but do proceed with caution and keep him contained."

The doctor bowed toward Titus and turned back to Theon. Titus crooked his finger at me, motioning for me to follow him out the door and into the hallway where we could be alone. I knew what he was going to ask me, and I didn't want to answer. I didn't want to talk about it. I would either be disobeying an order from my King to find Grayson and bring him home. Or I would be breaking a vow to my best friend to put him out of his misery.

Titus lowered his voice. "What of the Prince?"

"He still eludes us," I answered honestly.

"We need him contained as soon as possible." His voice was a deep whisper. "If anyone finds out that the heir is lost to madness, it will embolden them."

"We can't be doing with any more of that."

He placed his hand on my shoulder and gave it a little squeeze. "I know you've cleaned up the mess this curse has caused for years, and it's given you no hope for our Grayson, but I can't . . ." He cleared his throat and swiped at the corner of his eye as though brushing away a tear. "But I can't bear to think of losing him. Just bring him home."

"I will do my best, Your Highness."

"I know you will." He dropped his hand from my shoulder. "What of Piper? Are you two working together?"

"In a manner." I didn't want to lie to my King. "She's out there looking for him now."

"She's tireless in her pursuits." A slight smile played on his lips. "It must be exhausting."

I pictured that necklace Grayson had given her. He'd taken great pains to get it to ensure she didn't go feral once more. In his absence, I didn't think she was taking care as much as she should have. The memory of that pearl turning a darker shade of pink during our fight invaded my mind. I might be annoyed at her for getting in my way . . . I paused, thinking about that. Was I annoyed or was I grateful for her interference? She would need blood soon. As Grayson's soulmate, she could only drink from him or she would sicken and die. He was my best friend, my only friend, I couldn't let the only one he'd ever loved go feral.

"Yes, she is relentless." Again, not a lie. It felt odd standing in front of Titus and dancing around the truth of the situation. I lowered my voice. "She will need to feed soon."

His eyes darted up and down the hallway, checking to make sure no one was listening. "I believe Gray made sure he had a supply here for her."

"Indeed." I knew exactly where those bags of blood were kept. When she'd left the castle to go live with the Night Spawn, Gray *had* made sure she got regular deliveries of his blood and that there would be some left here for her. "I know where they are. I'll see that she gets it."

Titus gave me a tight-lipped smile. "Your loyalty knows no bounds."

Like a shot to the heart, his words cut me deep. I'd prided myself on my infallible loyalty, and yet I'd failed Grayson over and over again. I'd failed him out of selfishness, out of grief, and out of the need to keep my one and only friend.

"Thank you, Your Majesty." I nearly choked on the words. Without another word, he walked away, leaving me there with my self-loathing and doubt to suffer with. I pulled my phone from my pocket and hit the number. "I need something done and it needs to be done now."

She would have the blood she needed. I'd be damned if I would let her go feral on my watch. My best friend would be counting on me, and I'd never failed him. Not until now.

I relayed exactly what I wanted and quickly hung up. I had no other reason to stay here. It was my duty to return to my hunt. The heart that I'd long thought dead wretched in my chest, sending a dark wave of sadness through my whole body because there was only one thing left for me to do, and for all my faults, I was loyal until my very last breath. There was nothing left for me in this world.

I was bound to my vow, bound to kill my only friend.

CHAPTER THIRTY

SANCHITA

"You stick out like a sore thumb. I thought you were supposed to be good at undercover operations." I walked beside Jester as we moved through the lobby of the Night Spawn headquarters and right past the front desk.

Normally the lobby was full of vampires just before the sun came up. They would sit in the modern plush furniture and socialize. They'd laugh and joke like teenagers at a sleepover. Though things seemed to be normal, I could feel an edge in the air. The normal buzz of activity was muted. There were even less vampires moving about than usual. The front desk was usually as busy as the fanciest hotels in London, but as we passed the two women behind the desk, they just continued to play games on their computers and never looked up at us.

"I don't think anyone is paying attention to what I'm

wearing." Jester's voice was deep and smooth as he spoke to me.

Prisha looked him up and down. "You would be wrong."

"Trust me, you are noticeable." I gave him the side-eye. He looked so military-like in his crew neck long-sleeved black shirt and blue jeans. Even his boots were army grade. There was something about the way he walked that screamed *hunter*. Nothing about Jester said Night Spawn and everything said cop. This needed to be dealt with delicately or the other vampires would think I was taking sides.

"Or perhaps you're the only one noticing me." He smirked and gave me a wink as we walked down a long hallway full of shops.

"Or perhaps you've got a big head." Prisha looked at me with a *This guy? Really?* look in her eyes, and I couldn't agree more.

He waved his hand, letting us walk in front of him down the hallway. "Do you both always share the same opinions?"

"Always," we replied at the same time.

"Ah, so if I convince the sister to like me . . ." He let his words trail off.

"No, absolutely not."

He gave a dramatic sigh. "Shame."

I wasn't used to seeing the doors all closed up. Usually I was playing dodge the door. They opened and closed so many times it was difficult not to get smacked by one. The bar was always full of activity and loud music. Yet today it only played slower music, and a few regular vampires sat on the stools keeping to themselves. Next to the bar was a salon, and not a single chair was occupied. Nothing about this seemed right. Were all the vampires hiding after hearing about the attack on the castle? Perhaps, like me, they thought they would be in jeopardy for retaliation.

"Are you flirting with me at a time like this?" I asked. I'd never gone undercover before, and my nerves were frying me from the inside out. I didn't know if I was making the quiet out to be something more than it was or if my paranoia was justified.

"Merely pointing out that you like me," he replied.

Why did he have to be so damn calm? It was irritating at a time like this.

"You put me in prison." I looked away from him. "It was terrifying."

"You were where you shouldn't have been." He said it so simply, like that warranted his actions. "Any other vampire would've been treated the same."

"He does have a point," Prisha added, and I shot her a look that told her to shut her mouth. She pressed her lips together.

"Yes, because small women with no shoes hiding in the dark screams treason." I pursed my lips and tried not to roll my eyes at him.

"You never really can be sure."

I didn't want to respond to him. I needed to focus on the task at hand. I hooked my hand into the crook of

Prisha's arm, and when we got to the open floor where the apartments started, we turned to the right. There was a wide space between each apartment and the hallway was more like a hangout space with plush seating areas every few feet. As we walked, vampires paused their conversations to look at Jester.

"See? I told you."

He gave a dark chuckle and shook his head. "Think again, sweetie."

When two vampires approached us, I held my breath. They were a couple I'd known for some time. They were what I would describe as a cute goth couple. Mark was tall and thin with tight black pants and a ripped white V-neck shirt. His vest hung off his shoulders, making him look thinner.

His girlfriend was a mirror of him, only slightly shorter. She wore black skinny jeans and a loose-fitting white shirt. I plastered a smile on my face as they stopped in a small semi-circle in front of us. "Mark, Jessica, how are you?"

Mark eyed me closely. "Never mind how we are, how are you?"

"After your ordeal, it's all anyone can talk about." Jessica leaned in closer. "I mean, you were in the dungeon of the castle. You only hear rumors of how awful it is."

I wanted to kick Jester because I practically felt him gloating next to me. They weren't paying attention to him, and I was what got their interest. I kept my smile in place. "Oh, yeah. It was a total misunderstanding."

Jessica lowered her voice. "Yeah, but you were innocent. I can't imagine what they're going to do to the rest of us if they took you."

"It really wasn't like that." I swallowed. It was much worse. "Once they knew I was innocent, they let me go right away."

Not so right away. They held me for longer than I wanted, threatened me, and generally freaked me out. But the King had been kind, generous, and seemed to genuinely want what was best for his people, which was what brought me back here. Because I wanted to help.

Jessica's eyes widened. "Oh, I heard it was much longer."

"So, what's the dungeon like? Is it as scary as they make it out to be?" Mark shoved his hands in his pockets and rocked back and forth.

I sucked in a deep breath and held it in my chest. "I'll be honest, it wasn't great, but they didn't hurt me, and after an attack like that, I feel like they had to be overly cautious. The King was very kind though. I found him to be comforting."

Mark's jaw dropped. "You met King Titus?"

Just as I nodded, a group of vampires walked by, then another. Prisha followed them with her eyes. "Is there a party somewhere?"

Jessica stepped in closer to us. "It's a speak-on."

"What is that?" Jester softened his voice and made it sound innocently curious.

"It's a gathering of vampires to talk about what's going

on in the kingdom." She bit her bottom lip. "It's kind of interesting."

"You mean things get heated," Mark interjected. "It's all about what's next. Who do we trust? Was Marius even right about The House of Shade?"

Jessica nodded in the direction the others walked in. "You should come. You might have something to offer after being held there. You know, because you were innocent and all."

Prisha nodded. "I think it's a good idea. Let's see what it's all about."

She motioned for them to lead the way, and they turned to walk down the hallway. We filled in behind them. Jester gave me a sideways look, and I felt his narrow-eyed gaze mirror my suspicious feeling. We hopped on the underground train, and I was surprised to see how packed it was. There was barely standing room. The train descended in a circular motion like a corkscrew going deeper underground. When I first came here, the train shocked me with how fast it moved. If I were human, I'd likely be on the floor with sickness, but as a vampire, the speed and pull never bothered me.

When it finally stopped, I was in a part of the headquarters I didn't recognize. We were so deep in the Earth that it was cooler here. The smell of the streets above didn't touch us. The walls were rough like they'd been dug out by hand, and tunnels shot off in every direction. Yet there was a crowd of vampires all moving in the same direction. It was like going to a concert where the crowd moved like cattle.

We turned into a larger room that was about the size of a school gym. The walls were still rough like the hallways, but near the front there was a large boulder with a single vampire standing on it. She was tiny with dark skin and a shaved head. She wore bright, silvery make-up over her eyes like a mask that fanned out from her eyes all the way back to her temples. Her lips were coated in shining red lip gloss.

She placed her finger in front of her mouth. "Shhhhh."

Her voice boomed around the room like she had a microphone, yet I saw none.

Jester's chest rumbled with a low growl. "I have a bad feeling about this."

"Me too." I stared at the woman, recognizing her as one of the vampires who used to work as a bartender in the pub. "She's a Night Spawn."

"Quiet." Her voice boomed and echoed off the walls, but there were no speakers or microphone.

"How is it possible for her to have a power like that?" I lowered my voice.

"This way." Prisha waved toward us, and we followed behind her to a small space at the back of the room.

I pressed my back to the rough wall and Jester moved to my side and leaned there crossing his arms over his chest. The crowd quieted down to a low hum. The woman raised her hand, and the room went silent. She smirked and her eyes darted from one side of the room to the other. "I give you . . . Marius."

The room erupted into cheers and whistles. Jester stiffened at my side like he was going to leap forward and attack.

I placed my hand on his bicep and gave it a squeeze. "Not here, not now." He relaxed a fraction, but his body still thrummed, and when Marius ran out and leapt onto the boulder, a light hiss escaped his lips. The vampires around us gave him sideways glances and started to take steps away from us. I gave his arm another squeeze. "Bring it down a notch. You're drawing attention to us."

Marius threw his arms out and gave a hearty, fake laugh. "Stop, no. Really. Come on."

His false modesty made my stomach turn. This man had just killed people, attacked the innocent for no reason, and now seemed to have a growing fanbase for his treasonous ways. The thought of this was scary. How could anyone agree with what he'd done? And yet the applause was loud and unending. When I looked at their faces, it was as if they were looking at their savior. Marius raised his fist high above his head and gave a fist-pumping motion while pressing his lips together.

"Thank you!" He gave a small bow. "It has been a challenging few days."

The crowd quieted to hear what he had to say, and I took a step closer to Jester. He glanced down at me. "I won't let anything happen to you or your sister."

"Being outnumbered doesn't make me feel better." And we were outnumbered by a lot.

Prisha swayed from side to side the way she always did

when she was nervous. I brushed my fingers against her arm and she stilled. "Sorry."

"No worries."

"Smile and wave, ladies. Smile and wave." Jester spoke, smooth and calm.

I forced myself to look as excited as the others around us. "What's that supposed to mean?"

"If they think you're with them, then no one will suspect you." He glanced at me, then turned his full attention toward Marius. When the crowd erupted into applause, Jester joined in. I followed suit.

"We will make the Night Spawn a place for all to live and prosper! Why should we dwell in the shadows just because we are relegated to the night? They have the power to change that!" Everyone looked at each other in confusion. "I've seen it! The Blood Borns are hiding their relationship with the most powerful witches to ever walk this Earth. You think they can't find some way to give us immunity to the sun? No! They could help us. They just choose not to." When the crowd seemed to hesitate in surprise and their brows furrowed in confusion, Marius lowered his voice. "I will prove it . . . when I too walk in the sunlight."

Silence.

Marius chuckled. "Don't believe me? And what if I told you those witches had the power to do it *and* so much more? It's just another thing the crown has kept for themselves. Why not spread the wealth? Why keep us locked underground?"

"Because we'd burn to death otherwise?" I muttered under my breath. Jester and Prisha both gave light chuckles.

"They want us hidden away, trapped under the boot of superiority. They made us yet they refuse to offer us the same resources they've been privileged enough to have for centuries before any of us existed. Wealth is but a construct made to keep us down!"

The crowd broke out into yells of agreement. Jester leaned in closer to me. "He's not bad."

"He's a bit too good. To be honest." This wasn't what the Night Spawn needed. They didn't need their heads filled with dreams of walking during the day or lifestyles of the rich. The truth was that the Night Spawn made up a huge percentage of vampires, and no amount of shared wealth would save us all. Yet Marius made it sound like they had an infinite amount at their disposal.

"I know many of you have seen the new underground city. And the truth is, it is lovely. They have worked hard on it." He paused for dramatic effect. "But too little too late!" He hunched over with a loud cackle that the audience mirrored. He swiped his hand under his eyes at fake tears. "But really, though, we can do better. We deserve better."

Vampires cheered his words and whistled their approval. It was like one of those political rallies I saw on TV. I didn't know how much more of this I could stomach. The very air I breathed felt toxic. Grayson and Titus worked so hard to build that city, much of it coming from their own funds to help Night Spawn vampires live a better life. Marius made it sound like they kept us in hovels, when in truth even the older Night Spawn headquarters had every available luxury. It was just dark and dated. Yet they'd taken the time to build a new one. It wasn't right, and it wasn't fair. Marius was making zealots of normal vampires based on these lies and promises of a better future he could not keep.

"I've seen enough of this." Disgust rolled through my body.

I turned for the door and Prisha was by my side in an instant. "This does not bode well."

"Not in the least," Jester agreed as he stepped around us to take the lead.

When we exited the room, we walked down the hall and turned toward the train to leave. From the corner of my eye, I spotted the woman who'd introduced Marius to the crowd. She stood with two other of Marius' loyal followers. One was a huge vampire with muscles bulging from his body like he was a bodybuilder. The longer I looked at him, the surer I was that he was the one who'd picked me up and dragged me along the tunnels after the attack on the castle. The other one was a skinny, sleazy-looking vampire with greasy brown hair and dark-brown eyes. Though I couldn't make out their words, the woman seemed to be snapping at the other two. She gave them sharp gestures and cross looks while the two of them stood there taking it with their heads hung.

I grabbed Jester and Prisha, then pulled them around a

corner and against the wall with me. Jester lowered his voice. "What?"

"Look." I motioned around the corner, pointing toward that little meeting of the minds.

Jester leaned around the corner and watched the group. A moment later he waved his hand, motioning for us to follow him. He pressed his body to the wall and we followed suit as we moved down the hall.

"Where are we going?" I whispered.

He pressed a finger to lips and shook his head. We continued creeping down the hall, and slowly it became darker and more cave-like. The three minions all continued walking until they hit a line of doors. They were lined up one after the other. Windows were on one side of them like in a precinct.

They flung the door open and marched into the room like they were about to attack something or someone. A moment later, I heard the woman's booming voice. "Who are you?" There was a faint murmur I couldn't make out and her voice boomed again. "Take him."

She marched out of the room with the huge vampire right behind her. He had a smaller vampire draped limply over his shoulder with his arms dangling over his head. Sweat soaked his clothing and dripped from his hair. The huge vampire turned toward the woman. "Now what?"

"We'll add this one to our ranks." She gave a harsh look at the two doors at the end of the hallway and her lip sneered. "I don't think the other two are going to make it. We'll clean that up later."

Not going to make it? How could they be so callous? I watched as they walked away farther into the darkness and out of sight. Once they were gone, I hurried to one of the doors and placed my hand on the knob.

Jester put his hand over mine, stopping me. "Maybe you want me to call in backup to handle this?"

"Why?"

"Because what you're going to find behind that door is not going to be pretty. And there are certain things you can't unsee."

"She said *not going to make it*." I narrowed my eyes at him. "That means whoever or whatever is behind this door is alive . . . barely. We have to help."

Prisha licked her lips and looked through the window beside the door. "Oh god, get in there now."

Jester let my hand go and I yanked the door wide open. My adrenaline rushed through my veins as I walked into the dark room. There, on the floor, was a tiny vampire. She was slight, with dark, shaggy black hair and pale skin. She wore a thin grey sweater that seemed too big for her and baggy black jeans. Her body quivered in a pool of her own blood and sweat. Her eyes were closed up tight and her head lulled back and forth as she muttered incoherently to herself.

I dropped to my knees beside her and placed my hand on her head. "She's burning up."

"We need to get her out of here. Now." Jester placed his hands under her legs and around her back. In one fast move he was on his feet with this tiny vampire in his arms.

Prisha popped her head in the door. "I think there's more."

"More?" My voice went up an octave. "What the hell is he doing to these vampires?"

Jester started for the door. "I don't know exactly, but I have an idea."

Prisha looked down at the girl. "She looks like she's caught the sickness."

"What if it's not just the sickness? What if he's doing something to them to make them sick?" I didn't want to think this possible or that anyone would do this to anyone on purpose, but all arrows pointed toward Marius, especially because his people knew where these vampires were and were taking them somewhere.

"No, it can't be." Her lips turned down into a scowl. "On second thought . . ."

"I wouldn't put it past Marius." Jester hiked the tiny vampire up in his arms.

I nodded toward the girl. "Do you recognize her?"

Prisha shook her head. "No."

I leaned over her and held her cheek in my hand. "What's your name?"

"I'm no one," she murmured back.

"We have to go." Jester headed for the door, and I followed quickly behind him with Prisha beside me.

All the while, the tiny vampire repeated, "I'm no one. I'm no one."

CHAPTER THIRTY-ONE

PIPER

My head swam as a wave of dizziness overcame me. My stomach cramped with hunger and black dots swarmed my vision. *No, not now.* I fought for control over myself. When I glanced down at the pearl on my necklace, it was slowly turning darker. I hunched over and pressed my fist to my stomach, hoping to subside the pain. I needed Grayson or his blood and I needed him now. I thought I had longer. I wanted longer to handle this. But here we were in the middle of the midlands of England with no prospect of ending this chase.

"What can I do?" Astrid hovered over me and rubbed my back.

"Cage me." I gritted out the words through clenched teeth. Sweat broke out over my body, and I felt my fangs start to throb.

"What? No, I can't." She kept rubbing small circles on my back.

"Put me in a cage. I don't want to hurt you or anyone else." I knelt on the ground and curled in on myself. Pain shot through my stomach and nausea rolled up my throat.

Astrid took a step back and held her hand over me. Golden magic sparkled all around me, and a large cage with thick bars surrounded me in an instant. I sucked in a deep breath as the waves of hunger slowly receded. I dropped down onto the ground and sat there for a moment just sucking in deep breaths. It would only get worse from here, and I didn't want to lose my shit in front of them. I just met them, and although we had a common goal, I wanted to keep these friendships. They all seemed so accepting of whatever was thrown at them and genuinely wanted to help.

Astrid squatted down on the other side of the bars and met my eye. "Better?"

"Yeah, for now." I leaned back and rested on my hands. I crossed my legs and groaned.

"Maybe if you rest? We've been looking for Grayson for some time." Beckett walked up behind Astrid. "It might subside if we give you a minute."

I shook my head. "No, I'm . . . thirsty."

Kylian chuckled. "Aren't we all."

"Pervert." I rolled my eyes.

"You seem okay now?" Astrid tried to offer helpfully. "I mean, should we take you back to The House of Shade?"

"We can't. We have no idea if Atlas is there or what is

happening. We can't go there, not until we have Gray." I turned around in the cage, looking at the field. "Just let me think for a second. I really don't want to leave. What if Grayson shows up and we're not close enough?"

"I agree." Kylian spun in a small circle. "He's going to make a move. I feel it. I'm just not sure on the direction yet."

"How could we possibly know when he's going to do something?" Panic started to thread through my body and my breath came harder. "What if he summons more demons and it works this time?"

"Don't get worked up. That can't help." Astrid bit her bottom lip. "What if we have a warning system?"

"What do you mean?" I started to relax a little.

Astrid held her hand up. A single piece of paper lay in her palm with more of that scrawled writing across it. She glanced down at it, and it exploded into flames.

A second later, a ball of flames exploded next to Beckett. He reached up and plucked the paper from midair. "You could've just asked me."

"That's not from me." Astrid crossed her arms and smirked.

Beckett held the message up and raised his eyebrows at us. "Incoming."

He waved his hand and blue smoke poured from his fingers. A swirling portal opened up right next to him and Zinnia marched through it and out into the field. Her eyes widened when she looked at me, yet she said nothing.

"Thanks for the lift," she said, winking at Beckett.

Tuck walked out behind her. He was followed by a big guy with blond hair shaved close to his head. His eyes were bright green, almost feline-like. A tiger tattoo ran down the side of his neck and disappeared under his shirt. He was by far the biggest of the guys that hung out with Zinnia and her crew. I would have found him very intimidating if he wasn't wearing a baby carrier strapped to his chest. When I looked closer, there was a tiny pug sitting in the carrier with its legs dangling out. They swung up and down with each step he took.

"Good dog," he murmured in a thick Russian accent as he petted the top of the pug's head as he stepped out.

When he looked at me, I felt like prey for a moment, and I suddenly realized that since becoming a vampire, I never felt like prey. I never felt threatened in any way. In truth, I felt like the threat. As a human woman, I couldn't say the same thing. I'd been scared to walk the night, constantly vigilant at any point in time when I was alone. Now *I* was the predator and the thing to be scared of. I almost smiled at the thought.

"Do you look like that at everyone?" the big guy with the dog asked.

"Like what?"

"Like I'm a snack." He got closer to the cage. "I'm no snack. I'm Brax."

I looked him over. "I mean, you're *kind* of a snack."

Zinnia and Astrid both busted out into fits of laughter. Tuck and Beckett both stood there staring at them, not amused at all.

Kylian raised his eyebrows. "Now who's the perv? Pot kettle much, leech?"

I shrugged. "I'm just saying."

"No, I'm not snack," Brax protested.

Zinnia placed her hand on his shoulder. "It doesn't mean she's going to attack you. It means that you're . . . you know . . . attractive."

A wide grin spread across his face, and he ran his hand over the dog carrier in front of him. "Da, I am. But I have girlfriend."

I snickered from my spot in the cage as they all stood around me like this was not a big deal to keep a vampire in a cage so it couldn't kill them. But here we were.

Brax reached into his pocket and pulled out something wrapped in a small white towel. He shoved it between the bars, then backed away. He looked down at the ground and kicked at the dirt at his feet. "Is food." His words were a deep rumble.

I was afraid to look inside the towel. "What kind of food?"

"Is rat." He shrugged.

I backed away to the other side of the cage. I scrambled to my feet and pointed at it. "Why is there a dead rat in there? Wait, it is dead, right?"

"Rat is animal no one likes." He shrugged. "Glittery vampires on movie eat animals. You will eat animal and be okay."

I shook my head. "As much as I appreciate you hunting for me, I'm going to pass."

Astrid waved her hand, and the cloth-wrapped rat disappeared. "As curious as I would be about that, I don't think *rat* is Piper's brand of sustenance."

"How can we help, Piper?" Zinnia moved closer to the bars. She smelled so enticing. Like a buffet, she had all different scents seeping from her body. I didn't know how or why. Perhaps it was all the different magics she wielded that made her smell like that. But it was getting to be too much.

Astrid motioned toward me. "First, I think we could ease her mind a bit when it comes to Grayson, and then we need to figure out the blood thing."

Zinnia pursed her lips and nodded. "How so?"

"I have an idea, but I need your help to make it work." She held her hands out and her glittery, golden magic exploded from her palms. It spun and wove together until it turned into a glowing white box with a black front.

"What is it?" Zinnia tilted her head from side to side studying the box.

"It's an alarm system." Astrid glanced toward me. "So we'll know if Grayson tries to summon a demon, and we'll know we have to get there before he does, which Kylian can point us to."

"You're asking a lot there, Red." Kylian sat down on the ground and pulled his sword from the halter at his hip. He picked up a rock and his magic flowed around it, turning it into a sharpening stone. He ran it over the blade in a rhythmic motion. "But I can do it."

Zinnia crossed her arms. "So what do you need from me?"

"I need you to put a bit of Grayson's essence in here." Astrid held the box out toward Zinnia.

Tuck grimaced. "And what makes you think she just *has* that?"

Astrid raised her eyebrows at her.

Zinnia made a sound of frustration in the back of her throat. "Sometimes I can't help it, you know? Power like that lingers in the air, and my body just kinda takes it."

"It takes it?" Tucker spoke so slowly it almost sounded disbelieving. "Zinnia."

She shrugged. "I can't help it, really."

"Anyways," Astrid cut in, catching their attention. "Just give it a little something and we'll know if Gray is doing something fucked up."

Zinnia held her hand out, and her silvery magic wrapped around the box. I watched as hints of red mist filtered in with her power and seeped into the box.

The black front lit up like a radar screen and illuminated Astrid's face. "There, now we'll know if he's up to something. Now we can work on our next problem: Piper needs to eat, and I can't just manifest up some blood. Even I have my limits."

"Can we substitute it somehow?" Zinnia went into problem-solving mode. "Oh, I know."

She pulled her phone from her pocket and hit a number, then put it on speakerphone. It rang twice before it was answered.

"Go for O."

"We need some help, O."

"Just make an anonymous call to the cops. Tell them there's a body buried there."

Zinnia did a double take at the phone. "Wait, what?"

"That way there will be an empty hole where you need it, and they've already checked the area for a body. They won't go back and check it again. Work smarter not harder, sis." She sounded like she was chewing gum. "You're welcome."

Zinnia pinched the bridge of her nose and held the phone a bit higher. "Umm . . . no, that's not why I called. I'm calling to ask if you know where we can get some blood to feed a vampire."

"Just go grab a human."

"O, no, we can't do that." Zinnia shook her head, sending those wild black waves flying around her face.

Ophelia scoffed. "Why not? Just grab a bad one who deserves it. Orrrr I could grab one and throw it into one of Beckett's portals. Oh my god. Did I just come up with a new business? Free human delivery. It's brilliant."

"I'm not delivering humans to vampires, O," Beckett called out so that she could hear.

"Listen up, cuz, no one would miss them. We'll pick the worst of the worst and send them to their fate. The vamps get a snack and the world gets rid of a terrible human. It's really a win-win." She sounded so bubbly when talking about mass murder.

"No, O." He scrubbed a hand down his face.

"Don't tell me I didn't think of ways to make you rich," she snapped back at him.

"I already am rich," he said, leaning closer to the phone and raising his voice.

"Then those are all the ideas I've got."

The phone went dead. She didn't say goodbye or any kind of warning that would suggest the conversation was over.

"That was . . . super helpful," I said.

A second later Beckett's phone rang. He didn't look at the screen before answering it. "I said I'm not transporting humans for vampire snacks, O." He paused and his eyes widened. "Oh, um, yes. Sure."

"What was that?" Astrid arched her brow at him. "It didn't sound like Ophelia."

"It wasn't." He waved his hand, and his portal opened once more.

A perfectly tailored Martin strolled through and stopped just outside the portal. He looked at me, then looked around at the others. "Oh my. I see I've arrived just in time."

I sprang to my feet and wrapped my hands around the bars in front of me. "Martin!"

He pressed his lips into a thin line as he walked through the thick grass toward my cage. Martin seemed so out of place among the rest of us. He wore a perfectly pressed navy-blue suit, a crisp white shirt, and polished brown shoes. A cross-body satchel was draped over his shoulder. He moved closer to the bars. "They've put you in a cage."

"I asked them to."

He pulled the bag from his shoulder and pushed it through the bars. "Then I've arrived just in time."

I took the bag and flipped it open. There were three bags of blood inside. My stomach tightened. I wanted to dig into them right away, but I knew what would happen if I drank the wrong blood, and I knew we didn't have time for me to lose my damn mind. "I have to be careful."

"There's a note." He pointed to a small, folded piece of paper.

I yanked it from the bag and opened it quickly. "You've got to be kidding."

'Piper,

Though we find ourselves on opposite sides of the coin, I respect your choices as I'm sure you respect my own. Loyalty deserves loyalty in kind. You love him as I do. I don't fancy having to kill my best friend's soulmate, or worse, both of you. Do take the blood and avoid the tip of my knife.

Respectfully,

Atlas.'

"It's from Atlas." My jaw dropped, but I grabbed the first bag, eager to dig in and end my hunger pains.

"Wait." Kylian sprang to his feet. "Could be poisoned."

Martin squeaked and pressed his hand to his chest. His cheeks turned pink with annoyance. "Excuse me, I would never allow that to happen."

"Right, nerdy leech, because you look like the sort to stop a killer." Kylian gave a dark chuckle. "Errand boys don't use knives to make their deliveries."

Martin narrowed his eyes. "And yet I know everything there is to know about you, Kylian. Often referred to as the Dark Prince, wanted on multiple counts of treason, and you have several bounties on your head that I'm sure anyone would be happy to collect on." Martin straightened the sleeves of his already perfect jacket. "Perhaps I don't run around stabbing things with my little knife, but there are a thousand ways to get someone killed, and I'm efficient at nine hundred and ninety-nine of them."

Kylian jabbed a finger in his direction. "Him I like."

I couldn't wait any longer. I dug into the blood bag, sucking it down quickly. The taste was perfection on my tongue. Chocolate and red wine: the flawless combination. The moment I drank, everything receded: the pain, the dizziness, the weakness. It was gone in an instant. I moaned with how delicious it was. Before I knew it, all three bags had gone down like butter and I was full. My body felt so strong because of Grayson. But deep down the desire to find him redoubled. His flavor made me miss him with every fiber of my being.

Martin took the empty bags from me and put them back in the satchel. "Good. Now come out of there. You are not an animal."

"I got it." Astrid flicked her wrist and the cage was gone.

I hurried toward Martin and pulled him in for a hug. "Thank you."

"Don't thank me." He lowered his gaze to meet mine. "Thank Atlas. Someoneeee didn't call me personally."

"I know." I wanted to but I didn't know what kind of position he was in. The last time I'd seen Martin he was fighting with Theon and I was running after Grayson.

"You have my number." He winked and pulled a mirror from his pocket. He opened it up and placed it on the ground next to where he stood. "And on that note, I'm needed by the King."

Beckett motioned toward the portal. "Can I give you a lift home?"

"No, thank you." Martin held his hand up. "That was quite a ride, but now that I know where I'm going, I can make my way back."

Beckett chuckled. "All right. Call me if you need me. Apparently you have my number."

"Like you're hard to find, Beckett Dustwick." Martin stepped into the mirror and dropped as if he'd jumped into a pool.

I was about to relax when that damn box went off. It exploded into bright lights and loud sounds.

Astrid scooped it up and held it in her arms. "Shit, shit, shit."

I turned toward Kylian. "Where?"

He gave a harsh curse and closed his eyes. "Piccadilly Circus. No, wait . . . Westminster Bridge."

My breath caught in my throat, and I nearly choked on my panic. "If The Fallen catch him there, they'll—"

"—Kill him." Beckett motioned to the portal he'd held open for Martin, "Let's go."

I didn't know what we were running into, but I charged

forward with the others hot on my heels. *Please, God, don't let him die tonight. We're so close.* I sent a silent prayer to the heavens, hoping I wouldn't be too late. I jumped through the portal and ended up in pure chaos. Humans littered the streets. They were dressed up and celebrating.

I walked out onto the bridge. When I gazed across the river, the London Eye was lit up with bright colors. The buildings behind it were also brightly lit with dazzling lights. In the distance, Big Ben stood like a golden beacon against the dark night. I glanced around at the humans all milling about. There were so many . . . too many.

"What the hell is going on?"

Zinnia turned to me with wide eyes. "I forgot. No, this is bad . . . This is real bad."

I follow her gaze. "What?"

"Piper, it's New Year's Eve and we're standing right where their fireworks are going to go off . . ." she motioned toward Big Ben, ". . . in five minutes."

Kylian tapped my shoulder and pointed across the river. There behind the London eye stood Grayson. They'd closed the walkway between the Eye and building for the fireworks show, and there was Gray laughing and dancing around behind it. He bent down low and started drawing on the ground with another paintbrush.

"Oh no!" I tensed to run when from the corner of my eye I spotted Atlas standing on top of one of the cars. He held a bow and arrow and had a clear line for a kill shot at Grayson.

I grabbed Beckett's arm. "Get me there. NOW!"

CHAPTER THIRTY-TWO

ATLAS

Breathe in, breathe out. The cord of the bowstring pressed into my fingertips as I held it tight. My arrow would strike true. I'd sharpened the point to perfection and carved the rest of the arrow myself. It would be quick. It would be painless . . . for him. My friend laughed with madness as he drew odd symbols over the ground in blood. I didn't know what he was doing or why, but I knew this one shot would change it all. He would be no more, and once the King learned of what I'd done, I too would be no more. In fact, I was counting on that exact outcome. By using this bow, he'd know I killed Grayson from a distance. There would be no accident during capture. It would be known that I, Atlas Savage, killed the Prince of The House of Shade.

A blue portal opened a few feet from Grayson and Piper sprinted out, running between the two of us and blocking my shot. The others followed closely behind her, and they started to surround him. Grayson threw his arms up and blood magic exploded out of him and landed like fog over the symbols. The ground lit beneath his feet. It shined a brilliant white light and began to rumble under his feet. The crowd across the river cheered, thinking the light show would soon start.

New Year's Eve . . . the end of one cycle and beginning of another . . . How fitting.

I kept my eye trained on Gray, yet Piper stood there blocking me. She gave her back to Grayson and whatever was happening to stare me down. She gave a shake of her head, warning me not to do this. But my vow tugged at me, pushing me toward the end. My only friend in the world would be no more simply because he asked me to do this for him.

Big Ben struck midnight, and the tolling of the clock blocked out the cheers of the crowd. Fireworks exploded all around us, filling the air with a sparkling display. Bright reds, swirling greens, and showering golds all dazzled the oblivious crowd of humans. They didn't know how close they were to death. They were too busy celebrating their lives while a mad vampire unleashed hell on them.

The ground opened up around Grayson and demons flooded from it in all different directions. It was like watching fire ants swarm from their nest, ready to attack. Their grotesque bodies were shadows of whatever life-forms they'd once been. They were slightly humanoid with longer legs and arms. Their faces were contorted into elongated shapes, like horses, but their mouths were full of jagged, sharp teeth. Drool and slime seeped from their mouths and dripped to the ground in big wads. Their skin was charred to black, and embers rose up around them as they charged out.

The others all leapt into battle. Silvery magic whipped through the demons, slicing them in half. Balls of fire flew from a guy with dark-red hair and lit them aflame, yet that didn't seem to stop them one bit. It only angered them more. Then the guy who threw the fire leapt up into the air and his body transformed into a phoenix. He swooped into the fray, grabbing demons with his large talons and throwing them back into the pit. A guy with dark, inky hair and crystal eyes placed his hand on the ground and yelled something to another guy with blond hair and blue smoke seeping around him.

A moment later, the dark-haired guy let burgundy magic seep over the ground and fifty stone bullets suddenly lay at the feet of the one with the blue smoke. He smirked, then threw his arms out. The bullets shot from the ground and peppered the demons, turning them into Swiss cheese. My jaw dropped and I nearly lost aim at the display. When a tiger and giant pug frolicked side by side through the madness, taking turns ripping demons in half and throwing the parts to each other as if they were playing catch, I was tempted to join in their fight. But I had a duty to fulfill.

The fireworks exploded all around us, and scorching cinders fell to the ground and over me, burning my skin. I held fast, not moving from my position even as pain melted over my body. Grayson stood in the middle of it all, watching the demons fight his friends. But the Grayson I knew would've joined in this fight. He would've helped his friends defeat these hell demons. The Grayson I knew would not have stood there grinning and laughing at the chaos. I had to face the fact that this was no longer the Grayson I knew. I pulled the string tighter and straightened my arrow.

Piper jumped up and caught my eye. She didn't turn to fight with her friends. No, she stood there offering her life for Grayson's. Just as I was about to drop down and take up another position, a demon leapt from the pit at Gray's feet and dove right for her. It tackled her to the ground and pressed her face to the cobblestones. A scream ripped up her throat as she shoved her hands to the stones and flipped over on her back. The demon crawled on top of her, pinning her to the ground and out of my way. It snapped its teeth in her face as she shoved her hands into its jowls, barely holding it from her face. It raised its claw over her neck, about to strike and take her head.

I had to do what was needed. Deafening fireworks boomed over our heads. The light was so bright it was like walking in midday. And when Grayson spread his arms wide and smiled at the falling sparks, I took aim.

"Forgive me, friend." I let the arrow fly.

CHAPTER THIRTY-THREE

PIPER

I held the demon off, but I'd never felt anything this strong before. The body weight alone stole the breath from my chest. I shoved my hand into its jowls, holding it back from biting my head off. Drool and slime ran down my hands and over my arms. The smell of decay seeped from its hot breath and I nearly choked on the stench. I tried to kick out, to use my blood magic on it, but it wouldn't stop. Like a mindless animal, it raised its claws above me to take my head. I sucked in a sharp breath, bracing for the strike. The air whizzed and there was a wet *thunk* sound. The demon fell limply over my chest with an arrow jutting from its head.

Its dead body twitched on top of me, and I shoved my arms into its chest and threw it off me. That arrow was meant for Gray. I knew it was. When I glanced up to where Atlas had been perched, he gave a single nod and a small solute with the end of his bow. I turned toward Grayson to grab him but he was already running down the side of the riverbank. He glanced back at me with a hiss, then he leapt into the water. I ran to the edge to see if I could spot him, but the flashing lights and smoke from the fireworks made it impossible.

Just then Astrid lifted her arms and threw her magic out. It rolled over the ground like a thick fog. Zinnia joined in beside her and the two of them forced the ground to close up, trapping the demons left above ground. The demons were turned to dust by Tucker or shot to hell by Beckett and Kylian. Soon they were all dead and I was left standing there watching the water for any hint of Grayson.

When I looked up to where Atlas was, he leapt off his perch on The London Eye and took off running down the riverbank, searching for Grayson.

Kylian walked up to my side. "If we killed that one, this would be much easier."

I shook my head. "He had the shot. He saved me instead."

"So?" He shrugged.

"So I don't think he actually wants to kill Grayson." The others began to line up next to me one by one until we all looked out over the water. "This isn't working. We're always two steps behind."

Astrid gave a reluctant nod. "I agree. We have to go about this a different way."

"As much as I hate to admit it, my hunting skills have got us there, but the execution is lacking." Kylian plucked up a small stone from the stone wall and tossed it into the river.

"I've been thinking about this." I paused to gather my thoughts. "When I was in Gray's dreams the voice mentioned someone named Dracinda. Until we figure out who she is, we need to capture him and hold him. This curse is old as hell. We're going at it with more current methods. What if . . . what if we need something old? Something as old as the curse."

Zinnia turned to face me fully. "You might be onto something."

In my bones I felt like I might be. "So where can we get old magic?"

"Beck, I have an idea. Bring us home." Zinnia slid her hand into Tucker's and let their fingers wind together.

"With pleasure." Beckett waved his hand and opened a portal for us.

I hesitated for a moment, knowing we were leaving Grayson and London behind. But I knew this would be for the better. We needed to change tactics, otherwise we would always be chasing him and fighting demons. Whatever entity had a hold of Grayson, it was smart and we needed to fight fire with fire, so I would leave here only to come back stronger. I stepped through the portal and moved so quickly we were back in Evermore in an instant.

We were in the courtyard and surrounded by the rest of Zinnia's people. They all stood around as if we'd arrived on cue. Maze stood there holding a big white box in his hand

and a white plastic fork. He shoved it into the box and came back with a big bite of cake.

"We're going on a field trip." He took another fork from his pocket and offered it to Tilly who stood at his side.

She shook her head, declining it. "I'm full from the donuts we just had."

"You've got to eat to keep your strength up."

When she only looked at him he shrugged and put it back in his pocket.

"Where are we going, Maze?" Tuck put his hands on his hips as he peeked inside the box.

Maze turned away from him and put a protective arm over the cake. "Niche and Adrienne need to go to the library in Hexia. And stop looking at my cake or I'll stab you for it."

Tuck arched his eyebrows. "Is that a fact?"

"It's your future. Make better decisions," Maze snapped at him and shoved another piece of cake in his mouth.

Brax busted out into deep rumbling laughter. "Sparkle vampires says things like this. Is very funny."

"Sparkle vampires?" As far as I knew there was no such thing. Then I thought about it. "Do you mean Twilight?"

"Da." He nodded. I didn't have time to ponder his obsession with Twilight when it hit me, we were going to a place I'd never even heard of.

"Wait, hold up a second . . . Where is Hexia? What is Hexia?" I held my hand up. I'd been so ready to jump right into their suggestions that I hadn't even stopped to ask what was happening.

Zinnia gave herself a little facepalm. "I forgot that you don't know this world yet. Hexia is the seat of the oldest witches' city in the world. Our elders are there, and it's the only witch city that stood the test of time against my father, Alataris. They have knowledge we couldn't even dream of. Our histories, our spells, and pretty much anything we might need are there. The last time I was there it was pretty amazing. Even if there was drama."

"Drama?" That was the last thing I needed.

She waved my words away. "That's a story for another time."

Serrina motioned for the others to gather in closer to us. "Listen, we have to go to Hexia, but I think you're going to need us all, at least based on what Niche and Adrienne have been telling us. The spell we are going to do is going to be something huge and will require a lot of power.

Niche ran out from one of the hallways with her bright-red hair streaming out behind her. Adrienne followed quickly behind her with a stack of books in her arms. "Wait for us."

"This is your idea. We wouldn't leave without you." I felt the need to reassure her. "What did you guys find?"

Adrienne sucked in deep breaths, then came to a stop in front of our group. "There's mention of a spell to summon a vampire, but it's old magic and anything that took the power of the Witch Queens was sent to Hexia for safekeeping until they all rose. It's got to be there."

Beckett waved his hand, and the portal opened up

behind him. "Apparently, I'm playing taxi tonight. Everybody in."

I expected the portal to open into the middle of a big city buzzing with activity. Instead, he opened it right into the library. It was huge with high-vaulted ceilings that looked like a cathedral. The walls and large columns were made of light-gray stone carved with filigree from the floors all the way up to the ceilings. Stacks and stacks of books filled the cavernous space. They were spread out in all different directions, and there was no visible way of keeping track of them.

"How do we find what we're looking for?"

Before anyone could answer me, an older-looking woman hobbled from around one of the stacks. Her head was wrapped in a white silky material that fluttered around her face. It was so delicate it almost made the wrinkles around her eyes and mouth look soft. She was so tiny that her grey dress nearly looked like a robe draped about her body. When she strolled up to us, she walked right past Zinnia and the Queens and stopped in front of Maze. She held her hand out toward him, and he reached into his pocket and pulled out a small white box. It was tied with a simple white string. The box looked like the pastry one he'd held his cake in which was now somehow nowhere in sight. She gave him a small head nod.

Maze returned her nod. "This is Gerda, the librarian."

"It's very nice to meet you, Gerda." I gave her a tight-lipped smile so as not to show my fangs and startle her.

There was something so gentle about the older woman I didn't want to upset her in any way.

Again she said nothing but gave me a warm smile and motioned for us to all stand around a long rectangular wooden table. Adrienne dropped the books on the table with a light thud as Niche helped her straighten them into a nice pile.

As we all took our places, she hobbled her way to stand between Niche and Adrienne. "Why have you come?" Her voice was lighter than a whisper. It was less disturbing than the beat of a butterfly's wings and sounded even sweeter.

Adrienne lowered her voice to try and match her tone. "We are seeking a very old text."

Niche pushed her glasses up her nose. "One to help summon a vampire. There's reference to it in this book."

She reached up and pulled a book off the top of the pile and placed it on the table in front of Gerda. She pointed toward the lines on the page.

Then Adrienne pulled the next book down and opened it to a specific page as well. She ran her finger over the lines. "And here too."

Gerda gave a light nod and placed her hand over Niche's as she reached for another book, stopping her before she could grab it. "I know of what you speak."

"Then you can help us?" Hope sprang in my chest.

She shook her head. "The request must come from the Witch Queen. It is strictly prohibited to give this spell to anyone else."

Zinnia lifted her hand. "I respectfully request this spell. Please."

"I've been waiting for you to finally come to my library, child." She waved her hand and dusty brown magic fluttered down the rows of stacks. It was like watching a small gust of wind carrying leaves in a movie. "The knowledge here will help you along your way."

"I will remember that." Zinnia paused. "And we all will visit more often."

Gerda gave a knowing smile. "I know."

That little prediction brought everyone up short. Did she know something we all didn't? Her tone implied that she did. Maze and Tilly chuckled at the same time.

Tilly shrugged when all eyes swung toward her. "She's not wrong."

Astrid glanced toward Zinnia. "You know that's a little tidbit I'm going to think about later."

"Agreed," Serrina, Tabi, and Zinnia all said at the same time.

The fluttering of pages was the first sign that something was happening, then a thud that sounded like a book slamming into something. Then more page flutters. The book sailed out from the stacks and landed in the middle of the table. Dust sprinkled all around it. Brown and dark as they were, the pages were clearly ancient. The edges weren't square like in modern books. They were jagged and frayed all along the edges.

Gerda crooked her finger at the book and it slid across

the table toward where she stood. Then she gave the same motion to the other Queens. "Look here."

We all leaned forward, staring down at the ancient book. Adrienne leaned in closer and placed her hand over the pages. "But how do you interpret this?"

Silence. We all looked up to where Gerda stood and she was gone, disappearing into thin air. Adrienne made a tiny sound of annoyance in the back of her throat. "It'll take days to interpret this. The language is ancient, as are the drawings."

Niche nodded in agreement. "But you *know* who could translate it in seconds."

"No." Adrienne shook her head. "I don't want to."

"It'll make this go so much faster."

I didn't want to force anyone to do anything that would make them uncomfortable, but time was ticking. "We *need* faster."

Tabi leaned on the table. "I hate to say this, my friend, but Niche and Piper are right. We need this as quickly as possible."

"Ugh. Fineeeeee." She rolled her eyes and groaned. "Astrid, can I please have some paper and a pen?"

Astrid flicked her wrist and a pen and paper appeared in front of Adrienne. When she wrote her note across the page, her movements were sharp and punctuated with annoyance. She folded it up and handed it back to Astrid. "Can you please send that to . . . my mother?"

The paper burst into flames in Astrid's hand. "Done."

"Now what?" I glanced around at the others. We should

be doing something else, something to move us forward. My energy bounced around inside of me, and I felt the need to go and do something. Standing here waiting wasn't on my bingo card.

Kylian placed his hand on my shoulder. "Still."

"What?"

"You're making me feel how anxious you are, and it's making me uncomfortable."

I glared at him. "Yeah, I'm not sorry."

The room went black, cutting off whatever Kylian was about to say. Shadows of creeping spiders covered the walls of the library and crawled up toward the ceiling. They weren't small, average spiders. No, these were huge with legs as long and thick as my own. Webs dangled down from the ceiling and fell all around us like curtains.

"Always with the dramatics, Mom," Adrienne grumbled.

Astrid gave a visible shudder and stepped closer to Beckett. "I hate spiders."

A shadow slowly dropped down from the ceiling. My first reaction was to kill it with fire, but then I realized it wasn't a spider at all. It was a woman who was exotically beautiful. Her skin was as dark as night with a golden shimmer all over it. Her hair was cut short to her head, and a gold diadem came to a small point between her eyes. Her lips were full and so red I thought she might've been eating cherries. Her dress was impeccable, with thick golden straps that held up a loose-fitting, shiny golden dress that pooled around her feet. She held on to the webs and used them to drop down in front of us.

She narrowed her eyes at Astrid. "And they feel the same way about you. Rightly so, I might add."

"I still maintain my innocence." Astrid held her hands up in surrender.

"Do you?" She pursed her lips. "Perhaps—"

"—Mommm, please," Adrienne cut her off.

My eyes widened in realization. This was Athena in all her perfection and glory. Power rolled off her in waves, yet she was so much calmer than Morpheus. In total control.

Adrienne pointed toward the book in front of them. "Can you please help us translate this?"

"Yes." She didn't look at the words, she just stared at Adrienne.

"What's it going to cost me?" Adrienne sighed.

"Is it so wrong for a mother to want to spend time with her daughter?" Athena pressed her hand to her chest, trying to sound so innocent. She batted her eyelashes and ducked her chin shyly.

What an act. It was almost perfect the way she phrased her request and made herself look so innocent. . . almost. If it didn't visibly make Adrienne so uncomfortable the act might've worked.

"Fine, I'll extend my trip this summer by two weeks in exchange for this one page." She slid the book toward her mother.

Athena didn't look down at it. "Three weeks. You clearly need a lesson in ancient translations."

"Deal." She shoved the book right in front of Athena. "Now what does it say?"

Athena glanced down at it, then waved her hand over it. The words and images moved on the page. She placed a long, elegant finger on the page and suddenly the spell was written in modern English. "That should help. You see this symbol here? The circle with the shapes in it? It needs to be drawn on the ground of the cell you wish to keep your vampire in. You'll need salt, bone grindings, and blood of his own. Plus, all the powers of the Queens. It will take quite a bit of magic to pull this off."

"Can he be moved once he's trapped?" I needed to know where exactly this was going to happen, because there was only one place Grayson should be in this state . . . The House of Shade.

"No, go to the dungeon you want to trap him in. Guardians outside the cell. Witches inside the locked cell. Make a circle as directed in this picture. Witches stand outside of the circle of course. Unless you want to be trapped within the circle with him. Which I don't think you do. Then perform the spell as directed. You'll need *all* the Witch Queens for it to work."

I pulled my cell from the pocket of my jeans and fired off a text to Moira. *'Prepare the cell. We're bringing our guy home.'*

Zinnia glanced down at the book. "Nova is trapped in the underworld and won't be allowed out for this."

Athena shrugged and motioned toward me. "Piper can represent death as she's already died once and is still kind of dead. Summon your vampire and he'll be trapped within that circle. Seems simple enough."

Grayson had slipped past us so many times. I needed to make sure this time it would keep hold of him. "Can the circle be broken?"

Athena barely looked at me as she spoke, as though it pained her to explain things. She held her chin up higher and gazed down her nose at me. "Who has more power than all of you? No one. So, no. Unless The Fallen want him . . . But if that's the case, you're screwed regardless."

"She does have a point." Tucker crossed his arms over his chest. "We're all in on this. We need to help Gray."

Athena didn't acknowledge his words. She only turned toward Adrienne. "Three additional weeks."

"A deal is a deal, Mother." She didn't look happy about the prospect of being trapped with her mother. Judging how cold and exacting she was, I really couldn't blame her.

My phone buzzed with Moira's response. *'The cell is ready.'*

I shoved it into my back pocket and looked at all the Guardians and Queens that had come this far to help him and were willing to do more. I sucked in a deep breath, feeling the first threads of hope. Maybe we could help him, maybe we could break this curse, and maybe I would get my love back.

"Let's bring our boy home."

CHAPTER THIRTY-FOUR

MOIRA

"See that the bars are reinforced . . . twice." I stood in the dungeon for the second time in my whole life. It had not improved in two hundred years. It was damp, dark, and ominous. I held the hem of my dress up off the floor just in case the blood and muck here decided to seep into the material. The workers moved diligently about the cell as I directed them. "Remove anything not bolted into the floors or walls." When they all looked at me nervously, I lifted my chin. "If you don't want to be here when it arrives, I suggest you make haste."

They all scurried around the cell as I looked on. I checked every corner, anything that could possibly be used as a weapon. Once they were finished, I let them hurry away. It would come out eventually about Grayson, but I wanted to protect him for just a moment longer before the vampire world found out. I stood there for a moment wondering if I should have some kind of blinds hung outside his cell to block him from view.

I felt him behind me first, then I heard the deep rumble of his voice. "Moira, what are you doing here?"

"They're bringing Grayson home." I motioned to the cell. "I'm preparing for his arrival."

"We could have others attend to this. I'm not sure . . . I'm not sure you want to see this." Titus placed his arms on my shoulders, and I found myself leaning back into him. I knew I shouldn't, I knew it was wrong, I knew it crossed a line that should never be crossed, but I needed his support now more than ever, especially when Grayson was coming home. I hadn't ever been this nervous for him aside from the day he was born.

"I brought him into this world, and while I have a breath to draw, I will remain with him in it." The cell looked bleak but I'd rather him be here than anywhere else.

"Then I will be here with you every step of the way." "The kingdom needs you right now and until something can be done about Grayson's curse, I fear you being here might consume your time and draw unnecessary attention." I reached up about to place my hand over his, but it'd be too much. Being this close was too much. I dropped my hands and folded them in front of me as a reminder to never touch him.

His grasp slipped from my shoulders, and he took a step back. "I will always be here for him . . . always."

"As you always have been." I tried to reassure him, but the truth was I needed him away from this dungeon.

"If you need me, you'll call for me?" His voice was soft and rumbling as he spoke.

"Of course." But I wouldn't call for him. In this moment Titus felt like someone else I needed to protect.

He slipped away, leaving me there. He would always be here for Grayson. And for me it was forever at a perfect distance...

∽

200 Years Ago

"No, not again! NOOOOOOOOO." The pain hit me in waves. It started off slow, just a small ache, then it built, my muscles contracting until the pressure was so intense I thought my bones would break.

"Can you not do something?" Titus snapped to the midwife.

"Your Highness, we are doing all that we can." She hovered over my body with a wet rag in hand. She dabbed it over my head, trying to stop the sweat from rolling into my eyes.

"Thank you, Sarah." I let my head fall back into the pillows. The room felt oppressively hot and I wanted the plush blankets gone from my bed.

"Yes, thank you, Sarah, for doing nothing." Titus paced back and forth beside me.

"Brother, perhaps you should step out of the room for a moment," Graymont offered as he sat in the chair up by my head. "Find your calm."

"You find your bloody calm," he snapped back.

I'd never seen Titus like this before. His hair was wild and untamed, his jacket lay on a chair across the room, and he stood by me with his sleeves rolled up to his elbows like he himself would be catching the child. Just as I was about to tell him to sit down, another contraction hit. The child was going to render me in two. I threw my head back and a scream ripped from my throat. My back arched of its own accord, and I twisted to the side, fighting to keep myself on the bed. The pain only rose—it never peaked, it never dropped off, it never ended.

My breath left me and all I could feel was the pressure racking my whole body.

Graymont jumped to his feet. "She is not supposed to look like that."

Titus leaned over the bed and wrapped his hands around my upper arms. "Breathe, MOIRA!"

He shook me and I sucked in a gasping breath so hard it hurt my throat. Tears rolled from my eyes and down my cheeks as the contraction subsided. "It was," I fought to breathe, "too much."

The two midwives huddled together, whispering on the other side of the room. Sarah and Anne were mirrors of each other, both with mousy brown hair, brown eyes, and pasty skin. In my pain-induced mind, I could hardly tell one from the other. I tried to motion toward them, but my arms were too heavy for the effort.

"Her lips are blue," Graymont snapped while motioning to me.

"I bloody well see they're blue!" Titus growled.

"DO SOMETHING," Graymont bellowed back at him.

I sucked in another breath. "Dying."

"You're not dying." Titus slashed his hand through the air. "I refuse to believe this. You are the strongest female I know."

But he was wrong. I did feel like I was dying and taking the child in my belly with me. I crooked my fingers at the midwives, summoning them to my bedside. When they glided over to us, they couldn't look Titus in the eye. My throat was dry from my screams, and I found my strength waning. "Tell him."

My voice sounded weak even to myself. Sarah cleared her throat. "She is dying, my lord."

"What?" He ran his hands through his hair and tugged at the strands. "NO! How do we fix this?"

Sarah glanced toward Anna, and she motioned toward me, encouraging Sarah to speak. "You've got to lessen some of the baby's blood in her body, my lord."

"Graymont, you must bite her," Titus ordered.

Graymont pressed his lips together and gave him a tight-lipped nod. "Very well. I'll so it."

His fingers were soft and gentle as he took my arm in

his hand and turned it over, exposing my wrist to him. "I'll try to be gentle, Moira."

"Please just do it." My words were light and breathy.

I fought to stay conscious as black dots swarmed my vision. Graymont drew his lips back from his fangs and struck quickly. I barely felt the pain. It was nothing compared to having my insides torn out. Yet when he pulled away, I still felt just as weak.

Fighting was futile. I would die on this night. I was sure of it.

Titus turned toward the midwives, his eyes wide with panic. "IT'S NOT WORKING."

"It's got to be you, my lord," Sarah implored. "You must do it yourself. The baby comes soon, and only your blood magic can match the baby's in strength."

He shook his head. "I cannot."

I reached out toward him, and he dropped to his knees beside the bed and took my hand. He pressed a feather-light kiss on my knuckles. I would ask him for the things I swore I would not. I would ask him to bite me. I would ask him to love me. I would ask him to love *us*. "My lord, please, do it now or your son will die."

Another wave of contractions started, this one worse than the last. My muscles tightened and I held on to his hand, squeezing it as hard as I could. Titus let out a roar and turned my wrist over. His teeth sank into my skin, and with that first deep draw came relief. Power surged through my body and the pain lessened to a manageable point. His blood magic flowed through my body taking some of the power from the child so I could manage this delivery.

"Well done, Your Highness," Sarah encouraged him as she bent down between my legs. "Baby's coming."

He pulled his teeth from my skin, and I shot up to a sitting position, feeling the need to bear down.

Titus never let go of my hand. "I'm with Moira and him, for always. You can do it, love."

Graymont took my other hand. "You're doing great!"

I gritted my teeth and pushed as hard as I could, forcing him down. When I felt the baby free of my body, I sagged back on the bed and sucked in deep breaths. I'd done it. "Why isn't he crying?"

A moment later, there was a light smack and the first cry of my son, my beautiful son. Anna stayed with me, helping me to finish the last steps of delivery and clean up. Graymont shoved more pillows behind my head, helping me sit up. Titus rose to his feet as he stared at the little wailing bundle in Sarah's arms.

"Go check on him, my lord."

When he got to Sarah, she handed him over to Titus, and I'd never seen the King smile so much as I did the moment he saw his son. His hands looked too big as he awkwardly held him to his chest. He swayed back and forth, rocking him. Unshed tears gathered in his eyes. "I don't believe I've ever seen anything so perfect as our son."

"Nor I." Tears poured over my cheeks and I would forever remember the sight of him holding that tiny bundle.

Graymont leaned over me and placed a kiss on my cheek. "Well done, sister."

Titus bounced gently and lowered his voice. He ran the tip of his finger over the baby's cheek gently stroking him. "And what are we to name you, little one?"

"I love you, Titus . . ." In that moment, I broke my promise to Titus. I promised not to love him out loud. I told myself I would love him enough for both of us. Now I would love him enough for all three of us. My new, perfect family.

Titus looked up at me and met my eye with a tear-filled gaze. "I love you too, Moira.

A sharp gasp escaped Graymont's lips. "Brother, no."

Titus' head snapped to Graymont, and he took one last look at the baby and handed him to his brother. "Take the baby."

I sat up straighter. "What's happening?"

Titus backed away from me, from us. He shook his head and dropped his gaze to the ground. "No, no."

"Hold on, Brother." Graymont held the baby with one hand while he drew his sword with the other. "Fight this."

Panic and fear rose in my body. I wanted to get up to run to Titus, but I couldn't move. My body was still broken from the birth. "My lord, what is the matter?"

Titus' body shuddered from head to toe, and a growl rumbled deep in his chest. Gone were the dark eyes with mahogany flecks in them. Now his eyes were ruined by red veins that forked out over the whites of his eyes. Dark circles surrounded them, and his skin paled till it was nearly blue. His fangs descended down past his lips. He ran his tongue over the tip of one and smirked at me. I didn't know what was happening to him, but he grew bigger, his muscles more well-defined. His white shirt tore from his body as he growled once more and bent to lunge . . . for me.

The two midwives jumped into his path, taking the brunt of his strength. He slashed out with his claws, cutting their necks wide open and nearly decapitating them both. Blood sprayed across his body and over the room from their jugulars. I screamed as their bodies hit the ground.

Graymont shoved the baby into my arms and turned to face his brother. "Alright then."

He leapt across the room and dove for his brother, tackling him to the ground as tears streamed down my face and I held the baby close, praying that the King, his father, my husband, wouldn't kill us both.

A GLOWING blue light drew me from my memories. I quickly swiped at the tears on my cheeks and turned toward it. I did as I always had done for two hundred years: I hid my feelings, made my face placid, and carried on no matter how much I wanted to die.

Piper walked through the portal first and hurried toward me. She was radiant with excitement. "We've got it this time, Moria. I swear he's coming home today. I can feel it."

I forced a smile on my face. "This is excellent, dear. And what of the curse?"

"We're on it." She motioned toward the portal as more people walked through. "One step at a time."

"Indeed . . . one step at a time." It is what I'd told myself for the last two hundred years.

CHAPTER THIRTY-FIVE

PIPER

*D*are I let hope spring? What other choice did I have? This had to work. We had no other options. Grayson had the powers of Queens behind him. I had to believe that meant something. When we walked through the portal, Moira was waiting for us just outside the cell. She looked odd in her perfect elegance among the horrid aesthetic of the dungeon. The walls were made from thick, rough rock, and bars ran from the top of the ceiling all the way down to the floor. The sound of dripping water came from somewhere in the back of the dungeon, and it smelled damp. The air was moist and cool. It sent a shiver down my spine.

"How . . . depressing." It was dark here, nearly black. There were no windows, and it looked like there was only one way in or out.

Kylian moved to my side and wrapped his hand around

one of the bars. He tried to jerk it free but only ended up shaking his own body back and forth. "I've been in worse."

"That is not comforting." Moira met his eye. "And you are?"

"Kylian the elf." He gave a slight bow of the head, and I found myself surprised at the blatant show of respect.

Moira blinked up at him. "The Dark Prince. How interesting. I've heard things about you."

"All good I hope." He winked.

"Hardly."

I stepped closer to Moira. "Allow me to introduce you to the Queens. This is Zinnia, she's the Siphon Queen, Astrid is the Queen of the Occult, Tabi over there is Queen of Elements, and Serrina is the Queen of Desires." I turned toward the others. "And these are their Guardians. Tucker is a phoenix, Beckett is a Warlock, and Brax is a tiger shifter. That's Maze, he's a psychic, and this is his soulmate, Tilly. And of course, Niche and Adrienne."

Moira gave them a perfect curtsy. "Thank you all for being here to help my son. It means the world to me. Forgive me, but is that a dog strapped to your chest."

"Da, he goes where I go." Brax scratched his fingers over the pug's head.

Moira's eye widened for a second, then she forced her features to go back into place. "Right, of course. Are we missing two Queens?"

Zinnia nodded. "Well, Nova, our Queen of Death, is stuck in the underworld. Ironic, I know. And my sister Ophelia will be here soon. Actually, let me give her a call."

She pulled her cell out and dialed the number quickly. It rang once and O picked it up. "Go for O."

"Where are you?" Zinnia asked.

"Why? You need an alibi?" The scraping of metal against metal sounded in the background, as if she was sharpening something.

"No, I need you here."

"Can't. I'm busy."

Zinnia sighed. "Whatever it is you're doing, just bring it with you."

"Okayyyy, but you're not going to like it." She dropped whatever she was sharpening to the ground, and it clattered there. I was going to tell her not to bring Dice here. It was way too dangerous, and she was way too fragile. Too human.

"What? No." Maze stepped forward interjecting before I could. "O, leave it there with Cross. We won't need him for this."

"Okay, creepy dude, but if anything happens to him while I'm gone, you're gonna pay for it in flesh."

Maze's eyes went milky-white. "I checked. He'll be fine."

Ophelia gave a heavy sigh. "It's always hard work when you're the glue that keeps everyone together. Cuz, toss me a portal, will you?"

"On its way, O." Beckett waved his hand and the blue swirling portal appeared in the dungeon.

Ophelia sauntered through and my jaw dropped. She was not in her normal Ophelia gear, this was Ophelia times ten. Her hair was braided into buns on the sides of her head, and she wore leather shorts and a sports bra. Weapons were strapped to both her arms, her thighs, and around her ankles. When she turned around to look at all of us gathered here, I saw that there was a sword strapped to her back that ran the length of her spine.

"The gang's all here." She wrinkled her nose at our surroundings. "In a cell. Listen, if you've gotten arrested, the answer is not to let me join you afterwards. The answer is to let me join you before you do the crime so I can make sure you don't get caught."

Moira's eyebrows shot up. "I must say, that's a new way of thinking about things."

Ophelia pointed toward her temple. "It's because I'm a mastermind."

"Indeed." Moira nodded in agreement.

"So why am I here?" O crossed her arms over her chest. Though she was the smallest one in the room, she seemed to command attention.

Niche and Adrienne stepped forward with the book.

Adrienne flipped the pages open. "We're going to do this spell and summon Grayson here to this cell."

"Is it strong enough to hold him?" Ophelia pointed toward the bars.

"I gave it a try," Kylian offered.

She gave him the once over, then chuckled. "Right, because you're that strong." She nodded her head toward me. "You, crazy vamp girl, give it a yank, then we'll really know."

Moira stepped to the side, gesturing to the cell. "She has a point."

I moved over to the bars and wrapped my hands around them. I pulled back as hard as I could, and they didn't budge. I yanked three more times and still nothing moved.

Moira gave a single nod. "Very well. What now?"

Zinnia glanced around at the group of us. "Now we do the spell while the rest of you wait outside. Except Tuck and Beckett. We might need you in here—you know, just in case."

She didn't have to say *just in case this doesn't work and Grayson tries to kill us all*.

"Here you go." Adrienne passed the book over to Zinnia. "Just follow it perfectly."

"Perfect, right, got it." She took the book. "No big deal."

Moira placed her hand on my shoulder as she passed me on her way out. "Good luck."

When the door to the dungeon swung shut with a deafening thud, I was alone with Zinnia, Astrid, Ophelia, Tabi, and Serrina. My stomach twisted into knots and nervous energy shot through my body. I knew it wasn't a cure to the curse, but this was one step closer. If we captured Gray, they might be able to figure out what was wrong with him, and that meant I was one step closer to getting him back. I might end up killing him for not telling me any of this, but I had to save him . . . before I killed him.

"What now?"

Zinnia stepped into the cell, and we all followed her in. "Now they lock us in."

Tuck reached for the door to the cell and slammed it shut. "Love the idea of locking my soulmate in with a crazy bloodthirsty vampire."

"Hey, I've got it under control now," I teased, trying to break the tension of the moment.

Zinnia reached through the bars and cupped his cheek. "Now weld it shut. Once he's in, I don't want him to get out."

Tuck looked at the bars and hesitated. "Then how will you get out?"

"I think that's why I'm here." Beckett moved in closer to him and met Zinnia's eye. "I'll make sure you get out."

Astrid blew him a kiss. "I know you will."

"Enough with the PDA. Ew." Ophelia gave a visible shudder. "Are we here to summon a killing machine or what?"

Zinnia chuckled and shook her head as she stepped back from the bars. Tuck placed his hands on the seam between the bar and the door. Fire and sparks shot from between the two as the metal melted together into one solid block. He ran his hands over it like a sculptor molding clay. It looked molten and dripping, but as he moved his hands up and down, it smoothed over, quickly turning into a thick bar. When he stepped back, he crooked his finger at me.

"Give it a kick."

I moved toward the door, planted one foot, and kicked

out with the other. The room rocked and dust fell to the ground, but the bars didn't budge. "Well done."

"Yeah, welding seems to be a new talent." He stepped back and crossed his arms. "Now for the hard part."

Zinnia waved me closer. "Join us, Piper."

The others all stood in a circle. Zinnia placed the book on the ground and pointed toward it. "O, can you draw the symbol on the ground? Do you have the stuff we need?"

"Don't ask silly questions, sis. Do I have what we need? Duhhh." Ophelia reached into her potion pouch on her hip and pulled out a vial of white powder. She shook it up and let the dust fall into her palm. She closed her eyes and cupped her hands together, holding it close to her mouth. Grey smoke swirled around her hands, and when she held her palm up, the white powder glowed. She held it up to her lips and blew on it. The powder soared up into the air and mixed with her grey smoke. It spun around in a whirling circle and started to drift toward the floor in slow motion. The tiny particles landed in a perfect circle. She waved her hand and more lines ran through the middle of it.

I tilted my head to the side. "Is that a triquetra?"

"It's the symbol that'll let us tap into the powers of the Witches that came before us and those who will come after us. It represents the stages we go through: the maiden, the mother, and the crone." Zinnia waved toward the three points in the circle.

Ophelia dusted her hands off. "Piece of cake. You're up, vamp."

"Blood of the vampire." Zinnia read part of the spell. "You're his progeny so your blood will work."

I raised my wrist to my lips and gave my skin a little nip. Blood trickled from my arm and I held it over the symbol on the floor. The second my blood hit the mark it quaked beneath our feet. My eyes widened and I held my arms out to keep my balance until it ended. "Is that right? Did I do it right?"

Zinnia licked her lips. "Everyone has to let their power flow all around us, even you, Piper, you have to let your blood magic go for this to work."

"What do I do with it?" I was so new to all of this that I wasn't even sure what to do.

"Don't you worry. Just open it up to me, and I can do the rest." Zinnia let her silvery magic flow from her hands. It wound around her body in dazzling circles and struck the center of the symbol. The others followed suit. Streams of yellow ribbons came from Tabi. They bounced over the ground until they too struck the center of the symbol. Serrina was next, and her red sparks flew across the room and landed next to Tabi's. Astrid's golden, glittering power looked more like Zinnia's, except it was more direct as it arched over the others like a rainbow and landed in the middle. Ophelia opened her hands, and her grey smoke crept over the ground like fog in a graveyard. It rolled and slithered toward the symbol.

When they all looked toward me, I swallowed down my doubts and let my power flow from my body. I reached down deep into the well of my stomach and pulled at it, letting it go little by little. Red mist seeped from my body and moved toward the symbol. It wasn't as controlled as the others, it was more like a swarm of bees moving through the room. When it hit the symbol, the circle glowed even brighter.

"Good, Piper, now don't pull back, "Zinnia warned, "no matter what happens."

"Ominous."

The second their powers mixed with mine, I felt it. It was like having my insides pulled at. It was so strong I almost fell forward onto my knees. I wobbled back and forth but managed to keep my feet under me. A buzzing sounded between my ears, and it drowned out Zinnia's words.

The wind kicked up in the cell, and I felt my hair whipping around my head. The power swirled together in an array of colors and shapes, but it started to form a man out of magic. It flashed like lightning, slowly forming and disintegrating. For a moment, Grayson flashed into the cell. He curled his fists in front of his body as he hunched slightly and bellowed in agony, then he disappeared, his scream trailing him as an echo.

"He's fighting it!" Zinnia yelled over the howling wind. "Push harder!"

I felt my blood magic being sucked from my body. It pulled at my insides and ripped at my lungs. My breath left me, and my throat closed around a scream. I would endure, I would hold this, I would do whatever it took. The others all stood with their arms spread wide and their eyes closed.

Zinnia screamed the words, and as one, our feet lifted up off the ground and power swirled around us in a sphere of magic. It grew impossibly brighter, and Grayson flashed back into the center of the symbol. This time he was solid. He snarled in Zinnia's direction and blood magic poured from him out toward her.

"No!" I forced my power to meet his and stop it before it touched her.

The sphere around us shrank toward him. I felt it melt over my body and move toward Grayson. It surrounded him like a fish in a bowl. Magical white chains shot from the ground and wrapped around his wrist and ankles. They wove like a snake around his body, up his neck, and down over his shoulders. They grew so bright I could hardly look at them. Grayson struggled against their hold, but it was futile. When his power snapped back inside him, he threw his head back and bellowed. Magic exploded out of him, and we all soared back from the circle on the ground. My body slammed into the bars and I slipped to the ground. The others too were thrown back, but they landed on their feet and skidded to a halt.

Those white chains burned into his skin and smoke drifted up toward the ceiling. Grayson fell to his knees, his shoulders hunched over. All at once the magic stopped and the magical chains faded into his skin, letting us know that magic would hold him there.

I scrambled to my feet and sucked in a deep breath. "We did it!" Elation ran through my body. "We really did it!"

The others all stood there looking like we'd just run a marathon.

Grayson's face snapped up to mine. His voice was deep and rough with an edge of aggression to it. "Hello, Piper."

It sounded like him but didn't. My brow furrowed. "Gray?"

"Let me out, Piper." He looked manic with wild black eyes and red veins all over his face. His tongue darted over his lips, and he snarled at me.

The others moved to my side, and Ophelia gave me two awkward pats on the shoulder. "Want me to sew his mouth shut?"

"Dare you," Gray hissed in her direction.

Ophelia met that hiss with a wide, psychotic smile. She reached into her potion pouch and pulled a vial with a needle and thread in it. "With pleasure."

"O, no." Zinnia held her hand out, stopping us from getting closer to him. "No one goes near him. Beck, get us out of her. Now."

A blue portal opened up on the other side of the cell, and we all hurried toward it. Grayson leaned forward, but the circle under him illuminated and he was thrown back into place. We hurried through and ended up on the other side of the bars. Beckett quickly closed the portal, and we all stood there just staring at Gray. He was a shadow of himself. His movements were jerky as he turned his head from side to side, talking to himself incoherently. He rocked back and forth with his arms wrapped around his body. I hated seeing him like this. The others all just stared at him in silence.

The dungeon door creaked open, and Moira walked in with Maze and Tilly right behind her. The others all followed her in, and Brax slid the dungeon door shut behind them. Moira moved to my side, looking like she was fighting to keep her face passive, but when her lip started to quiver and unshed tears glistened in her eyes, I felt myself almost wanting to cry with her.

She dabbed her finger under her eyes. "What now?"

Zinnia cleared her throat. "Now we try to get the damn thing out of him."

"What about what the voice said? Bring him Dracinda and he will free Grayson." I didn't know why those words kept lingering in my mind, but I couldn't seem to stop thinking about them.

"Dracinda?" Moira's eyebrows shot up.

"You know her?"

"Yes but," She paused and glanced around at us. "She's dead."

"What? How?" That couldn't be possible. I wanted all the details and why this voice was obsessed with this Dracinda person. It had to mean something.

"I doubt whatever he's hearing could be trusted. We need to focus on what's in front of us now." Zinnia sounded so confident.

"How?" Moira tried to sound confident, I could tell that she did, but her voice quivered ever so slightly. I couldn't imagine what it must be like to watch her child in this state and know that she'd lost her soulmate to this very same thing. The threat of death was very real to her, much more real than it was to any of us.

"Like this." Zinnia opened her hand and her power flowed from her body. It drifted over the floor and wrapped around Grayson. "I'll siphon it out of him now that we've got him."

"No!" But it was too late she already surrounded him with her silvery power.

Gray threw his head back and bellowed to the ceiling. Blackness flowed through Zinnia's power right toward her. The moment it touched her skin, she sucked in a sharp breath and her eyes rolled into the back of her head. Her body fell to the ground. Convulsions racked her from head to toe, yet the flow of magic didn't break off between her and Grayson. Everyone leapt into action at once, trying to get to her.

"Back up!" Ophelia reached into her potion bag and pulled out a vial. It was a glittering purple liquid. She pulled the cork out with her teeth and dumped the contents over Zinnia's face.

Zinnia stopped convulsing and her body went limp. She sucked in a deep breath and rolled to her back as if she was sleeping. Tuck staggered back and hunched over and vomited . . . tar.

Astrid threw her hand out and a bucket appeared in front of him. "What the hell is this? Beckett?"

"Dark, dark shit." He turned to Ophelia. "Any ideas?"

"How would I know? I'm not the one killing them with

black magic!" She reached into that pouch and began rummaging around. "If I was they'd be dead already."

Moira pushed her out of the way and dropped down to her knees right next to Zinnia. She held her hands over her and a pinkish mist flowed into her body.

For a few moments it looked like nothing was happening, then Zinnia's eyes fluttered open and she sucked in a deep breath. "What happened?"

"You're an idiot." Ophelia shoved her shoulder. "I thought we all agreed that the only one who gets to play with dark magic is the most responsible one: me."

Tucker stood up straight and ran his hand over the back of his mouth. Sweat beaded his brow, and his skin was sickly pale. "I don't usually like to say your sister is right but . . ."

"From now on we do not test any magic on Grayson until we discuss it." Astrid held her hands out like she was stopping traffic. "To avoid any of whatever the hell that was."

Moira rose to her feet. "I quite agree."

I nodded. "The only way we're going to help Grayson is if we all work together and get as much information as we can, then we form a plan and do it."

They all nodded in agreement.

Grayson just cackled. "Come on. Let's play. I wanna play."

Moira turned to face me, and her face turned deadly serious. "Piper, there's something I need to tell you. Actually, I need to tell all of you."

CHAPTER THIRTY-SIX

MOIRA

I hadn't spoken these words to anyone ever. I swore that I would take them to my grave when the time came. The world would never know the truth, yet here I stood about to tell them exactly what happened all those years ago and how things came to be like this now. My son was mad with dark black magic, and I could no longer bear to see him like this. These powerful Queens were going to help him, and I truly believed they'd do everything in their power, which meant I had to do everything in mine.

"Piper, there's something I need to tell you. Actually, I need to tell all of you."

"You can tell me anything." She was so lovely, caring, and beautiful. The perfect soulmate for my son.

I glanced toward the dungeon door. "What I have to say cannot go beyond this room."

Serrina opened her arms wide and red sparks covered

the walls. "Anyone outside this room will have the sudden desire to walk away and not listen to a word you speak."

The reassurance made me feel better, like I could trust them. "I am trusting you with the most delicate information of my life. And up until this point, I am the only person who has a memory of the events I'm going to tell you about."

Piper took a step closer to me and rested her hand on my arm. "Whatever it is, I just want you to know that I trust the Queens and Guardians."

"We want to save Gray as much as you do." Zinnia rose to her feet. "I swear it."

"Very well. What is it the kids say these days? Oh yes, buckle up." I knew if I didn't tell them the whole truth, they'd get themselves killed dealing with this curse.

200 Years Ago

THE BABY SQUEALED and squirmed in my arms. He was so strong and held the looks of his father. Sometimes it was difficult to see those mahogany eyes staring back at me. Titus only had flecks, but Grayson had full, deep mahogany eyes. Even the tiny hairs on his head matched Graymont and Titus' hair. My heart sank at the thought that he would never know his father, the man I'd grown to love in so many ways.

Graymont stood beside me with his arm wrapped

around my shoulder. He gave me a little squeeze. "We will see to it, Moira. We will have him back."

"The way he just killed those two midwives." I shook my head. "I can't put the image out of my mind."

"I've written to The Fallen, letting them know of our situation. They're on their way now."

Titus bellowed from the cell, the madness wracking his mind and body. He'd ripped most of his clothing from his body, leaving him only in his trousers. Deep scratches marred his body from where he'd hurt himself. Rivers of blood covered his body and flowed down the sides of his face. The bed I'd had brought down was smashed to pieces. They littered the cell. He paced around in circles, muttering to himself words I didn't understand. The sight would forever haunt my nightmares. Yet still I found myself willing to do anything to have him back. Grayson let out a little wail in my arms, and Titus charged the bars, ramming his head against them. His breath hissed through his teeth, and he bared his fangs at the two of us. I curled my arm over the baby and took a step back from the bars.

Graymont stepped between us and blocked Titus' vision. "Control yourself, Brother."

"Perhaps I should give the baby to the nurse?" I rocked him back and forth. "He seems to make him more crazed."

"Yes, let's get my nephew to the nurse."

We turned for the dungeon door, and there stood two of The Fallen. Matteaus was covered in battle armor from head to toe. Tristen was by his side in very much the same gear. They both looked down at me with grave expressions, as though my mate had died, but he hadn't, and I refused to accept this situation.

I froze. I hadn't heard them enter. They were silent, despite their hulking black wings and overpowering energy. I gave a deep bow to Matteaus. "Thank you for coming."

"I would always come for one I call a friend." Matteaus placed his hands on my shoulders and raised me up to stand before him. "And for you, Moira."

Tears sprang to my eyes, and I held them at bay. "Please, is there anything, anything, that can be done?"

They turned toward Titus' cell watching him in his madness. "If only I could. But you know we can not interfere with this."

"Please." I held Grayson tighter in my arms. "He'd only just become a father. He deserves this life."

"None more than I believe that he does. But this curse is based on love, and he loves you more than anything." Matteaus gave me a sad smile. "For most, a blessing. For you and Titus, a curse."

I'd only wanted to love him enough for both of us. In my selfishness, I'd done this to us. I'd done this to him. "So my love did this to him?"

"No." Graymont slashed his hand through the air. "That's a load of bollocks. Dracinda did this to him, not your love and not his love for you. It was done by a bitter, loveless hag."

Tristen nodded. "You are correct, and yet it was the love

that triggered the curse to activate. I have never known love to be a blessing."

"Now who savors of bitterness?" Graymont ran his hand through his hair and pulled at the strands with a frustrated yank. "The Angel of Love who doesn't actually believe in love."

"If my love did this to him, then take it away," I pleaded. "Please, if you take it, if you make me not love him and him not love me, then he might come back."

Tristan gave me a sad smile. "Would you be able to live in such a way?"

"To have him back, I could live in any way. I would stand next to him as a friend day in and day out just to have him, for Grayson to have his father." Desperation made me want to make these promises, but deep down I didn't want to lose Titus. He'd been the best part of my life. But for my son to have his father, I would live as a friend. For Titus to have his life back, I would endure him being only feet away from me but never to touch him, never to love him again. "Please take it from me and be done with this."

Matteaus gazed at Titus, and his lips pressed into a hard line. He hung his head. "I cannot take this curse. It's in his blood so deep now it's got a hold on his entire body."

I didn't have the words to answer him. I wanted to scream. I wanted to cry. He was the most powerful being to walk the Earth, yet he could only stand there and do nothing. Anger ran through my body. I didn't know where to direct it—at him, at myself, or at the witch who did this to us all? The truth was that there was enough rage for me to aim it at all of us. I was angry for losing my love, I was angry at them for keeping this a secret, I was angry at how helpless we all were, and I was angry that my brand-new baby came into the world on the very same day that we both lost everything. It was no way to start a life.

I turned toward Tristan. "And you, what about you? Can you take my love and be rid of it? Will that end this?"

I had to think of something, do something. I couldn't stand by and watch him slowly descend into madness and eventually die.

Matteaus shifted from one foot to the other. "We cannot. I fear our presence here is only upsetting you all more. We will take our leave and check in at a more convenient time."

When would there be a convenient time? I reached out and grabbed on to Tristan's arm as he turned to follow Matteaus out the door. "Please."

"That's not the kind of magic *I* can do." He glanced over my head toward Graymont and stared at him for a moment before he turned and left for the door.

I felt my legs start to give out. How could they not have helped? They'd been friends for ages.

Graymont caught my arms and held me up. "Do not give up hope, Moira. Did you not hear what he said?"

"They said they wouldn't help us. How could they after they'd been friends for so long?" I held the baby a little too tightly in my arms and he gave a little cry. I loosened my hold and tried to sway to soothe him, though I myself felt as though the world was coming to an end.

"No, he said that's not the kind magic *he* can do. It doesn't mean someone else can't do it."

"But we barely have relations with the witches because of Alataris. How could we possibly . . ." My eyes widened. "You don't think *he* could, do you?"

"I think he could, and I think he would." Graymont perked with excitement. "Put the child to bed and meet me back here in moments. I will have him here, and we will see what can be done."

"Do you think this will work?" I didn't dare hope, not after what The Fallen had said to us.

"I think we have to keep trying and never give up." He hurried for the door.

I turned back toward Titus. "I know you're in there, my love. Please fight it for us. Please."

In answer he arched his back and threw his head back, bellowing toward the ceiling. His screams echoed off the walls and shook the castle. I hurried out the door and moved through the castle like a ghost. Everyone looked at me with pitying glances as I hurried by. They knew their King had gone mad and I was the dutifully wife who stood by him. When I reached the nursery, I went through the motions of handing the baby over and making sure he was okay, but my thoughts were already trying to get back to Titus. I didn't recall the walk back to the dungeon or anyone I'd spoken with. My mind was focused only on getting back to Titus and Graymont to see what could be done.

I arrived just as Graymont and Marius walked into the dungeon. I stopped before the two of them and held my breath. "Can you do it?"

Marius glanced through the bars at Titus. "The curse and the magic run deep. It will take dramatic effort on both your parts."

I reached for his hands and cupped them in my own. "I swear you will have anything you desire if you do this for us."

"As you know, I've kept my magic hidden. I would prefer Alataris not hear of this. It is why I've chosen to live among the vampires though my warlock power would love nothing more than to be used more readily." He glanced between the two of us. "I must admit it was a blessing to befriend you both in such a time of need."

"Marius, what we're asking . . . it could be dangerous," I tried to warn him. "They said the curse is in his blood."

"If that is the case, then we must be rid of that blood." He said it so simply, like draining the Vampire King was just as easy as that.

"He will surely die." Graymont shook his head. "We don't want to kill him."

"I didn't say drain him dry. We have to replace it with new blood, royal blood . . . family blood."

Graymont's eyebrows shot up. "You want to take his blood and replace it with mine?"

"In theory, if you exchange blood, then your body

won't react to the curse. As lovely as Moira is, you're not in love with her." Marius motioned between the two of us.

"Yes, but once his blood is clean. what's to stop him from falling to the curse again once he wakes?" I didn't want to go through this again. I wanted to ensure my family was protected.

Marius steepled his fingers and pressed his mouth to them. "That's going to be the tricky part, I'm afraid."

"*That's* the tricky part? Not the blood exchange?" This all seemed so far-fetched.

"My particular magic is very strong when it comes to memory. In order for this to work and for the curse to not come back, we have to make Titus believe he never loved you. He must think you were only ever friends."

My jaw dropped. "You want to rid me from his memory completely?"

"Yes, it's the only way to ensure he won't fall once more." Marius nodded.

"And what about Grayson? He's his son. We can't just hide a baby from his father!" He was only days old, and this was his start. I wanted the best for him, and now he was getting erased from people's memories after barely coming into the world. And how would that affect him as he got older?

Marius nodded toward Graymont. "You tell her."

I looked back and forth between the two of them. "Tell me what?"

Graymont took my hand in his and held it while

catching my eye. "We're going to make Titus think that Grayson is mine and that you were my wife."

"Have you both gone mad?" I pulled my hand free of his. "That is insane."

"Think about it, Moira. Grayson looks like us. Titus will remember you, and you can stay here in the castle. Grayson will be close to his father, even if he thinks of him as an uncle."

I slashed my hands through the air. "This is . . . Graymont, what of the life you want? Don't you want children of your own? A family of your own?"

"No, absolutely not." He shook his head. "Moira, you're my best friend. I love my brother. To me there is no choice left. You will have a life here, and so will Grayson. To me there is no other option. Let me do this for you."

"Of course, you will have to remain friends with Titus. You can never let him love you, and you can never tell him you love him," Marius added. "It is the only way to avoid this from happening again."

I turned toward Titus as he rammed his head into the bars once more. This time his skin split and blood trickled down the side of his face and into the corner of his lip. His tongue darted out and he tasted it. I couldn't imagine he would last much longer with the way he was abusing himself. Or worse, he'd hurt someone else. I wanted his son to know him, no matter what capacity that was in. But could I hide my love? Live a life at a close distance? For both my husband and son . . . I would do anything.

"Very well." Either way, I'd lose my husband, my love, tonight. But at least he would gain his life back.

Marius reached into the pocket of his suit coat and pulled out a hand full of blue powder. He walked over to the bars and kicked them, getting Titus' attention. When Titus charged for the bars, he lifted his hand and blew the powder into his face. Titus jerked back, rubbing at his face for a moment before his eyes rolled into the back of his head and he collapsed to the ground.

Marius motioned to Graymont. "Help me get him into the other cell and strap him down before he wakes. That powder won't last long on him."

"We're doing this now?" My eyes widened.

"You'd prefer we wait until he actually kills himself?" Marius rushed into the cell and placed his hands under Titus' shoulders while Graymont got his legs.

I hurried to the other cell door and swung it wide open. "I suppose not."

They carried him into the cell and laid him on the table there.

Graymont took the thick metal bindings and wound them around Titus' legs and arms. He stood beside his brother and gazed down at him. "What next?"

Marius moved closer to him. "I need you to hold your hands over his heart and let your own blood magic flow. I will guide it where it needs to go."

Graymont held his hands over Titus and closed his eyes. Red mist drifted from one of his hands and Marius grabbed his wrist. White magic drifted down like spiderwebs from Marius' hand and wound around Graymont's wrist. They shot down toward Titus like an arrow and right into his chest. Titus' body jerked, and I found myself stepping closer, but Marius shook his head and I stopped, holding myself still.

Blood ran up his white web-like magic toward Graymont. Marius moved to his other wrist and placed his hand there. More of the white webs wrapped around Graymont's wrist and shot down toward Titus' chest. This time drops of blood flowed from Graymont into Titus. It was a give and take. Graymont looked as though he was going to vomit. His face turned a sickly pale and he staggered forward.

"Gray." I took a step forward.

Marius held his arm out to stop me. "He can hold on long enough. If you touch him, it won't work."

"He looks dreadful." I didn't want anything to happen to Graymont. He was my friend and Titus' brother. He brought light and fun to our world of duty and honor.

"He's filtering cursed blood with his body. Of course he does." Marius moved to stand next to Titus' head.

He leaned his elbows on the table and held his hands on either side of Titus' head. The magical white webs shot from his fingertips and right into Titus' temples. They glowed white and looked like little white drops of magic going into his head one by one, as though Marius were placing the thoughts into his mind and leaving them there. An eerie feeling settled over me and I couldn't shake the feeling something was going to go wrong.

When Graymont's body started to quake and sweat poured from him, I hurried to Marius' side. "Stop this now."

"It's too late. We can't." He spoke through gritted teeth.

Titus' eyes flashed wide open and every muscle in his body went tight with tension. Every alarm bell went off in my mind. I moved closer to the table, but I didn't want to touch any of them, not when they were all tied together with magic. Titus jerked in the chains and red mist exploded from his body. The webs that were taking blood from Titus snapped from Graymont's wrist. Blood poured from Graymont's other wrist and flowed right into Titus.

"STOP THIS NOW!" I screamed toward Marius, but Titus' blood magic was expanding.

Graymont fell to his knees and bellowed in pain. Blood flowed from him to Titus. He tried to jerk his hand away, but those webs of magic were more like chains. Marius' hands were glued to Titus' head. He tried to stand up and pull away, but he was pulled closer by the blood magic. The chains around Titus snapped and flew around the cell. Magic exploded out of Titus in a huge wave that shook the entire castle. Dust rained down on us all, and the bars cracked from the force of the explosion. Shards of chains snapped across Graymont's chest and face, cutting his skin wide open. Yet blood didn't flow from his wounds because Titus was draining him dry. Titus leapt on top of the table and the last drops of blood sucked from Graymont's body and went right into his heart.

Graymont dropped to the ground beside the table. His

body lay there completely lifeless, with his eyes wide open but completely sightless. I ran to his side and dropped to the ground. "GRAYMONT, NO!"

I placed my hands on his chest and felt nothing, no heartbeat, no breath. Titus turned toward Marius and leapt off the table.

Marius backed away from him. "Now, Titus, we were only trying to help you."

Titus moved toward Marius, hunting him down. He darted across the room and wrapped his hands around Marius' face. He jerked him against his body and sank his teeth into Marius' neck. Blood trickled from the bite, and Titus pulled in greedy sucks, taking as much as he could. *No!* I wouldn't stand by and watch as he killed someone else in front of me. He was too distracted by his thirst and drinking. I ran up behind him and placed my hand on his chin and the back of his head. I jerked his teeth free from Marius and twisted as hard as I could, snapping his neck. Titus' fell to the ground at my feet. I stood there among a room full of bodies. The only one I knew would survive was Titus.

I ran to Marius and placed my hand over the wound on his neck, but he was too far gone. Warlocks didn't heal from things like this. I crawled to my hands and knees, shaking as I held them over his body. I called on my own blood magic and pink mist covered his wound. But nothing happened. "No! No, come on. No. Oh god, no."

His breath was shallow and soon he would be dead. I didn't know what else to do, so I bit my own wrist and held his mouth wide open. I let my blood trickle down his throat then forced his mouth shut. With his last dying breath, he swallowed it. I let him lie there on the floor as I crawled over to Graymont. I pulled his lifeless body into my lap and held him there, letting my magic flow over him and praying that he would heal from this. I rocked him back and forth as tears poured down my face.

"Come on, Gray. Breathe. Just breathe." I didn't know how long I held him there, but I couldn't let him go, couldn't stop rocking him as I held him and just cried.

Silence.

I waited for them to say something. But they didn't move, didn't speak. I tried to drown out the others and just focus on Piper. Her jaw dropped. She snapped it back shut and shook her head. Her eyebrows shot up, then she straightened her features. "I, um . . . What?" She held her hand up, stopping me from talking. "What I mean to say is WHAT?"

"I know it's a lot—" I started.

"A lot doesn't even begin to cover it." She started pacing. "So, Titus is Grayson's real father?"

"Yes," I answered honestly.

"And everyone thinks Graymont is really his father because . . ." She trailed off, waiting for me to finish.

"My theory is when Marius' magic mixed with Titus', it backfired and spread over the entire kingdom. I waited for someone to say something, anything. But they never did. They all just said their condolences for Graymont. For better or worse, I went with it. Because when Titus woke up, he didn't remember a thing."

Zinnia raised her hand, looking like she was about to explode with questions. "So Titus has no idea he's Grayson's father?"

I shook my head. "No."

Ophelia sauntered around me in a little circle. "Well, well, well, Moira with the surprises. Bagging two brothers. Impressive."

"I didn't bag two brothers." I threw my arms up. "Really, were you not paying attention?"

Ophelia winked at me. "Then you played friends for two hundred years? That's badass."

"It saved my son and my husband. What else was I supposed to do? There was no other choice. If I stayed, then at least I had some semblance of a family and Gray had his father."

"I mean, I get it . . ." She paused and her face fell. "I think."

"So Marius was a Warlock?" Beckett crossed his arms over his chest.

"And you're his sire?" Piper continued pacing.

"I buried him just outside the castle walls. I didn't know what would happen, if he would rise or not, but when he rose, I knew I was. I've been watching him, and I still can't tell if he knows what happened or not." I shrugged. "But he changed after that. He lost his magic and it did something to him in his head."

"It would do something awful to any of us." Serrina glanced around at the group. "Our magic is who we are. I would imagine he's been harboring some resentment."

"You think?" Piper rocked back and forth as she paced. "I mean, he's got two hundred years of resentment built up, and he attacked the castle on Christmas. I'd say he's pissed off."

I sighed. "But the truth is, it was all his idea. He didn't wait. He didn't think it out. He just acted."

Zinnia held her hands up in surrender. "Point taken."

"I don't know about you guys, but my mind is blownnnn." Piper hunched over and sucked in a deep breath. "Titus is Grayson's real father and your husband. Graymont is only his uncle and wasn't even killed by the curse. Marius was a warlock and now a vampire with a vendetta. And you have been holding on to this by yourself for two hundred years. Oh, Moira . . . I'm so sorry."

It was the first time I'd been able to talk about any of this. I blew out a long breath and tears fell from my eyes. "It feels good to get it off my chest. I mean it's so silly. Titus and I didn't even like each other when we first met."

"I somehow find that hard to believe." Piper waved her hand through the air. "You've been by his side this whole time and never even tried to tell him once."

"I didn't want to lose him to the curse again. And I knew if he knew he would try to make it right. And there is no making this right." I gave a humorless chuckle. "He used to sneak out of the castle and come to my home to find me wandering around in the forest to spend time with me. It was a lifetime ago and all seems so trivial now."

"No Moira, none of this is silly." She shook her head.

I hated to admit to any of this. "In truth, it has been very lonely."

Piper hurried toward me and wrapped me up in a tight hug. "I bet." She froze in my arms and pulled back. She quickly shoved me behind her and turned to face into the darkness of the dungeon. "There's something back there."

The others all let their magic flow around them, ready to attack. I sucked in a sharp breath. "*What* is that?"

CHAPTER THIRTY-SEVEN

ATLAS

I held my hand up and stepped from the shadows, letting it peel away from me. I moved into the light where they all could see me. The dungeon had many secrets, one of which was a way for me to get in that no one else knew about. Lying in wait was my specialty. I hunted for my prey and then waited for the perfect moment to strike. The idea had always suited me well, and tonight it had once more.

Moira stepped around Piper. "Atlas, what did you hear?"

What hadn't I heard? "Everything."

"You swear to me right here and now it does not go beyond this room," she snapped at me.

I pressed my hand to my chest. "You have my word, Moira. And you know I always keep my word."

Zinnia raised her hands and glowing silver magic ran

up and down her arms. "Yes, I remember how well you keep it."

"Secrets." Grayson cackled wildly. They startled, as if in his silence they'd forgotten he was there. "Mother, all the secrets." He rocked back and forth, biting at his nails and spitting the pieces all over the cell. His eyes were wide and unfocused. "She's got secrets."

Piper stepped to the side so I could see her perfectly. "What are you doing here, Atlas?"

"I came here to kill him," I answered honestly.

"You came here to do *what*?" Moira put her hands on her hips. "Atlas Savage, you had better not be saying what I think you're saying."

"Oh, he is." Piper crossed her arms, and for a moment she looked like the little sister who was tattling to mother.

"I heard everything you said, and it's given me the hope I scarcely allowed myself to have." I wasn't lying. I'd never thought for one moment that Grayson would survive this. Though he looked madder than anything I'd ever seen, I knew now there might be a way.

"What about that story gave you hope?" Ophelia sat down on the ground and pulled one of her knives out. She placed the tip of it on the floor and held the hilt with her pointer finger. She flicked it and it spun around. "And it better be good or this knife will find a new home in your rectum."

Tucker wrinkled his nose. "Ew. Graphic."

"I've been studying body parts. That's just the first one

that came to mind." She peeked up at me. "Based on his answer, the parts might change."

She let her eyes drift down to my bollocks, and I fought the need to cover myself. But I stood still. "If Titus could survive this, then so can Gray."

"He took all the blood Graymont had, and it killed him." Moira's hands were still on her hips. "Do you think Titus would be able to live with himself if he knew he killed Graymont?"

"That's not what's important." I was sorry for their loss. Deep down, I felt Graymont's death too much for a vampire I'd never known but always heard about. Somehow losing him felt like a loss that they all felt every day, which meant that I felt it too.

"Grayson would need a blood relative to drain and replace his own cursed blood. There are no more living relatives in The House of Shade," Moira pointed out.

"That you know of," I countered. "Rakes were in abundance for quite some time within The House of Shade. How do you know one of them hasn't begotten a bastard?"

Moira's eyes widened. "Atlas, you can't possibly be thinking of . . ."

"That's precisely what I'm thinking." I would do anything not to have to kill my best friend. Anything. "I will hunt one down, and they will be sacrificed. Grayson will live."

"Whoa. Hold on a second." Piper held her hands up. "That is not what he'd want."

A guy with milky-white eyes and neon-green magic

chuckled from the back of the group. "Are you sure that is what you want, Atlas Savage, last member of The House of Savage?"

"I don't believe I've made your acquaintance." I'd seen a lot of things, killed a lot of things, but the power that these supernaturals wielded was something I'd never expected.

"No, but I've made yours. I'm Maze." He gave a dark chuckle. "Be careful what you wish for, Sav. You just might get it."

"I'm used to getting what I want. In this I will not fail. I never had an inclination to kill my best friend. In fact, the mere thought of it pained me so. But hearing Moira made me realize I didn't have to do the one thing I'd loathe myself for eternity over. For that, I am grateful." I gave Moira a small bow.

"When this is over, you and I will speak on this in great detail." Moira glared at me. "I am not pleased with you, Atlas."

Her words struck me, and for a moment I felt like a child being scolded by his mother. "Of course, Your Highness."

"So you want to just grab a dude, steal all his blood, and give it to Grayson so he will live?" Ophelia tilted her head to the side, studying me.

"Essentially."

She jumped to her feet. "I'm in."

The redheaded witch spread her arms out wide. "Hold on. No one is killing anyone. If anything, we've learned that with this curse, we do not act rashly."

"You're all fools!" Grayson's voice turned deadly serious. It was darker and smoother than his normal tone. It was almost a voice I didn't recognize. "I'm going to kill you all for getting in my way."

"Are we really going to trust this guy?" A dark-haired elf pointed a knife in my direction. "After all that he's done."

Piper gave me a scrutinizing look. I arched my eyebrows at her. She of all people would know I never wanted to hurt Gray. "You know I had the kill shot."

She gave a heavy sigh. "As much as I'd like to say no, he can be trusted. He had the shot, and he didn't take it. He loves Gray as much as any of us here."

More so. Before I could answer, a loud boom sounded from outside the castle and the walls shook. Dust and rock fell from the dingy ceiling. "What the devil was that?"

Another boom like a battering ram hitting the side of the castle crashed all around us, and when I looked at the others, they all had the same face I did. We were under attack. The dungeon door flew open, and a small maid ran into the room. She was tiny and round with dark hair and a tear-stained face. Her cleaning uniform was covered in dirt.

"You must come quickly. They've taken the King!"

CHAPTER THIRTY-EIGHT

PIPER

"They've taken the King!" The maid ran into the room pointing toward the doors.

The group didn't hesitate. We all turned and ran for the door.

"We have to split up and check all the exits," I called out toward them as another loud explosion sounded from outside.

Zinnia barked out orders, sending her people to all corners of the castle. "Cover the outside and inside! Spread out!"

They all sprinted in different directions. It was chaos. The explosions came louder and faster now, each one hitting the side of the castle and rocking it. The sound of screams from the vampires inside echoed up and down the halls as they too ran for cover. Members of the court huddled in corners as I ran by, while the staff that worked there fled down toward the basement. When I reached the main level of the castle, I looked up and down the hall.

The little maid appeared out of nowhere. She waved her hand at me. "Come on, miss, I saw them go this way!"

She ran down the long hallway and took a turn down toward the throne room. I hesitated, why would they go to the throne room? She waved me on and picked up her skirts to run through the doors. I slowed my pace. Something didn't feel right about this, yet I took cautious steps forward. When I entered the throne room, it was completely empty, but there were no signs of a struggle or anything.

"Pssssst." She was pressed against the back corner, peeking around a doorway I'd never seen before.

I crept closer, regretting the decision to come here by myself. I should've brought backup, but we'd all run into the fray without a backwards glance. "What's in there?"

The little chubby vampire turned around to face me. One minute she was the little vampire with a round face and big eyes, and in the next her body morphed into a tall, statuesque ginger-haired woman with dark-brown eyes. When she looked at me, a sneer covered her face and a deep chuckle rumbled in her chest. Five other vampires strolled out from that one dark opening. They moved slowly, arranging themselves in a circle surrounding me. They were all dressed similarly with black shirts and combat pants, as if they were some kind of army.

I opened my hands and let my blood magic flow. "Bring it, bitches."

The redhead came at me first, swinging her fist toward my face. I ducked under it and threw my magic at her. She turned to stand in front of me like a shield. With the flick of my fingers, I used her body as my own personal puppet. She punched and kicked at the others any time they got near me. A cackle ran up my throat, and I knew I could take them all this way. They were no match for my power, and I would make them regret walking into this castle to ambush me.

The vampire standing in front of me glanced over my shoulder, and a wild smile spread across his face. I turned to look when a thick metal pipe came right for the side of my head. It connected with my skull and my body flew through the air. I soared across the room and smashed headfirst into the wall. Black dots exploded behind my eyes, and I tried to think, tried to move, but I couldn't hold the offending dots off any longer. They filled my whole vision as pain exploded across the other side of my head. Another vicious hit came, and I welcomed the blackness. My body went limp. I was unable to move or even fight back . . . I had no choice but to let the darkness take me.

CHAPTER THIRTY-NINE

PIPER

My fingers felt numb and hushed voices surrounded me. Pain throbbed through my temples, around my head, and deep into my eyes. My body felt so heavy I couldn't move. Ice-cold water splashed over my face and soaked my shirt. I sucked in a gasping breath, and my body swung back and forth before I put my feet down and steadied myself. There were two things I realized in this moment:

One, being woken up by being doused by ice water was only something a douche would do.

Two, I was absolutely fucking screwed.

"Hello, Marius." I blew drops of water out of my mouth onto the floor between us. My hands were wrapped and bound. They were chained high above my head. I didn't know how long I'd been there, but my arms and fingers were completely numb. I couldn't open my fist with the bindings holding them shut. I didn't know how else to let my magic flow.

He leaned against a table across from me with his arms crossed over his chest. An empty bucket sat next to him. *I give you the douche.* "Hello, Piper."

"You'll never get away with this." I knew it sounded cliché, but I'd made friends in high places, and with Atlas now on my side, I knew I'd be hunted down soon enough.

"I already have." He shoved away from the table. "You're referring to your very powerful friends, I gather."

"Perhaps." I wasn't going to give anything away. "Or perhaps I plan on killing you myself."

He gave a humorless laugh. "Your magic isn't powerful enough to take me."

"At least I have magic." *Low blow, Piper.* But I couldn't help myself. He had me chained here like an animal. It wasn't in my nature to cower or beg. Whatever he was going to do, I wanted to get it over and done with. There was no use hanging here dreading what I knew would already be awful.

"Do not speak to me of magic!" He bellowed, and his voice carried and bounced off the rough, rocky walls.

I glanced around, trying to figure out where I was, but the best I got was *underground.* Which meant that I could've been anywhere. My gut told me I was still in England, but even that could be wrong. He could've carried me through a mirror to anywhere in the world. I tried to make my voice sound bored.

"What the hell am I doing here, Marius?"

"Did you know magic resides in the blood? It's a life force of its own." He moved in closer to me, so close our bodies were mere inches apart. He reached up and ran the backs of his fingers over my cheek.

I threw my head back, jerking away from his touch. The chains rattled and jostled but had little give. Even my ankles were chained to the floor. Panic and fear rose in my stomach, but if life had taught me anything, it was to hide those emotions at all costs. Fear only encouraged bullies to do worse things.

I cleared my throat, giving myself a minute to gather my courage. When dealing with a bully, there was only one thing to do . . . show no fear. "Your point being?"

"I wish to feel the sun on my skin again, the magic in my veins, the power at my fingertips. I had a life stolen from me. Now I want it back." He reached out and put his hands on my hips, taking a moment to press his fingers into the skin where my shirt had ridden up.

"That doesn't answer my question. What am I doing here?" I had the sinking feeling he thought I would be the answer to all his desires.

Marius smirked at me. "Serving my purposes."

I threw my body around, struggling against the restraints. I tried to call upon my power, but it was trapped within my fists. I glared at him. "I'll never serve you anything."

"I bet you taste delicious." He opened his mouth and

extended his fangs, then leaned in so close his cheek brushed against mine as he sucked in a deep breath, running his nose over my skin, smelling me. His hot breath fanned over my ear, and I wanted to gag as he whispered, "I wasn't asking."

He leaned back and parted his lips, about to strike . . .

EPILOGUE

Grayson

Cold. So cold. Relief. Trapped.

I traced the edge of the circle with my finger, debating how long it would be until death would take me. "Take me. Take me, pleaseeee," I whispered to myself.

How I'd gotten here, I had no idea. Yet I lay on the floor in the dungeon of my castle . . . alone. The sounds of dripping water in another cell and my own heartbeat were too loud. I shoved my hands over my ears and curled into a ball on my side.

Grayyyyyyyssssooooonnn, the voice breathed through my mind.

"No." I curled myself tighter, holding my hands harder against my ears. "Trapped."

The dark chuckle started in my mind or was it my own? I didn't know. Then it was there with me in the cell. I peeked my eyes open as he stood over me. His shoes were polished to a shine, and when I looked up, he wore pressed black dress pants, a black vest, a dark burgundy shirt, and a black suit jacket.

He squatted down next to me. "Trapped you say?"

I nodded, praying that it was true. I wanted it to end here. If he couldn't use me, he would kill me, and this torture would be over. From the inside of my circle, the air shimmered with the powers of the Queens. I'd poked at it, ran into it, kicked it, punched it, and used my magic against it, all under his direction.

"How pathetic you are." He reached forward and I waited for the boundary to stop him. But it didn't. The magic just peeled away from his head. He wrapped his fingers around my jaw and squeezed. Pain shot up my jaw and into my head. He forced my head up until I could meet his eyes.

I didn't want to meet his eyes. To look into his eyes was to view a sea of nightmares. I was already in one. He tilted his head from one side to the other, studying my face. "You know what I want?"

"Yes." I was helpless to move against his hold.

"You will do this, and then I will kill you quickly." He shoved my face away from him, and I smacked the back of my head on the hard floor. "Now get up and bring her to me."

"Trapped," I repeated, not wanting to argue with him any longer.

He scoffed and kicked his perfectly shining shoe through the white drawing on the floor. The magic broke as the white powder scattered across the floor and drifted over my skin. "Now. Get. Up."

"No." The word sounded feeble coming from me. "I will not."

He turned and leered down at me. "Silly vampire." Pain exploded behind my eyes. I couldn't think, couldn't speak, couldn't see. There was only me and the fire I lay in. My skin peeled from my body, and my insides boiled. Nothing would be left of me this time. I was sure of it. Finally, I would die and be rid of this madness. I'd be rid of *him*. All at once it stopped and he stood staring down at me. "Remember, there are far worse things than death, and I am capable of them all. Now bring her to me."

I couldn't fight this anymore. The madness, the pain . . . it was too much. Perhaps he would kill me quickly and I would be done forever. "Yes."

"Yes, what?" he snapped with that smooth, calm voice that made my ears bleed.

I slowly began to rise from my trap. "Yes, Lucifer."

ARE you ready for the epic conclusion of The Royals: Vampire Court?

Click the link and pre-order Wicked Blood now!
https://mybook.to/wickedblood

Curious about what Dice and Ophelia have been up to? Come join my book for a free scene!

Click here to join the Wicked Readers

DON'T MISS OUT ON THIS FREE BOOK!

THIS POWER CHOSE *ME*...

Within the supernatural world of Evermore everyone prays their child will be born with the Mark of the Guardian for they have unparalleled strength, intelligence, and *power*...but they have no idea what it's actually like. I didn't wish for this *gift* and I definitely don't want it. I was born a prince, I already had it all. This Mark on my neck stole all of it from me and forced me into a dangerous life I'd gladly trade away if I could...

But now the Witch Queens have ascended and it's time to try and defeat the evil King once and for all. For over a thousand years his cruelty has spared no one as his torturous power grows stronger. He must be stopped now, before his reign destroys everything and anything in his way. So I must push aside my dreams of returning home to the family that cast me out. I must step up and claim the power that chose me. I *must* enter the Trials and become a Knight in the Witch's Court.

There's only one way to prevent the tyrannical king from destroying everything I love…I must become the one thing he can't beat.

Click here to get your FREE book now!

IN CASE YOU MISSED the first season of The Royals: Witch Court check it out now!

CLICK HERE TO GET YOUR WITCH COURT BOXSET

It's time to claim my power...

ALL MY LIFE I've lived under lock and key, always following the strict rules my mother set for me. A week before my sixteenth birthday I sneak out of my house and discover why. Turns out I am not just a normal teenager. I'm a witch blessed with a gift someone wants to steal from me.

And not just anyone…the evil King Alataris.

For a thousand years the people of Evermore have suffered under his tyranny. The Mark on my shoulder says I am the Siphon Witch, one of five Witch Queens fated to come together and finally destroy him. The only thing keeping Evermore safe is the Stone that shields the witch kingdoms from Alataris's magic…and now he's found a way to steal it. Suddenly, I'm sent on a quest to find the ancient spell to protect the Stone. My only hope for surviving is through my strikingly beautiful and immensely powerful Guardian, Tucker. The laws of Evermore state that love between us is strictly forbidden, and it appears I'm the only one willing to give in to the attraction…

When the quest turns more dangerous than expected I realize I have absolutely no idea what I'm doing. I was raised human. But I have to learn my magic fast because If

King Alataris gets his hands on me he'll steal my magic and my life…but if he gets his hands on that Stone we all die.

THE MAGIC CONTINUES in the second season of The Royals: Warlock Court Now in this completely set!
CLICK HERE TO GET WARLOCK COURT

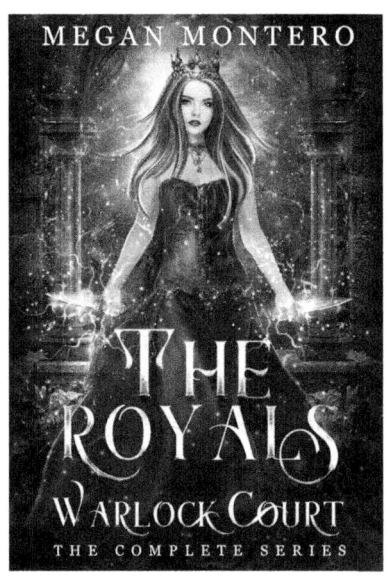

THERE'S **no such thing as magical powers. . .**
All my life the only kind of magic I'd ever seen was the sparkling jewels on fifth avenue. On the night of my sixteenth birthday all hell breaks loose, and by hell I mean

me! I never felt power like this, so dark, so tempting, so out of my control! No one is safe around me. And now I'm being thrown into Warwick Academy.

An academy for the darker side of magic...the warlock side.

My captor, my savior, and the bane of my existence, Beckett Dust insists on keeping me here even though we can't stand each other. I don't care how drop dead gorgeous he is or that he rules the school like he owns it, I need to stay as far away from him as I can. His deepest desire is to turn me into a weapon in the great war to come. My deepest desire is . . . him. There's a thin line between love and hate and right now I'm walking it.

IF YOU'RE all caught up on The Royals don't worry there's more to come. In the mean time check out The Night Realm: Magic Marked my awesome co-written series with Chandelle LaVaun.

CLICK HERE TO GET MAGIC MARKED

He put a spell on me...

Or at least he *must* have, because none of this makes any sense. None of this can be *real*. I'm not a mage with magical powers...I'm just *me*. Ellie Sutton. Your average, everyday seventeen-year-old high school *human* student. My biggest concerns are bullies, failed exams, and missing the express subway twice in one day.

Magic is something I read about in comic books, it's not real. People don't move things with their minds or summon lightning with their hands. I don't care what Stellan Wentworth says. It doesn't matter that he's breathtakingly beautiful or that his eyes sparkled when I challenge him. He's the kind of hero found in romance novels, not my real life. I'm dreaming, I have to be.

Because if I'm not, then what he's telling me is true. This gorgeous, terrifying world is in turmoil...and if I don't learn how to use my magic overnight...they'll all die.

Published by Leo Press

Copyright © 2024 by Megan Montero

Cover Design by Lori Grundy @ Cover Reveal Designs

Artwork by Samaiya Beaumont @ Samaiya Beaumont Art

This book is a work of fiction. Though some actual towns, cities, and locations may be mentioned, they are used in a fictitious manner and the events and occurrences were invented I the mind and imagination of the author. Any similarities of characters or names used within to any person past, present, or future is coincidental.

All rights reserved.

No part of this book may be reproduced in any form or by any electronic or mechanical means, including information storage and retrieval systems, without written permission from the author, except for the use of brief quotations in a book review.

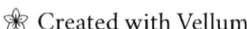 Created with Vellum

For my London Wankers! We don't do emotions so thanks for EVERYTHING you crazy bitches.

ABOUT THE AUTHOR

Megan Montero was born and raised as sassy Jersey girl. After devouring series like the Immortals After Dark, the Arcana Chronicles, Harry Potter and Mortal Instruments she decided then and there that she would write her own series. When she's not putting pen to paper you can find her cuddled up under a thick blanket (even in the summer) with a book in her hands. When she's not reading or writing you can find her playing with her dogs, watching movies, listening to music or moving the furniture around her house…again. She loves finding magic in all aspects of her life and that's why she writes Urban Fantasy and Paranormal.

Learn about Megan and her books by visiting her website at:
Www.meganmontero.com

ALSO BY MEGAN MONTERO

The Royals: Witch Court

Wicked Witch

Wicked Magic

Wicked Hex

Wicked Potion

Wicked Queen

The Royals: Witch Court Boxset

The Royals: Warlock Court

Wicked Omen

Wicked Wish

Wicked Hunt (A Warlock Court Novella: Ophelia)

Wicked Lies

Wicked Curse

Wicked Warlock

Wicked Ties

The Royals: Vampire Court

Wicked Bite

Wicked Vampire

Wicked Thirst

Wicked Blood (Coming Soon)

The Night Realm (Co-Write With Chandelle LaVaun)

Magic Marked

Midnight Mage

Marvel Mage

Master Mage

Court Marked

Fatal Fae

Fiery Fae

Final Fae

Christmas Marked

Bite Me, Santa

Jingle My Bells

Trim My Tree

Ride My Sleigh

Stuff My Stocking

Printed in Great Britain
by Amazon